LAUREN GREENE

Fight for It

Palm Cove Book 1

For Crystal, my Krav partner forever and always

Content Warning

Dear readers,

Fight For It is a standalone romance that contains consensual sexual activity and explicit language. The novel explores mental health themes. Content warnings for panic attacks, flashbacks to violence, SA, and anxiety. Depictions of sexism are discussed as well. Please read with care.

-Lauren

Chapter 1

Mia

My shoulders brushed up against the exterior brick wall of Krav Maga on Main, a local gym that offered self-defense focused workout classes. As the minutes ticked by, I watched the sun dip toward the horizon, transforming puffy white clouds into cotton candy swirls. I was supposed to be meeting my best friend Kendahl in this spot, five minutes ago but she was nowhere to be seen.

Where was she? I was right on time, and she hated tardiness. Her ex-boyfriend, Ben, thought that an arrival time was just a suggestion, and it drove her insane. I shifted from one foot to the other, watching people head into the glass gym door behind me. They were all dressed in workout clothes and wearing matching navy blue shirts that bore the name of the gym on the front. The sun may have been setting, but sweat was already beading on my brow and under the band of my sports bra. *Florida heat was the worst.*

I took another look around and saw no sign of my friend. Tired of sweating my butt off, I went into the cool air-conditioning of the gym's waiting area.

Finding a spot close to the door, I took one more peek out the window for Kendahl before tapping my phone screen. Even though I had been listening closely for the familiar ding, I was still a bit surprised that no new messages were waiting for me, only the background image I'd chosen a few months ago. A photo of a crashing wave that I took last time Ken and I went to the beach. It was meant to be one of those focus images to help me radiate calm. It wasn't working. I sighed, trying to decide if I was more anxious or irritated that she hadn't messaged me.

Groups of people stood around idly chatting or checking their phones, waiting for class to begin. I decided to text her and see if she was okay, while I still had time.

Me: *Hey I'm here*

Me: *You ok?*

Drawing in an anxious breath, I willed it down into my belly. I didn't want to bail, but I probably still could. There was no way I could go through with a class like this alone. She knew that when we decided we'd try this class together. Maybe it was too soon for her to come to something like this after what happened the other night. God, I felt like such an idiot for pushing her.

My phone lit up.

Ken Doll: *Hey sorry... not going to make it.*

Ken Doll: *It's too soon.*

I knew it.

Me: *Okay, I understand.*

Ken Doll: *I'm not ready yet.*

Me: *No worries! Get some rest and text me if you want me to come hang out.*

For someone who said no worries as much as I did, I sure worried a ton. I looked around the waiting area. Everyone was still hanging out. Now was my chance to take off.

Ken Doll: *You go though… let me know how it is. XOX*

Me: *I'm gonna bail. I'll call the gym owner and tell him something came up.*

As I turned away from the door someone tapped my shoulder. I spun around ready to apologize and tell them I was leaving when I came face-to-face with a gruff-looking man flashing me a beaming smile. The combination was dizzying.

"You must be Mia." He reached out a hand, which was attached to the most muscular forearm I'd ever seen. I blinked and looked around before grasping his palm and giving it a shake.

"Uh, hi. Yes, I'm Mia." I had to get out of this. "I was actually leaving… My friend couldn't make it tonight—family emergency. And I… need to get home to feed my cat." *My cat?* What the heck was I even yammering on about? I had no cat, no pets whatsoever. I couldn't even keep a cactus alive.

This dude looked intimidating even with his wide smile. He wasn't super tall, only a few inches taller than my five-foot-five-inch frame. What he lacked in height, he made up for in muscle. His bald head seemed to gleam from reflected drop lights. He had sleeves of ink that were visible thanks to his cut-off T-shirt, and his tan skin seemed to glow—the picture of fitness.

He chuckled and it instantly brought me back to my first day of kindergarten when my teacher, Mr. Thomas, hauled me into the classroom. He wore the same grin when he tried to placate me and all the other crying kids who were afraid of school. "Don't worry, Mia. We don't bite here." He reached around and placed his hand on the small of my back ushering me into the next room.

"I'm Mark Ward, but you can call me Sifu. No need to be nervous. We all started where you are now." He gestured to all the students now taking their spots.

I looked around the space. Crimson walls stood out against the gray concrete flooring. The room was bare except for a few random weight machines along one wall and a cubby to hold bags and water bottles along the other. Stale sweat with a hint of men's body spray lingered in the air. I willed air into my lungs, knowing I probably looked like a complete idiot here surrounded by these muscular men and women. Thankfully I didn't have to shake any hands since mine were so clammy I had to keep wiping them on my pant legs.

Mark led me to the front of the room. Come on Higher Power, help me here. Maybe make the power go out. Or what if I could somehow spontaneously combust, but not die? Just combust enough to get me out of here.

My mind whirled with all the excuses I wanted to give Mark so I could get out of there. There was no way I could go through this alone. But I had no words. Did someone suddenly fill my mouth with Elmer's glue? My tongue was definitely stuck to the roof of my mouth.

"Hey guys, nice to see you all tonight," Mark bellowed out to his class, his hand still at the small of my back.

"Hi, Sifu!" Everyone hollered back and then they watched us intently. I might literally die right here and now—in my workout clothes. RIP, me.

"We have a new student here. It's her first class, so let's be easy on her." He chuckled as if they all had some kind of inside joke. "Her partner couldn't make it tonight. Shawn, where you at?"

Mark searched the room. As he did, I willed myself to look throughout the room too. Maybe my eyes were playing tricks on me before, but now as I scrutinized the surrounding people it was like a veil had been lifted. There were a few super-fit-looking guys and one or two women who looked like they could hold their own in a fight. But the majority of the twenty or so students were average sized and different ages. Some gawky teenagers giggled in the back row, and I could make out a mother-daughter duo to the side. The former had to be in her mid-to late-forties.

I breathed a sigh of relief. Okay, it sucked that Kendahl bailed on me, but I wasn't the only non-gym rat there. I could try this. If not for me, then I could do it for Kendahl or for my sister, Olivia, who, despite being an athlete herself, still endured the worst kind of thing that could happen to a person. I squared my shoulders and stood up a little straighter. Yes, I would do this class and I would kick ass. I was Wonder Woman, minus the lasso and amazing body. I was the embodiment of power.

I brought my water bottle to my lips and sipped, trying to unglue my tongue when the most gorgeous man I'd ever laid my eyes on walked into the gym from the waiting area. His hair caught my eye first, sandy blond and tousled. It was long enough that I could run my fingers through it and get a handful of the thick strands. Then there were his eyes. Holy hell. I'd never seen eyes like his, cobalt blue with lashes that any woman would pay good money for.

When he zeroed his gaze directly into my eyes, my pulse kicked up a few beats. I knew in an instant he was one of those people whose eyes showed their every emotion. They were stormy and complicated and pulled me in like a boat to shore.

When I was finally able to tear my eyes away from his perfect face, I realized I was looking at a body that could have been in magazines. His biceps were like barrels bursting out of his tight-fitted T-shirt, and ink snaked up his arms making me wish I had special goggles that would let me peek underneath those annoying clothes.

Damn woman, chill.

"Shawn, there you are, man. I was just asking for you." Mark gave me a little push in Shawn's direction. My mouth gaped open, like a freaking fish, and water dribbled out onto my chest. "This is Mia, your new partner."

Chapter 2

Shawn

Great, another newbie here to waste my time. I tried to remember how many first timers there had been last month but came up blank. It happened that often. They'd come in, try one class, and then we'd never see them again.

I nodded at Mark, noticing his shit-eating grin. I bet he was doing this to me because I was late for the second time this week. He knew how much I loathed working with newbies. I looked over at the woman he had practically shoved at me, her brown eyes were wide open and blinking rapidly. She literally had water dribbling down her shirt and onto her huge tits while she shifted from one foot to the other. I'd give her half of class before she's excusing herself to the bathroom to puke.

Awesome.

I figured I should put on my assistant teacher hat and try not to be a complete ass, but it was a long, rough day at the shop. I spent an hour dealing with a customer who decided he wanted a different shade of stain after I'd already finished his cabinets. I'm drained and tired of being around people.

"Hey, what was your name again?" I motioned for her to sit down next to me as Mark led us through warm-up stretches.

"Mia," she squeaked out.

I looked at her closer and noticed she was inhaling breaths faster than she should. Damn, she was really nervous. Okay, I changed my original guess. She'd make it through fifteen minutes, not thirty.

"You ever do anything like this before?"

We followed Mark into a butterfly stretch. Shit, my hamstrings felt tight. I inhaled a deep breath and willed my body to stretch further. Mia followed my movement and sank into a deeper stretch than I could ever muster.

"No, I... uh...," she cleared her throat and stood back up. "I'm not the athletic type, but I have done some yoga."

I leered. Yoga. That's what all the women who came in here said.

We got to our feet and started rotating our shoulder joints in large circles. Sometimes this was my favorite part of a class. After working at the shop all day, it was rare if I took five minutes to stop and stretch. Most of the time, I felt like a rubber band ready to snap.

"Well, buckle-up sweetheart, you're in for a whole new experience."

A strangled sort of laugh escaped her lips and she turned back to Mark. I'd bet my paycheck that she was calculating how and when she could skip out of here with no one noticing.

After a series of jump squats and burpees, Mark deemed us thoroughly warmed up. I glanced over at the woman a few times and couldn't help but notice her perfectly round ass as she squatted. Those leggings left nothing to the imagination.

"Alright, pair off and go grab a pad. Then gather around for the demonstration," Mark boomed.

Mia looked around, her eyes were wide in confusion.

"I'll get what we need. You can go on and watch Sifu," I said. She nodded, her chest was still visibly rising and falling, and her brow line was moist with sweat.

I turned to the wall and grabbed a black training pad, finding one that was nice and firm. Coby, another assistant, was slouched against the wall, waiting to jump in and help out.

He jerked his head in the new girl's direction and said in a low voice, "You're lucky. Mark stuck me with an old hairy dude yesterday that came in for a trial. What I wouldn't give to tumble around with her."

"I didn't notice," I huffed. "And you know Mark only gives you dudes because you're way too creepy, man."

He laughed. "Hey, a man's gotta charge up images for his spank bank whenever he can, am I right?"

I shook my head and headed back over to the group where Mark was demonstrating how to do a stomp kick on his wife Dina. I loved to watch her kick his ass when they sparred. It cracked me up every time to see a tiny five-foot-nothing woman flip her husband and pin him down.

Everyone scattered into pairs, and the newbie looked around for me. Her eyes were no longer the size of dinner plates as if the demonstration had put her mind at ease.

She found me lingering near the stack of remaining pads, and our eyes locked. I was in no rush to start what I knew would be another frustrating chunk of my already irritating day.

I gestured at her to come over. In my serious teacher voice said, "Okay, so I'm going to hold the pad and you can practice for a while. We can switch it up when you need a break."

She nodded and then took up the stance that Dina had demoed, one leg a step behind the other. Her first kick missed the pad completely and landed on my shin—hard.

"Oh crap, I'm sorry," she sputtered, "I have no idea what I'm doing. My friend was supposed to be here, and this is so crazy. I should go."

Yup, there it was. One kick in and she was ready to bounce. Mark looked over at me and nodded with that look of his that told me not to be an asshole. I huffed and rubbed my now throbbing shin.

"It's fine, happens all the time," I said through gritted teeth. No, it really doesn't, but whatever. "Just try again."

She started mumbling out another apology but she reset her stance. This time, her kick touched the pad right in the center, but with barely any power behind it. She stopped and looked at me for approval.

"You can just keep going. No need to stop in between each kick," I affirm.

"Right," she whispered.

She breathed deeply and swung her leg with another kick, the heel of her foot connected with the pad that time. Again and again, she repeated until her chest heaved and her face was red.

"You need a break?"

"Uh, some water would be good, actually," she replied through labored breaths. I nodded in response.

She turned to the shelf, moving around other pairs who were huffing and sweating while I leaned back waiting. Normally I'd take these short breaks in the waiting area, in hopes of avoiding small talk with the students. I knew if I stepped away though, newbie might get lost. After a couple of minutes, she joined me again. Her shoulders were squared, her chin held higher.

"Can I try holding the pad for you now? I mean, I should probably learn how to, right?" she asked.

"Sure, if you want. I wouldn't mind getting a workout in too," I said.

I handed the pad to her and watched her get into position. She was a fast learner. I'd give her that. I took a deep breath and focused. There was nothing in this room except for the thump of Mark's awful house music playing in the background, the cool air that came out of the vent above me, and the black pad in front of me.

I launched into a stomp kick with only a fraction of the power I'd normally give. The newbie went down on her ass in what felt like a flash of a second, the pad tossed to the side on the concrete ground.

It was no longer the new girl I saw sprawled out before me, but Michelle. The music was gone, and all I could hear were sirens wailing. She was lifeless on the ground in front of me in the pitch dark.

My breaths came in short gasps. I was frozen. I needed air. I needed quiet. I needed to not be here where the room was closing in on me.

"I'm sorry... I just..." The words fumbled from my lips as my vision came back to the here and now. I turned and got the fuck out of there.

The last thing I saw was her face, honey-brown eyes wide in shock. I left the newbie there on her ass. Just like I had left Michelle.

Chapter 3

Mia

WHAT THE HECK? HAD he really walked out and left me on the ground?

I watched his large frame push through the front door without even a glance back in my direction. I know I'm new here, but was I that terrible of a partner that he had to up and leave? His expression had looked far away, haunted even. Something must have been going on with him. It was like he was staring at a movie screen, only the picture was fuzzy, and he couldn't make out what was happening. Whatever it had shown terrified him.

A hand reached out to help me up, and I stood, wiping my sweaty palms on my leggings.

"Hey, I'm Dina, Mark's better half." She gestured to the door. "Did Shawn bail? I was helping another pair, so I didn't see him leave, but I saw you by yourself."

I nodded. "Yeah, not really sure what happened, but he kind of just left. Do you think he's alright?"

Her brows raised and she shook her head, not looking as surprised as I would have thought. "Yeah, I'm sure he's fine. I'll text him later to see what's up." She looked like she had more to say but shrugged and grabbed the practice pad.

"Why don't we finish practicing together? You go ahead and get some more stomp kicks in. This time I'll move around, so it's more realistic. In the real world, our attacker wouldn't be standing still like a statue." I wiped my brow and then stepped back, readying to strike.

With the thumping of the music and the gentle directions Dina gave me, the rest of the class flew by. I managed to stay upright the whole time and even enjoyed myself.

Dina was a great teacher. She reminded me when my posture was off and taught me to always keep my hands up to guard my face. It felt weird, at first, like everyone would watch me or laugh because I looked out of place. I wasn't a jock and had never been a fighter. Maybe that was the problem, though, I thought I had to fit myself into certain boxes to enjoy activities.

Mark gathered the class around in a circle, everyone out of breath and sweating.

"Impressive job tonight, level one. Remember, everything takes time and hard work. No one, not even me," he said with a smirk, "wakes up perfect at Krav."

Nods and mumbled agreements filled the space.

"Let's commit right now to show up this week. I want to see every one of you again at the next class." He pointed his finger at a dark-haired middle-aged guy with tan skin who had a small grin on his face. "Yeah, even you, Mike. I know you've got a baseball game tomorrow night. Don't get too hungover."

Everyone chuckled, even me. I already felt a sense of ease I didn't have when the class first started. This place felt welcoming, despite what happened with Shawn. Here with these people, I felt like I could reach my potential and finally gain some confidence. That by being here, I could learn to keep myself safe.

Once the other students dispersed, Dina motioned for me to come into their office to chat. She and Mark gave me a sales pitch about joining as a student and explained about how their class levels and testing worked. Little did they know, I had already decided to join before the end of class.

"Oh, and again, we're sorry about Shawn." Dina smiled graciously. "He… uh. He's gone through some tough stuff in his life."

I looked from Dina to Mark as they sat next to each other. Mark gave Dina a wide-eyed look as if to say, enough.

"It's fine. I don't need an explanation. Hopefully, he's okay. That's all I'm worried about," I said.

I mean, yes, I'd love an explanation, but it wasn't my place. Obviously, they valued Shawn as an assistant, or they wouldn't place him with new students.

"Well, we're glad to have you, Mia. Here's your shirt and gloves." She handed me a navy-blue shirt with "Level 1" written on it. I smiled, proud of myself. "We'll see you in the next class," Dina said as she stood up to show me out.

I drove back to my apartment with the windows rolled down, bopping along to the local pop station. The springtime humidity had subsided, and a light breeze dried some of the lingering sweat on my brow. Even so, I couldn't wait to take a long, hot shower.

I breathed deeply when I reached the warm familiarity of my second story apartment. What my building lacked in grandness, it made up with cool neighbors who left my introverted self alone. Except for sweet Mrs. Vega next door, who loved to treat me like an adopted grandchild. I could smell whatever deliciousness she made for dinner floating through the walls somehow. My mouth watered and my stomach made a sound like an alien was attempting to escape. I would do dinner before my shower.

Moments later, I settled down onto the plush couch with a plate of leftover noodles and a cold sparkling water in my lap. I didn't really want to get my sweaty stink onto my cushions, but, oh well. It was only me that had to smell my stank, anyway. The noodles tasted decent warmed up, even if the corners were hard enough for me to bust a tooth

I flipped on the TV for background noise while I ate and scrolled through my phone. I'd take this any day over dating random guys. Netflix never cheated. Hulu never drank too much. Instagram never slipped drugs into drinks. Maybe I was jaded, but the handful of dates I went on since I left college gave me more anxiety than it was worth.

My phone pinged twice with texts from Kendahl. I was still irritated at her for bailing, even though I understood why she did. I looked at it anyway.

Ken Doll: *Hey*

Ken Doll: *How'd it go? Did you end up leaving?*

I set my half-eaten meal down and nestled into the corner of the couch.

Me: *No. I stayed.*

Me: *Kind of got lassoed into it by the owner.*

I chewed my lip thinking of what else to text.

Me: *It went pretty well. I only fell once. Haha lol*

Ken Doll: *Haha, of course you did...*

Ken Doll: *I'm sorry I didn't show. I know you get anxious in new situations.*

Me: *It's really okay. It felt good to get over my fear a little and push through it.*

Me: *How are you though?*

I waited, watching those three little dots appear and disappear.

Ken Doll: *I'm okay... taking today to just chill at home helped.*

Me: *Any more thoughts on letting a Dr. check you out?*

Ken Doll: *No, they're just bruises. They'll heal. The real trauma was realizing a guy could do a complete one-eighty like that.*

Ken Doll: *Tell me more about your class. Did you get to punch anyone?*

I huffed. There would be no talking her into anything. She was my best friend, feisty, tough, and always brushing things off. Maybe I could talk her into finding a therapist. I know how much that helped Olivia when we were younger. I wouldn't push her into talking about herself. I knew if I did, she'd cut me off, and she was already emotionally drained.

Me: *No, not today at least. We did kicking moves... I kind of... kicked my partner in the shin.*

Me: *He took it like a champ. At least before he knocked me on my ass and left me there.*

Ken Doll: *Wait, what?!*

Ken Doll: *A guy knocked you down and just walked away?*

Ken Doll: *What a fucking dick!!!*

Ken Doll: *What's with guys in this city?!*

She had a point there. Neither of us has had any luck on the dating scene.

Me: *He seemed okay before that. Serious and kind of grumpy...*

Me: *Idk he acted kind of out of it after I fell.*

Me: *It was fine. I ended up working with the owner's wife.*

Ken Doll: *Hmm... well I guess I'm glad it worked out.*

Ken Doll: *Were there any hot guys?*

Me: *Omg your head is in the gutter!!! I thought you were all torn up and had sworn off guys.*

I wanted to add that after Ben cheated on her, her first attempt back in the dating pool had gotten her assaulted. I knew better than to voice those reminders.

Ken Doll: *Come on! I may be taking a break but you shouldn't.*

Ken Doll: *It's been way too long since your last date.*

Me: *I know. It's fine. Guys are dicks, especially in Palm Cove. Didn't we just emphasize that? Lol.*

Me: *Lungberg is keeping me busy enough at work that I low key want to change my identity and move to Switzerland.*

Ken Doll: *But you could never leave meeee. Lol*

Ken Doll: *Back to the good stuff.*

Ken Doll: *Any sweaty, muscular guys that you'll be fantasizing about when you use your lightsaber later?*

Me: *OMG!!! You're insane.*

I burst out laughing. I wish I had never told her about my little purchase. Little isn't exactly the best word for it—okay, *big* purchase.

Me: *With my luck every hot guy I encounter is either gay or a complete jerk.*

Me: *Ugh fine... the douchey guy was pretty hot. He had this sort of Ryan Gosling look to him, but way buffer.*

Ken Doll: *Damn girl... you should have led with that info. Maybe I will come to this gym after all.*

Me: *Haha... I know you're just being an ass and you are so not ready yet*

Me: *Which is why I'm going to let you off the hook. For now...*

Me: *I signed up for a membership. I'll give it a month or two and if I think it's worth it, then I'll drag your booty in. That way, you'll have time to do a bit of healing first.*

A few minutes went by with the three little dots at the bottom of my screen. Kendahl was all talk. As tough as she was, I knew she was probably still camped out on her couch in her fuzzy pajamas, not ready to deal with the outside world.

Ken Doll: *Okay... I'll give it another month or two.*

Ken Doll: *Mi, I'm proud of you.*

There she went and made me get all choked up.

Me: *Thanks K, love you girl.*

It felt good to hear that someone was proud of me. It wasn't something I heard often as a kid. I was always trying to fill the footsteps left by my sister. At least until her senior year, when her life went to hell and my parents stopped looking at her as their perfect older daughter. It's not that I didn't love my family. I did, especially Olivia, and my rascal of a nephew, Alex. It's just always been hard to fit in with them. I was never pretty enough, thin enough, or prim enough for my mother. And with my father, I never did as well in school and athletics as Olivia. I also refused to date his golf buddies' sons. Their life in politics was as far from what I wanted as possible. It was laughable to me that Olivia and I came from them. Everything was about image for my parents. My father seemed genuinely glad when I chose accounting as a career. But he won't give me a pat on the back until I make it up the ladder.

Olivia was only two years older, but in so many ways, she was more like a mother to me than a sister. At least until the incident that changed her life. Afterward, she just collapsed into herself. The trauma of what she went through completely wrecked her. My parents, instead of being there for her, made it all about them and the family shame. In the aftermath, they did what they were good at, emotionally shutting us both out. It was then that our roles reversed. With Olivia no longer able to care for either of us, I needed to make sure she ate and kept up with her online schoolwork so she could graduate. I vowed I would never let anyone I cared for suffer through what she did without feeling supported and loved.

Kendahl reminded me so much of Olivia, before that night, when I met her at freshman orientation of college. Her free spirit called to me and let me release some of the burdens I had been carrying for years. We were both free of our family situations. After a few months, I let go of trying to be the perfect daughter and sister and to being someone I wasn't, just to win my parents' love. But with that came a vulnerability I hadn't felt in years. My safety net of hiding myself away was gone.

Kendahl had never lived full of anxiety and fear, the way I did before. She may have had a difficult upbringing, but she somehow let things roll off her shoulders, never stewing and ruminating the way I did. Even with all my mother-henning, she was just herself. She scared me then, and she scares me now. If anything were to happen to her for real, I know that the spark that is Kendahl would go out, just like Olivia's did.

I breathed deeply and shoved that worry aside. I couldn't protect everyone I loved, but at least I was working on being able to protect myself.

After a hot shower, I cuddled up in my bed with my phone and scrolled to Krav Maga on Main's Facebook page. Looking through their photos; I couldn't believe that I'd gone through with the class and that I loved every minute of it. Well, almost every minute. The beginning was a little rough.

I trailed over a picture of a familiar face. Shawn, with his sandy brown hair and his piercing blue eyes. In the photo, he had less facial hair than he did today, only a faint shadow of scruff spread across his chiseled jawline. The tattoos, that I was dying to see more of, peeked out of his shirt. The picture looked like someone had taken it in the middle of class. He was knocking a fake weapon out of his partner's pointed hand.

I was dumbstruck. I had no idea we'd be practicing stuff like that. It made sense because this gym is all about protecting ourselves in the real world. But weapon defense? Would I ever be ready for that?

I looked back at the picture, his expression was one of determination, eyes focused on his target. And damn, if just looking at him didn't turn me on. I needed to get a grip; the guy is obviously a douche. Who cares if he could be Chris Hemsworth's body double? I had enough asshole guys on my plate at work and didn't need to add any more to my life.

Eventually, I drifted to sleep with my phone propped next to my pillow, and I dreamed of house music and red walls.

Chapter 4

Mia

My work email pinged with a new message from my evil boss, Evan Lungberg. Even his name was horrible. It sounded like a disgusting type of smelly cheese. Or an undiscovered deep-dwelling ocean creature, one that feeds on faceless worms living in the sand and never sees the light of day. A short scan of the subject line had my left eye twitching:

***Mandatory* Client Appreciation Golf Event Meeting at 10:00 a.m.**

God no, I hated this event. I'd rather get a root canal by a blind man than have to deal with the weeks-long buildup of office hell leading up to the horrible event itself.

Jared, my best friend in the office, and I glanced up at each other with knowing looks. A second later, my phone beeped, showing Jared's, self-appointed, nickname.

Pretty Boy: *Please tell me we can get lunch after this meeting? We're both going to need a vent session.*

Me: *Kill me now.*

Me: *The only thing worse than stupid golf, is golf in Florida's ninety-degree weather.*

Me: *So... yes, lunch, please.*

Jared silently chuckled at my response, showing his beautiful white teeth and adorable dimples, before he gave me a covert thumbs-up. I didn't know how I'd get through my workdays without him.

I buckled in for the next hour, trying to get my work done before this meeting inevitably ruined my still positive mood thanks to the previous night's class.

At five minutes to ten, I pushed out of my chair, straightened my navy pencil skirt, and adjusted my glasses. Lungberg was already out of his office and had given me the stink eye on his way into the conference room, along with a remark about him wanting me to bring a legal pad and pen into the meeting. I wish, somewhere inside his pig-headed brain, he would remember that I'm a junior accountant and not his assistant. But it is what it is. Not much I could do about him and his nasty demeanor.

The conference room at our firm was a rectangular room that was not nearly as comfortable as Bosch or Lungberg's lush offices. It was small and had one window overlooking the street. It was jam-packed with a large table and twelve chairs. Because of this, there were always one or two stragglers that had to stand during whole office meetings. I took my seat next to Jared and steeled myself. I was one of only two women in this office. The other woman was Cathy, Mr. Bosch's assistant. I had known that I'd be working in a male-dominated field when I got into accounting, but I hadn't realized how much I would always feel like a piece of meat being dangled into shark-infested waters during large group meetings.

Lungberg cleared his throat, and the idle chitchat in the room fell silent.

"Let's begin. None of us have time to waste here. Jared is going to pass around a document that assigns each of you tasks for the upcoming golf event. These tasks must be completed prior to the event." His eyes were laser-focused on Jared who jumped up and got to passing out the paperwork. "You'll notice a couple of changes from last year. The main one being that it is at a new location. The second being that there is a change in leadership."

I looked down at the paper in front of me and froze.

No. Absolutely not. My name was listed, in bold, as leading the entire event. I had no time or desire to take on this huge task. I was an accountant, not a damn party planner. I drew in a deep breath and raised my eyes to meet Lungberg's, a fake smile plastered on my face. Everyone in the conference room stared at me and waited for me to acknowledge the change.

"Uh, Mr. Lungberg, while I appreciate this opportunity, I'm afraid I won't have the time to be the lead organizer. It's almost the end of the second quarter and I have a lot on my plate as it is." I glanced around, noticing a few snickers from some of the other junior accountants. Those bastards knew I was swamped just like they were.

Lungberg looked at Bosch before he turned to me. His face was reddening to the shade of a ripe raspberry. "This is non-negotiable, Miss Murphy. You are the only woman in this office, therefore, the party planning falls to you." I turned and locked eyes with Cathy before she lowered her head, making herself seem smaller. *Thanks a lot, Cathy. I'll remember this next time you bombard me with pictures of your grandchildren.*

A throat cleared, "Mr. Lungberg, I'd be happy to take over most of the organizing. I have a knack for event planning." I turned to see Jared had spoken up.

Lungberg winced and then raised his bushy brows. "While I'm sure that is true, you're not experienced enough to take the lead. Mia is in charge. That is final." He coughed and added, "But she may delegate some minor tasks to you."

Jared reached beneath the table squeezing my clenched hand. He didn't realize how much I needed that to redirect me from reaching for the nearest blunt object and launching it at Lungberg's bloated face.

Bosch took over to give other team members menial tasks and to ask if there were any questions. Of course, no one piped up. That would have risked the bosses thinking they were interested in helping with more than what they were already assigned.

"If that is all, everyone is free to get back to work. The second quarter is ending soon and we need to make sure we have met our clients' needs first and foremost." I rolled my eyes. That's exactly why I couldn't take on organizing a party for a hundred or more people. "Mia, I'll have Jared bring forward the files from my last assistant with vendor information. And remember, this is our biggest event of the year. If it fails, it's your head on the chopping block."

I don't remember getting through the next hour of work. I think there was a filter of red over my vision as I punched at my keyboard silently willing every golf course in a hundred-mile radius to cease to exist. My brain didn't reboot itself until Jared shoved a burrito in my face and said, "Earth to Mia."

"Ugh, I'm sorry. I think I've been having a brain malfunction since the meeting." I took a big bite of my veggie and bean burrito and sighed. Taco Bout It had the best veggie burrito in all of Florida or maybe even the country. "Thanks for dragging me out of the office. I needed this."

Jared shook his head at me. "I knew you would. That's why I texted you as soon as we got that stupid email." He looked me over with his head tilted. He was the only other person I knew who mother-henned as much as I did. I was grateful for him. "It's going to be okay. I know what Lungberg said about me not taking the lead but screw him. I'll do as much as I can, so you don't fall behind on clients." He popped a chip from his nacho platter into his mouth while still watching me curiously.

It's not that I hated parties. I didn't mind throwing them. What I hated were pretentious golf clubs and sexist asshole bosses.

"I don't know what I've done to that man for him to hate me so damn much," I said, my mouth full of burrito. "All I do is smile and nod and do whatever he asks of me, yet he's trying to make my life hell every chance he gets."

"It's because you haven't kissed his ass or flirted with him. Men like him will always think women are below them. That women should treat them like Hugh Hefner because they make six figures. It's fucking gross."

"Yeah, I guess you're right. I mean, remember the rumors going around a while back about that payroll clerk and him?

Jared chewed another chip, staring intently at a cute guy in line to order. I almost didn't want to break him out of his obvious daydream.

"Wait, I think that was before you started." I shook my head, "Ew. I don't even want to think about it while I'm trying to eat and I'm sure you don't want to either while you're checking out that guy."

"Am not," he said, although his reddened cheeks gave him away. "I know what you're talking about with Lungberg." He sipped his drink while flailing his hand for emphasis. "I bet that clerk was let go because it got back to his wife. It's okay, girl. I got your back. We'll get through this hell, and you'll get the satisfaction of being awesome and taking all the credit."

Jared's phone beeped with a text. "Speak of the devil. He wants me to bring him lunch. You think I can spit in it and get away with it?" He narrowed his eyes and waggled his brows at me causing me to almost choke on my water.

"Listen, I can pretend I never saw a thing," I retorted. We finished up the last few bites of our meal chatting about Jared's latest family drama. His cousin broke up with her fiancé a week before their wedding, devastating his aunt. With his big boisterous family there was always something going on.

"I forgot to ask you about that class last night. How'd it go?" Jared asked, as he grabbed our to-go bag from the counter.

We started walking toward the door with Lungberg's untainted steak burrito bagged up at Jared's side.

I smiled. "Believe it or not, I actually loved it. Not at first, but once my anxiety subsided, I had fun. I'm going again tonight."

"That's awesome, girl. You should totally picture Lungberg's face when you punch something later." I would definitely do that. Maybe it would help my nerves. Butterflies fluttered when I thought about the class ahead and I still had hours to go.

We were still laughing as we reached the office entrance.

I pushed through the doors of the Krav gym precisely five minutes before class time with a racing heart and a stomach that housed tiny acrobats. I contemplated waiting outside until the exact minute class began but decided that would make me look super weird. I know I wasn't here to make friends—but it wasn't like the other students would bite.

In times like these, I wished I had a better handle on my anxiety. It was like my body was constantly fighting with my brain over if I was in danger, even when I was fine.

I forced controlled breaths in through my nose and out through my mouth, while I stood in the back of the waiting area, staring way too intently at an inspirational poster. It said, **Never Give Up**, in bold lettering above a silhouetted image of boxing gloves. With how entranced I was by the poster, one would think it was the most prolific piece of literature to exist, but it was better than staring at the students gathered around talking.

I jumped when I felt a tap on my shoulder. A woman who looked to be in her sixties, with short platinum hair, and more defined muscles than I'd ever seen on a woman of her age, smiled at me, showing a mouthful of porcelain white teeth.

"Hi there. I didn't mean to make you jump," she said. Her voice was raspy as if she spent most of her time laughing. "I'm Evelyn, but everyone calls me Evie. You must be new, huh?"

A shy smile crossed my lips. "I guess that's pretty obvious." I let out an uncomfortable laugh. "I'm Mia. It's my second class tonight."

Evie squeezed my shoulder and the tightness in my chest relaxed an inch.

"Come on, doll, let me introduce you to the other girls. Us ladies have to stick together in this land of testosterone," Evie said.

She guided me the few steps over to a small circle of women. I overheard one of them laughing about something her kid did.

"Y'all, we got ourselves a newbie. This is Mia," Evie interrupted, "she just signed up. Reminds me of you, Avery, when you first started. I remember how I could practically see you giving yourself an inner pep talk that first night."

Everyone chuckled, and Evie went around introducing them. There was Avery, a woman in her mid-twenties like me, with cropped brown hair, a colorful sleeve of tattoos, and a very slim build. She was tall, had to be around six feet. Next to her was Anna, she had been the one who was talking about her kid. She must have been in her forties, but like Evie, looked in shape and kind of intimidating. Maybe it was her perfectly straight bob haircut or just a severeness in her face. Either way, I wouldn't want to mess with her.

Last, was the mother-daughter duo I noticed yesterday. Evie introduced them as Jill and Kayla. Jill smiled warmly at me, and Kayla gave a small wave. They looked alike, both with round, friendly faces, tan skin, and dark brown hair. Other than their age, their main difference was Kayla's studded nose ring and her loads of black eyeliner.

Without missing a beat, everyone continued with their conversation. Anna's little boy was asking about the birds and the bees last night at bedtime because of something he heard at school. She had almost fallen over it was so unexpected. She called in her husband, Jake, whom Anna pointed out across the room, talking to that guy Mike whom Sifu singled out at the last class.

"I told Jake he could handle the talk with Ryder, and I'd take it with Brynlee. Hopefully, I won't have to worry about it for a good five years since she just turned three."

Anna is a badass for being a mom to little ones and coming in here learning how to fight. She was setting such a good example for her kids. My thoughts drifted to my mother. I imagined her in a class like this and almost laughed. Pamela Murphy would never break a sweat.

I looked around the room again discreetly searching for my partner from yesterday, Shawn. If I was being honest with myself, I had thought about him about a dozen times since this morning. I didn't see him here when I walked in. Part of me wanted to ask the ladies about him, but what would I ask? This wasn't high school, and I barely knew the other students to start a conversation, especially one that could come across as gossip.

Just as my heartbeat had slowed to a normal rate, Mark came out of his office followed by Shawn. Our eyes locked immediately and only for a second before I angled my gaze downward. His biceps rippled beneath the black T-shirt he wore. And there were most definitely visible pecs pressing against his shirt. I hadn't imagined his attractiveness yesterday. Oh, to be the shirt on that man's body. My heart rate picked back up, but this time, anxiety had nothing to do with it.

"Level ones, let's get started," Mark hollered. "Shawn's going to run you through most of the class today."

This should be interesting.

We shuffled into the open gym space, and I found a spot near the back after stashing my purse in a cubby. Everyone spread out to give each other space for warming up.

I noticed Shawn at the front of the room still wearing a serious expression but looking more at ease than he had yesterday. He said something to the guys in the front row that caused the corner of his lips to perk up in the slightest way. I couldn't hear what it was before he raised his voice to the full group and told us to start with shoulder rolls. He spoke with a type of authority that came from sheer masculine confidence. It irked me how I was almost happily anticipating his next command.

I stretched my hamstrings and quads. They were always pulled taut because of my desk job. The gentle release stretching gave me sent a wave of relaxation up my spine.

That feeling was short lived, though. Shawn didn't let us off easy as he called out for the group to do sets of jump squats, burpees, and crunches. By the time Mark joined him at the front of the room a slight sheen of sweat coated my forehead and my pulse pounded.

I took slow inhales, willing my breathing back to normal. Mark, in his black jogging shorts and frayed gray tank, demonstrated what we'd be learning with the much larger Shawn.

They slowly went through two different types of punches. Shawn's arms moved fluidly toward Mark's pad, he almost made it look like they were dancing. I tried to memorize their steps.

His sandy hair fell forward into his face a few times, but he pushed it back showing a completely sweat-free face.

"Okay, everyone, find a partner and practice both types of punches. Switch every ten reps. Shawn and I will come around to see how everyone does," Mark said.

I watched the others around the room gravitate toward their normal partners. Anna and her husband came together as well as Jill with Kayla. Evie met my gaze, but she gestured to Avery with an apologetic look. I smiled back, but it didn't quite reach my eyes. I would not ask Shawn to partner with me again. No way would I humiliate myself a second time. Plus, he was sort of teaching today, so that probably meant he couldn't be my partner, anyway. I took one more desperate glance around. I was about to ask Mark to help me out when I felt a presence behind me. Turning, I came face to face with a grinning man.

"Mia, right? Do you need a partner?" He must have been an assistant like Shawn because he wore the same shirt. That was about their only similarity. This man was tall too but had a lean muscular build, whereas Shawn was just straight-up jacked. His hair was dark and cut short on the sides but left longer on top where it curled slightly. He beamed at me with a bright smile and perfect teeth as I nodded like an idiot, unable to form words. He squeezed my shoulder chuckling, "I'm Coby. Come on, let's go over to the other side of the room. There's more space for you to practice." He already held a pad in his arms, and I weaved through partners who were hard at work punching with reckless abandon.

Chapter 5

Shawn

I KNEW COBY WOULD go in for the newbie like a shark who just scented fresh blood. She was exactly his type. Curves on curves with a shy demeanor. I could see a playboy like him winning her over by the end of class. I'd seen him hit on women like her countless times in the past few years. Makes me wonder if his proclivities played a part in his marriage ending.

I ground my teeth as I circled the floor. I'd stay away from them. It's not like I'm interested, anyway, may as well let him do what he does so well.

Mark walked back into his office. After five years here, he finally trusted me to run some level-one classes, and I can't say it didn't fill me with a small amount of pride. Mark's been like a big brother to me all these years and to have him trust me with his livelihood meant a great deal. It surprised me when he texted me to ask earlier, especially after I walked out yesterday. Lord knows, I wouldn't trust anyone with my business, especially not someone with my issues. Not since my Gramps passed away has anyone other than me laid a hand on any of my pieces of furniture, not even the ones commissioned for me to refurbish.

As soon as the office door closed, I changed the music from that horrible electronica. That was Mark's one major flaw—his taste in music. Pantera pumped through the speakers and instantly I could see the mood in the room shift. Punches became harder and more precise, and pairs paced around instead of staying glued to one spot.

This class was improving. There were students with real potential. I loved that, at the very least, they all seemed to take the class seriously. The last thing I needed were punks who wasted my time.

I inclined my head to a few pairs and gave positive reinforcement as I walked around the room. I only had to correct one or two posture issues.

Like a magnetic pull, I soon found myself watching Coby with the new girl. He had taken her to the back corner where they were basically as alone as you could be in this room full of people. She bit her lower lip in concentration as she jabbed each punch, her messy bun bobbing with the movement.

I watched Coby drop the pad and come around behind her. He practically had her back up against his chest as he held her arms out teaching her the correct form. She laughed at something he said, turning her body so they were almost flush against each other.

Watching him with her pissed me off. I couldn't hear shit over the music and the pounding of pads and for some unknown reason I wanted to hear what they were talking about. A muscle ticked in my jaw as I bounced on my heels. Normally, it didn't bother me to see Coby flirt, but she just had this innocence about her that I knew he'd completely wreck. I thought about her wide, amber eyes as she had looked at me for guidance the night before. The anxiety had poured from her like an open faucet.

I huffed and forced myself to circle the room again and help someone else before I jumped in and made this woman think I was an even bigger dick. I still couldn't believe I'd reacted so strongly to seeing her on the ground like that. It's been over a year since I'd had a flashback while I was awake. I shook my head, bringing my attention to the present and dismissing those unhelpful thoughts. Setbacks would happen. At least that's what Dr. Glover said. It killed me to feel that out of control and let it affect someone else, too. I'd have to apologize to her. It was the right thing to do since it seemed she was here to stay.

I eyed them again. Coby had given her the pad. He was showing her how to properly hold it by literally pressing it against her chest for her. His fingers curled around the edge of the pad, brushing up against her breasts. She didn't look creeped out or anything. Actually, she was smiling broadly and laughing again.

Her smile completely lit up her face. Those wide eyes crinkled at the edges and seemed to glitter. Something tightened in my chest as Coby tucked a loose curl of hair behind her ear.

"Water break!" I yelled over the music and waited to watch them separate and go to their cubbies. I checked the clock. We still had about fifteen minutes left before class ended. Coby sauntered over sipping out of his water bottle.

"Hey man, I like the music change." He leaned casually against the wall next to me. I wanted to ignore him. That would be petty, but I knew if I turned to look at his face, he'd have that smug grin on.

"I can't stand that house shit." I kept my eyes trained straight ahead.

"Same, give me heavy metal any day over house," he chuckled. "So, I'm shocked Mark asked you to lead today. Congrats man."

I had no response for that. Shocked was a strong word, but I guess he wasn't entirely wrong. Mark rarely took breaks from teaching.

"I'm glad it's you and not me. Now I can get up close and personal with our new level one." He nodded in her direction, smiling. Mia gazed our way and her face lit up at his attention. "It's been too long of a dry spell for me. Hopefully, this one will change that."

I clenched my fists at my side and pushed away from the wall without responding. What could I say? Good for you? Atta boy? He was a grown, thirty-three-year-old man, for fuck's sake.

If she fell for him, then maybe they deserved each other. I just wish I knew why it pissed me off so much.

"Alright, we're going to switch things up a bit. Everyone gather around so I can demonstrate our three main choking defenses." I kept my voice as level as I could, pushing my shitty attitude down deep.

The group circled me at the front of the room. I called for Coby to come join me since I'd need someone to work with. Although me squeezing his neck probably wasn't the best idea.

"I'm going to choke Coby from the front, and he'll break my hold." Most of the group had done this move hundreds of times by now, but not the newbie. I glanced at her and the look of horror on her face told me that she hadn't mentally prepared for this.

"Do your worst boss-man," Coby quipped.

I shook my head, thinking, *yeah you really wouldn't want that, buddy.*

The whole demo took all of two minutes, with me putting pressure on his neck from different positions and him easily breaking my hold.

I dismissed each pair to practice taking turns on each other. Coby walked slowly back to the newbie. He made another joke that got a tense laugh out of her and that irritated the hell out of me. This wasn't a joking matter and, obviously, by the look on her face, she was nervous as fuck about this drill. I watched them closely. Coby let her choke him first. I knew he was loving this—the pervy fuck.

Looking closely, I could see her hands shaking the smallest amount. You wouldn't notice it unless you were paying close attention. That was it.

I needed to step in.

Walking over, I brushed aside her quivering fingers from Coby's neck. A jolt of electricity shot up my arm at the small touch of our skin. Coby looked at me, eyes questioning.

"Since this is your first time with this move, I wanted to come over and make sure you were okay with the form," I said.

She nodded loosening a breath. "Thanks, it..." she stuttered, "it isn't something I realized we'd be learning."

"I understand. We want to teach you how to fight in real-world situations. Because of that chokeholds are a big deal in Krav," I said.

I walked her back through the move using Coby's neck as our dummy, much to his aggravation according to his shifting eyes and slouching posture.

"I get that. Do you think I can try now? I mean... getting out of the choke..." Her voice wavered.

I met her eyes. They were the lightest shade of brown, almost amber, and reminded me of a fall day somehow. "Are you sure you're ready?" I asked.

Why was I coddling her? I shouldn't. If she wasn't serious about being here then she didn't deserve all this attention. But seeing the way she shook I couldn't leave her with Coby. Not that he isn't a decent assistant. He is. He just doesn't take most things seriously.

She nodded. "Yeah, I can do this." She took a step back and asked, "Who am I working with though?" She looked between me and Coby, unsure.

"I'll work with you. Coby, you can go help whoever needs it," I said.

Coby gave me a raised brow but didn't argue.

She looked at me curiously, likely trying to get a read on me.

"Shawn," she said, as she backed toward the wall, "go easy on me, okay?" Her voice sounded so small, I had to talk myself into putting my hands on her neck at all. She was safe though. I'd make sure of it.

I moved closer and gently cupped her neck. It was warm and smooth. Her skin was fair with a smattering of freckles that I hadn't noticed yesterday. Touching her like this made me want to trail my fingers down the slope of her neck to the curve that met her shoulders, even though I knew it was wrong.

Before I knew it, she had broken my loose grip, much quicker than I expected.

"How was that?" She smiled. I noticed the trembling was gone in her hands.

"That was perfect." I appraised her beaming face and let the corner of my lip turn up a touch. "You're a fast learner."

"Yeah, well, I want to take this seriously. Even though it's pulling me way out of my comfort zone." I cupped her neck again. She twisted and broke free a second time.

"I'm glad to hear that." We grew silent as she broke free of my hold again and again. I moved around to let her try to escape a choke from the side and back as well.

"Uh, about yesterday..." The class was nearly over, I knew I had to swallow my pride and apologize to her. "I just wanted to apologize for leaving you in the lurch like that. I was having a bad day and I don't know what came over me."

She stepped back, pausing the drill for a moment to look at me. "It's fine, Shawn. We all have bad days sometimes."

"It won't happen again. I don't make a habit of leaving women knocked flat on their asses."

She nodded as I met her gaze again. I liked how she didn't pry or try to make me feel worse than I already did. We continued the drill for a few more minutes, with the newbie getting more confident with the technique each time she released my grip on her neck.

"By the way, my name is Mia." She gave a cocky smile. "I over-heard you talking to Coby earlier and calling me 'the newbie.'" She twisted and brought her hand down on my arm to break my hold. "And soon enough, I'll be able to knock you on your ass too. Don't you worry."

Mark came out of his office and turned the music off right at that moment. He hollered for everyone to circle up. Mia gave me a wink and went to join the other women.

I'd be lying if I said I didn't watch her full ass walk away from me. That wink and her last comment had my mind spinning.

She was pulling me in, and I didn't think there was anything I could do to fight it at this point.

"Great job level one and thank you to Shawn for leading class tonight." A few people gave a slight applause and Mark continued, "I wanted to announce that this weekend we'll be hosting another gym family party. It'll be at my place and you're all invited. It was a blast last time. You know if you were there." Chuckles sounded around me and even I laughed. I wasn't there, but I had heard all about people getting hammered and jumping into their pool fully clothed. "It's a potluck, so everyone sign up to bring a snack or drink. There's a sign-up sheet hanging on my office door and an email will be sent out tonight with our address. Other than that, have a good night, all, and see you soon."

By the time I gathered my stuff the room was sparse. On my way out, I glanced at the sign-up sheet. People had already sprawled a few names along the lines. Mark caught me by the door.

"Thanks again, man. You're a good leader out there," he said.

I let the praise roll off my shoulders. I had a lot more to learn before I would ever consider myself a good enough teacher.

"I better see your mean mug at the party this weekend." He gestured to the hanging paper. "As a matter of fact, I think I'll sign you up now."

"Mark, I can't make it. I have pieces to finish in the shop this weekend."

"I call bullshit," He chuckled. "There. Shawn signed up to bring chips." He patted me on the shoulder. "You'll thank me one day for pushing you out of that shell you hide in."

I sighed, "You're lucky I love you and Dina, or I wouldn't take this abuse."

"Abuse? Me? I'd never." He walked back into his office laughing at himself. Man was he infuriating in the most lovable way.

I pulled my pickup into the long winding drive of my home, noticing the overgrown brush creeping toward the path. This house was far too large for just me, but I couldn't bring myself to sell it. My grandfather put his heart and soul into fixing it up. On top of that, my woodshop took up the entire backside of the property. I took notice of the creak in the stairs leading up to the wraparound porch, another thing I'd been meaning to fix. I wished this place wasn't so much damn upkeep.

I sighed. Maybe this weekend I'd have the energy.

As soon as the front door opened, Remy, my golden retriever, trotted toward me and nuzzled my legs.

"Hey, Bud, did you miss me?" His big brown eyes bore into mine. "Yeah, I know. You want your dinner. Come on, let's go to the kitchen." I gave his scruffy head a rub, and he followed me around as I gathered both our dinners.

After I fed Remy, I settled myself down onto the couch with a beer and one of my previously prepped meals of grilled chicken, brown rice, and broccoli and flipped on the TV for background noise. My mind wandered back to class, and I replayed each interaction with Mia. The way she raised her brow and told me I'd be on my ass soon enough. Damn, I hadn't seen that coming. It was like a piece of her real personality broke through all the nervousness and anxiety. I wanted to see more. I thought about the way she had laughed with Coby, and how casually they touched each other. Fuck, if that didn't make me wish I was the only one she smiled at or touched.

I thought about that party this weekend. As much as I hated parties, I knew Mark was right. Sitting here in the silence of this big house, eating alone every night with only my dog for company, I get why he probably pitied me.

Remy was stretched out on the floor waiting for me to finish eating so we could go on our nightly walk before bed. "What do you think, boy? Should I get out more?" He looked up at me with a head tilt. "The fact that I'm talking to you tells me all that I need to know."

While shaking my head, I gave him a rub. I thought of Mia and her big brown eyes one last time, and I promised myself I wouldn't bail out. It was time I tried a little harder. Michelle wouldn't have wanted this life for me.

Chapter 6

Mia

THE ICY BLAST OF the air-conditioner was a welcome reprieve as Kendahl and I walked into Cove Mall on Saturday afternoon. As far as malls go, this one was your typical run of the mill. Nothing too bougie like Chanel or Louis Vuitton, but it did have a few decent boutiques that we'd frequent every month in search of cute work outfits or sundresses on sale.

My thighs burned as we walked up the flight of stairs leading to our favorite shop. I was still getting used to all this exercise. Thankfully, Kendahl was looking and acting much more like her old self again and, from what I could tell, only faint bruises remained from her encounter with that drunk, crazy asshole. She still covered up way more than she normally would have in this spring heat, so the bruises had to be there still.

As she sipped her iced coffee and slid her hand through a rack of dresses she leaned to one side, appraising me. "You look different today, Mi, like you're standing straighter or something. I bet it's that class."

I laughed. "Who knows, maybe I am. I mean, I feel pretty good after the first week. But it's only been a week."

"What do you think of this?" She grabbed a cream-colored sundress and held it up against herself, "Cute with one of my beachy straw hats, right?"

I sized it up. "Yeah, it's a cute daytime date dress."

She huffed and shoved it back on the rack.

"What? Come on, eventually, you're going to date again. I know you too well."

Dress after dress in the circular rack slid aside. She pulled out a hideous frock. It looked like a cross between prairie wear and old lady curtains.

"This is more like it. It'll keep all men far away." She squished her face into a weird, wrinkled state and slid the frock back. "Not that it would stop my mother from giving randos my number. I could wear a garbage bag and she'd say, 'I know just the man who would love that on you.'" She was right. I could picture her mother saying that.

I suppressed a giggle. "You're nuts, girl. Correct. But nuts."

I sipped my iced green tea and wandered over to another rack. I needed to find something modest but wouldn't die of heatstroke in for the golf event. I shivered uncomfortably thinking about wearing one of my sleeveless sundresses. I could picture

Lungberg's hungry eyes on my exposed skin. I grabbed two blouses that were light and would pair well with a skirt.

When I looked up, I saw Kendahl staring at her phone screen in front of a swimsuit display. She looked like she was about to cry or throw something. Either way, it wasn't good.

"What's wrong? I walked away for like ten minutes." I came up next to her and peered over at her screen.

Her screen had Facebook open and, front and center, was an engagement announcement for her ex-boyfriend, Ben. Oh no, this was bad.

"Oh, shit. Ken, I'm so sorry. Wait..." I didn't know what to say. "That's not *the* woman, is it?"

"Of course, it is." She shook her head and wiped a tear away. "The very one he was cheating on me with."

"Let's get out of here." I pulled her in for a side hug and tossed my blouses aside. Reaching across her chest, I pried her phone out of her death grip and pulled her toward the fountain benches.

Luckily, the fountain area only had a lone elderly man occupying a bench. I directed her to another bench in a more private spot and steeled myself for a best friend pep talk. Couples holding hands and mothers pushing baby strollers walked by consumed with their own shopping needs. Kendahl reached her hand into the water and idly splashed, staring off into space.

"Did you know that over a thousand dollars per year end up in this fountain?" she said.

"You know, I wouldn't be surprised. I wonder who gets it? Maybe there's some kind of mystery fountain diver that comes and collects his loot every night," I joked.

That got a small chuckle out of her.

"It's going to be okay. I know that asshole broke your heart, but just last week, you were already back on the dating scene. Don't let this bring you back under that cloud. You're too much sunshine to be that way again," I encouraged.

She leaned in and rested her head on my shoulder. "I know you're right, but it still hurts. Why is she good enough to marry, and I was the girlfriend who got cheated on? It's not fair."

If I could see Ben now I'd show him some of my new Krav moves. That asshole was at the top of my shit list.

"It's not fair," I said while I rubbed her shoulder, "but the universe did you a favor. You found out who he really was before you got even deeper. Plus, I bet he'll end up cheating on her, too. Once a cheater, always a cheater." I learned that from my big sister. It was one of her early sisterly life-lesson chats after her first boyfriend broke her heart at age eleven. She loved to watch morning talk show reruns back then and thought she was a relationship counselor.

"You should come to this party with me tonight. I was going to invite you anyway, but we got absorbed in shopping," I supplied.

She lifted her head and bit her lower lip, her light eyes still damp. "I don't know. I don't think I'm ready for a party."

"You think I'd let anything happen to you?" I flexed my biceps obnoxiously. "I'm super ripped after a week of Krav Maga. I can take anyone down."

She snort laughed and leaned over coughing into her hand. Drips of iced coffee spewed out of her mouth.

"Oh my God, you're such a dork. I almost choked on my iced coffee!"

At least she was smiling now. I smiled back brightly and gave her my huge, very pathetic puppy dog eye look.

"It's at my Krav teacher's house. I promise I'll stay with you the whole time. Pretty please! I wuv you Ken dolly."

"You're a five-year-old." She rolled her eyes.

"Only when I want something." I flashed another bright smile. I had her, hook, line, and sinker.

"Fine. I'll come. But only because I know you're an anxious mess at parties."

"You're the best. It'll be great, and it'll take your mind off everything. They're nice people. You'll see."

We walked back toward the boutique. I really wanted those blouses. Maybe I could get Kendahl absorbed in finding a new outfit for the party. A little retail therapy never hurt.

This time we went to the back where more of the night time outfits were. "Come on, let's find something cute for tonight." Then, remembering the bruises, I added, "There are some longer dresses here."

We walked out with two big shopping bags full of stuff and Kendahl looked much happier. I was glad she wasn't alone when she saw the news about Ben.

She bumped my hip. "So, you said everyone would be nice tonight? Does that include the hottie assistant you told me about?" A sly look graced her face.

I guess I deserved the teasing. I was the one dragging her to a party.

"The jury is still out on that one. All I can say is he seems very... intense."

"Intense? That can be hot. Like brooding intense? Or like in-your-face-doesn't-know-personal-space, stage-five-clinger intense?"

I laughed. "God no, nothing like that. I guess brooding would be a good description. Maybe a bit gruff. He just seems kind of sad."

"Aww, maybe he needs a little cheering up?" She winked and laughed again.

I shook my head and made my way toward the exit.

"He probably won't even be there. He doesn't seem like the social type. Not that I've been paying attention or anything, but he doesn't seem to talk to many of the other students."

"Not paying attention? Right." There was way too much sarcasm in her voice than I would have liked to hear. "He sounds like your type. I know you can't resist a fixer-upper. I mean, you are best friends with me."

I almost face-palmed myself. "You're too much."

We hugged and agreed to meet up later to get ready for the party together. Nights like these reminded me of college, only back then it was Kendahl dragging me to parties and not the other way around.

I hopped in my car to head home. I'd have to slog through some work before I met with her. This stupid golf thing wasn't going to plan itself. As I drove, I wondered if Shawn would be there tonight. It didn't seem likely, and maybe Ken was right about me liking a challenge, but I couldn't help but wonder what he'd look like with a smile on his face.

Chapter 7

Mia

As the sun set and the temperature fell, Kendahl and I made our way to Dina and Mark's place. It felt weird seeing these people while I was wearing something other than workout clothes. Kendahl practically shoved me into one of her little black dresses, since I had found nothing that fit both her fashion standards and my curves at the mall. I realized too late that her dress was way shorter than anything I'd normally wear. I let her tame my curls into sleek waves and spruce up my makeup, giving me a smoky eye with winged liner. The results made me feel equal parts sexy and uncomfortable that I'd potentially stand out in the crowd.

Fifteen minutes of driving and my GPS announced that we had arrived. Mark and Dina lived in a well-maintained gated community. They had a modern-looking house, not my style, but beautiful with its sharp edges and lines. Cars filled their street and the driveway.

That's a lot of people.

Beads of sweat collected at the nape of my neck and my temple, having nothing to do with the heat. My instincts were telling me to turn around and leave. I looked over at Kendahl in my passenger seat, whose normal sparkle was dimmed, and I knew I'd have to push through. At least I'd have her to lean on if things got awkward in there.

Parking was a mess, but I squeezed my tiny Civic between two pickup trucks. I tossed my keys in my beaded clutch, grabbed the bottle of wine I brought, and put a reassuring hand on my best friend's shoulder. "Okay, it's now or never."

She flipped open the overhead mirror and checked her lip gloss for the fifth time.

While squeezing Kendahl's shoulder, I spoke to her in a soft voice, "You look great. Stop fussing. You're going to make me even more self-conscious than I already feel."

I stepped out and tugged my dress down knowing damn well that a strip of duct tape could have done a better job covering my ass. Kendahl followed looking hot as hell in her faux leather pants and tucked-in white shirt. There was a sign tacked to the door that read, Krav Family Come On In.

Without hesitating, I pushed it open and we walked inside. The entryway of the house welcomed us with modern art and fresh flowers. Voices were coming from down the hall, so I tugged Kendahl toward the party. Dina spotted us immediately and came over to say hi, smiling brightly. Her long dark hair hung in waves, framing her face, and her dark skin glowed. Her wobbly gait told me she'd already enjoyed a few drinks.

"Hey Mia, glad you could make it. Come on in." She grabbed onto our arms pulling us into a big hug. "Let's get you both a drink. It's a rule that everyone has to do a shot when they get here. You know, loosen the nerves a bit." We followed her into the kitchen. I wasn't going to argue about taking a shot, my nerves needed it.

"Dina, this is my best friend, Kendahl. I hope it's okay that she came along?"

Thinking about it, I really should have called and asked but with all the drama while shopping today, it slipped my mind.

"Of course, the more the merrier," Dina responded.

"I brought this." I handed her the bottle of wine that I carried in. "I'm not the best cook. I figured you can't go wrong with wine." That and it had also slipped my mind to buy groceries to make something. This extra workload was killing me. She grabbed it, putting it in the ice bucket along with another bottle.

"Perfect. We can always use more drinks at these parties." Dina busied herself around the kitchen, tossing out trash and replenishing glassware. Ever the hostess, even while mildly drunk. Her white slab countertops gleamed thanks to the hanging pendant lights. She grabbed a bottle of clear liquid and filled three shot glasses, like a pro, and handed them to us. "Bottoms up."

With a glance at each other, Kendahl and I downed the shots. It burned sliding down my throat, but I immediately felt my limbs loosen up.

"That's better," Dina whooped as she took our empty glasses. "I saved up my first shot of the night to have with you, Mia. So far, it's been wine for me."

My chest relaxed even more. I could tell Dina had a read on me and my anxiety.

"That was so sweet of you. And you have a lovely home, thank you for having us." I said, feeling my cheeks flush from the shot.

"Thank you. So, help yourselves. Drinks are in here and most of the food is in the dining room. I'm going to go check in on things outside. Don't be shy, okay?"

An awkward laugh burst out of me. The sound made me think of an elephant's trumpet. I cringed hard. Thankfully Kendahl replied with a bright thanks.

Dina raised a brow. "Okay, then. See you both in a bit."

I guess it was that obvious that I was socially inept.

Wine in hand, I steadied myself and turned to Kendahl.

"Okay, if you see me turning into Awkward Accountant Girl, you know what to do," I told her.

She cracked a smile. "Oh my God, it's been so long since you've brought up Awkward Accountant Girl." She laughed. "She's my favorite version of you, though. Do I really need to step in?"

"Yes. I'm trying to at least make it look like this isn't the first non-work party that I've been to in over a year." She loved to tease me. "Be my wing woman, you know I need you."

"Okay...," she sighed. "But you owe me. You know I'm still not myself, but I'll channel my amazing, glowing personality just for you."

I pinched her nose causing her to squeal a little. "That's why I keep you around."

She swallowed a sip of white wine and pulled me out of the kitchen and into the fray. Keeping with the modern decor, the house had a huge open great room, with sleek furnishings and neutral colors throughout. A few people I didn't recognize were scattered around on couches, holding beers and plates of food. They must have been in higher-level classes. Most of the noise was coming from beyond the French doors.

As we walked in that direction, a couple of interested faces looked up from their conversations to stare at us. Or at least I felt like they were staring. I looked down at my shoes willing my feet to step forward. Kendahl, being herself, waved and greeted them with a cheerful hello.

She whispered to me, "Head up, lady or I'm not going to wing woman for you. You can do this. I'm sure once we get outside there will be at least someone else that you know."

I gulped more delicious wine and noticed my glass was already almost empty, as we made our way outside into the humid night air.

Their patio was gorgeous, with white twinkle lights hanging from a large wooden pergola and cushioned birch couches set up around coffee tables. In their yard, front and center was a large pool with an attached spa. A few chatty people already floated in it. To the left of the pool, I spotted Dina and Mark talking animatedly to a small group around a gas firepit.

I kept scanning and it was then that I noticed Anna and, her husband, Jake in their group, as well as Avery. I inhaled, the air finally reaching my chest. At least I wasn't the only level one here.

"I know a few of them," I said to Kendahl in hushed tones.

"Oh good, because we were just about to say hello."

I introduced Kendahl to everyone, and she quickly steered the conversation away from Krav to her job in PR.

Dina refilled my wine at least once, and the conversation went more smoothly with each glass. Anna complimented me on my first week of class and my chest swelled with pride since I was trying so hard to not suck. I kept quiet, absorbing everyone else's stories unless a question was directed my way.

It wasn't long before Coby showed up, he surprised me by sneaking up behind me and giving my shoulder a light squeeze.

A small yelp escaped my lips from the contact. When I whipped my head around, there he was smiling like the Cheshire Cat, dimples and all.

"Jumpy aren't you, Mia?" Coby said, "Sorry, I didn't mean to startle you that badly."

I shifted from one foot to the other and let out an awkward laugh. "It's fine, I guess I am kind of on edge."

And maybe, I was hoping the teeniest bit that there would be a certain sandy haired assistant behind me instead. But I'd never voice that out loud.

Kendahl, sidled up next to us and in that instant I saw all of Coby's attention shift to my best friend. His hazel eyes lit up and it could have been the wine getting to me but the way they were eyeing each other made it warmer all the sudden.

"Mia, who's your friend?" Coby asked before bringing his glass of amber liquid to his lips.

Kendahl jumped right in, stepping in closer to Coby and introducing herself with a flirtatious grin.

After a few minutes of listening to them chat back and forth, inching closer to each other, I took the hint and excused myself.

At least Kendahl was smiling genuinely again. I knew bringing her to the party was a good idea. She needed a little distraction, and from what I could tell about Coby, he was a huge flirt and exactly her type.

I decided I should find something to eat as I was wobbling on my feet a bit. I hadn't eaten dinner yet and after that shot and at least two glasses of wine, I was feeling pretty buzzed.

The quieter vibe inside the house was exactly what I needed. Without my wing woman the large groups on the patio were a lot to handle. So much small talk with people I'd just met. They were all incredibly nice, and I felt welcome, but baby steps. I scanned the room and there were no familiar faces. *It's fine,* I thought. I was just happy Kendahl was having a good time.

They filled the long dining table with bowls of chips, different dips, and appetizers. My focus went to the cookie platters and mini cupcake trays at the end of the table. Desserts were my weakness, especially when I was drinking.

I grabbed a plate and started loading treats onto it when I felt the back of my neck prickle with awareness. Turning on my heels my gaze locked directly onto cobalt-blue eyes framed with thick, dark lashes. Shawn was here, and he was staring at me with intensity from a few feet away.

I looked him up and down, more slowly than I would have in a sober state. *Thanks, wine.* But I couldn't help myself. This man was insanely hot. Dressed in a black T-shirt that barely contained his inked biceps, and a pair of fitted dark wash jeans, he looked mouthwatering. Light brown stubble, a shade darker than the hair on his head covered his prominent jaw line. Something about the intensity of his stare only added to my attraction. Having his full attention on me made me squirm internally with nervous excitement.

Heat pooled between my thighs, and I quickly looked away forcing myself to focus on the dips in front of me. I needed my pulse to slow down so I wouldn't be a stumbling idiot in front of him, for a second time.

I could sense him coming closer thanks to that tingle back on my neck and exposed shoulders. I turned. I couldn't help it. There he was, right next to me. Breathing deeply, his scent invaded my senses. It reminded me of a rainy day in my hometown in rural New York mixed with something woodsy and smoky. I wanted to bury my face in his chest and inhale more of it.

Holy shit, I was a creeper. This is why I needed Kendahl by my side, especially when I was drinking and my everyday awkwardness became tipsy awkwardness. She'd have nudged me for staring and told me to stop being a baby and go talk to him already.

Shawn opened a bag of chips, set them on the table and looked right at me again.

"I love them." I mumbled the first thing that came to mind.

His brows raised, "Huh?"

Oh God, why was I allowed to speak? I should become mute. I should've taken a vow of silence and maybe joined a convent while I was at it.

"The chips," I muttered, "kettle… they're my favorite."

He smirked, and his brows raised again. "I'd have to agree."

He leaned back on his heels watching me finish scooping dip onto my paper plate. My cheeks flushed from his attention.

"I love a good crunch, especially with dips." I should have just stuffed this delicious food into my face. Then maybe I would have stopped rambling.

Shawn kept his casual posture with his hands slung in the pocket of his jeans. He seemed to think about what he wanted to say. "Who doesn't love a good crunch?"

I noticed a glob of dip smeared on the outside of my hand and cursed myself. Where were the napkins? I couldn't lick the damn dip off my hand in front of this guy. I looked around hoping to find something to nonchalantly clean myself up with. I'd be ninja-quick, no need to draw attention to my mess. Until, no more than a second later, I got an itch from hell on my chest and idiotically scratched it with said dip hand. Now I was a jabbering fool with a big white splotch front and center on my boobs.

"Crap." I dabbed at the mess with my bare hand only smearing it worse.

Shawn stepped closer holding a napkin he must have summoned out of thin air. "Here, this might help." There was a gleam in his eyes that told me he was barely suppressing a smile.

The napkin didn't help. The damage was done. Oh well.

"I'm just going to... uh..." I pointed to the nearest couch with the plate still in my hand to indicate I was heading that way.

"I'll join you," he said.

"No, it's okay. You don't have to. I'm sure you have plenty of friends here to go talk with."

I finished off my wine while holding my embarrassingly full plate of junk food willing myself not to drop it. Before I even reached the couch, Shawn's fingers grazed mine.

"Here, let me take your glass. I'll go refill it for you and grab a beer. White wine, right?"

How'd he know? "Uh...," I stumbled, "I'll come with you. No offense or anything, but I just don't trust anyone else to touch my drinks." A flash of approval crossed his face.

"That's very smart of you. You can trust me, but of course, someone who wanted to take advantage of you would also say that."

"Exactly. I can't be too careful." I knew firsthand what could happen when a person trusted too easily.

With refilled beverages in hand, we settled into the leather couch. I closed my eyes and gave myself a quick pep talk.

Mia, don't make things weird. Yes, he's hotter than any guy you've ever laid eyes on in real life. Yes, his muscles could rival Henry Cavill's in Superman, but he's just a guy. Just a guy. You got this.

My pep talk wasn't going to do a thing. I knew it. Shawn moved closer to me, leaning back into the cushion, and that incredible scent overtook me again.

He took a swig from his beer bottle. Meanwhile, I was shifting around trying to keep at least most of my thighs covered by this barely there, now stained, dress. I turned to him. "So, fun party, huh? Is this your first time coming to one?"

He was quiet for a moment. His eyes kept jumping from my face to my plate and back again. "Aren't you going to eat your food?" he responded.

"Huh?" The noise slipped out of me.

"Your food. You haven't touched it." He nodded at my plate causing a piece of his hair to fall forward. I wanted to reach out and tuck it back in.

"Oh." I picked up a cookie and took a nibble. I was hungry, but I had a tough time eating in front of people. It started when

I was young with my mother always making such a fuss over everything I ate saying I had to watch my figure. Olivia was always naturally slim with an athletic build, but I went from a small-child body to a curvy-adult body the moment puberty hit.

He brought his beer to his lips and pulled. I sat so close that I could hear the sip slide down his throat and see his Adam's apple bob.

"To answer your question," he looked away toward the window, "no, I haven't been to these parties before." That surprised me. He seemed close to Mark and Dina. He must have been a student for a long time to be assistant teaching.

"I never really had a reason to come," he finished.

His intense gaze met my eyes again, and I knew my face was crimson. I cleared my throat and bit into the cookie again needing to distract myself from staring back at him.

He reached over and gingerly touched my bottom lip. "You had a little crumb right there."

Holy God. His finger felt calloused against my lip. My thighs clenched together and I cleared my throat again. "Uh, thanks."

"You always eat dessert first? Or is it just a party thing?"

I tried to remember how to use words before I answered. "Not always. I do have a bit of a sweet tooth, though. If the choice is between a veggie platter and cookies, I'm going for the chocolate."

An easy smile curved the corner of his lips, not quite reaching his eyes, but it was the closest to a full smile I'd seen on him.

"You?" I leaned forward and set the plate on the table in front of me. He followed my gaze and then his eyes landed on my lap. I realized my plate had been covering most of my exposed thighs and I clenched them together again.

"Do you mean, am I more of a dessert guy?" He leaned in closer, so close that I could feel the warm puff of air escape his lips as he exhaled. His voice sounded rich and smooth with a tiny amount of shakiness. "It depends on what's for dessert."

I was mid-sip as those words left his mouth. The wine slid down the wrong tube in my throat making me choke.

Then I was leaning forward and hacking into my hand. Shawn patted my back. His palm felt as large as a baseball mitt.

"I'm okay...," I cleared my throat, "just went down wrong."

He gave a knowing smirk again, that twinkle back in his eyes.

I took another sip of wine. Not the brightest idea as I was still wheezing from my near-death-by-wine experience.

Shawn went to pat my back again, but I put my hand up. "I'm fine," sucking a breath in, "just need a second."

He slid his hand back settling it in the space between us. So. Damn. Close to my thigh. I only needed to scoot an inch and our skin would be touching. The longer we sat quietly, the more I noticed our closeness.

"So... uh... you did a great job teaching yesterday. I enjoyed watching you." *Backtrack, Mia.* "I mean, I enjoyed how you demoed." Was I sweating? I was sweating.

With a husky laugh, he replied thanks and took another swig of his beer. "You're doing well. I wore extra shin protection yesterday and didn't even need it."

The hand holding my wineglass stopped halfway to my mouth, and I winced. "Oh God. I'm sorry again."

Shaking his head, he gave another half-smile. "I'm kidding, Mia. Although now that I think about it, it's not a bad idea to keep shin guards in my gym bag."

I gulped down more wine, leaned back, and groaned. "You're probably right. The way I'm going, you'll need them next time we partner up." What was I saying? He wouldn't be my partner again. That had to be a one time thing. "I mean, *if* we do," I corrected.

He shook his head. An easy laugh escaped his lips, and he brought his intense gaze back to me. "I meant it when I said you were doing well." He reached out and moved a curl from my face. So gently that if I hadn't seen his hand moving, I may not have registered him doing it. "And I'd be lucky to work with you again."

He was saying all the right things. And looking at me like *that* with those eyes and that face and—oh my God—those forearms. Why hadn't I noticed them before? My body was on fire. I needed a water hose. Or a fan. More wine too—that was most important.

I looked out the window, breaking our gaze, and cleared my throat. Some air would be good.

"I should probably go check on my guest," I said.

"Oh, you brought someone?" His shoulders drooped slightly as he looked toward his knees.

I stood up carefully, gripping the arm of the couch for stability. "I brought my best friend, Kendahl. She needed a night out. I think she's talking with Coby still."

Something flickered in his eyes as he raised himself up next to me taking one last sip of his beer and leaving it on the table with my untouched plate. "I'll come with you."

"You don't have to," I said, pulling my dress lower and adjusting an unruly hair behind my ear. "I'm sure Mark wants to hang out with you and everything."

He didn't respond, just walked slowly toward the patio.

"Okay, then... I guess you're coming with me." I mumbled under my breath and followed him out back.

Chapter 8

Shawn

I GUESS I COULD call Coby my buddy, or the closest thing I had to one these days, but that didn't mean I trusted the guy. It was bad enough that he was all over Mia in class, but now he was probably pulling out all the same moves on her friend too.

A protective urge bubbled up inside of me wanting to break free and bring Mia closer. That protection also included anyone important to her, and while I knew Coby wouldn't be a complete piece of shit and ever harm a woman, I didn't trust him not to take advantage of the situation.

We made it onto the patio, Mia trailing behind me. I chuckled a little at her awkwardness.

"Is everything okay?" Mia asked as she closed the patio door. Her voice was starting to slur the smallest amount.

"Yeah," I said in reply.

"Oh." She paused to adjust her dress. "I was just asking because you seemed kind of upset?"

I let my gaze linger on her flushed face, thinking of a response. "Not upset. Let's find your friend."

"Yes sir. No conversation necessary." She faked a comically awful drill sergeant tone that almost had me cracking a smile. I'd relax when we saw that her friend was okay.

As we searched the large backyard for Mia's friend I thought over her comment. She seemed to have pegged me correctly. I am a man of few words, at least with most people. I'm always observing the situation in front of me, whether it be a person or an action, to be ready for anything. I wanted to be one step ahead. I found mindless chatter hindered my focus. Plus, I had to make enough exhausting small talk with clients, so why would I want to keep that shit up when I didn't have to?

But, seeing Mia at such a loss for words that she had resorted to talking about chips was pretty good. The way her face flushed when she noticed me staring at her, I could feel my cock tighten. Then that ranch dip dripped onto her chest. It was like a higher-powered being was trying to fuck with me.

Mark noticed us come outside and cut off his conversation. "Hey!" he hollered and gave a quick wave, brows raised. That smug prick was happy to see me here. He's bugged me dozens of times to come over for barbeques or even small get-togethers. He had to have been positive I'd bail on this party.

"Hey, we were just about to do shots. You two in?" Mark asked.

I glanced back at Mia, and she stopped in her tracks, looking ecstatic. What I really wanted to do was say a quick hello and go find her friend but if Mia was stopping to talk then I would too.

I shook my head, "Nah, I'm good on the shot, man. But I'll come hang out."

Mia was fitting right in with them. Her head tilted back, shooting whatever concoction was in that glass more than once. If I guessed, it was most likely tequila, but at least Mark didn't skimp. He only bought the good stuff. I didn't pay any mind to their conversations; I was too busy noticing the blush of Mia's cheeks, and the way her face glowed when she felt comfortable.

Mia laughed heartily at something Mark said and when she saw me watching her a few paces outside the circle, she excused herself and joined me again, albeit slowly and less balanced than before.

"You okay?" I asked, even though I knew those shots would have put her from buzzed into drunk territory, but she was a grown woman, and I wouldn't tell her what to do or not to do.

"All good here," Mia chirped, her voice higher than usual.

On the couches behind the pool, I spotted Coby with Mia's friend. They were alone and looked to be chatting like old friends. I focused on them, and to my surprise, Coby's hands were to himself. Maybe I misjudged him.

They must have heard our footsteps because Coby broke his gaze from the friend and looked between Mia and me.

"Hey you two, we were just saying we should check in with Mia." Coby looked at the friend for clarification.

"I didn't realize how long we had been talking until I got a text from my mom and saw the time. It's been a while." She beamed at Mia. "You all good, Mi?"

Mia swayed a bit and grabbed the couch for balance. "Yup, am fantastical."

I grabbed her waist and held her firmly so she wouldn't topple over. Her waist was soft and warm through the thin material of her dress. Up close, she smelled feminine and floral. Intoxicating.

"Whoa, girlfriend. How much wine have you had?" her friend asked, face glued to where my hands wrapped around Mia's waist. "And who is your, um, friend?"

Mia leaned into me, a small sound escaping her throat like a hum. It was adorable. I led her around the furniture to sit next to her friend on the couch. She grabbed my arm and trailed her hand lightly over my palm before leaning against her friend's shoulder. Goosebumps came to life all over my body, sending a tremble to my toes. It had been so long since I'd been touched that way.

"Him?" She poked at my stomach. "Oh, that's hard."

I shook my head, laughter threatening to escape. Sticking my hand out, I introduced myself. "I'm Shawn. And Mia, here, she just had a run-in with some of Mark's strong tequila."

"I'm Kendahl." Then she gave Mia a knowing smile. "Tequila? Girl, you know better," she huffed, appraising her friend. "I guess this is what happens when I leave her for a little while." She stroked Mia's wavy hair as Mia rested on her shoulder.

I clenched my jaw wishing it were my hands running through her hair. I caught Coby watching them too, a gleam in his eye.

Mia's eyes drifted shut. She looked so peaceful.

"I should get her home," Kendahl said, shifting in her seat. "I wasn't planning on leaving yet. I was going to give myself another hour to sober up, but I think I'm fine to drive."

I caught Coby's gaze at that moment. I knew he was about to offer, so I cut him off.

"I'll bring you both home. We can pick up your car tomorrow." Coby's lips formed a straight line. He may have been a gentleman so far, but no way in hell would I let him drive two drunk girls home. I didn't trust any man to do that.

Kendahl looked between the two of us and a realization formed that she barely knew me, and she had been talking with Coby all night. She breathed in, clearly torn.

"I promise, nothing will happen to either of you."

The seriousness in my tone had her nodding. "Okay, but I'm taking a picture of your driver's license, just in case."

That made me chuckle under my breath. I couldn't blame her for being cautious.

She gently shook Mia, whispering something into her ear. Mia sat up a bit, her wavy hair hiding half of her face.

"Did I fall asleep?" she asked yawning and pulling her hair back into a hair tie. Then she shifted her gaze to me. "You're here? Oh man, was I snoring?"

Kendahl laughed, "No, don't worry. You were every bit as dignified as you always are. Come on, Shawn's going to drive us home."

Mia started to protest, but, like a sleepy child, Kendahl helped her up off the couch. Coby stood too, still wearing an expectant look on his face.

"It was really nice to meet you," he murmured to her, but I could still hear what he was saying. "Can I get your number? I'd love to take you out sometime."

Kendahl struggled with a half-limp Mia and flashed him a smile. "Yeah, sure. One second, let me just adjust her." Mia played with Kendahl's hair, twirling it around her finger. Kendahl glanced at me, eyes wide.

"Here, I'll help her. You two take a minute." She flashed an appreciative grin my way, and I reached out to cradle Mia's waist. "We'll meet you out front. I have the gray pickup."

Nodding, she turned to talk with Coby quietly.

"Let's head out front, okay?" I asked, guiding her through the yard. She grabbed onto my hand, her small purse dangling from her other hand.

"Lemme take off these heels. Hold on." She murmured through a yawn.

With the grace of a baby giraffe, she lurched over, ass half out to undo the strap of her black heel. As much as I liked the view, I didn't want anyone else getting a free show.

I scooped her up into my arms before she could register what was happening. "What...?" she stammered, then giggled.

"You're like a superhero." Her head rested against my shoulder. I grabbed her purse and held onto it before she dropped it.

I shook my head and tried to ignore the way her body felt against mine, but it was near impossible. Her hair brushed against my neck and her ass was two inches from sitting in my palm. My breathing hitched, but I soldiered on and gave Mark a quick wave. His face instantly morphed into a shit-eating grin. I was going to be razzed for this tomorrow.

Halfway to the front door, Mia's head came up, "Wait! Hafta pee. Where's the bathroom?"

"Okay. I think there's one over here. Do you want to wait for Kendahl in case you need help?"

She shook her head. "I'll be 'kay... 'm all good."

I turned to see if Kendahl was behind us, but she hadn't come inside yet. Sighing, I carried Mia over to the half-bathroom and put her down gingerly in front of the open door.

"Be out inna sec," she mumbled while pushing through the door with more force than necessary. "Whoopsie, that's lighter thennit looked."

I nodded my head curbing the laughter that was bursting to escape. "I'll wait right here."

She closed the door, and I stood against the wall waiting. My mind reeled thinking over our interactions tonight. There was no doubt about it. I felt something for Mia. Not sure what those feelings meant but they were there. Which only meant I should keep her away from me. She was too young and sweet to deal with my baggage. It was bad enough that I hadn't stayed away thus far, but after tonight, I had to keep our relationship purely professional. I was her assistant teacher, and she was my student. I was fucked in the head, and she was baggage free.

Outside, I could see Kendahl still talking with Coby. I wondered if I should offer to let her stay and just take Mia home. I'd be a judgmental prick if she took me up on the offer, and let her drunk friend leave with a stranger. Friends should watch each other's backs. But still, maybe I should, anyway. I didn't want to leave Mia here, that was for sure.

"Mia? You okay in there?" I knocked lightly. "Should I see if your friend wants to stay?"

No reply.

Damn, did she fall asleep on the toilet? That tequila hit her hard.

"Mia? All good?"

She mumbled something from behind the door. Okay, at least she was awake. But I had no idea what the hell she said.

For a few seconds, I debated with myself: should I go in or give her a few more minutes? I didn't want her to get the wrong idea, but I'd be a complete asshole to leave her here. Outside, I could only see the back of Kendahl's blonde head. She and Coby were most definitely making out.

"Christ," I grumbled running my hand through my hair. I knocked again.

No answer.

"I'm coming in," I announced.

In the tiny bathroom, Mia sat on the floor in front of the toilet. I kind of figured she'd gotten sick. What I hadn't expected was the top half of her dress to be hanging down showing pretty much all of her strapless bra. My words caught in my throat. She was beautiful, even like this, getting sick in a bathroom. What the fuck was I just thinking five minutes ago about staying away?

I crouched down and rubbed her shoulder unfortunately getting a look into the bowl. She looked up.

"Mia, you okay?" I asked. Her eyes were glassy, but she nodded with her head slumping forward as if it were heavier than normal. "Here, let me help."

I reached out and flushed the toilet, but not before shutting the lid to the bowl. "Let's sit you down for a second." Instinct took over as I carefully wiped her face and hands using a warm washcloth.

"My dress! Oh no," she pointed to the folded-over front, "wait... this is Kendahl's dress." She slumped back against the toilet.

"It's fine. Nothing a good washing can't fix." I reassured her remembering the dip stain that already soiled her front.

I pulled my T-shirt off and tucked it over her head. She sighed.

"Better now?" I asked, trying not to think of the fact that I hadn't been shirtless in front of a woman in years and that seeing her in my shirt did all kinds of things to my chest and cock.

"Mush better." She looked up at me, eyes widening. The air inside this small space suddenly became much warmer.

"Here, I got you. Let's go outside."

I picked her up again, and I could still smell her floral scent over the faint hint of vomit. Luckily, I had a tough stomach for these kinds of things. Her face veered closer to mine and she licked her bottom lip. I had to look away until she rested her head on my bare shoulder again. It wasn't lost on me that her head fit in the curve of my shoulder perfectly. Once outside, I noticed a few people lingering near their cars and I nodded their way. If they thought the sight of me, shirtless, and carrying a woman was odd, they didn't show it.

As I buckled Mia into my front passenger seat she took my face into her hands. "Your eyes—they're sooo shiny, like two crystals." She ran her finger along the stubble of my cheek down to the divot in my chin and said, with more clarity than she'd had most of the night, "You're beautiful."

I stared at her full lips knowing damn well if I kissed her now, I'd be doomed. Blinking, I noticed her breaths, warm and fast, anticipating. Her eyes slid closed.

I jerked myself upright.

"Crystals, huh?" That pulled a smile out of me. "That's a first."

She was already asleep. I would have to ask Mark what the hell kind of tequila he gave this poor woman. She would be hurting tomorrow.

A few moments later, Kendahl reached my truck, Coby following closely behind her.

"Shawwwn... there you are. 'M so sorry!" She stumbled a bit over the curb. "Since you're driving us I figured I could finish my drink. Then Mark showed up with shots and made me do one."

Oh, I bet it was so forced. I held back an eye roll. "It's alright. Coby, can you help her in?"

"Yeah." He opened the back door and practically lifted her into the truck while whispering something into her ear that only she could hear. Whatever it was caused her to kiss him.

I cleared my throat. "See you later, Coby."

He looked up at me, in a daze. "Sorry, man. See you later. Get them home safe, okay?" He gave the top of my truck a light pound and then shut her door.

"Can you give me an address?" I asked hopefully to the beaming face behind me.

"Les just go to my apartment. I forget Mia's address. I only know it's near Grand Street—or is it Juniper Street?" She took out her phone, the blue light blinding. "Wait, I think it's Palm something." That described about half of the town.

"It's okay. I can bring you guys to your place."

She rambled off her address, which wasn't very far from Mark's.

The ride home was quiet with Mia still sound asleep and Kendahl furiously texting someone on her phone. Within a half hour, I had them both walked up to the second-story apartment. Kendahl thanked me and assured me she was fine and could get Mia settled in.

My jaw ticked and I left worried Mia would end up vomiting again or something. But she was out of my hands now.

By the time I walked Remy and climbed into bed, my thoughts drifted back to Mia saying I was beautiful. She found me attractive too. *God damn*. If only I was a man who was worthy of such a beautiful woman. I pictured Mia lying beside me, her curly hair splayed out around her head like a halo. Did I finally want to try again? Even if I did, I had to stop imagining what could be with Mia. She deserved better.

My only question was, did I have the strength to stay away?

Chapter 9

Shawn

The following Monday, I forced my mind to focus on work. Sleep had evaded me after I woke-up in a cold sweat around two o'clock in the morning because of another night terror. I could never remember the details, but I could feel the pure panic course through my veins.

Opening my shop a couple of hours early, so I could get a head start on a set of custom cabinets I've been building seemed like the best idea. The whirring of my table saw and the steady riffs of classic rock coming from the speaker nearby worked to keep me from focusing on the night terrors. But today it wasn't enough to keep me from thinking of Mia and the way we were so close to kissing the other night.

There was no doubt in my mind that she was into me. Cocky as it may seem, I picked up on those signals. Unfortunately for her, she has no idea what she'd be getting herself into.

I looked up at the clock and realized it was already past nine and I'd been at it for hours. It was time for coffee and to stretch my aching limbs. I whistled for Remy to follow me back up to the house and he abandoned the tennis ball he was ripping apart, tail wagging as he followed.

A few minutes later, coffee in hand and Remy behind me, I walked back into the shop and almost collided with Camila, my part-time assistant and organization aide. Coffee sloshed over the top of my mug, and I used my other hand to steady it. Camila turned, an apologetic look on her face.

"Sorry—I didn't hear you come in behind me." She grabbed some tissues from her nearby desk and reached to wipe away the coffee splashed on my arm. "There, that's better." She beamed and scrambled to toss the soiled tissues away.

"Thanks." I nodded and walked back toward my work area.

Remy sidled over to her and started rubbing his head against her leg. She bent over to give him a pet and then followed me. This was another reason I tried to get into the shop early each day. Not that Camila wasn't a nice woman, but when I worked I liked the quiet, where I could focus on my craft.

"So, when I got in this morning, I noticed the yard could use some work. If you want, I could come over on Saturday and help you?" She smiled at me with her mouth abnormally wide. "I don't mind. I actually enjoy gardening."

"Thanks, for the offer. I'm sure you have better things to do than help me in the yard on your Saturday."

Assessing the wood in front of me, I grabbed my sander and turned it on low. Camila's face dropped and she let out a low, "Okay," before turning back to her desk. I knew I was being a dick, and she's a sweet woman, but I can see the pity in her eyes when she looks at me. She's another one who's too good for me and my baggage.

The afternoon went by with no interruptions. I nearly finished the cabinets. They just needed another coat of sealant. By four o'clock in the afternoon on a late spring day, the heat was oppressive even with the portable air-conditioning units I had installed a few years ago.

I ran a hand through my sweaty hair, and then I got to cleaning up the area. Clutter has always caused my shoulders to tighten and stomach to churn. Gramps was a neat freak, especially with his workshop. Maybe his tendencies rubbed off on me.

I stored my tools safely on the workbench and capped the spray bottles tightly. Remy looked up at me from his dog bed where he was currently waking up from his afternoon snooze.

"Come on, boy. Time to be done for the day." I wanted to get a shower and a meal before class tonight.

Camila looked up at me, still at her desk, "Wow, is it four already?"

"Thanks for coming in today. Don't forget to lock up on your way out."

"Hold on. An email came in earlier, but I didn't want to bother you." She clicked away on the laptop in front of her and pulled up an email from my accountant. "It looks like Dan is finally retiring."

I quickly read over the letter. "Looks like it. Good for him, but what a pain in the ass for me."

Dan had been my accountant and bookkeeper since my grandpa was still running things. They were buddies who bonded over their love of baseball. I've been grateful for him, since I knew absolutely nothing about the financial aspect of running my business. Between Camila and Dan handling all that, I've been free to only worry about the physical side, building and refinishing.

"I'll look up some local accountants so the transfer will be seamless. I bet Dan would have some recommendations, possibly." She looked up at me with bright eyes.

"That would be great, thank you."

"Oh, and I'll send Dan and his wife a card on our behalf, congratulating him on his retirement."

Nodding, I headed toward the door.

Camila gave another, "Good night, Shawn," but I was already outside.

I was the first person at the gym for the evening, wanting some quiet time to warm up before all the level ones came in. Mark spotted me from his office and gave me a slight nod then went back to the paperwork in front of him.

I breathed in the comforting scent of metal with a tinge of sweat and made my way toward the mat. Here, with the large room to myself, I could breathe and center while connecting with the tight muscles from a day of labor. I could release my pent-up tension through stretching and shadowboxing.

I heard the front door open and glanced up, hoping to see a head of brown curls, but it was only Coby. He usually came in early too, so that we could chat with Mark before class and find out what he needed from us.

I kept my eyes down not wanting to engage with Coby yet. I still needed a few more minutes to ground myself. Plus, starting a conversation with Coby was never likely to end quickly.

Standing, I went through a few more rounds of shadowboxing, roundhouse kicking, and punching an invisible target. I spun around, kicking out low, then higher, keeping my stance tight and my arms blocking my face. I could sense Coby across the room doing the same thing, but I was in my head and my own space.

Sweat coated my forehead by the time I finally looked out toward the office, a noise breaking me from my trance. My eyes immediately locked with Mia's, but she quickly looked away, blushing. One of the women from the class was chatting with her, flapping her hands around for emphasis.

Mia probably felt awkward after the party on Saturday night. There was no reason to, although if the tables were turned, I'd be embarrassed. I wondered how much she remembered. The blush on her cheeks reminded me of her face as she looked up at me from my passenger seat. I thought about that look for the rest of the weekend.

Mark leaned against his office door talking with Coby. After grabbing a sip of water and a towel for my neck, I joined them.

"You look like you already got a good workout in," Mark teased, breaking me from my thoughts. "Hope you have enough energy to assist today. I've got a good one planned for level one."

I chugged another gulp of water and wiped my brow. "You know me. I'm just getting started."

"Can't wait to see what ass-kicking you're handing out tonight." Coby lightly punched Mark's arm garnering himself a death look.

"You know I'd square up if I didn't have to teach a class right now." They laughed and walked into the gym.

Following behind them, I searched again, instinctively looking for Mia. She had taken up a spot in the back of the room near the side wall. Her confidence still wasn't where it should be, but I guess that's to be expected for a newbie. I wondered what Mark had in store for today and if Mia would have a partner to work with.

Mark's voice rose above all the banter and the room silenced. He paced against the length of the wall at the front of the room. "If any of you have thought previous classes were out of your comfort zone, well, tonight think of your comfort zone as being catapulted away."

A few light chuckles sounded around the space, but mostly everyone stayed silent, listening. I knew what was coming. He gave this same speech back when I was in level one.

"This next drill is likely the most critical thing you'll learn in here. It's also the most difficult." Coby sported an easy grin. "I see that face, Coby. It's ground fighting time," Mark said.

He spent the next few minutes going from straddling Coby and fake punching or choking him to being flat on his back on the concrete floor. I watched them take turns bucking hips, bear-hugging, rolling, and getting out of each other's grips so fast it looked like a choreographed scene. It wasn't as easy as it looked. These skills took time, strength, and a certain level of comfort to execute properly.

"Do you see how Coby is hooking his leg around mine and using his body weight to turn me?" The group looked on, determination on their faces. "Don't worry, it'll take time and we'll be walking around to check in with each pair. Find a partner who you feel most comfortable with and take turns. Each person will try to roll their partner three times." He clapped like a proper coach and turned up the music.

More shitty house music.

I knew I'd have to walk around and assist all the pairs, but I immediately gravitated toward Mia, who thankfully partnered up with another woman. For a minute there I tensed up thinking I'd have to watch her straddle one of these dudes.

The pair sat on the ground, hands fumbling at their sides before I heard the other woman rasp that she'd go first in trying to flip Mia. Mia nodded and they got into position. I kneeled next to them and Mia's eyes met mine. Looking deeply into them was like freezing time and space around me and it pulled me into her spell.

"Hey Shawn, want to give us some pointers?" I snapped back into the present. She turned back to the woman below her. "Mark went so fast that we have no clue where to start," she said, her voice was soft but determined.

"Uh… yeah… yes, that's what I'm here for," I stammered and then stood up, skimming my eyes over their form. "Ideally, you'd want your attacker to sit a bit lower, but you both look good."

I didn't miss the slight blush on Mia's face.

"Mia, pretend to punch, uh… I'm sorry, I didn't catch your name," I said to her partner.

She cackled. "Honey, I've been coming here for a few months now. I'm Evelyn, Evie, for short. I guess I'm not a looker like this one up here." She gestured to Mia, hovering over her. "I should say, not anymore. But back when I was her age, the guys were lining up for me—women too." She winked and squeezed my thigh.

The only thing I could do was shake my head laughing lightly. Mia joined me.

"Evie! You're still a total hottie. Your body is fire. I'm semi-afraid you're going to launch me into the air when you roll me off of you."

"Doll, you're too funny. Now come on and pretend to choke me out." She cackled a laugh again. "Reminds me of spring break '89, but that's a story for another day."

Jesus, this woman is a trip. "Okay, Evie, let's see what you've got," I directed.

Mia placed her hands around Evie's throat. I could see how gentle she was, barely touching skin. Her eyes shifted back to mine, and I nodded at her. *You got this, baby.*

Clumsily, but with great force, Evie rolled Mia off of her with a grunt that could rival a feral boar. Mia ended up flat on her back, messy curls floating above her head, her face flushed with laughter. Her smile was infectious, and I found myself laughing with them as they reset two more times and Evie heaved like her life depended on it.

I pulled her up from the floor the third time. Evie had sort of flung her and she had ended up a few feet away somehow. I needed to remember to never underestimate an older woman's strength. Without thinking, I reached out and ruffled Mia's messy bun giving her hair a light squeeze. It was just as soft as I remembered when her head laid against my shoulder on Saturday. I wanted nothing more than to feel those strands against my bare chest again.

Her breath hitched at my touch. "Thanks. I guess she's a lot stronger than she looks."

"Hey, I heard that. You ready for me, little one?" Evie squeezed my arm, a sweet smile lighting up her face.

Mia and I gave each other knowing looks. "As ready as I'll ever be."

Chapter 10

Mia

I couldn't have been more grateful to Evie for loosening the tension gnawing away at me. Mark wasn't kidding when he said this would be uncomfortable. I wasn't even close to coming to terms with the chokeholds, but this brought a whole new level of real-life self-defense right to me. While I sat on Evie, lightly choking her, I willed away the thoughts of my sister. They kept coming back like ants attacking a picnic basket. Was this how her attacker had pinned her? Maybe things would have been different if only she knew how to do these moves. Although, with drugs involved, there was no telling if she'd have been able to defend herself, anyway.

"Little one? I like that," Shawn chuckled, and I scowled at him.

"Only my partner gets to call me that." I gestured down to my curvy hips and full thighs. *Plus, I'm not exactly little, anyway.*

I hoped they couldn't see the trepidation on my face, especially Shawn. He already saw me completely panicking the first night when I kicked him in the shin, and then totally drunk two days ago. He must think I'm some fragile doll. Although the way he's been looking at me has me thinking either I'm his type or he just pities me and wants to take me under his wing.

The concrete floor was ice cold against my back. Evie settled herself on top of me and, in that moment, something sparked inside my chest. All the words that Mark had been saying about needing to have the upper hand and protecting yourself seemed clear now. Maybe it took feeling the body weight of another person bearing down on me or seeing them reach for my neck. I only flinched slightly as her hand wrapped around my throat. They were rough and much stronger than I would have imagined.

Evie nodded at me, and louder than the thoughts in my head, I heard Shawn at my side. "You've got this. Clear your head." He was on his knees beside me, leaning over, his face inches from my ear. His voice was warm and solid, bringing me back to the present. I nodded, as well as I could, with Evie's hands still wrapped around my neck with gentle pressure.

"Release her chokehold, just like you practiced," Shawn instructed.

That I could do. Olivia's face flashed in my mind, but only for a second before instinct took over. The strength of my upper body came down on Evie's arms ripping them from my neck.

"Okay good. Now, buck your hips hard, so you can knock her back a bit. Then hook your leg under hers and bear-hug her."

In an instant, I did as he said and tried to throw all of my body weight into the flip, but Evie felt like a ton of bricks on top of me. I heaved again, squeezing her tightly, but to no avail. At most, we moved an inch to the side.

I huffed, "Evie, are you a freaking spider monkey? Your thigh grip could win a bull riding competition, geez." She laughed, which loosened her grip on my torso slightly.

We reset and I tried again to flip her, but I couldn't get her to move.

I felt weak, especially when I glanced around the room and saw pairs rolling and grappling. How was it so effortless for them?

"I think I'm done for today," I said, wiping my sweaty brow. The resolve I felt a few minutes ago was diminishing by the second.

"You sure, little one?" Evie pushed herself up to standing. "I don't mind if you want to practice a few more times."

I sat up, giving my neck a rub. "It's alright, maybe I'll get it next time."

"No. You're going to do this or you're not leaving class tonight." Shawn's blue eyes bore into mine. The look he was giving me would probably freak me out if I didn't already know he had a flair for intensity.

"Thanks for your support, Shawn, but I think I've had enough." Of course, he thought this was a piece of cake. I'd bet he flung his partner off him, like Superman, his first try. "Plus, I doubt Evie wants to stay here all night long."

"Well, you're not going to roll Evie," he wrung his hands in front of him making the tattoos on his forearm flex. "You're going to roll me."

I studied his face for a moment. His jaw set and eyes blazing. He was serious. I busted out laughing.

"You? If I couldn't roll Evie—who is what? Fifty pounds lighter than you? What makes you think that *I*," I pointed at my chest for emphasis, "could roll *you*?"

He crouched down and, with his voice low but firm, said, "It's all about having the right partner. I could teach you a lot of things, Mia." The way he said my name, growling it low and deep, had my mouth hanging open at a loss for words.

My core heated and I knew there must have been a blush spreading up my face. He stood up again, and I watched the thick muscles of his thighs flex. I had to respond, but my mouth felt like it was filled with sand.

"On your back. I'm going to walk you through this, nice and slow," he instructed.

To have a guy command me like that would normally piss me the hell off, but, with Shawn, it sent my mind into a spiral, imagining all the commands I'd like to hear him give me.

Again, I looked around the room as I laid back on the hard floor. My tailbone was already aching. Most of the groups were gathering around the cubbies and drinking water. Evie was already chatting with Anna across the room.

"Don't worry about what they're doing. It's just you and me here."

I met his gaze and nodded. "This is so awkward."

He chuckled, the sound husky. "Only if you make it that way. I'm going to straddle you. I want you to pay close attention to where my body is on yours."

Holy shit, pay close attention? How was I supposed to focus on doing this move with him on top of me? What if I felt his bulge? My face was definitely red. I could feel it burning. But before I got the chance to reply, he climbed on top of me. His eyes crinkled at the sides as his face angled down toward mine in a look that radiated smugness.

The only thing that registered in my brain was the feel of his thighs pressed against mine and the delicious weight of his body settling right above my pelvic bone. With only a slight change in position, I knew I would feel him pressed against me, right over my most sensitive area.

I cleared my throat, desert mouth feeling drier than ever, "Can you walk me through this again?"

"Of course," he said with that smirk still on his face. He was totally enjoying this. I could see the fight on his face on whether to be the professional assistant or the cocky flirt that I'd only seen bits and pieces of.

I took a deep breath to steady myself before wrapping my arms around him as tightly as I could and pulling him onto me. He felt hard and warm. The woodsy scent of him flooded my senses. My leg, which I had wrapped around his, dragged him closer, and then his chest was right above my face. I could feel his heart pounding, sure that mine matched his staccato rhythm.

His chin grazed the top of my head where my messy bun flopped to the side. Did he rub my hair with his chin or had I just imagined that? I craned my neck to find his eyes. "You know what to do now. Give it your all and roll me," he said.

I took another deep breath in, filling my lungs with his scent, and I heaved to the left with all the strength I could muster.

We moved an inch. After Shawn scooted off of me, I collapsed on my back again, groaning and missing the weight of him on top of me. "I managed to shift you a little." I rolled to my side to look at where he was sitting, knees folded. "You are a big dude."

"Are you calling me fat?" One corner of his mouth lifted in a slight grin. "You're going to give me a complex."

I laughed. "Oh yeah? You're fat alright." He quirked a brow. "If you're talking about that head of yours. That massive ego... must weigh a ton."

He gave me a full smile that made his eyes twinkle before moving closer to me. "You wound me, Mia." He leaned even closer, his face inches from mine, and whispered into my ear, "It's not just my ego that's massive."

I licked my dry lips, and, for the second time that night, felt a weight settle in the juncture between my thighs. I turned my head and was about to tell him to prove it when Mark turned off the music and hollered at us to gather around.

Shawn stood, breaking our trance, and grabbed my hands to help me up. My body was already feeling the brunt of the night. Beside me, he said, "Good job tonight."

I tried to think of a rebuttal. "Good" would not be the word I'd use to describe how I did tonight, but he interrupted my thoughts. "Talk after class?"

I swallowed and nodded, bringing my attention back to Mark.

"You all impressed me tonight, level ones." Mark paced along the front wall. His features were energetic. "As I said, this skill is essential, and the more you practice it, the easier and less awkward it'll be. We're going to be working on ground fighting a lot in the coming weeks, so don't worry if you struggled tonight."

As he said this, I could sense Shawn glancing over at me.

"Get some rest, and I'll see you in the next class." Everyone clapped lightly, me included. As the students dispersed, I couldn't help but smile slightly. Like Mark said, the class was incredibly difficult and awkward, but I hadn't let my fear and anxiety get the best of me.

"I like to see that smile on your face." Shawn and I walked side by side to gather our things. "You should be smiling. You did well."

I sighed, "I guess. But it's impossible not to compare myself to the other students. I know I just started and I'll get stronger." The smile left my face, and I turned toward him. "Let's face reality, though. If this were real life, and you weren't," I gestured with my hands, "you. I'd be attacked or worse."

Shawn's face fell, and his eyes looked past me to a spot on the wall before coming back to mine. I could have sworn his cheeks lost all color.

"Practice with me outside of class." His expression grew more serious by the second. I could've sworn I saw his hands tremble as he slid them into his hair. I contemplated what he just suggested.

"I don't know. I feel like that's not the best idea." I shifted from one foot to the other and took a small sip out of my water bottle. "I'm busy with work, and I'm sure you have other things going on."

He clenched his jaw and stepped closer, making me almost drop my water bottle. "Nothing is more important than making sure you're safe." He showed absolutely no signs of relenting and damn if that didn't make my heart crack open in my chest.

"Umm..." I looked down and then back out at the room. Anywhere to avoid the intense look he was giving me. "I mean, I do need the help."

Sixteen-year-old Olivia's tear-streaked face flashed through my mind again. I could almost hear the desperate sobs leaving her lips. I looked back up into Shawn's eyes. His gaze was as far away as my own. "Okay, let's do it. You and me, Big Guy. Teach me your Krav ways."

He released a breath and lifted the corner of his lips. "Nothing would make me happier."

Chapter 11

Mia

THIS WAS ACTUALLY GOING to happen. Shawn and I, working out together outside of class. We exchanged numbers. The anxious fluttering of nerves that felt like tiny creatures forced their way up my stomach into my rib cage.

I don't know what it was about him that made me feel like I wanted to prove that I was tough, yet simultaneously wanting to expose all the things that make me feel vulnerable. He was a puzzle. The caretaker in me called to the broken pieces of him. When I looked into his blue eyes, I wanted to fit those puzzle pieces together. I wanted to open up and tell him why I was so anxious about self-defense and even more so about men in general.

I sighed as I reached my apartment door, my back was aching, and my legs felt like lead bricks. It was a fact that I had loads of baggage and lacked confidence. Those were my burdens. No matter how sassy or silly I could get when I got comfortable with someone, I'd need to keep my guard up working with Shawn. Men had proved time and again to be untrustworthy.

Every guy I dated, which wasn't many, either used me for a good time or tossed me aside when things got too serious. Then there were the Lungberg types and every other asshole guy at work. Not to forget Olivia and Kendahl and all their horrible encounters. Even my father was an asshole that I never fully trusted.

I plopped down on the couch not caring that a layer of moisture coated my body. My mind was reeling, and I needed my best friend.

I grabbed my water bottle and sipped while I slipped off my sneakers and tossed them aside. My legs were tucked underneath me as I grabbed my phone, found Kendahl's name and hit video call. I hadn't seen her for long Sunday morning when we both woke up in her bed still dressed in the previous night's clothes, hair a wreck, and faces lined with smudged makeup. It was a miracle I made it home in one piece to sleep it off the rest of the day. I still had Shawn's T-shirt folded up on my dresser. How did I forget to mention that to him earlier? It definitely wasn't because I kept randomly smelling it every time I walked by it. *No, not that.*

She answered on the second ring with a groggy "Hello," blinking into the screen, her voice gravelly with sleep. I glanced at the time; it was about nine o'clock at night. She must be exhausted.

"Sorry, were you sleeping?" I asked.

She yawned and ruffled her head of hair. "No, I was just watching TV." She reached over and clicked the remote. I shot my best Samuel L. Jackson are-you-serious face into the camera.

"Be honest, the TV was watching you, wasn't it?" I retort.

"You got me. The party did me in. I'm still tired two days later. I think I'm becoming a lightweight like you."

I laughed, "Yet somehow I wasn't too hungover the next morning."

"You did barf your brains out. Or at least I think you did from the stains on my dress." She stuck her tongue out at me.

That must have been why I felt alright today. The alcohol left my system—or most of it—soon after it went in. I groaned as a realization hit me. I puked in front of Shawn, and he was such a gentleman he hadn't even mentioned it tonight. "You know, I hadn't thought of that."

Kendahl started munching on some popcorn. "What's up? I figured if you video called instead of texted it must be something big. Was class all right?"

"We exchanged numbers," I said and sucked in a breath.

Her face lit up. "Oh really? By 'we' I'm assuming you mean you and Shawn."

I nodded my head bobbing like a buoy in the waves.

"And this is freaking you out I'm assuming?" Kendahl continued.

I nodded more.

She sighed, "Look, I know you haven't had luck with guys. I mean, obviously, same here. But Mia, you're amazing, and you deserve a chance at love." Moisture began to collect in the corners of my eyes.

Kendahl shifted on her bed sitting up straighter. "I want you to push your anxiety aside and tell yourself that you are amazing."

I let out a laugh. "If only it were that easy."

"Not the right response. Come on, let me hear it," she kept on.

Sighing, I repeated her words, with about the same amount of gusto as a dead fish. "I am amazing."

"Oh no. That won't do. Come on. You're constantly mothering me and building me up. It's time I give you my best friend's pep talk, too. Say 'I, Mia Murphy, am amazing. My anxiety is stupid, and I will not let myself get hurt.'"

She nudged her head in my direction and waited for me to repeat her little speech. This time, I took a deep breath and let myself imagine for a moment what it could be like with Shawn. How well he took care of me the other night, and how he never made me feel uncomfortable. I was drunk and all my inhibitions were down, but he didn't even try to take advantage. In class, he's been nothing but kind. Yes, a little brooding, and a little mysterious, but he's made me feel warm and comfortable. And I deserved a chance at love. I knew that deep down. If only I wasn't wearing these stupid, imaginary VR goggles that clouded everything I saw with a tinge of anxiety and fear. They showed me that men were bad and untrustworthy, that opening up to people meant leaving me vulnerable to pain and heartache, and that the worst would always happen.

"Mi, I see the wheels spinning in that pretty head of yours. Come on, say it."

"Ugh, okay, fine." I repeated, "I, Mia Murphy, am amazing. My anxiety is stupid, and I will not let myself get hurt." I looked up into her smiling face. "But really, Ken, how can I not get hurt? That's not something I can control."

She took a moment, clearly digesting what I asked. "You're right, but you know what? Sometimes we need to take chances and put ourselves out there, Mi. We may get hurt, but I have faith in you. You're stronger than you think. Look how many times you've picked my sorry ass up after getting my heart broken."

The moisture in my eyes gathered again. "I love you, Ken. I know you're right."

"Damn skippy, I'm right," she laughed. "Now, if only I could take my own advice."

"Isn't that how it always is? Freaking way of the world," I said.

Nodding, she stuffed more popcorn into her mouth. "Anyway, speaking of numbers..." She blushed. I knew that look.

"Oh my God! Have you been texting with Coby?" How could I have forgotten how hard they were flirting the other night? Crap, now I felt like a bad friend for forgetting to ask about that whole situation.

The corner of her lips lifted with a small smile. "We've texted a few times since Saturday night. Am I crazy for wanting to see where this goes?"

A small bubble of trepidation tightened in my chest. I felt like this any time Kendahl started dating a new guy. At least with Coby, he wasn't a total stranger and from what I have seen, he came across as decent, albeit a huge flirt.

"No, of course not. He seems like a good guy. If it makes you feel better though, I'll ask around the gym about him. Do a little recon work." I waggled my brows. "Reminds me of college with that TA... What was his name?"

"Hunter. Don't remind me. Thank God you looked into him, or I would have been dating an engaged dude without knowing a damn thing."

"I'm always here for you. Detective Best Friend is on the case."

Kendahl yawned again and rubbed her eyes. "Okay, Sherlock Holmes, I gotta get some rest. Back to work tomorrow for me. I don't even want to think about the amount of crap that I've missed while being out."

"I feel for you. You did the right thing in staying home for a while. You needed it."

"I know, I'm glad I did too, but I may sing a different tune come mid-week."

I stretched back on my couch, kicking my feet out in front of me. "Same. I'm about to pull out my files for the golf party. Eff. My. Life."

She chuckled. "Well, get some rest. And Mi?" She paused. "I'm happy for you."

I smiled and pictured Shawn's intense gaze as he told me he would keep me safe.

"I'm happy too. I feel much better. Thanks, Ken doll."

"Love you, boo. I'll talk to you tomorrow."

I hit end with a new sense of calm. She was right. I needed her to reel me in from my spiral. I liked Shawn and deserved to see where this would go. I was probably reading into things too much, anyway. He hasn't asked me out on a date or professed his undying love for me. For all I know, he's just being a good assistant teacher.

I climbed off the couch to get a snack, using the arm to pull me up like I was an eighty-year-old woman. My muscles felt like I had run a marathon. Who would have thought that rolling around on the ground would take so much out of me?

My thoughts shifted to thoughts of Shawn's body on top of mine. The way his biceps were flexing against the sides of my face, his strong thighs gripping mine, his hard chest just inches from touching my face.

I needed a cold shower.

Just as I was about to abandon my files for the night, my phone beeped.

It was after ten. *Who would message me now?*

A lump formed in my throat, and my heart pumped faster. Maybe it was Shawn. If it was, that would totally clarify what was going on in his head. Or at least I hoped it would.

The screen came to life and my stomach dropped. It was a text from my sister.

Olivia: *Hey. Sorry, I know it's late. I wanted to talk to you about our summer plans.*

Olivia: *Give me a call when you get a chance. Long story short, Alex and I are coming to Florida for the summer... Mom and Dad too. Can't wait to see you!*

My family was coming here? *No way.* I could see Olivia wanted to get away from New York for the summer, but my parents never left for long. They were usually busy with campaigning and charity events. Plus my father rarely took time off of work. Why the hell were they coming to Florida? And why for the entire summer?

It had been over two years since I'd seen any of them in person. Olivia and I kept in touch somewhat regularly, but my parents? We spoke once a month, and the conversations always left me with a bitter taste in my mouth.

I didn't have the mental capacity to respond to her texts. It would have to wait until morning. Maybe it was my stupid, invisible goggles again, but my gut was telling me that their reason for coming here would not be good.

Chapter 12

Shawn

I STARED AT MY phone all night after class, wanting to text Mia, but not wanting to come across as a stage-five clinger. Why did liking someone have to be so complicated? It was never like this with Michelle. I had made it clear that I wanted her; she wanted me, and there was nothing else to it. I had no recollection of this waiting game.

I reached out to pet Remy and then adjusted my collared T-shirt. Camila and I were going to meet with a new accountant today and she had recommended I dress "professionally". What she meant was don't wear the ripped and stained work clothes I normally wore or my other attire of training clothes. So, I wore my only collared shirt, and I felt like a complete ass in it.

First, it was too tight around my arms which made me feel like I was wearing a straitjacket. Second, the collar came up too high on my neck giving me a feeling of being suffocated.

Third, it was white, and I hated wearing white. After I lost Michelle, every time I'd see someone wearing a white shirt it would bring me back to the hospital. Doctors in lab coats rushing around her gurney, and people holding me back from being by her side.

"I can do this, right boy?" I scratched behind Remy's floppy ear while he gazed up at me. "Mental note though, run to Walmart and pick up a different fancy shirt so I can toss this one in the trash." Was I having a full-on conversation with my dog? I'd really lost it.

The clock on my microwave read ten. I could have been getting so much work done in the shop. I wished Camila would have handled this meeting on her own. She'd be the one dealing with the accountant all the time, anyway. But, like she said, it's my business, and I at the very least needed to meet the guy.

My phone vibrated against the kitchen table and my heart leaped. I wondered if Mia was texting me first. This woman had me by the balls. My chest sank as I picked it up and saw Camila's name.

Camila: *Just left my house. Want me to pick you up since I know where the office is? Maybe early lunch after?*

I'd be trapped with her in her vehicle. Stuck with no way out. The shirt started to feel even tighter on me, constricting my throat. Breathe in.

Three...

Two...

One...

Counting off a few more times, my chest opened again, my mouth sucked in air.

I quickly typed a reply.

Me: *No all good. I'll drive myself. Will meet you there.*

She replied with a thumbs-up emoji. I could picture her crest-fallen face. She's given me that look quite a few times when I've turned her down. I wish she'd stop trying, but I didn't want to hurt her feelings by being straight with her. Maybe that made me a dick, but I feared losing her as my assistant.

I took another deep breath, in and then out. Before I could argue with myself anymore, I shrugged the white shirt off my body and tossed it onto the nearest chair. I had a few minutes to change into something more me, and if the accountant didn't like it, then I guess he wouldn't have my business.

Feeling much more like myself in a black T-shirt, I pulled into the parking garage behind the address Camila had texted me. The office building was a short walk around the corner. I looked around, leaning against the door of my pickup, wondering if I should wait for Camila. Maybe she was already waiting for me inside. I figured we were going to the same place either way, and I hated to be late.

Stuffing my hands inside the pocket of my khaki shorts, I made my way into the three-story building. It wasn't modern by any standards, but the air-conditioning was cool and it didn't have that musty, humidity smell so many buildings in this town had.

The sign in the lobby showed that I needed to go to the third floor, suite 303. I glanced over at the elevator. *Fuck that.* I hated those claustrophobic boxes. Instead, I walked around the corner and pushed open the door to the stairwell. Clearly, only maintenance workers used it. Dim florescent lights flickered overhead showing the peeling beige paint and cement steps. Where the lobby had cool, fresh air, the stairwell smelled of spilled Simple Green and metal.

Glancing at the time on my phone I saw that I only had two minutes until our appointment time. I sprinted up the steps relishing the feeling of moving my legs after a morning of sitting around.

When I reached the entrance door to floor three, I yanked it open only to run into a warm, small body. Something hard clanked against the floor with a thunk.

"Shit, I'm sorry," I apologized panting. I held onto the woman's shoulders to steady her. When I looked down at her all the breath whooshed out of my lungs.

"Mia?"

"Shawn?"

We both spoke. Her eyes widened in confusion. I had plowed into her hard. My first instinct was to look her over. If I hurt her, I swear I'd never forgive myself.

She looked fine, if not a little flustered, but that was understandable. She shifted to one side, her hand on her hip, and gave a glance out into the hallway. From where the door peeked open, I could see Camila getting off the elevator. I must have just missed her in the lobby.

Mia gently nudged me back onto the stairwell landing, then bent down to pick up her dropped phone. She spoke in a hushed tone, "Shawn, what are you doing here?"

I rocked on my heels. "I have a meeting. What are you doing here?"

She pointed at her chest. "This is where I work. I'm an accountant."

The universe was definitely fucking with me. "No shit? What a coincidence. I happen to be meeting with a new accountant."

Her voice went up an octave in surprise. "Seriously? Well, that's some craziness. I thought you were stalking me or something."

I laughed, "I don't need to stalk you to see you, Mia."

She looked down, her face coloring, and I took that moment to fully take her in. She was beautiful at the gym in her leggings that hugged her curves perfectly, but here in her work clothes, she looked absolutely fuckable. She wore a tight black pencil skirt that hugged every inch of her full hips and ended just above her knees with a tucked-in button-down shirt. Even with all the buttons done up, I could see them barely holding on against her full chest. Her chestnut curls hung wildly around her face making me want to fist them and pull her to me. She had on some makeup, not too much from what I could tell, but it made the amber in her eyes stand out. The clencher, the one thing I wasn't expecting, and never realized I was into before, were the black frame glasses she wore.

And I had thought that at the party the other night wearing that little black dress that barely covered her ass made my dick hard. One look at Mia the accountant and I knew this would be how I'd picture her in my dreams from now on.

She cleared her throat, face still pink. I was ogling her, and she knew it.

I shoved my hands into my pockets to stop myself from reaching out to her. "You wear glasses?"

Confusion wracked her face, and she grabbed them, taking them off. "Oh," giggling nervously, "I forgot I had them on. Yeah, I normally wear contacts to the gym, but the air in here is so dry that they bother my eyes." She held up the glasses. "So, these have to do at work, or I'd basically be blind as a bat."

She was rambling again. I loved that about her.

"They suit you."

She fiddled with them, twirling them around, before sliding them back on.

"So," she pointed back to the door. "We should probably get back out there. My boss will go ballistic if I'm late for your meeting."

"Your boss? I thought I was meeting with you."

She chuckled nervously again. "Yeah, well, I'll probably be the one who ends up doing your books, but it's Lungberg, my boss, who meets with new clients. I'm just a junior accountant."

"Lead the way." I opened the door, holding it so she could go ahead of me. With one last glance at her ass, I followed her into the hallway and through her office door.

Chapter 13

Mia

I COULD NOT BELIEVE that I ran straight into Shawn—in my office. My heart was still pounding at the shock of seeing him here. During our brief conversations, we had never exchanged details about our careers, so unless he truly was a stalker, there was no way he could have known I worked here. And what were the odds that the one time I step onto the stairwell to make a call—bam, I collide with the person I'd been thinking about all morning.

I glanced back at him as I led him through the reception area where Cathy followed us with her gaze, mouth slightly agape. *Yeah, Cathy, I know he's hot.* Even grandmas weren't immune to Shawn's presence. We'd both been quiet as we walked through the office passing by my co-workers on phones or working at their computers.

Reaching my desk, I turned to look at Shawn. Out of the corner of my eye, I noticed Jared peeking around his computer monitor likely trying to figure out the identity of the hot man gracing our presence. His eyes widened and he mouthed the question, "Who's that?" But I waved him away, pointing toward Lungberg's office, eager to get our meeting going so we weren't late. Maybe Jared would put two and two together and realize this was Lungberg's ten-thirty new client appointment.

Grabbing a legal pad and pen from my desk, I then shifted back toward Shawn.

"Right there," I pointed to the office twenty feet away from my desk area, "is my boss' office. That's where the meeting is." He nodded, and I looked past him to see a woman already sitting in a chair chatting with Lungberg. "It looks like he's with someone." I chewed my lower lip. "I guess we can wait here. It shouldn't be long."

He looked through the open office door. "That's Camila Torres, my assistant. We came in separate cars."

"Oh. Okay." Not that I was jealous, but it was a small shock to hear that he worked with another woman. "Let's go in."

I knocked lightly on the door, causing Lungberg to glance up at me with a scowl and the beautiful dark-haired woman in front of him to raise her gaze my way. "Mia, here you are, finally."

"Mr. Lungberg, this is Mister..." my mind blanked, and I searched my legal pad for the quick notes I had sprawled earlier. *There must be a last name here somewhere.*

"Shawn Brooks," Shawn's voice cut off my search, and he reached out his hand to shake Mr. Lungberg's. Then he pulled out the chair next to Camila, looking at me like I should sit down in it.

I gave my head a quick shake and stood on Lungberg's side of the desk against the wall. Shawn's eyes narrowed, but he took a seat.

"Thanks for meeting with us," Shawn continued.

Lungberg's voice became a velvety timber, which was the extreme opposite of the harsh edge he used to speak with Jared and me.

"The pleasure is all mine." He grinned from ear to ear. "I was just speaking with your lovely assistant about the needs of your business. Now that you're here, we men can get everything squared away. It sounds like we can onboard you before the end of the second quarter."

I gritted my teeth, watching him rake over Shawn's poor assistant. She wore an uncomfortable smile but kept nodding at his words. Shawn's eyes drifted to mine quickly searching for something on my face.

"That's good news." Shawn leaned back in his chair. "We used to work with Dan Henderson, but he just let us know he's retiring."

"He's a good man. I've met him many times," Lungberg steepled his fingers in front of his face. "Although, from what I've heard, his old age has gotten the best of him." It was just like Lungberg to be putting someone else down to make himself seem bigger. I glanced at Shawn, whose eyes had narrowed and nostrils flared.

"He's an old family friend as well, so I'd trust him with more than my books. Plus, Camila has done a great job, too."

Seeing that he crossed a line, Lungberg pivoted. He added, chuckling, "That's good to hear. I hope our relationship will be the same as yours with old Dan. We pride ourselves on treating clients like family."

I had to hold in my scoff.

"You'll be signing on just in time for our client appreciation event, actually." Lungberg tilted his head in my direction. "Why don't you tell them about what you're planning, Mia?"

I cleared my throat. "It's our annual golf event. I'm firming up plans now, so I wouldn't want to spoil anything."

Lungberg puffed up his chest. "It's a great time. We spare no expense." Yeah right, a kindergarten classroom had a bigger budget for paints than I had for this entire shindig.

"If Ms. Murphy is planning it, I'm sure it'll be great," Shawn said.

I looked down, trying to hide the sure flush that was spreading across my cheeks. Both Camila and Lungberg looked from me to Shawn, surely trying to figure out Shawn's comment.

"Yes, yes. It's best to let the women in the office handle these things." Lungberg said before he shuffled some papers around. "Now, let's have you fill out some of these so we can get started right away. The rest you can email to us sometime this week."

Shawn and Camila nodded, both reaching for the documents.

"Mia, why don't you make yourself useful and go get our new friends here some refreshments? Coffee, tea, water?" He asked. "Let her know what you want, and she can scurry along and get it for you."

I tried to hide my grimace behind my legal pad. Scurry along? The last time I checked, I wasn't a rodent. I didn't want to make a big deal, especially not in front of Shawn.

"Sure, what would you both li—"

"Isn't Ms. Murphy also an accountant?" Shawn interrupted my question. "Or am I mistaken?"

Lungberg's smile twisted. "She is. A *junior* accountant. But she is also very much my assistant."

I wanted to jump in and say, *no you prick, I'm not your assistant,* but bit my tongue.

Shawn's piercing blue eyes speared into Lungberg's. "I wasn't aware it was an accountant's duty to fetch coffee."

You could cut the tension in the room with a knife. I wanted to hide under a rock. Yes, it enraged me that Lungberg treated me like his personal errand girl. And yes, he was a chauvinistic asshole. But I was always quiet, and I never made a scene, because it wasn't worth it.

"It's really no bother. What would you both like?" I slid on a mask of easy cheerfulness, hoping they didn't see through to how uncomfortable I was.

"I can join you." Camila looked at me with kind eyes. "I know how Shawn takes his coffee."

Why did her knowing that information cause a burning sensation to spread throughout my gut? It wasn't like the way a person took their coffee was the same as knowing where an intimately hidden freckle was on their body. Anyone could retain that knowledge. A grandparent, a neighbor, the barista at Dunkin'.

Camila smiled warmly at me and started to rise from her chair. Shawn reached out and placed his hand on her arm.

"No." He glanced back at Lungberg. "You know what Mr. Lungberg?"

Lungberg ran a hand through his thinning hair. "Please, call me Evan."

"Okay, Evan. I'd like Ms. Murphy to handle all my business. We'll be taking this meeting into her office now."

Lungberg's jaw hinged open and his eyes bulged out of his head. I'd never seen his face contort in that way.

"Mia? She's not equipped. She is just my errand girl," he stuttered and spittle leached from the corner of his lip. "She doesn't even have a proper office."

Shawn stood up, flashing a shit-eating grin. "Well, this errand girl just got her first account."

Without letting Lungberg get another word in, he slowly walked to my side, put a hand at the small of my back, and led me out the door.

To say I was in shock was an understatement. My emotions swung between making me want to kiss Shawn for standing up to my asshole boss and simultaneously making me want to smack him for causing Lungberg to internally combust. Every fiber of my being knew he would make my life hell after this.

Camila stayed behind in Lungberg's office for a moment speaking quietly to him. His face went from strawberry red back to his normal cotton-candy pink. I silently reminded myself to get her email, so I could thank her for helping diffuse the situation.

Shawn and I reached my desk, and I leaned on it for support. Breathing in, I looked up at Shawn. He had his head cocked to the side. There was no look of concern as he studied me, only that smirk he so often wore. He was proud of himself, that much was for sure.

"You know you just made my work situation a living hell?"

He leaned against my desk crossing his arms against his wide chest. "I didn't like how he was speaking to you."

I turned to face him, running a hand through my hair and taking a moment to collect my thoughts. I lowered my voice, "Look, I know he's an asshole. But I've been dealing with him for a long time without ruffling any feathers."

Reaching across my desk, I grabbed my water bottle and took a sip. "Now he probably thinks you're my boyfriend or something," I blurted.

I wished I could reel that back into my stupid mouth.

Shawn inched closer to me, stealing the very air I was breathing. "And what would be so wrong with that?"

"Well...," I gulped, trying to calm the organ in my chest that was beating so hard I thought I'd need a medic. I was looking into those blue eyes, and it made the words harder to find. "It wouldn't be true. That, and it would bruise his gross old man ego. I think he gets some perverse pleasure in knowing that I'm single."

Shawn rubbed the stubble on his chin and stood taller. Clearly, he was choosing his next words carefully.

"I don't give a fuck about that douchebag's ego. I only care about you being treated the way you deserve to be treated," he said finally.

He reached out and lifted a tendril of hair that had fallen in front of my face, rubbing the strand between his thumb and forefinger before tucking it behind my ear. His gaze boring into my soul.

"And you, Mia? You deserve to be treated like a queen."

Warmth flooded through me, his words covering me like a soft blanket. What was this man doing to me?

I was trying to think of a coherent response to him bursting my heart when Camila came up behind him. Looking from Shawn to me, she coughed a little, "Am I interrupting something?"

"No, you're all good." The spell now broken, I shook my head. But Shawn's gaze was still fixed on me.

The look on her face told me she didn't believe me.

"Let me go grab some chairs and we can finish up." I motioned for Jared to come over but didn't really need to as he was already halfway to my desk before I looked in his direction. He flashed me his sweetest innocent smile, but I knew he was only coming over to be a nosy meddler.

"Can I help you with anything, Mia?" He batted his thick lashes, more at Shawn, than at me before sticking his hand out to introduce himself. I beat him to it.

"This is Jared. Mr. Lungberg's *actual* administrative assistant." A small smile graced my lips. "And he's one of my good friends."

Shawn looked Jared over appraisingly and stayed silent as Jared stuck his hand out to Camila next. They exchanged first names and Jared opened his mouth to start a conversation but I beat him to it yet again. My nerves were already frayed and I had no idea what Jared would come out with. When it came to being in the same air space as attractive men, he had the tendency to flirt shamelessly.

"Jared," I widened my eyes at him, using one of our most common silent looks to convey that I needed him to zip it. "Could you grab us some extra chairs please?"

"Of course." He narrowed his eyes at me before shifting his attention back toward Shawn and Camila. "Good to meet you both. I'll go help Mia with those chairs. Be right back."

"He seems nice," Camila said.

Nervously chuckling, I nodded in agreement before awkward silence commenced. *Where was Jared?*

Like he could read my mind he showed up a few minutes later, arms full of folding chairs. Not the most glamorous pieces of furniture but they'd do. Finally, with the three of us seated around my desk, we could finish up the meeting.

"I think I smoothed things over with Mr. Lungberg." Camila eyed Shawn. "I didn't want things to be awkward if we're going to be working together."

"Thank you." I smiled, hoping it relayed my gratitude. "He's a piece of work, but I do like working here despite having to deal with him."

Shawn was still silently filling out paperwork and glancing up at me every few seconds.

Camila went on, "I've worked for a few men like him, before meeting Shawn." Her voice was filled with respect. "Do the two of you know each other? It's just that I've worked with Shawn for a long time and I've never seen him so protective of someone." She laughed it off, but her face bunched with insecurity. "I can barely get two words out of him most days."

Pushing my glasses up my nose, I laughed, "I could picture that." I gave her an easy smile and looked at Shawn for his approval. I wasn't sure if it was a good idea to share that we knew each other personally. He nodded. "I kicked Shawn in the shin the first time I met him."

Camila blinked and knit her brows together.

"We met at the Krav Maga gym," I clarified.

"That hurt more than I let on," he laughed, the sound rich and deep.

I scrunched up my nose. "I'm so sorry. Hopefully, it won't happen again, but I make no promises."

Camila, looked up from her paperwork with a slight frown, "It makes more sense now that I know the two of you are personally acquainted." And then she added, "Good for you keeping at it, even after kicking Shawn."

She definitely didn't like the fact that I had a connection with Shawn. I made a mental note to ask Shawn about their relationship when the timing was right. For now, I just smiled and steered the conversation back to work.

Thirty minutes of paperwork and questions about Shawn's business later, I closed their file and made plans to email Camila about the rest of the information I would need. Camila stood up, collecting her purse and sunglasses.

"Thanks, Camila, I'll speak to you tomorrow at the shop," Shawn said, dismissing her. Although his voice was warm, nothing like the way Lungberg spoke to me. She nodded, but that same small frown lined her lips.

"It was nice to meet you, Mia. I look forward to our professional relationship." She turned and left with a small wave at Jared and Lungberg, who were both watching us from their desks.

Shawn leaned in and lowered his voice, "Have dinner with me tonight."

I looked up and saw Lungberg sitting forward in his seat trying to hear our every word. I felt flustered. "We have an audience. Text me, okay?"

Shawn took a glance over his shoulder toward our onlookers, which caused Lungberg to grab his phone to try to make himself appear busy.

Nodding, Shawn left, but not before reaching out again to that same stray curl and tucking it away with the others.

I leaned back, my head whirling. What in the name of all that's holy had just occurred? Why do I feel like the last hour of my life changed everything?

Chapter 14

Mia

A FEW MINUTES AFTER leaving my side, he texted me just like he implied he would. My head had just stopped spinning, and I was settling back into my email box when my phone pinged.

Shawn: *Want to come to my place to practice? It helps to work on ground moves while they're fresh in your mind. We can eat something after.*

I sat back, puzzled. Why on earth did he sound like a totally different guy in text? Maybe I was reading it wrong. It sounded to me like he was backtracking into assistant teacher Shawn and the intense guy who said I was a queen was taking a backseat.

I typed out: *Uh is this a date? Or...? Because a few minutes ago it seemed like you were asking me out.* Huffing, I backspaced.

That was too forward. I gnawed my lower lip, thinking of a different response.

Me: *Sure. Sounds good.*

There. I was clear and to the point. And it did sound good. We already talked about practicing on the side and that's exactly what we should be doing. Maybe I was wrong for thinking he wanted to get to know me in a more personal way.

My phone pinged.

Shawn: *Cool*

Wow. It took everything in me to not physically face-palm. Another ping.

Shawn: *17 Woodland Dr.*

Shawn: *See you at six.*

Either Shawn had no idea how to hold a text conversation with a woman, or he was doing a full one-eighty. I didn't have time to dissect the situation with the entire morning already throwing off my day.

After stashing my phone in my purse, I got back to my work tasks. I had a long list of confirmations to make regarding the golf event, plus a few clients to follow up with, and forms to send to the state. I had no time to focus on one frustrating man and his ping-pong personality. On top of that, Lungberg was still pissed about the meeting and kept beckoning me into his office for the dumbest reasons. He, clearly, didn't know how to handle Shawn having requested me as his primary accountant. On one hand, he didn't want to lose a client, but on the other, he'd have to accept that I was more than just his errand girl. If he continued to stew this hard, his head would explode. *Wishful thinking.*

I arrived at his house right on time, six o'clock in the evening; I had stopped at home to change into workout shorts and a loose shirt after work because if this wasn't a date, then there was no need for me to dress up.

As I turned onto the long, sandy dirt drive, the exterior of his house surprised me. While the house wasn't huge, it was certainly larger than one person would need. It was a white two-story bungalow with one of the nicest wraparound porches I'd ever seen. It looked like a home ready and waiting for parents, two kids, and a family pet.

I parked my car, got out, and walked up the pathway lined with greenery and overgrown fragrant bushes leading to the creaky porch steps. I'd always dreamed of having a porch like this where I could sit in a cozy chair each morning and drink my coffee. Before I had the chance to knock, the front door opened and a shaggy golden retriever barreled toward me immediately sniffing my legs and feet. I looked up and locked eyes with Shawn.

"Remy!" he hollered. "Come boy, leave her be." Remy obeyed, trotting inside like a good boy. "Sorry about that. We don't get many visitors, so his manners aren't what they should be." Shawn opened the door wide, gesturing at the entryway with his spread palm. "Come on in."

As I entered, Shawn's scent, that woodsy earthy smell, enveloped me. His home was warm and spacious with a cozy living room to my left and the kitchen straight ahead. To the right, large double doors opened to a space the size of an office. Shawn had it set up as a home gym with weights, a bench, and padded mats.

"It's not much, but it works for me."

I leaned from one foot to the other, taking it all in.

"Your home is way different than I imagined," I laughed. "I guess when I think of a single guy's home, I don't have high expectations."

His mouth curved up. "Not all of us live off of futons and Goodwill furniture."

The anxious flutters in my belly started to subside. "You may be the first single guy to show me that."

With a husky laugh he added, "Brownie points to me then."

He led me into the living room, ducking slightly to avoid hitting his head on the wide doorframe, and I put my purse down on the wooden coffee table. It was then that I noticed beautiful wooden furniture filled the room, end tables holding framed photos and a maple bookshelf lined with books.

"Did you build all of this?" I asked, now that I knew what he did for a living.

"Some, but my grandfather built most of it years ago. He's the one who started the business and taught me everything I know." He settled down on the couch, Remy coming to lie at his feet, and patted the cushion next to him.

Some pieces were coming together now. "Was this his house?"

"Yeah, he practically built it from the ground up for my grandma. They left everything to me when they passed away." Emotion clouded his vision, and he turned to grab a framed photo from the side table. "This is them back when they were younger, around the time my mom was a kid."

The photo showed two people beaming, each of them with a hand on the shoulder of a little girl. The decorations hanging in the background told me it was a celebration. "They look really happy."

"I'm sure they were happy back then. Life was simpler, right?" he said somberly, before he snapped back into the present. "Anyway, there's a bit more time until dinner. Ready for your boot camp?"

I was enjoying our conversation especially since Shawn was such a mystery to me. It was nice to learn a bit about his past. But I sensed that my chance to learn more was dead in the water, so I nodded and pushed myself to standing.

"Just a warning. I had my Wheaties this morning. I came prepared."

A smirk grazed his lips, crinkling his eyes. "Bring it on. I can take whatever you throw my way."

"Oh, really?" I walked closer to him, feeling emboldened by our flirtatious banter. "Why don't we make a bet?" *What the hell was I doing?* There was no way I could beat Shawn in anything physical. It was the main reason I was here in the first place, to practice.

His brow raised while he ran a hand across the scratchy stubble on his chin. "I'm normally not a gambling man, but I like these odds." He closed the last few inches between us, so we were almost chest-to-chest. "What are your terms, Mia?"

I swallowed, finding it hard to make words come out. His smell, this close, was pure bliss. I could bury my head in his chest and inhale deeply. If I could bottle it up and spritz it throughout my house, I would. He shifted his weight from one foot to the other, eyeing me intensely.

Determination lined my features. "If I roll you..." I took another second, thinking of what I wanted. His stare intensified even more.

"Go on. If you roll me, what?"

"If I roll you, you have to come to a yoga class with me."

I smiled widely. I'd pay money to see this ever-composed man wobbling around in chair pose. The smirk came back, and he rocked on his heels. "Okay, I'll admit that would be torture for me—nice."

"And I know I'm going to win. I feel it in my bones." I didn't feel it in my bones, but bluffing was the most important part of every bet, right?

"And what do I get if you don't succeed?"

"I hadn't thought that far ahead. I'm confident that there will be no need to consider it." If there was a picture next to smug in the dictionary, they could glue my expression on the page.

"How about this?" he started. "You can owe me a favor of my choosing if you lose."

"What kind of favor are we talking about here? Yardwork? Personal shopping? Buying you lunch for a week?"

"Oh, don't worry. I'll be creative with my reward." He stared at my mouth for what felt like a full minute before stepping back. Instantly, I felt cooler with space between us. My heart rate was elevated, and we hadn't even started working out yet. I needed to prepare myself more mentally than physically.

I followed Shawn into his small gym and noticed a few things I had missed at first glance. Bright white walls and black rubber mats made this space stand out from the rest of the house. The corner held stacks of pads like we used at the gym and a pile of sparring gear along with your average gym equipment. Every item was neatly arranged, not a dumbbell or resistance band misplaced.

"Do you wear this stuff in level five?" I bent over to take a closer look at the sparring gear. It looked completely intimidating, a helmet, and a full set of body pads.

"The gear? Yeah, but only sometimes. It can get intense, so Mark only has us wear it for certain drills."

"Gotcha." I doubted I'd ever get to that point in the classes but thinking about being at that level one day filled me with a rush of excitement.

"Let's warm up a bit, stretch, and do a few exercises to wake our muscles up."

Shawn was back to using his teacher voice. It was weird how he switched from hot to cold in seconds.

I took his lead, shaking out my arms. "Whatever you think, I'm down for."

We rotated our shoulders, stretched our leg muscles, and rolled out our necks before doing a few jumping jacks and burpees. I was grateful for the rubber mat that covered his hardwood floor.

When we were all warmed up, Shawn grabbed a large pad from the stack. "Want to try some drills before we roll?" His tone was all business, not an ounce of the playful teasing from earlier.

"Sure, why not? I'm here for the full boot camp package. May as well take advantage of your time." I put one hand on my hip and gave him a playful smack on the arm with the other, hoping to get a smile out of him. Even a quirk of his lip would suffice. But nothing. He just held the pad low for me to stomp kick, and then higher for me to punch. We did a few rounds of this before I stopped and put my hands on my knees, breathing heavily.

"You did well. I could feel the power behind your moves." He opened the mini fridge in the corner and grabbed us bottles of cold water.

Chugging, I said, "You know, you could have your own little gym here. Maybe take on paying students." The accountant in me started to calculate how much extra income he could make, but he stopped me.

"Nah, I wouldn't want to step in on Mark's students. Plus, I don't have the time with all my projects."

"So, I'm just special then?" I stood back up to stretch my sore calves, willing him to smile or laugh. He looked so damn good when he laughed. His whole face became lighter.

"I guess so," he said quietly, almost too low for me to hear.

"Time for our bet?" I asked, hopefully. I was losing steam fast, especially being so hungry.

"I'm ready if you are." He rubbed his hands together and kneeled on the mat.

I swallowed hard as I laid on my back. There was no one here to distract me this time. It was just Shawn and me, his towering presence as he hovered over my body.

I closed my eyes. Now that we were in position, it became more real. I wanted to prove to myself that I could do this. I blocked out the way his hair fell forward into his face. I pinned my hands to my sides to stop myself from reaching out to touch the strands. I was strong, and I refused to be in a situation like Olivia or Kendahl without any means of protecting myself. I tried not to let his scent make me dizzy or to let the weight of him feel like anything more than what it was, a drill.

Opening my eyes, I found Shawn staring down at me. His body weight still only barely on me as he hovered.

"You okay?" He sounded so soft, so sincere, it made me gulp.

"Yeah, I just needed a second. But I'm good now."

He nodded and sunk onto me. It wasn't his full weight. I could tell. His thighs grazed mine as he tightened them around me.

"You remember the steps?" I nodded.

Buck my hips.

Bear-hug.

Hook legs.

Throw my body weight into the flip.

I could do this. A vision of Shawn wearing yoga pants passed through my mind, and I gave a small snort.

He looked at me like I had five heads, lips drawn in a tight line. "This is serious, you know. If I had bad intentions toward you, laughing would be the last thing you'd do."

God, he had a stick up his ass. This was just a drill, and I was perfectly safe.

"Sorry, teacher," I teased. "I just had a flash of you in yoga pants and the laugh slipped out." I smiled up at him, but his expression stayed hard. "Okay, Mr. Serious, I'll stop playing around."

He was infuriating. Learn how to joke around a little, Shawn, I thought, still stewing from his grumpiness.

Before he had the chance to scold me again about the seriousness of this drill, which newsflash, I already knew, I used all of my pent-up frustration to haul every inch of my strength into rolling Shawn to my left.

He thudded over and I ended up on top of him, disheveled as hell, but that didn't matter. I did it. I had rolled Shawn—a huge guy—off me. My chest heaved up and down from the force of the roll, and I looked down at Shawn with my smuggest expression.

He smiled, a small, brief smile, but I caught it. "Good job. Now let's do it again."

Was he serious? After the bet and all the buildup, that's all I was getting out of him? No sir, I wanted more than that. I didn't know where this was coming from, but at that moment, I wanted actual praise for something I had accomplished.

I poked him in the chest, still straddling him low on his abdomen. I moved to push myself up to standing but decided I was going to let him have it while I had him in this position. I was loving this control, and I let the feeling of my accomplishment run through my veins.

"That's all I get? 'Good job. Let's do it again'?" I leaned in closer to him to make my point. "You know this was hard for me, physically, but most of all, emotionally. And the bet... what was the point of all the buildup and then nothing?"

I barely registered Shawn's face during my rant. Was he trying to cut in and say something? I didn't even know.

"Why am I even bothering with this anyway? Stupid men, and their stupid ways. This is all Kendahl's fault. Yeah. If she just came to class with me like she was supposed to I'd have a real partner. But no, she didn't want to leave her apartment bubble. And here I am. Alone again with no one to share in my happy moment."

Aggravation clouded my mind too completely. I thought of my parents always doting on Olivia and her volleyball wins and straight A's. I thought of Lungberg never giving me credit for my hard work, and finally, I thought of myself. How could I expect others to praise me when I told myself I was never good enough?

"Mia..." Shawn started. But I cut him off, finally registering that I was still on top of him with fire in my veins.

"What is this between us, Shawn? Tell me. Because I'm sick of your back and forth. Are you into me? Or are you just being a good teacher because—"

Shawn cut off my rant with his lips and oh my God. I was not prepared for that. The kiss was firm and quick, answering my questions without any words. It was as if he stole my anger away, along with my breath. He looked up at me with a gleam in his eye that stoked my irritation and sent my heart hammering.

"This doesn't mean our conversation is over, you know." I would hold my ground. I would get him to have a real conversation. But first I had to wipe that proud expression off his face.

I leaned in slowly, our bodies flush, and kissed him. I explored the planes of his lips softly, barely a touch. Then his mouth opened, deepening the kiss and he parted my mouth with his tongue. A soft moan escaped my lips as he wrapped his arms around me, bringing me tight to his chest so that the heat of his body seared through me. One of his hands came up to bunch into my hair, pulling gently on the bun that was barely held in place. Holy shit, if I could burrow myself inside of him, it still wouldn't be enough.

He brought that same intensity of his stare into his kisses. They were searching and urgent. I could feel the muscles deep within me tighten with each slide of our tongues. My shaky arms screamed for relief from hovering over him. He shifted us, maneuvering me easily so that we were on our sides.

From this angle, I was free to run my hands through his thick hair, gently tugging. A light hiss escaped his lips, and he deepened our kiss, barely giving me a moment to breathe. He was like a man starved, and I was his long-awaited meal.

With my top leg still wrapped around him, I could feel his arousal against my belly and it was large. *Damn.* It had been years since I'd been intimate with someone, not since college, but I don't remember anyone else pressing into me this way.

I ground my hips against him. He broke free of my lips, murmuring some unintelligible explicative. I did it again, loving the fact that I was breaking down his barriers and getting a reaction out of him. In answer, he peppered my neck with kisses, reaching my ear and sucking my earlobe into his mouth. His warm, hot breath made me squeeze my legs tighter around him, and I rubbed my face against his delicious stubble.

"I've been wanting to taste you since I met you, Mia," He hummed into my ear.

All the air whooshed out of me. I had no words. Not that words were all that important in that moment. Instead of responding, I pulled his face back up to mine, devouring his mouth and stealing his breath.

A loud beeping started trilling from the other room and I jumped, almost as if something had forcefully awoken me. Panting, Shawn cursed under his breath, "Shit, that's the lasagna." He scurried into the kitchen to check on the timer.

I rolled onto my back and used my forearms to half-sit up. My chest still heaving and face flushed I flopped back down to collect myself. That was the hottest make out session I'd ever had. No comparison. Panties drenched and lips swollen, I couldn't help but wonder how far we would have gone had that timer not gone off.

Chapter 15

Shawn

THE LASAGNA COULD HAVE been burning my house down and I wouldn't have realized it. Damn timer. I guess it was a good thing I had had the foresight to set it.

My cock threatened to break through my shorts after that kiss. I wasn't planning for that to happen, even if I'd pictured it since I laid eyes on Mia and even if the thought crossed my mind when I invited her over here. I tried to be professional and keep my attraction at bay. The last thing she needed when she was being vulnerable was a guy with an entire truckload of baggage.

It had been no use. As soon as her fiery temper came out, her beautiful face getting flustered, I couldn't hold back. And shit, now that I had a taste of Mia, I don't think I'll ever have my fill.

I pulled out the tray of lasagna, mozzarella cheese bubbling to perfection, the smell of marinara sauce wafting through the house. I'll never be able to look at lasagna without being pissed again. I laughed to myself. I was losing it.

Remy meandered in, the click of his nails loud on the wooden floor. Anytime he smelled food, he was right there, my little shadow. Mia followed shortly behind him. Her face was still rosy from where my stubble rubbed against her, and her ruffled hair bobbed on top of her head. She was beautiful like that. "That smells amazing," Mia said wistfully.

She poked around the kitchen, glancing over at our cooling dinner. I cleared my throat, grabbing two glasses and the sparkling water out of the fridge. "Thanks. It's one of the few vegetarian things I can cook well. Or at least I think it's pretty tasty."

Mia beamed, "How did you know I don't eat meat?"

"I'm very observant," I hoped that didn't make me sound like a stalker, but she didn't seem to be anything other than happy. Truth was, I noticed her avoiding all the meat dishes at the party. I took a guess, and it turned out to be right. "How long have you been a vegetarian?"

She chewed her bottom lip and followed me to the kitchen table, which I had set earlier. "I think fully since I graduated college, but I was never really a big meat eater. It was one of the things about me that drove my father nuts."

I laughed, "Why? Is he one of those typical grilling dads who wears an apron that says Master of Meat and has ten different barbeque sauces at all times?"

"I wish he were that way. That sounds wholesome and sweet," she sighed. "Sadly, no. I think I can count on one hand the number of times my father prepared a meal in my lifetime. Knowing him, he probably viewed my choice as a control thing. He always hosted dinner parties at these fancy steakhouses and would bring up how I lived on rabbit food as a joke to make others laugh."

I scoffed, "Sounds like a real nice guy." I knew guys like that. They had to put people down to build themselves up. I glanced at Mia, already looking dejected from bringing up her father. "While I eat meat, I always buy it at the farmer's market and make sure it's responsibly sourced." I grabbed a spatula and sliced up the still-steaming pasta and plated it for us.

"I'll have to make you my famous chickpea curry one day. It's to die for. My best friend, Kendahl, is obsessed with it." A blush ran up her neck, to her cheeks. "You've met Kendahl, my bad. Parts of that night are still somewhat blurry for me."

I scooped lasagna onto my fork and shoveled it into my mouth. It was nice to have someone else to cook for. It had been a long time since I'd eaten a meal with another person. I watched Mia bring a bite to her lips and gently blow to cool it down before sliding it into her mouth. She chewed slowly, a small moan escaping her lips. A jolt shot straight to my cock. I needed to stop watching her mouth.

Mia's gaze slid to mine, and she noticed I was watching her intently. Her eyes quickly shifted back down to her plate, and she sipped her seltzer. I decided to quit gawking at her full lips and forced myself to focus on eating. "This is amazing lasagna. You weren't boasting."

"I'd never boast." I shot her my widest cheese grin.

"Why, Shawn Brooks, if I didn't know better, I'd say you were getting an actual personality."

"Hmm, I don't know about that. Does being a stubborn ass count as a personality? Because I think it would fit." Teasing her was so much more enjoyable than I would have thought. My chair squeaked as I leaned back.

"Not sure if that counts." She rested her chin on her hand. "I'd be willing to bet you're definitely an introverted, observant type—maybe an ISTJ."

I put my fork down. "What kind of psych language is that?"

"You've never heard of the Myers-Briggs personality types? You will so have to do the quiz one day. I'm curious now."

"Whatever you say," I shrugged. "I guess stubborn ass isn't one of them?" I shoveled another bite of lasagna into my face while she laughed lightly.

"Nope. We can submit a petition to have it added, though. They can make you a case study. The scientists would have a field day with you."

Baby, if you only knew.

"What's your type?" I guess this is the new age dating lingo. What used to be "What's your favorite color or animal," has now become this nonsense.

"I'm an INFP." She sat back, wiping her lip with a napkin. "It's also called the mediator."

A fuller picture of this woman formed in my mind. I could see her in that role. Even with that fiery temper that occasionally came out, she still seemed full of empathy and peacemaking skills. That had to be why her piece-of-shit boss walked all over her. Personality type or not, I'd make sure this woman toughened up and took what she deserved.

"I could see that, even from the short time we've known each other." I took a long drink out of my glass, wiping my scruff with the back of my hand, "Now here's the real question. Can these types change over time? What if you wake up one morning and you're sick of always playing the referee?"

She smoothed a wayward piece of hair back from her face. "I'm no psych major. Accountant. Remember? But I'd be willing to guess that they could change a little bit, but it would have to happen over a long period. No one can just wake up one morning being that different. Plus, I think these are more intrinsic to who we are deep inside, you know?"

I sat back in my seat, belly full but comfortable. "You know you're pretty sexy when you talk all scientific, those big words." I leaned in closer, loving the flush on her cheeks.

She was quick to reply, "I can talk wordy to you anytime."

This woman put me at a loss for words. I looked at her lips again, remembering the feel and taste of her. Reaching across the table, I covered her hand with my own. She flipped her hand up so we were palm to palm and she threaded her fingers through mine. The kiss had been mind blowing, but this simple gesture meant so much more.

"I like this side of you, Shawn." She was genuine and had a soft smile curving her lips.

I wanted to open up to her, to tell her everything. There was a reason I was so closed off. Looking at her gorgeous face, so open and caring, I wanted to get some of it off my chest. But fuck, I was afraid I'd send her running for the hills. If I wanted to see where this thing would go, I'd have to give her that part of me. I rubbed circles around her palm with my thumb, her hand was so small and soft in mine.

"I'm going to clean up, and then I'd like to talk. If you're up for it?" Of course, she would be. She just admitted to me she was a damn mediator. I'd have to be sure she understood that I wasn't here for her to fix me.

"Talk about you coming to a yoga class, you mean?" Her brows perked up.

I grasped her palm and brought it to my lips, kissing the outside of her hand gently before releasing it. I loved her teasing me. It almost made me want to forget about this whole serious conversation. "Oh, I know I'm not getting out of that."

"Nope. I'm going to find the cutest pair of yoga pants for you to wear, too. It'll give me the perfect view of that bubble butt of yours."

"That's it. I feel objectified and slightly self-conscious now. Are you calling me fat again?" I joked.

I stood up, taking our plates while Mia grabbed the paper towels from the countertop and wiped the table down. "I'd never," she teased with a full smile on her face. "A girl can appreciate a little junk in the trunk, though."

She could ogle my ass any day if it got her smiling like that.

With the majority of the dinner mess cleared away and the lasagna leftovers packed up, we moved into the living room. My fingers itched to touch her again. Anywhere. As long as I could feel her heat beneath my hands. We slid, facing each other, onto my deep brown couch, her thigh grazed the edge of mine. She fiddled with the hem of her shirt, bunching it up between her fist and letting it go. I assumed she was nervous about what I had to say. The easy, teasing atmosphere we had had at the dinner table changed once we stood up as if coming into a different room set an entirely new scene emotionally.

Sensing my heightened emotions, Remy came to my side and leaned his warm head against my leg. *Good boy.* I gave him a gentle scratch behind the ear, garnering a grunt-like sound from him and a head nudge for more.

Mia was waiting for me to start the conversation, just like I knew she would. I reached out for her hand, that small connection anchoring me.

"I'm not usually a big talker." I expected her to laugh and throw some teasing remark at me, but she just looked expectant. It took every ounce of willpower in me to not get up and pace. "I like you, Mia. I tried not to..." I reached out and held her hand firmly. "Fuck... I'm terrible at this. What I mean to say is, I want you in my life."

I met her wide gaze, brown eyes softening. I wished I could read minds. This shit was terrifying. It was so much easier to hide away like the hermit I was than to lay it all out there.

Mia leaned in and, the second her floral scent hit my nostrils, my heart calmed. Her lips met mine, soft and warm, coursing through me like a drug. This must have been her way of saying she wanted me too. I could feel it in the way she kissed. *Fuck.* It took every ounce of restraint in me to stop her before I got carried away. I kissed her forehead gently and leaned back to put physical distance between us, but I kept her hand in mine.

"In case you didn't realize, that was me saying I want you in my life, too." She gave me a coy look, her eyes still glazed from our kiss.

I shifted in my seat from the uncomfortable bulge now in my pants, I nodded, "I figured as much, not to be presumptuous, but I figured my amazing lasagna sealed the deal."

"That was it. I only like you for your lasagna skills." She reached down and scratched Remy behind the ear. "And your dog, he gave you brownie points too."

Her smile while she pet Remy, on my couch, was enough to make me want to sling her over my shoulder and carry her into my bed. First, I had to be sure she had the full picture of me. And that meant talking about Michelle.

I quieted, rubbing circles on her palm. "As much as I like you, I want to be sure you know what you're getting into with me." A heavy weight settled onto my chest, like a fucking boulder.

I hated to recount this and hoped it didn't set me off. She deserved to know, though.

Mia chewed her bottom lip, anxious but still teasing me. "Are you going to tell me you have the body of your dead mother down in the basement, Norman Bates style?" Her voice softened, and she squeezed my hand. "Whatever it is, Shawn, I can handle it. I'm not as fragile as I look. I've been through some shit, too." That was a knife straight to my heart. Whoever or whatever hurt her, I hoped they got what they deserved.

"Remember the first time we met?" Mia nodded, about to cut in but I held my hand out. "When I said I was having a bad day..."

My cheeks burned from the intensity of her gaze but I couldn't meet her eyes. Not while I was bearing a part of my soul.

"I have PTSD. What you saw was me on the edge of a flashback."

Gripping the edge of the couch, I finally met her gaze. I don't know what I expected to see in her face. Fear? Nervousness? I never thought she'd be biting the corner of her lip with a look of resolve across her face.

"Thank you for telling me."

"I was expecting a different response." I loosened my grip on the couch and bent to pet Remy again. Anything to avoid the warmth emanating from her expression.

"I don't know why you would? Having a mental health condition doesn't change the fact that I like you and think you're a good person. I know that there are a lot of myths out there about people who have PTSD."

She was right about all the myths out there. I learned from Dr. Glover that when many people heard of post-traumatic stress disorder or PTSD, they automatically thought of violent outbursts. Of course, there are many levels of post-traumatic stress disorder, so I'm sure that could be possible, but I'm thankful every day that I don't have those symptoms.

"I'm not sure how much you know about it, but baby, I have a lot of baggage. I've been working on my shit for years, and I still have night terrors most nights. I get a shitty attitude out of nowhere sometimes, and there're times when I feel like something bad is going to happen. I lose myself, and I swear, Remy is the only one that is able to pull me back when that happens," I sighed.

Telling her about all of this reaffirmed for me that she'd be better off without me. I should be alone, like the waste of space I am. This world is a bad place, and she didn't need me making it any worse for her.

"As much as I want you, and, God, Mia, you're the fucking sunshine that's broken through my wall of clouds, I can't let you get sucked into my bullshit. I want to do what's best for you, and not be a selfish prick. We need to end this before it starts."

I was spiraling. How did I start this conversation intending it to go one way, and it derailed onto a completely different track? Mia was silent, biting her lip, her eyes narrowed. I needed to know what she was thinking.

Chapter 16

Mia

I'VE BEEN CAUTIOUS ABOUT getting into relationships my entire life, and I would be lying if I said his PTSD didn't concern me at all. I experienced it firsthand with Olivia. The sleepless nights, the crippling fear, the guilt. Each and every symptom ripped away who my sister was bit by bit, shaping her into a hardened version of herself.

Anyone would be cautious after seeing what she went through as intimately as I did. Then, once I hit college, it seemed like every guy had only one reason for showing interest, and once they scored, they bounced. So, I've guarded my heart. If I never started a relationship than there was no way I'd end up with my soul shattered. But Shawn has been the first guy—maybe ever—to stir something in me. Something genuine that made me want to peel back his layers and see more. Not just to help him, like I did with everyone else, but because he's made me start feeling things I'd long given up on. We both deserved love. I've been waiting for the right guy to come around, someone worth my heart and someone I could trust with my full being. Shawn could be that person for me. I'd be damned if I was about to let him push me away. I was done letting men tell me how to feel.

"Shawn," I dropped my hands to my sides, fisting them in my shirt, "I'm not going to let you push me away."

His face fell. He obviously expected a different response. "Mia, I'm being serious. I like you so much, but that's why we can't do this."

I steeled myself, "No. First, since we sat down on this couch you talked in a circle. You started out with how much you wanted us to work to pushing me away. I'm saying no to that."

He stared at me, mouth parted. "I haven't told you everything."

I put my hand out to stop him. "Like I said, unless you're secretly hiding bodies in your basement, I'm here, Shawn. You don't have to tell me everything tonight. You don't have to tell me tomorrow, or the next day, or the next month. I am patient. I know when someone is worth it."

He ran a hand through his hair and stood up, pacing the length of the coffee table. He stopped in front of me. "I'm not worth it, though. That's the thing."

I didn't want to pry. Like I said, I was a patient woman, but it was killing me that I didn't know why he felt this way. What happened in Shawn's life to make him hate himself so much?

Remy grunted and scooted closer to Shawn's feet. Shawn bent over to rub his neck, sucking a breath into his nose.

"In the short time I've known you, this is what I've seen," I started. He stilled, eyes blazing into mine. "I've seen a stubborn ass of a man." That got a small smile out of him. "But that stubborn ass has cared for me when I was sick, made me feel safe and secure in vulnerable situations, stood up to my chauvinistic boss, and, most importantly, made me lasagna."

He shook his head lightly, one corner of his mouth turned up.

"He's taken care of my best friend, and he's pushed me to do my best in a situation where I'd normally quit." I heaved myself up to stand and then walked directly in front of him. Being this close, chest to chest, made me realize just how tall he was compared to me. I placed both of my hands against his torso, feeling the steady rhythm of his heart.

"That is a worthy man. So, you can try to push me away, but I see you, Shawn. I see what you have in here," I patted his chest. "It's a heart that anyone would be lucky to hold."

I went to remove my hands and go back to the couch. I had said my piece and could see that he needed time to absorb my words. Before I could move an inch, his calloused hands were wrapping around mine, pulling them from his chest up to his mouth. He planted one firm kiss on the outside of my stacked hands and then let them drop, stepping back from me.

This was it. He was really going to push me away. I couldn't force him into anything. If he was this stubborn, the only thing I could do was leave. A stupid tear welled in the corner of my eye. Rejection always hurt, but never more than when you had laid your feelings on the line. I had to get out of here before the waterworks came out like a floodgate opening.

I turned and rushed into the kitchen for my purse. Being next to him and looking at his gorgeous face would only make it harder to hide my emotions. My purse was slung on a chair, my phone peeking out of it. Frantically, I grabbed it and turned to head for the front door, another tear slipping out.

Come on Mia, hold it together until you get in the car.

I made myself think of the fact that I succeeded in flipping Shawn, and how badass that felt. I was strong. I was powerful. I did not need to cry.

With my head down, I hadn't noticed Shawn blocking the kitchen entryway with his huge fighter's body. I refused to look up at him. He didn't need to see me upset. He was already beating himself up enough.

"I'm going to go, Shawn. We can talk about this another time, okay?"

He didn't budge. I huffed, trying to slide between him and the door frame.

"Come on, message received. I'll go. You sit here in your self-loathing. Thank you for dinner. Goodbye." Like a freaking stone statue, he stayed in place, his body so close to mine that I was losing my resolve with each passing second. I could feel his warm breath against the top of my head. I wanted to look up into those blue eyes but knew if I did, I'd break.

I tried to wiggle my way past him again, but he reached an arm out and steadied my shoulders. At that, I finally looked at him. His face held the expression of a man tormented. "Let me go, Shawn. I'll leave you alone."

He trailed one hand from my shoulder up my neck, gently, like I was made of porcelain, before reaching my curls and fisting his hand into them. "What if I don't want you to leave?" His eyes were pleading, darting from my eyes to my lips, trying to read my expression. "What if I want you right here, with me?"

I scoffed, even though his touch had me melting like warm chocolate. "Your back and forth gives me whiplash, Shawn. It doesn't feel good to be pushed away." I drew my gaze down to my feet again. "You've made yourself clear."

He grazed my jaw with his hand, lifting my face back up so my eyes could meet his. A tear spilled down my cheek. Stupid thing. I told myself, *keep it together*.

He reached out and wiped it with his finger, stroking over the planes of my face from my cheek, over my lower lip, and back down to my jaw. The gentleness of his touch had me reeling. I wanted to nuzzle into him and succumb to the shivers that were making their way down my body.

"Nothing is clear, not when it comes to you."

His warm lips crashed into mine, stealing my breath. Emotions be damned. I met his force with my own, parting my mouth slightly to let his tongue slide in. He groaned into me and it was the hottest sound I'd ever heard. I slid my tongue into his mouth, exploring, grazing his teeth, the top of his mouth, reaching everywhere I could. I came alive with him against my lips.

He yanked on the scrunchie that held up my mass of curls so he could bury his hand into them, gently tugging on the strands. My pulse skyrocketed and more shivers slid down my body, settling right in my center. His other hand moved down my back, stopping at the curve of my low back. His fingers were mere centimeters from the swell of my ass, but I didn't want him to stop there. I wanted to feel his hands cupping me. I wanted his strong palms to explore my bare skin. Our kisses were hot and needy. I savored the taste of him, sucking his lower lip and teasing my tongue around it.

He pulled back, panting. "Fuck, if you keep doing that with your tongue, I'm going to back you up to that counter and take you right now."

This stoic man, who observed everything around him and rarely lost control in any situation, coming apart for me was like a drug. I wanted to see every ounce of his control slip and feel him melt around me.

I usually let my anxiety control me, but for once I wanted to tell off my emotions. I'd sort them out later. At that moment, what I wanted was right in front of me.

I raised a brow to challenge him and slowly teased his lower lip, licking and sucking it before gliding my lips up to pull his earlobe into my mouth. I could feel the scar from a piercing that hadn't fully healed and imagining Shawn with metal in his ear turned me on more.

He growled into my ear his hands sliding down and finally cupping my ass, grinding me into him as we crowded in the doorframe.

"You're testing me, aren't you?" His voice trembled as much as my body. "You don't think I'll really take you on that countertop?"

From the feeling of his thick erection pushing against his gym shorts, there was no doubt in my mind that he wasn't bluffing. I wanted this. Badly. Answering him with movement, I ground myself into his hardness. With our height difference, he was rubbing against my lower abdomen, but it didn't matter, the movement did what I wanted it to.

Shawn hissed a breath through his teeth and kissed me again, running his tongue over mine until I was practically gasping for air. Turning us so that I was against the doorframe, he grabbed both of my legs, hoisting me up so his thick length was hitting right at the sensitive nub between my legs. Thank the gods above that he was holding me fully because, with that first connection, I shuddered. My body gave into the intensity it felt.

"Oh God," I panted.

Was it possible that Shawn could make me come while fully clothed? I guess there could be a first time for everything.

He pushed into me again, his hands gripping my ass and squeezing, while I grasped at his neck, frantically kissing and sucking anywhere my mouth would reach.

"Mia, tell me what you want," Shawn said as he continued his teasing of my lips, his palm still kneading my backside. "I need to hear it from your perfect lips."

I wanted...

God, I didn't know what to say. I wanted everything with this man. Maybe it was lust talking, but I'd let him devour me whole if he wanted to. I panted against him while trying to get as close to his body as I could. My panties were flooded with wetness.

"I... I don't know. Just..." I tugged on his hair, and he rubbed his face against mine. The scratch of his stubble a painful pleasure against my sensitive skin.

"Words, baby. Where's that fiery girl who came out earlier, huh? She would tell me exactly what she wanted."

Why was this so hard for me? His husky voice set my body on fire. I knew what I wanted, but I couldn't let the words escape my lips.

With one more push of his hips into my core, he loosened his grip on me, and let me slide back to the ground. No, that wasn't what I wanted at all. I climbed him, spider monkey style, and he chuckled, "So eager, aren't you?"

I scrambled for purchase, panting into the warm curve of his neck. His hands reached for my ass again, holding me steady.

"I want to lay you out on that counter and taste you for dessert, Mia," his voice rasped against my ear as he leaned into me. "I want to make you come so hard you fucking see stars."

Oh. My. God.

"Uh hmm," I nodded, nuzzling his face.

"Tell me you want that. Let your fire out, baby."

I opened my mouth to say "Yes, I want that," but what came out was, "Please, I—"

That was all he needed to hear. He hefted me up like I weighed no more than five pounds and plopped me down onto the kitchen counter. I turned to move shit out of the way. The salt and pepper shakers, a napkin holder thing, and a few other random items left out from dinner still littered the counter.

"Leave it," he guided my hands back. "Look at me. I want to see your beautiful face when you come all over mine."

My breath caught in my throat. Pure need wrung through me until I felt nothing else. I scrambled back, resting my forearms on the cold counter while Shawn brushed his lips against my neck. He worked his way lower, pulling my shirt up over my head in one swift motion. His eyes were blazing as he took in my breasts. They were spilling out of the sports bra I still wore.

"Off," he growled, barely taking his mouth from my neck. I yanked it off and Shawn's eyes lit up like twin flames.

"Fucking hell, Mia. I knew your tits would be perfect." His tongue swiped against his lower lip.

Exposed to the cool air, my nipples hardened to firm points, and when Shawn made his way down my body and popped one into his warm mouth, my hips jutted off the counter. He tugged, filling me with more need, but he didn't stay there long.

"You ready for me? Lift those hips. These shorts need to come off."

A quick wave of self-consciousness hit me. The overhead lights were bright as hell and illuminated every inch of skin. Was I ready for this perfect specimen of a man to see all of me on full display? My small belly roll was already laid bare, but my abundant thighs with lines of stretch marks and my very un-waxed pussy were still hidden under clothing. I wasn't sporting an eighties porno bush or anything, but it had been some time since hot wax had touched my sensitive areas.

Seeing my hesitation, Shawn's face softened. He stood up to his full height. "You say the word and we can stop."

I bit my lower lip, covering my exposed breasts. "No, that's not what I want." God, why was this so hard for me? "It's just you look like that," I said as I rubbed my hands down his chest. "And I look like this," I finish as I gave my thigh a squeeze.

He narrowed his eyes as he got on his knees before me. The only sound to be heard were my anticipating breaths. He cupped my calf in his hands, gently kneading his way up toward my knee. How could every touch feel so incredible? "This calf right here," He planted a slow kiss right below my knee, "is the sexiest calf I've ever seen."

I closed my eyes, a small smile playing on my lips. He kept going up my leg, grasping my thighs, one large hand on each. "These right here, the strength in them, I want nothing more than to feel them pressed against my cheeks." He nuzzled my thighs, slowly kissing each one. He kept traveling further and further upward until he was hovering right above my center. His face an inch from my throbbing middle.

My eyes still closed, I tilted my head back and rasped, "Please."

Inching forward, I lifted my hips and he pulled my shorts and underwear off in one tug. The care he took with his words, and the way he savored every inch of me before we ever even got fully undressed made my cloud of self-doubt dissipate as quickly as it had come on.

I opened for him, the cold countertop biting at my bottom, and he took a moment to take me in this way. "So fucking beautiful." Without another word, his face was buried in my pussy. With the first press of his tongue, I nearly launched myself off of the counter, but one of his hands reached up and pressed the tops of my thighs to keep me steady. His tongue parted me, spreading wetness to my clit.

Shawn started a punishing rhythm, swirling his tongue over my bundle of nerves. It took every ounce of restraint in me not to buck against his face. I was close, my stomach tightened, every nerve wound so tight I could snap. He gave me a soft, teasing suck before looking up at me. His eyes were deep pools, and my wetness glistened on his lips.

"You're fucking dripping for me, and you taste like heaven."

He went back to devouring me and sucking my clit so hard that I jolted. His finger slid inside of me, hitting my wall at the perfect angle. He pumped into me with his finger, matching the steady flick of his tongue.

I threw my head back and dug my fingers into his hair, pulling. "Oh my God, Shawn."

He reached up to pinch my nipple with his free hand, and with that tiny movement, I shattered into a million pieces.

I shuddered for what felt like hours, clenching around his finger until he lifted his head with one last kiss right above my pelvic bone. When it subsided, I tried to lift myself, but I felt utterly exhausted. Still, I wanted to make Shawn feel as good as he just made me feel. I wanted to see him come apart at my hands.

I reached for him, wanting to squeeze his thick cock, wanting to taste it. But Shawn took my hand, covering it with his.

"Shawn?" I asked, confused. But he lifted me and started carrying me back out to the couch.

"I want to feel you," I rasped out, my body still letting out tiny aftershocks.

He plopped down on the couch, arranging my naked body on top of his lap. "You will, eager girl. Just not tonight. Tonight was about you."

He smoothed the hair back from my face and I put my head against his chest, completely confused, but too tired to argue. Between working out earlier, the emotional rollercoaster after dinner, and that mind-blowing orgasm, sleep threatened to take me.

Shawn grabbed a thick blanket from the corner of the couch and spread it out over us. Kissing the top of my head once we were both covered. "Thank you," he murmured.

"Hmm?" I asked, but by the time I looked up at him, his head was resting against the cushion, and he was fast asleep.

Chapter 17

Mia

Fifteen minutes later, I managed to extricate myself from Shawn's lap before I, too, was knocked out from exhaustion. Shivering from the air-conditioning and no longer being tucked against his warm body, I searched the kitchen for the wrinkled pile of my clothes.

Dressed and purse slung over my shoulder, I tiptoed past Shawn, giving him one more appreciative look. Sleep caused all the tightness that his face normally held to be erased and replaced with a peaceful softness. I hated to run out on him like this, especially with so much left to discuss, but I had work tomorrow and no clothes to wear.

Besides, even with as intimate as we just got, I didn't think we were ready for a sleepover. Shawn barely knew how he felt and finding me next to him in the morning may send him into another spiral.

Remy poked his head up from the couch beside Shawn as I reached the front door, his head tilting as if to ask, "Where are ya going?" I pushed down the desire to curl back up with Shawn and slipped out the door.

I woke up the next morning feeling equal parts sore and soothed; an odd combination. My thighs ached. Heat spread to my face at the thoughts, from last night, of Shawn between my legs. I couldn't believe the night went the way it did. I wouldn't change it, though. When I thought of Shawn and his obnoxiously beautiful face (even when he acted indifferent), the gentle way he rubbed his thumb over my palm... *gah*, even his intoxicating scent. It reminded me of the forests in my New York hometown.

That man was a damn drug.

Stretching out on the queen-sized bed, polka dot duvet hanging precariously off the edge, I grabbed my phone to check my messages. I needed a minute before I committed to the whole "getting up for work like a functioning adult" thing. I had meant to text Shawn when I got home to apologize for slipping out like a wraith, but I had barely managed to plug in my phone before passing out.

There were already three message alerts. Why were people so eager to converse before seven o'clock in the morning?

The first two were a given, Lungberg almost always assaulted my inbox before my first cup of coffee. It was nothing important, just him telling me I only had a few more days until the big soirée. Like I didn't know. This party had taken up every nook and cranny of my free time, even with Jared's help.

My face broke into a grin at the next message. It was from Shawn, sent at four-thirty in the morning, so either he was a super early riser or the couch didn't prove to be the best spot for a good night's sleep.

Shawn: *Sorry I passed out on you. I woke up to Remy next to me and for a second I wondered if I had fallen for a werewolf. *Wink emoji**

Fallen for? Were my eyes working? I stuck my lip out of the corner of my mouth. It's something I'd done since childhood when trying to think of witty retorts. Coffee would have helped a lot with making the words come.

I type out: *Well, you haven't seen me during the winter. My leg fur could rival Remy's coat...* Oh my God. No. Not saying that.

Delete.

I try again.

Me: *Haha, if only I could be as cuddly as Remy. * Wink emoji *

Okay, that was better. I was putting the conversation back in his hands. I rolled over in bed, flopping my legs over the edge. I didn't have a ton of time before I had to leave for work, but coffee was a necessity at this point. With the grace of a porpoise, I pawed at my Keurig until the sweet sound of coffee brewing filled the room. I reached for my favorite I heart NY mug that I've had since a sixth-grade field trip, and I prepped my cup with some sugar and oat milk. My phone trilled again, and I had that thing unlocked in a second.

Shawn: *You're pretty cuddly. You made me fall fast asleep… which was a miracle with how hard I was…*

The large gulp of coffee I was chugging almost got spit across my kitchen counter. Holy shit.

Shawn: *Will I see you in class later?*

Thank God he was changing the subject to something neutral. Dirty talk and I before seven in the morning did not work well together.

As sore as I was, there was no way I'd miss class tonight. Even with the last-minute planning I needed to finish up for the golf event. This was my me-time and seeing a certain hot man who made me want to drop my panties with one look sealed the deal.

Me: *I'll be there. Want to partner up?*

A cheesy grin lit up my face as I took my coffee and got myself together for the day. I needed a shower, badly. Maybe a cold one, if he texted me any more about his hardness. I felt like a southern belle, fanning herself and thinking dear me.

Shawn: *I want to be your only partner from now on.*

Shawn: *Unless I have to assist or teach. In that case, I'm keeping Coby and every other guy far away from you.*

I snorted. Possessive much?

Me: *Okay Big Guy lower your testosterone. We don't need any violence being incited this early in the morning. *Laughing emoji**

Me: *I'm hopping in the shower to get ready for another fun-filled day at work. I'll see you tonight.*

I started the water, chugging the last sips of my coffee while it warmed up.

Me: *Oh and don't think you're getting out of yoga class. We are checking the schedule tonight and making plans for that. *Tongue out emoji**

It elated me to think that we already had plans in the works. I couldn't wait to text Kendahl later and tell her everything.

Without waiting for his reply, I showered and ran the razor quickly over my legs and bikini area. A girl had to be prepared now that she was semi-dating. Or whatever it was that we were doing. I scrambled around my apartment, throwing on a fitted blue dress and tossing my still-damp hair up into a bun. I gathered some gym clothes and put them in a bag for later along with my sneakers. There were a few minutes before I had to leave, so I added earrings and a quick coat of mascara to brighten up my eyes.

I skipped my usual walk to work and drove instead because this heat plus me in a dress equaled a massive sweaty mess. By the time I plopped down at my desk after a quick hello to Jared, who assessed me with a raised brow, I was finally able to check my phone.

Shawn: *I already ordered my yoga pants.*

Shawn: *The reviews said these were the best for making butts look amazing. I figured the least I can do is give you something to ogle.*

Below the text was a screenshot of a woman in yoga pants that had ruching on the entire back seam. I laughed—hard. Her butt did look amazing, like a big juicy peach. If Shawn was serious, there was no way in hell I'd get through a class without passing out from laughter.

Shawn: *Have a good day at work. Don't let that boss of yours push you around. You've got fire in you, remember that.*

Just like Shawn to end the text in an endearing way that made my heart skip an actual beat.

Me: *You may make some ladies faint if you show up with your ass in those pants. I'd pay to see what happens. Haha. Thanks for brightening my morning.*

Was it possible that grumpy, man-of-few-words Shawn, had a silly, goofy personality underneath all that brooding? I loved what I was seeing and needed to see more of this side of him.

Precisely five minutes before class time, I pushed through the glass door. I don't know how I did it, considering Lungberg was on my ass all day micromanaging every little detail for the event this upcoming weekend. Jared saved me more than once, sweeping over to my desk with lists and confirmations that he had handled for me. He also pried me for information, saying not subtly that I looked like I had been "thoroughly fucked," and he wanted every damn detail or he would withhold every baked good his mother sent in for me for all of eternity.

Knowing Jared, once he found out, he'd hound me daily. He was like the little brother I'd never had. I wanted to tell him about Shawn; the words were on the tip of my tongue, but I still wasn't sure what we were doing. I wanted to keep things to myself for a teensy bit longer. I'd have to tell Kendahl though because damn, I don't think I'd ever had an orgasm that good.

My cheeks heated, and I'm sure I looked like a weirdo standing in the corner of the waiting area of the gym. Mark's office door was closed, and I guessed Shawn was in there prepping for class.

"It's pretty dead tonight." Avery had joined me, each of us shifting from one foot to the other. I looked around for some of the chattier women, like Evie, but they weren't there. She was right. Besides the two of us, about five others were waiting for the class to start. That number was usually double.

"Maybe he'll go easy on us," I hoped out loud. I was sore as hell, and work stress was not helping the situation.

"Not likely," she scoffed and brought her hands behind her back to stretch her shoulders. "From what I've seen, when the class is small, he does a whole group activity."

Huh, that sounded... terrifying. But I was always a little scared before class started.

Mark came out moments later, followed by Dina and Shawn. My heart did a weird involuntary squeeze thing at seeing him.

"Okay, level ones, let's go," Mark shouted and we followed him in like little ducklings.

Shawn reached my side and squeezed my shoulder. "Hey, you."

"Hey yourself," I couldn't help the smile that spread across my face. "Are you teaching tonight?"

"Nah, but I'll probably have to walk around and help out." He scanned the room before adding, "Not sure what he'll have us do tonight with such a small group."

I chewed the inside of my lip. "Avery mentioned he liked to change things up with a group this small."

Shawn rubbed his hands together before taking my hand and leading me into the gym. It was a small gesture but having his hand in mine helped push away my nervous energy.

"Gather around," Mark sat on the cool gray floor with his back against the wall. "Let's have a little chat before we start."

I looked over at Shawn. He raised a brow and whispered, "No idea."

Mark truly looked the part of a leader with all of us seated around him. We waited with bated breath for him to go on.

"I know we're each here for different reasons. Some of us wanted to get in shape, de-stress, or maybe you've had martial arts experience in the past. For some, it's about safety and learning how to protect yourselves and the people you love."

Goosebumps trailed up my arms, and I squeezed Shawn's hand.

Mark cleared his throat, "Here's a statistic that doesn't sit well with me. Over one million violent crimes are committed each year in the United States. That includes assault with a weapon, rape, and murder."

I fidgeted in my seat, hands sweating. The tension in the room was thick as Mark held each person's gaze. "This is why I do what I do. I want each of you to have a fighting chance at protecting yourselves. In here, drills aren't going to be cushy. We're not going to do some synchronized Tae Bo shit. These are real-life get-out-of-a-deadly situation drills because you'll need to neutralize any threat quickly and efficiently. Since we have a smaller group, our drill for tonight is going to include the whole class," he glanced at Shawn, "assistants too. Shawn, come on up here."

I looked over at Shawn, who was clenching his jaw so tightly it looked as though he might crack a tooth. He stood to join Mark in front of us, grabbing a pad first.

"We've been practicing choke defenses, kicks, and elbow strikes but in a very controlled environment." Mark maneuvered each of those combative moves on Shawn. "What we haven't done is practiced with the element of surprise."

My stomach clenched. What did he mean by surprise?

"Half of you will be our attackers. Go grab a pad. Everyone else, you'll have your eyes closed and be standing on one foot." Murmurs sounded around me from a few classmates. "You'll either feel a pad tap you or you'll start getting choked. Be ready for anything. You'll need to act fast, figure out what to do, and where the attackers are coming from. Attackers, once they've neutralized the threat, move on to someone else. Are we ready?"

Shit, I wasn't ready for this. I could barely do these drills in fully controlled situations. I searched for Shawn's face through the small crowd. When I caught his gaze he gave me a nod and a look that said, you got this.

Mark started some eighties rock on low, which helped break the tension.

As I stood there on one foot, eyes closed, the only thing going through my mind was survival. I could do this. I'd make myself proud and Shawn too.

I felt the first tap against my back. Eyes flying open, I launched out a low punch, then a stomp kick. Avery, who held the pad, smiled, and backed away.

I breathed heavily.

That wasn't so bad. I was certainly caught off guard and it majorly tested my balance, but I did it. Resetting my stance, I waited.

I could hear my classmates, their breathing, their hisses as they punched and kicked. Suddenly, I was being choked from the front by a pair of strong hands. My eyes flew open, but the room was dark. I acted on instinct and plucked the man's arms as hard as I could.

The student nodded and moved on, letting me reset again.

My eyes were only closed for a second when I felt another push from behind. Turning on my heels, I met the pad with a hard front kick. I looked up and saw Shawn's signature half grin. "Keep going, fiery girl." He lowered the pad, and I struck it with two low punches, followed up by a knee strike.

Damn, I felt good.

Shawn, upright again, leaned in, whispering in my ear, "I've never been so turned on while getting my ass kicked." He walked away, leaving me speechless and panting.

The drill lasted another few minutes until we switched roles. I made sure to approach Shawn a few times, the first time being with my hands wrapped around his throat. We finished the forty-five-minute class in what felt like ten minutes. Sweat coated my forehead and pooled underneath my bra, but I felt amazing.

Shawn joined me near the cubbies where we stood collecting our water bottles and phones. I peeked at mine, noticing a missed call from my mother and a few messages. She had to have been calling to talk about her and my father coming to Florida. But why was she calling so late? Usually, at this time of night, she and my father were already at the country club, three drinks in.

"Everything okay?" He peeked over at my phone, no doubt noticing my scowl.

I tucked it away. I'd deal with it later. "Yeah, all good. My mother called me, but I'm in too good a mood to call her back."

A raised brow told me he most definitely had something to say. "There's a story here, isn't there?"

I huffed, "Too much to unpack at the moment. Let's just say, Mr. and Mrs. Murphy, aren't my biggest fans."

He was quiet while we walked out to the parking lot. I enjoyed his silent contemplating as much as his teasing, witty comebacks.

"It took me a long time, and trust me, I'm still working on it, but at some point, I realized I was done trying to make other people proud. The only person I needed to live up to was myself. Now, I'm still shit at that, but that's all on me."

He was absolutely right. If I couldn't truly be my own number one fan, then no one else would.

"Such a philosopher, aren't you?" I joked. "You're not shit at it. What you are is way too hard on yourself. You set up these mammoth expectations that no one could ever reach."

Shawn leaned against the driver's side door of my older-than-dirt Civic. The air-conditioning still cranked, and it only intermittently made suspicious groaning sounds, so in my book it was perfect. Shawn looked kind of ridiculous next to such a small car.

He smirked, "Who's the philosopher now?"

"Me of course." I laughed and gave his arm a playful smack adding, "And this is me after a day of work and anxiety inducing Krav class. Imagine me when my brain is fresh."

"You'd be the new Aristotle." When his cheeks lifted, giving me a peek of his genuine smile my stomach flipped. He should definitely smile more, I'd have to see to that. "So, if I'm not mistaken, I was told we would be scheduling a yoga class tonight?" he teased.

Everything I had to do for work flashed through my head, then the call from my mother, and then catching up with Kendahl. It wasn't like me to be impulsive and shirk my responsibilities, especially for a guy. But there he was, arms crossed, looking down at me like I was the sole person on this earth. The part of my brain that controlled responsibility and reasoning shut down like a lantern being blown out. I could picture it happening inside my head in slow motion. Little cartoon character versions of me physically squashing each other for power. I pushed my bun back up on top of my head and bit my lip, feigning contemplation. "Too bad those yoga pants didn't come in yet. I'd love a preview."

He laughed, leaning his head down, "I'm sure I can find something else to show you."

"You're too much," I shook my head, a light laugh escaping my lips. He opened my car door so I could hop in. "Meet you at your place. I'm going to stop at home and grab a few things."

He leaned in and buckled my seatbelt. His lips grazed my ear. "Does this mean you want to spend the night?" My cheeks heated like a kettle beginning to boil.

"I wasn't... I was going to grab my laptop. I mean...," I stuttered in response.

He placed a slow, soft kiss on my lips, shutting up my stumbling words. "Grab your toothbrush and a change of clothes," he whispered. "Just in case."

As I watched him climb into his truck, one thought crossed my mind. *Mia, you're deeper than the diving area of an Olympic swimming pool.*

Chapter 18

Shawn

I scrambled around my bedroom tossing dirty underwear into the hamper and straightening out my tangled bedding so that it didn't look like a cave dweller lived there. I was half hard the entire time I cleaned up, picturing Mia in my bed did all kinds of things to me. Not that I wanted to falsely advertise or anything, but I haven't had much of a reason to keep my bedroom presentable for a long time. The photo of Michelle and me from our wedding stared at me from my bedside table.

Should I put it in the drawer? That seemed wrong. But sleeping with another woman in the bed that we shared with our wedding photo on full display seemed even worse. God, it had been almost five years since I'd been with anyone. Quickly, I slid it into the top drawer. There were other photos throughout the house, and I knew the conversation would come soon if things became as serious with Mia as they were heading. I only hoped it didn't change things for her. I was closing the lid on the toilet seat after wiping down a smear of toothpaste from the sink when Remy barked letting me know we had a visitor.

Mark and Dina had tried to set me up a few times. The first was about a year after Michelle. It was a joke. I could barely look at another woman without guilt eating me alive inside. After the second setup, I felt even more like shit because I was making these perfectly nice women feel like there was something wrong with them. They seemed fine; it was all me and my fucked-up head.

Dr. Glover, my shrink, and I finally agreed it was best for me to put dating aside for a while to focus on my healing. After all these years, even he's been getting on me at this point to get back out there. What I hadn't told him is that the longer I waited, the harder it became to connect with people, especially on a romantic level. When I woke the other morning to Mia gone, I had to jerk off twice to calm myself down before I could go to the shop and work without the thought of her taste driving me insane. He'll be happy as a pig in shit when I finally tell him about Mia.

I opened my front door to Mia's gorgeous smile. She was still in her workout clothes with her purse and a small bag at her side. She reached out to pet Remy, whose tail was shaking a mile a minute. "I think you've made a good impression on him."

"I'd take animals over humans any day." Remy rolled over for a belly rub and she crouched down to oblige. "Right boy? Humans are the worst."

I stepped beside her, taking her bags and setting them aside. "I feel so hurt. I thought I was getting on your good side."

She gave me a sideways glance, "Nah, I'm only using you because I like your dog."

I clutched my chest. "Just push the knife in deeper."

She cracked a grin up at me. "And because I need a teacher. Oh! And I like good lasagna!"

I flopped back onto the couch, playing dead. Remy jumped up, sniffing me, tail wagging. We both laughed. "It's okay, boy." I pet his neck, sitting back up. "Only my ego is dead."

"Don't worry," Mia made a small noise while pushing herself to a stand. "I'll think of a few ways to boost your ego later. I'm starved. Got any leftover lasagna?"

While I warmed up some plates and fed Remy his dinner, Mia sat perched on a kitchen chair, legs folded beneath her. She had her phone out and was scrunching her brows in the cutest way, reading something. I joined her, placing two plates on the table in front of us. She clicked her screen off and pushed the phone away. The lasagna smelled as good tonight as it did last night, and my stomach growled.

"Everything okay?" Her brows knit together in a line as she took a bite, blowing to cool it.

"I was just reading the texts from my mother." I focused my attention on her, letting the plate cool.

"Do you want to talk about it?" I surprised myself by asking. I wanted to see that crease between her brows smooth out. Normally, I wouldn't give a shit about someone's family life. I didn't get involved in things that didn't concern me. It would be none of my business. But I genuinely wanted to know. Her lips turned up in a smile.

She huffed. "My mom just confirmed that she and my dad are staying here for the summer. Well, not in Palm Cove, but about twenty minutes away on the beach. I guess they want a change of scenery, and a few of my dad's colleagues have houses here."

"And that's a bad thing?" I asked gently.

"I mean no, but yes." She thought for a minute. "I don't know, it's complicated. I haven't seen them in person in years. I stopped going home for holidays when I started at my job, and they've never made any attempts to visit me here. I have a monthly conversation or two with my mom, which usually ends up with me drowning in the nearest bottle of wine or pint of Ben and Jerry's." She slumped down, moving her knees so they were crossed and jiggling. I tried to be optimistic even though I wanted to bash them for not caring about her.

"Maybe they've realized they've been dicks and want to be a part of your life?"

"Doubtful," she sighed. "I'll call her back tomorrow. She wants to have lunch at their place this weekend." She chewed thoughtfully on a bite of pasta. "I'm going to turn them down. I have that golf thing on Saturday, and I know I'm going to be exhausted."

"Whatever you think is best." The last thing I wanted to see was Mia losing her fire again.

"I'll think about it." I reached out to rub her hand, tracing calming circles around her palm. She closed her eyes. The hum escaping her lips made my cock twitch. "Just you touching my hand makes me feel better."

"I'm glad. You did too good tonight to have your night ruined."

"You're right." The smile that I loved lit up across her face. We both polished off the rest of our plates. Finally, we sat back satisfied.

"It's not only my parents coming." She glanced back at her phone and unlocked the screen. "My older sister, Olivia, is joining them with my nephew, Alex. He's ten years old."

She pointed her phone in my direction to show me a photo of a woman who looked eerily similar to her. They had the same chestnut hair, only her sister's hair was somewhat wavy and shorter, and they had the same cheekbones. Olivia's smile didn't reach her eyes the same way Mia's did. Her expression looked far off as if she was on the other side of a mirror looking in. Her arm was slung over a boy's shoulder. Freckles covered his face, and, like his aunt, he had a head of unruly brown curls.

"I can see the resemblance. Is your relationship," I struggled to find the right word, "strained?"

Standing up to clear the table, she took a moment to answer. "So-so. We talk a decent amount when I'm not too busy with work. I love my nephew. He's a trip. Olivia kind of pushed me out of her life a bit when I made the move down here. I don't know. It's a long story and a mood killer."

I didn't give a shit about her killing any mood. If she needed to talk about her family, I'd listen. "Mia, you don't have to keep your feelings in because you think other people don't want to hear what you have to say. I don't care about any mood being ruined. I care about you and how you feel." I pulled the empty lasagna tray out of her hands, stopping her from flitting around the island cleaning. "Look at me, beautiful girl." I tilted her face in my direction. I saw what she was trying to hide. A single tear fell to her cheek and her eyes were glossy with emotion. "What's going on inside that perfect head of yours?"

She swallowed, blinking away the tears forming. "Stop saying all the right things. You're making it hard for me to find reasons to keep you away."

"I'm not going anywhere, Mia." I pressed my lips to her forehead then trailed soft kisses down her face, tasting the salty tears on her cheek. "Leave the damn dishes. I'll deal with them later."

She hesitated. "No, you cooked. I can clean up."

I growled, "Mia, I warmed up leftovers. I'd hardly call that cooking. Now get that beautiful ass over here."

She didn't give much of a fight as she followed me into the living room. I was about to sit down and pull her to me when Remy shuffled to the door and gave it a scratch.

Shit, I forgot about our after-dinner walk. Amazing how a small change in my night threw off my whole routine.

"Looks like he has to go out," Mia said, her eyes on Remy.

I stretched my arms above my head and reached for the leash hanging on a hook on the wall next to the front door. "I always take him for a walk after dinner. Want to come?"

"Just don't let any monsters get me, okay?" She grabbed her sneakers and slipped them back on.

She was back to teasing. That made me smile. "No monsters, maybe just an alligator or two, though."

"Ugh, I've been scared of a gator encounter since I moved here." I shut the door behind us and led the way down my front porch and stone walkway. "Have you seen any?"

I laughed. I was born and raised here. I've seen so many that I hardly batted an eye anymore. She was obviously terrified of them, though, so I didn't need to freak her out more. "Just a few. They're harmless really, just don't go swimming in any of those man-made lakes they keep building."

"You'd never catch me dead in one of those—or any lake. Dark murky water," she shuddered.

The temperature dropped a few degrees since we left the gym. A light breeze in the air made the humidity less oppressive. The black sky was clear, which didn't happen often as we approached summer and storm season. Crickets sang and mosquitos buzzed around us, but the only sound I could focus on was the breathing of the woman next to me.

"Seriously?" I laughed. "I was going to ask you on a lake swimming date for next weekend."

She turned, reading my face. I tried to keep my poker face on but couldn't. My stone serious look turned into a grin under her stare.

"You're an ass," she laughed.

"Never claimed not to be," I said lightheartedly.

"No way will I swim in anything where I can't see the bottom," she shivered again. "Especially not here."

"I sense a story."

"Not so much. Back in New York, I used to occasionally fish with my father, but it was never my thing. I always hated seeing the hooks in the poor fish. But I usually stuck to swimming pools in the summer. I avoided lakes even back then." I could picture a young Mia staging a fishing protest, hands on her hips, declaring all the ways fishing was wrong. Knowing what I did about her father he probably didn't give a damn and fished in front of her anyway.

Remy tugged me along prodding his nose into a bush on the side of a neighbor's yard.

"I feel like I always spent my summers messing around in the lakes nearby with my buddies. My grandma used to call me her jellyfish when I'd come home waterlogged and covered in seaweed."

"You're lucky you didn't catch some kind of brain-eating amoeba." She swatted at a mosquito that landed on her arm.

"Yeah, I guess so," I laughed. "I'd much preferred to go to the beaches, but my grandma didn't drive, and my grandpa was always busy working."

She thought for a moment, "You don't have to answer this, but where were your parents?"

I figured this question would come up once we got on the topic of family. I surprised myself by not even hesitating before talking about them. "My mom had me when she was a teenager, seventeen, I think. My father was never really in the picture. He ran off after graduating and we never saw him again."

She grabbed my hand. "God, I'm sorry. I could never understand how a person could abandon their child."

"From what my grandpa told me, he wasn't a real winner. Maybe I was better off." I shrugged, "Anyway, my mom did the best she could with me for a while, but we always lived here with my grandparents, and when I was around five or so my mom bolted. Said she needed to live her life and spread her wings." I could tell Mia was holding her tongue and I went on, "I was surrounded by so much love from my grandparents who were raising me, anyway. It wasn't a huge loss.

"She came and went for a few years, and I found out, much later, she became an addict and was traveling around with another loser. She'd show up for money and give a sob story that she was changed and that things would be better, but we'd wake up a day or two later and she'd be gone again. Finally, my grandparents stopped giving in. They weren't going to be her enablers. I was almost a teenager by then and getting into some trouble of my own." I flashed a grin, "Believe it or not, I wasn't always this evenly keeled."

She shook her head, inviting me to go on. I swallowed and took a deep breath, leading both Mia and Remy around a corner.

"When I was fifteen, we got a call that my mom had passed away—overdosed apparently. She was brought into a hospital down near the border by someone and left there."

"I'm so sorry, Shawn. I don't know what to say." She squeezed my hand and my chest tightened at the same time. I felt relief in telling that small part of my story. I hadn't talked about my mother since Michelle unless you counted the person I paid weekly to listen to my tragic life history.

There had been no reason to dredge up the past bullshit before. My mother made her choices and they led her down a bad road. Why dwell on something I couldn't change? I never realized how much of a release it would be to just let it out for a minute, though.

"You don't have to say anything. The only thing I want you to take away from that story is that I had the world's best grandparents who took care of me and dealt with my crap. I was lucky to have them."

We walked a few more feet in comfortable silence. There was something to be said for being with a person you felt contented with in conversation and silence. Crickets sang around us in the warm breeze. I wanted Mia next to me all the time. More than I could put into words. Her skin, her taste, the curve of her hips. But most of all, her company. She put me at ease, more than I'd been in years.

"I'm sorry about your parents. I'm assuming your grandparents aren't with us either, from the way you speak of them?"

"They've passed. I think once my grandpa died of cancer, my grandma's broken heart couldn't take any more loss. She passed about nine months later." Remy broke the tension by barking at something in the distance. "We don't have to talk about all this heavy stuff. What can I do to make you smile?"

"You already make me smile. Plus, I'm still getting used to this sweet version of you. I haven't seen your scowl in a while and it feels unnatural."

I shot her my most brooding of scowls. "Better?"

A sliver of moonlight touched her face, making her cheeks almost glisten when she smiled up at me.

"Much better, all is right with the world now."

"Well, if that's so, then I guess we can turn around."

We walked on the other side of the road to give Remy more options to sniff. He did his business in a nearby bush, and we picked up our pace. I sure as hell was ready to get her back home and into my bed.

"I feel like someone poured syrup all over me—so sticky," Mia said.

"That's a visual I'll save for later."

She elbowed me. "Ew! I mean I'm sweaty and gross, so I'll have to use your shower."

Me being the horny bastard that I was, I let the scene play out in my mind: Mia, water dripping down her full breasts, hair hanging down her back. Me, soaping her up, paying extra attention to her taut nipples before trailing down her body.

"You're thinking dirty thoughts, aren't you?" She laughed, her voice husky.

"No comment," I deadpanned, getting another laugh out of her.

Walking along the side of the road, my porch light became visible.

"Shit—" In a split second, Mia was on the ground. She pushed herself up and brushed dirt off her knees. I dropped Remy's leash, knowing he wouldn't go anywhere, and crouched down.

"Fuck! Are you okay? What happened?"

"Yeah," she winced, looking at the ground next to her. "I must have stepped in that pothole."

"Here, let me help." Gripping her under the arms, I lifted her to standing. She wobbled a bit on her feet when she tried to take a step, hissing under her breath.

"Crap, I think I twisted my ankle. I'm so damn clumsy."

Chapter 19

Shawn

We made it back to my house. Mia hobbled along while I held her up. Once inside, I sat her down on the couch and started to take off her sneakers. "Let me take a look at it."

She winced. "I'm all sweaty. It's really okay. I can take care of it." She reached down, rolling up her leggings, but I brushed her hand away.

"You think I care about a little sweat? Give it here." She huffed and leaned back against the soft cushion. Her ankle was already swollen. "Damn, looks like you sprained it for sure. I'll grab an ice pack and a wrap I bought when I messed up my knee."

She sat up. "I can come with you. Really, I'm fine."

I narrowed my eyes. "Stay put, woman."

Her eyes narrowed like she wanted to argue, but she was also grinning the tiniest amount, which told me she wouldn't dare.

"Fine, but I'm telling you, there's no need to fuss over me. I'm clumsy. I'm always hurting myself, even sitting down."

I raised a brow, gathering her foot and twisting her body so that she was sideways on the couch with her injured foot elevated on a couple of cushions. "Sitting down?"

"I'm the paper cut queen at work. I find a new one daily, literally."

Shaking my head, I went into the bathroom to grab what I needed, an ice pack, a bandage, and some ibuprofen. She would give me a hard time, no doubt, but the hell did I care. I couldn't let an injured woman hobble around my house while I sat on my ass. It made me wonder what type of men she'd known if she expected me to do that. Before heading back into the living room I grabbed a cold bottle of water from the fridge. When I returned with the supplies, she was petting Remy who hadn't left her side as she chewed the corner of her lip.

"You look like you robbed a CVS or broke into my great-aunt Mary's bathroom cabinet."

"Didn't you know I'm the world's fastest criminal? I can get in and out of an old folks' home in under two minutes." I gave her a wry grin.

"I bet if I checked your pockets, they'd be full of ancient hard candies and folded-up tissue."

"You can poke around in my pockets anytime."

She blew a small laugh out of the corner of her mouth. "Slick."

"See," I shrugged, "I took your mind off the pain. Now scoot over and let me get you all fixed up."

Holding her leg in my hands, I noticed how smooth the skin of her shapely calf felt. I rubbed gentle circles along her leg, moving from her knee down to her ankle. She made a small sigh that sent blood straight to my dick. I needed to keep it in my pants tonight; she had a fucking sprained ankle. I'd been celibate for five years. What was another night, right?

Mia's eyes closed, but her lips were still drawn in a thin line. Sprained ankles were no joke. I wrapped the stretchy bandage around the swollen joint, light enough not to hurt her but with enough pressure to help calm the swelling.

"You're good at that." I glanced back up and saw her watching me with an intent expression. The air between us felt charged. It was always like that when I was close to her.

I laughed, "Like I said earlier, I was kind of a hell-raiser when I was younger. Definitely had my fair share of bumps and bruises. My poor grandparents must have schlepped me out to the ER more times than I could count back then." Her eyes twinkled. She got that look right before she was going to tease the shit out of me. I fucking loved it.

"Why can't I picture you causing trouble? You seem like such a rule follower."

"You calling me a stick in the mud?" I rubbed her foot gently in an upward direction.

Her smirk lit up her face, whereas moments ago she was wincing. "Actions speak for themselves."

I folded the soft ice pack around her foot and covered her lower half with a throw blanket. "Here, take two of these for the pain," I said while unscrewing the medicine bottle. She grabbed the two ibuprofens from my outstretched palm, grazing her fingers against my hand. Our bodies pressed lightly against each other on the couch and it reminded me of the sweaty film coating my skin. I needed a shower too—badly—but I wasn't going to leave her until she felt better.

"If you don't believe me, look at these." Pulling up my T-shirt, I showed her the fine line just above my hip bone. I swore I heard her take in a sharp breath. "This one is from a fishing accident. Well, more like a sharp rock accident by a lake." I yanked up my shorts a bit, exposing the much lighter skin of my upper thigh.

"And here?" she traced her finger around the circular scar halfway between my knee and hip. Her fingernails were barely scraping my skin. I stumbled on my words.

"What happened here?" She kept her tracing, completely ignoring the response her touch had on my body.

"Bike accident," I gulped. "Stupid trick on TV."

"Hmm," she hummed. "Someone was very reckless." Her fingertips trailed higher stopping just short of where my boxer briefs ended. She circled lightly and moved back down to my knee driving me fucking insane.

"I'm not always calm and collected." Fuck. My voice sounded like it had dropped a full octave and I did the stupidest thing and met her gaze. Her wide brown eyes were warm, like liquid amber. She knew what her touch did to me.

"I think I'd like to see that." She stopped on my knee again, tracing lightly. I reached out and took her hand in mine, placing kisses on each finger.

"See what?" My head was full of her, her smell, the way her skin felt like silk under my rough, calloused hands. I couldn't think straight. I paid extra attention to her index finger drawing it into my mouth and sucking gently. Her eyes closed and her tongue darted out to moisten her lips.

"See you come undone," she rasped.

I crushed my mouth against hers opening her lips open with my tongue. She had to know I was already undone, with just one look, one touch. She owned me. Her hands felt like they were everywhere all at once, in my hair, squeezing against my thighs, against the rough stubble of my cheeks. She touched me like she was trying to memorize the planes of my body. I broke away but let my tongue linger on her full lower lip before drawing it into my mouth sucking gently.

"You don't know how much your touch makes me come apart, Mia."

She maneuvered her body so that her leg was still on the pillows, but her soft lips could caress down my neck. "I want to be the one to make you come apart," she whispered as her lips met my ear. Her hand moved down to the waistband of my shorts lifting the elastic and sliding her warm palm inside.

"God…" I rasped and kissed the corner of her lips. She hadn't even touched my cock yet, and I was so fucking hard I could explode. I needed to calm down or I'd either come right here or I'd push her belly against the couch and sink so deep into her she'd forget her name. "You should rest…"

She teased the tangle of coarse hair above my cock, making my heart hammer.

"Fuck. Mia… you're hurt… " Saying that took every ounce of my restraint. If I was a good guy, like I was trying to show her I was, I would get my ass up and move to the other side of the couch. She was wrapped in a damn bandage. What if she hurt herself more because she was too busy making me feel good? I couldn't let that happen.

"What if I don't want to rest?" Her hand slid lower, and she gripped the base of my cock sliding her palm slowly up to my wet tip and spreading the pre-cum along my shaft. The way she stroked me like her hand was made for this, for me, I wasn't a strong enough man to stop her. I kissed her furiously, my hands sinking into her hair, pulling it free and letting her floral scent overtake me. She smelled like springtime in a fucking field of wildflowers. Her hand rubbed me expertly, circling my head while we devoured each other's mouths. I needed to feel more of her.

"Mia, you're gonna make me come if you keep doing that." My words came out in a strangled rasp.

She didn't stop, only maneuvered herself so she was facing me and gently pushed me back onto the cushion. My thoughts drifted to the fact that I was coated in sweat, and she was sporting a swollen ankle, but that quickly subsided when she straddled my lap. I went to pull off her shirt, to feel those perfect tits and take each nipple into my mouth, but she pushed me back down again. I knew she could be fiery, but I never pictured her to be the type to take what she wanted like this.

"You took care of me. Now, let me take care of you." She pulled my shirt off and trailed her fingers down from my chest to my hips. She shimmied her body to the floor and onto her knees. Her eyes blazed and her hair was wild and in her face. She looked like my personal siren. She could devour me whole and I'd let her.

"Mia, you don't have to do anything." I gave it one last plea. "I—"

My words were cut off in a hiss by her pulling my cock out with one hand and my shorts down with the other. She slid her tongue up my length getting me nice and wet before she opened wide and brought my whole cock into her mouth.

I bucked my hips. She felt so damn good, her mouth so warm and tight and perfect. A moan escaped her lips. She was enjoying this just as much as I was, and I abandoned every thought that told me she shouldn't be doing this, that she should've been resting, and that I was being a selfish prick. I let myself completely lose control.

"Your mouth feels perfect, baby," I crooned. "God, I'm going to come so quickly."

She stroked the base in a rhythmic pace while sucking and swirling at my wet tip. Again and again, pumping me and suctioning at a punishing pace. I fisted my hands into her mass of curls, holding tight while her head bobbed. "Look at me, baby. Let me see those beautiful eyes while you take my cock." I felt a humming noise of satisfaction that drove me wild.

She met my gaze looking up at me from underneath thick black lashes. That was all it took. One look and I was driving my hips up off the couch, my balls tightened and twitched as I emptied myself into her mouth. She kept sucking, drawing every last drop out of me until my eyes were rolling back into my head.

Limp and panting, I watched her swallow my cum down her throat. She gave me a sly smile. If I wasn't already completely infatuated with this woman, I was now. There were so many of her layers unfolding each day.

She crawled up into my lap and kissed me softly with those bee-stung lips.

"You're too good for me." I leaned back, every muscle in my body felt like mush.

"You're just realizing that?" Curled up on my lap, she stroked my hair. I wondered what she was thinking about. I was going to pass out on her again if I didn't rouse. I wanted to have a more serious conversation, but I was always afraid of ruining everything. But at that moment, with her soft body against mine and her hands in my hair, I was content.

"Hmm," incoherent sounds escaped me. "I've known that since I first saw you."

She gave a small tug on my hair. "You know I'm kidding, right? I don't think I'm too good for you, you stubborn ass."

"How's your ankle?" I sat up to check if she had it elevated. She did.

"It's fine. The meds kicked in. I'm sure it'll hurt like hell tomorrow, though."

Pulling her head against my chest, I let my breathing return to normal. "If you rest it, it should feel better quickly. It may be weak for a while, though."

She groaned, "I'll have to miss class... and hobble around for that stupid work party."

"Don't worry about class. You won't miss much. And we can do extra training here when it's not swollen." She made a small noise of agreement. "As far as your job goes, if you need to sit down at that thing, you do it. Your asshole boss can deal with it, or deal with me."

Mia twisted so that she was facing me. "You can't fight my battles, Shawn. I've been dealing with Lungberg for years. I'm used to it. Eventually, I'll make my way up the ladder and get offered a partner position." I knew guys like her boss, and hell would freeze over before they promoted a woman as their peer.

I threw my hands up. "Okay, I won't get involved. But you need to take care of yourself. A bunch of uptight pricks can manage to play golf and eat some appetizers without you directly serving them. That's all I'm saying."

Her shoulders drooped, "It pains me to say you're right... it is what it is. Jared will be there too, so I'm sure he'll help me as much as he can."

"Plus, I'll be there." She raised her brow. "Being supportive in every way I can that doesn't include staging a carting accident on your boss."

Her grin lit up her face, and my chest swelled. I'd do whatever it took to keep her smiling. "Do you want to stay tonight? It's getting late, and you should keep off that ankle for a few more hours."

"Yeah, I don't think climbing the steps to my apartment would be super fun right now."

"I'd drive you myself and carry you if I needed to, but your incredible mouth made me basically boneless."

"That would be overkill. I didn't break a bone."

"Overkill, huh?" I raised my brow and pushed myself up to standing. Before she had the chance to object, I scooped her into my arms.

She squealed my name, and I gave her round ass a smack. My cock was ready to go again since that movement alone had me half hard already.

I grabbed the ice pack. "Here, hold this."

"Shawn, put me down. I'm fine." She swung her legs back and forth for emphasis.

"Soon enough you'll learn to just let me take care of you."

I walked through the house, meticulously locking each door, checking each window, and switching off lights. It was a habit

I had gotten into years ago, and I couldn't sleep unless I knew everything was locked up. I knew she was probably wondering why I was so meticulous about this ritual. With her here for the night, I wanted the house to be extra safe. I felt her head rest against my shoulder, her breaths even. I took in her scent. It calmed me, even with my dick at attention from the feel of her ass in my hand.

Remy followed us up the stairs and down the hallway to my bedroom. When my grandparents passed, it had taken me years, but I finally moved into the largest bedroom in the house. At first, it was weird as hell to be in the space that had been theirs all my life, but I slowly made it my own.

I switched on the bedside lamp and gently plopped Mia down onto my king-sized bed. She looked around, taking in the space. I had painted the walls a neutral slate gray and hung up a few homemade wooden floating shelves and a painting from a local artist in Miami. I had a few framed photos on the shelves and a small potted plant that I somehow had kept alive for years. With the laundry tidied up and my bed made, the room almost looked homey, not like a space I barely occupied. Remy's plush dog bed sat in the corner, and he wandered over to it, groaning as he laid.

"Get some sleep, buddy." It never took him long to knock out and snore louder than a fully grown man. Mia ran her hand over my duvet still taking in my room. "So, this is my room…"

Why was I stumbling over my words?

She flushed. "I wasn't sure if we would be sleeping together."

Shit. I was an idiot. Did she want her own room? I could make up the guest bedroom quickly. "Sorry, I just assumed. Did you want your own bed?" I cleared my throat. "After earlier—" She cut me off.

"No, I want to be in here. With you."

My heart calmed. I wanted that more than anything. But only if it was mutual.

"We don't have to *do* anything. I mean... you know what I mean?" I sounded like an awkward teenager. Fifteen minutes ago this woman had my dick in her mouth and we'd done just about everything but fuck. Why did sleeping in a bed together seem so intimate?

"I should really take a shower." She ran her fingers through her curls, pulling apart a knot that had formed. "I'll just have to take off this wrap first."

"The bathroom is right next door. I can help you."

She went to stand, but I scooped her up again. This time, she didn't argue.

"I guess I should just get used to being carried around like a bride on her wedding night." The tone of her voice was light and teasing, but what she said made me stop in my tracks momentarily.

Michelle, in a white shift dress, popped into my mind. I had carried her, just like this, into our hotel room on our wedding night, and then again, the next day when we went home to our shitty studio apartment. I shook the memory away and continued into the bathroom. Mia climbed down and started to unwrap her ankle, her foot resting on the toilet seat cover for support. "Do you want me to help you?"

"I've got it." She looked around my master bathroom. My razor and shaving cream sat on one side of the sink with my toothbrush, toothpaste, and a bar of soap on the other side. There were no decorations in here, just necessities. I fished a clean towel out of the cabinet, set it on the sink, and turned to leave her to it.

Our eyes met as I went to close the door. "Let me know if you need help with the water. It's an old house and sometimes the pipes don't like to cooperate."

"Shawn?"

The way she said my name, sweet and innocent, stopped me in my tracks.

I cracked the door open and poked my head back in, my mind full of the dirty things I wanted to do to her in that shower.

"Yeah?"

"Don't you need to shower, too?" Her eyes were wide amber pools. How she went from spunky to angelic in a matter of minutes was beyond me.

She slowly pulled her shirt up, tossing it to the floor. She still wore her black sports bra that zipped in the front, her cleavage spilling out of it. She didn't wait for me to respond. Next, she shed her leggings, slowly peeling them off her lower half, leaving her in nothing but a black thong and her sports bra.

My eyes roamed over her like I was discovering a new planet. I may have had her splayed out on my counter, but that was fast and hungry. I barely had a chance to see all of her.

"I do?" It came out as more of a question.

Standing there facing me in just her bra and barely-there panties, hair wild, she said, "Yes, you do."

I cracked the door open more, as she turned her back to me and slowly bent over to start the shower. She was a damn vixen with that apple-shaped ass. I snapped out of my trance when I noticed her wobble and grab at the towel bar for balance.

"Here, sit down for a second."

"There goes my sexy strip tease," she laughed. "I was doing great. Then that ankle almost gave out again."

I shook my head. This woman was going to be the death of me.

Chapter 20

Mia

PERCHED ON THE EDGE of the tub, still in my thong and bra, I watched Shawn morph into caretaker mode. I officially felt like the world's worst seductress. For that short moment, with his hungry eyes watching me undress, I had him. It's my fault for trying to be hot while I was basically one legged. I think I was becoming addicted to seeing this man come undone.

He pulled a knob and switched the shower from sprayer to faucet and plugged up the drain hole. "You'll be much safer with a bath. If you put any more pressure on that foot, I'm worried you'll slip."

"Stolen any shower seats from the old folks home while you were there?" I quipped watching his lips turn up in the corner.

"Unfortunately, my hands were already too full of knitted blankets and checkerboards. Next time, though." I couldn't help but laugh through the throbbing pain. "The water temp feels good. Do you need help getting in?"

"I think I can handle it." I went for the zipper of my bra, pulling it down, my eyes watched Shawn's the entire time. I needed to see him shift, to see his desire plain on his face.

But before my breasts were fully out, he turned on his heel and left the bathroom, closing the door behind him.

"I'm right outside the door if you need me," he said, his voice barely audible over the noise of the faucet.

Dumbfounded was the only word that entered my mind. It was clear he wanted me. Why was he being so weird?

"Uh, you know I don't mind if you want to stay. Or join me?"

I cracked the door open to make sure he had heard me. There was pure struggle in his eyes. They shifted from my face to the hall in front of him. "I'm trying to be a good guy here. You almost fell before, and I know you're not used to someone taking care of you, but I plan on changing that."

Emotion swelled in the back of my throat making it hard to respond. He was right; I was used to being the one caring for others, but he was being overly cautious. This must be how Kendahl and Olivia always felt when I would meddle in their lives, like a risk assessment agent.

I found my voice. "You know, I appreciate you taking care of me." He edged closer to the door.

"I sense a *but* here." His eyes stayed put on my face, but every second, or so, I could see them inching down lower.

"*But,* I am a big girl. If you're not interested, that's one thing…"

"You're kidding, right?" He bit back a laugh. "If you felt how hard I am right now… Mia, I have wanted you since the first time I met you. Of course, I'm interested."

I shuttered.

I opened the door wide and pulled him in. "I'm not a fragile doll, Shawn. Come on, let's just get clean." I slid down my panties while batting my lashes and giving him my most adorable expression, the one that worked on Kendahl to get my way, except this time I didn't make a big show of it. I barely gave him enough time to register my movement before I hobbled into the tub and sank low. The water was deliciously warm and came up to my breasts. Without even realizing it, I slumped back against the cool porcelain. "You don't know what you're missing," I teased, letting out a low moan and closing my eyes.

A moment later, I felt the water rise. "Slide up a bit. I'm going to get behind you."

I wasn't even able to fully take in Shawn's, completely bare, body before he slid into the water settling himself against my back. Water splashed out of the tub onto the tile floor as he situated himself, and I couldn't help but notice the firm length against my back.

He exhaled deeply. "You were right. This is nice."

I turned and splashed him. "See, told you. When was the last time you soaked in the tub?"

"No idea. I'm always a quick shower guy."

He grabbed the green bar of soap off the ledge and lathered his hands. It smelled faintly of lavender and mint with the distinct scent of clean. His warm, soapy hands massaged my shoulders, and he swept my damp hair aside. He washed my back, rubbing circles around my shoulder blades before going underneath the water toward the spot where our bodies met. I leaned into him, practically purring. I could get used to this feeling of contentedness. He lathered some more and went to work on his own body, while I rested my hands atop his thighs. I had to keep this bath PG-13 because it was hard enough to get him in here.

"I haven't relaxed in a bathtub in lord knows how long either. Life is always too busy." Not that I was *fully* relaxed with Shawn's sculpted naked body against mine. Is there such a thing as being wound up from sexual frustration but also relaxed at the same time? If so, I was there.

He started washing my hair, and I turned to wash his giving him a scalp massage that had his eyes closing and breath slowing. Sex was great, but this was a new level of intimacy for me. I'd never showered or bathed with a guy before.

When we were both thoroughly scrubbed with drooping, exhausted eyes, Shawn pulled the drain and helped me to stand. My ankle didn't throb quite as much thanks to the warm soak, but I was grateful for Shawn's steadying hands.

After we toweled off, I slid into one of Shawn's old broken-in T-shirts. It smelled woodsy and clean, and if he wasn't watching me, I'd have stuck my nose in it and inhaled deeply.

"I packed something to wear to bed. Something sexier than this. Want to see?"

Shawn pressed himself beside me, running his eyes up my body, clad only in a pair of boxer briefs. "There's nothing sexier than seeing you in my clothes."

Tilting my head up, I planted a kiss on the corner of his lips. "Who would have known you were such a sweetie?"

He climbed into bed and arranged a stack of pillows for me to elevate my ankle, and then patted the spot beside him. "Don't spread it around too much. I might lose my asshole reputation."

I climbed in and nuzzled into his chest, feeling like we fit together perfectly. "I love your house. It's so cozy and warm. I didn't know what to expect the first time I came here. I mean, you are a single guy and I've seen some pretty gross dude apartments."

He wrapped his arm around my body, squeezing me into his side, and then pulled the blankets over us. My pulse sped up at the closeness, especially after having his naked body against mine just a few minutes earlier.

"Thanks, I love it too. Being here, and in my shop outside, are the only places I feel truly comfortable. Although, it is too big for just Remy and me."

Did he want a family one day? The question was at the tip of my tongue. Why would he keep this big house if he didn't? Now wasn't the time to ask.

"Hopefully it won't just be me and my furball hanging around alone anymore." He turned his head down to look at me. "I kind of like having you here."

"Yeah, well, I kind of like being here with you, too." I rubbed circles on his chest, twirling my fingers through the light waves of hair. "Even if I'm not used to anyone taking care of me."

Kissing the top of my head and holding me close, Shawn breathed out, "Get used to it, because I take care of what's mine." My breath caught in my throat.

We hadn't really talked about where this was going, or if it was serious. He's said he had something huge to tell me still. But... *mine?* He considered me as his and the more time I spent with this man, the more I felt he was mine, too.

While my mind whirled with his last comment, thinking of a response, I felt Shawn's breath deepen. His eyes were closed and his light snores mixed with Remy's from his dog bed. He'd fallen fast asleep. I smiled like an idiot. How were snores so endearing? Not only had I seen this man come undone, but now seeing him vulnerable, fallen asleep against me. It was something I could get used to.

Chapter 21

Shawn

My eyes spring open and the first thing I see is the flickering streetlamp casting a faint glow around me in the darkness. I'm sprawled out on the concrete sidewalk by the feel of it. It's too quiet. No noise from cars, no people anywhere. My head feels heavy like it's being held down by some unknown force.

"Hello?" Someone must be here. There's a deli close by. I can see the half-lit sign. It's missing the "D" so it reads "eli."

I plant my hands fighting against the invisible force. I need to get up. My hands land in a puddle. I need to figure out where I am. What am I doing here? I can't see what the liquid is, but it feels warm, sticky. What the—? I try using the flickering light to help my eyes adjust. I look at them closer blinking my eyes into focus. They're drenched—deep red, almost brown, and warm. So warm that I instantly wipe them down the front of my pants.

Why am I in a suit? I never wear suits. Buttons are missing from my shirt, and, for some reason, that is all I can focus on. Counting the buttons: one... two... three.... By the fourth button, I realize the rest of my shirt is hanging open like a curtain.

Wait a second, this shirt... it too has that strange brown substance all over it.

I look toward the deli again and shout into the silence. "Hello? Anyone?"

That's when I see her. She is a few feet away from me stretched out on her back. Her dress looks all wrong. I have seen it before. The woman's long blonde hair looked familiar too.

I push to a stand. Each step toward the woman feels like wading through muddy water. Every foot closer is making my heart thud in my chest like it's rattling against a cage trying to break free.

Fear, all I know, is crippling fear and the feeling that this is all wrong.

"Miss?" I call to her.

Maybe she will snap out of it like I did? We'll have a laugh and figure out why we both fell asleep on the sidewalk.

I'm right in front of her now, so close that I could smell her perfume. Amber and vanilla mixed with something sharper, something metallic. I reach out to shake her and wake her up.

Fear is eating me alive.

She is too still.

No.

"Come on, miss. We should call someone for help." I prod around in my disheveled jacket pocket for a phone but come up

empty. When I turn my gaze back to her, I choke on a scream. Bile rising in my throat. She's turned over; I don't know how, but she's sitting up pointing at me.

Her eyes are haunted. Deep black pits. But that wasn't what was making my stomach clench, and my throat scream itself raw. There is a gaping hole in the center of her chest, where blood was pooling thick and slow like molasses.

"Michelle?" I cry, her name barely escaping my lips.

Her white finger crooks my way accusingly.

I fall back onto the sidewalk and try to crawl to her, but something is holding me down. "Michelle!" I scream her name again and again fighting the invisible force while crimson flows to the ground coating every inch of me.

"Shawn! Shawn, wake up!"

A pair of hands were shaking me. A voice was calling my name. I sat bolt upright. My chest heaved as I took in the familiar room. My bedroom.

Remy was panting loudly, next to me, pawing at my thighs. I rubbed his head, every stroke of his soft fur bringing me back into my body, willing my breathing to calm. I closed my eyes for a few seconds before opening them to meet wide brown eyes peering into mine.

"Mia?"

Kneeling beside me, her breaths matched mine at a frantic pace. She reached out tentatively to push my hair back from my face. "It's okay, you're safe. It's me and Remy here."

Her soothing touch and hushed whisper helped my chest to loosen and my breathing to calm. *Fucking nightmares.* It normally took me much longer to come to after one this bad, but having Mia here anchored me somehow.

We both nestled back into my pillows, pulling the thrashed blanket back over us.

"I'm sorry." It gutted me that she had to witness that. What would she think of me now?

Mia pressed her head into my chest, which let the scent of her hair drift up to my nostrils. "There's nothing to be sorry for. Bad dreams happen to us all."

I let my fingers rub circles over her soft abdomen. The smooth curves of her skin threatened to bring my mind in a completely different direction.

"Do you want to talk about it?" She whispered.

I knew I should. Maybe it would help with the sheer guilt I felt every-fucking-day. Just having Mia here, after what happened to Michelle, was enough to set that spiral out of control again. That must have been why the dream came back tonight after it had been so long.

I kissed the top of her head. "Not tonight. I want to enjoy having you here against me." Before she surely got rid of me or before I did what I always did and pushed her away again.

"Well, I'm here whenever you're ready." Her hand settled against mine and her breathing slowed.

Would I ever be ready, though?

Within ten minutes, Mia was asleep again, her body was warm velvet against mine. I checked the clock on my side table—4:32 a.m. There was no way I was falling back asleep, not after that dream.

I rolled out of bed, without disturbing Mia, and shrugged on a pair of shorts and a T-shirt. A sheen of sweat coated my body, and I desperately needed to rinse off, but I didn't want to wake her again. Remy poked his head up from the bottom of the bed but quickly put it back down, nuzzling into the thick duvet.

"Lazy mutt," I laughed under my breath. I didn't blame him. I'd be back in bed with Mia if my brain wasn't forcing my body to move. The adrenaline burst from my nightmare had my limbs antsy to do something.

An inky blue sky stretched out beyond the trees, but peeks of gold rising up from the horizon told me dawn was approaching. As much as I hated being woken by my nightmare, I didn't mind being awake this early. There was a quiet in the world right before dawn that was calming. Plus, it gave me extra hours to work in the shop before the sweltering heat set in for the day.

I'd been refinishing a beautiful antique chest for a local client. It was her great-grandmother's and had traveled to America with her from Europe in the early eighteenth-century. The divots and dents told a story of their own, one that I didn't want to erase completely. Luckily, my client also didn't want me to make the piece look like any other mass-produced thing you could pick up at Pottery Barn. She wanted to keep its history, but just spruce it up a bit. Every piece of furniture like this told a story, much like their owners and they deserved to be seen, not covered up.

I spent a good thirty minutes going over it with the sander, sloughing off the old stain, and getting the wood prepared. With each pass of the sander, I felt my frantic energy dissolve bit by bit. My brain focused entirely on the piece in front of me and the whirring of power tools drowned out every other thought.

Warmth wiggled its way throughout my body, as I took a step back to admire the chest, stripped and ready for stain. This was my grandfather's favorite type of work, restoring old family heirlooms and keeping the integrity of a piece of history but giving them a new shine. I'd love to think that he'd be proud of me and the work that I've done.

Turning away from the chest, I grabbed the can of stain the client and I had selected earlier and gave it a shake. As I poured it into a tray, I willed my brain to not think back on the dream and the thick, sticky blood that had coated everything around me. I closed my eyes and counted down from five.

When I opened them, I focused on the very real and tangible things in front of me, the grains of wood along the chest, the metallic buckle edges, and the chemical smell of stain mixed with the earthy smell of sawdust. Rays of sunlight were creeping through the open door land birds were waking up with their morning calls. I took a centering breath and began to rub the stain onto the chest like a moving meditation.

In my relaxed state, I didn't notice when Mia came in until she was halfway to me holding two mugs. She looked beautiful with her eyes hooded from sleep, hair messier than usual and wearing my T-shirt.

"Coffee? I wasn't sure how you took it, so I guessed." She placed the steaming mug of coffee on the workbench beside me. "I figured when I woke up next to only Remy that you had come out here to get some work done."

She circled the chest and drank from her mug. "This is beautiful. Did you build it?"

I took a sip of mine, grateful for the caffeine. It was a little too sweet, but I'd drink anything she made me. "No, I wish though. It's an antique. I'm just prettying it up a bit for the owner."

A small smile settled on her lips. "That must be so cool to take something old and beat up and make it like new again."

"It is." I slouched against a countertop. "Sometimes I like it more than building something brand new. There's a fine line between preserving the original beauty of a piece and sprucing it up. I don't like to change it too much."

"I get that. Especially with really old stuff. They just don't make 'em that way anymore."

I sipped again, letting the warm liquid wake me up. "Not unless you come to a small business owner like me. But, of course, that kind of craftmanship costs good money. I can't compete with IKEA much these days. But I do well enough."

I could see her brain working as she was scanning my workshop. "Have you ever thought of putting some revenue into advertising? I bet you could get clients from all over the country."

I shook my head. "Nah, I have a lot of clients here that keep me busy. Plus, there's assisting at the gym."

She nodded, "Just a thought."

We stood in silence, listening to nature wake up. My nightmare sat like a mountain in between us.

"I'll let you get back to it. I brought my laptop so I can get some last-minute work done for the event tomorrow." With a hand against the doorframe she nodded, and it surprised me that she wasn't pushing for information. Either she was the most patient person in the world, or she didn't give a shit. I hoped it was the former, not the latter. She turned, coffee in hand, ready to head back to the house.

"Mia, wait a second."

I ran my hand through my hair, no doubt getting stain in it.

"About my dream, I'm sorry that I woke you. It must have scared the shit out of you."

"I told you earlier, it's fine, and I meant it." Putting her mug down, she walked until she was inches from me. "You were screaming and shaking. Of course, it was scary. I won't lie. But I could see how terrified you were, and all I wanted to do was pull you to me and help you come back."

I released a shaky breath. "You're too fucking good for me, Mia. I said it before, and I'll say it again every day."

Her face softened. "I don't want to hear it. I'm going to start a collection jar and every time you put yourself down, you add a buck."

I huffed a laugh and leaned back on the counter. "You'll be rich quick then."

She grabbed my hand. "I'm serious, I'm here for you. Just like you've been there for me."

"Shit, I almost forgot about your ankle." I crouched down to check it out. "Is it hurting? The swelling looks like it's barely there."

She pulled me up. "I'm fine. Someone took very good care of me last night, and I'm hardly even wobbling anymore."

Thank God.

I swallowed down the knot that had quickly formed in my throat. She was okay.

"I'm glad. You still shouldn't be putting too much weight on it today. Give it time. Here, come sit on the couch."

I led her over to an old sagging futon I kept in the shop. Remy usually claimed it as his napping spot, but it was good for a nice rest when I didn't feel like going back up to the house.

She laughed. "Seriously, you can get back to work. I'm fine."

She plopped down and put her coffee mug next to her on the side table.

"I was going to take a break soon anyway," I hedged.

"Yeah, right. You were in a trance when I came in here. I felt bad for breaking you out of it."

"You can interrupt me anytime." I joined her on the couch, our thighs touching, and reached out to push a curl from her face.

"You're smooth, Mr. Brooks," she crooned.

"Hmm, I enjoy hearing you call me Mr. Brooks. So very professional accountant of you. If only you were wearing those sexy glasses."

She leaned back and wet her lips. "You like those?"

"I do. Very much." I leaned in and kissed her gently. Not knowing how she'd respond. Did she want me as badly as I wanted her? Her lips were soft pillows, her breath a tinge of mint mixed with the coffee she had just drank. She leaned into me, opening her lips so I could slide my tongue in. I slowly and languidly explored her mouth taking my time to savor her. Each exhale and little moan that escaped her lips sent blood straight to my cock.

"If you're like this without the glasses, I can't imagine how you'd be with me wearing them." I nuzzled her cheek, and she planted kisses around the corner of my jaw, slowly reaching my neck.

"Oh, I can imagine," I breathed. She nibbled my earlobe gently, and I pulled her mouth back to mine. My T-shirt bunched up around her thighs, and my hands itched to feel her. She must have felt the same way. Her palms traveled up my shirt, gliding along my muscles. I shivered as she grazed my side with the tips of her nails.

"I think this should come off." Her eyes were blazing.

I yanked my shirt up over my head and tossed it aside. I didn't give a shit if it landed in a pile of sawdust or a paint can. This woman wanted me, and I'd give her anything. I slid my palms up her thick thighs, causing her to press them together.

"Shawn, please."

Her mouth crashed into mine again. There was nothing slow about it. Once our hands started exploring each other it was like they ignited a fire. She pulled away to tear my shirt off her, letting her full breasts into the air.

"I knew you weren't wearing a bra under there," I growled. "Jesus, Mia, you're going to give me a heart attack." She held my gaze and raised a brow at me before grazing her breasts with her palms pushing them together and pinching her tight nipples. The sound that came out of her told me I was a goner.

Before I knew it, we were both completely bare and Mia was straddling me, grinding my erection against her clit. Her hair hung in my face and we were kissing frantically. I was so close to coming from just feeling her wetness against me and the friction of her grinding her hips.

"I want you in me, Shawn."

I'd lose my damn mind if I wasn't inside her in two seconds.

"I don't have a condom in here." My breathing kicked up as Mia continued to kiss my neck and grind against me.

"It's okay. I'm on the pill and clean. Are you?"

"I uh..." I wasn't about to kill the mood and tell her I hadn't been with a woman in the five years since my wife died. "Yes."

She reached down and guided me to her entrance. I stilled letting her sink onto me inch by inch until there wasn't space between us.

"Holt shit," I grunted. "Baby, you feel so good."

"Mmm...," she purred something unintelligible and rocked against me.

I brought my palms to knead her round ass while thrusting my hips up into her until she threw her head back. She felt better than I imagined. Her on top of me, hair wild, beautiful tits in my face. I knew I wouldn't last long. She was so fucking tight.

"I'm close, Shawn."

I squeezed my hand between us and rubbed her clit spreading the wetness there. I could feel her clenching around me. I circled that spot in a rhythm matching each rock of our hips. My free hand dug into her hip guiding her against me harder. I wanted to hit the deepest reaches of her sweet pussy.

"Come for me, baby."

I pinched her clit and pushed into her one last time. She buried her head in my shoulder calling my name and we fell over the edge together. My cock pulsed as I bit my lip so fucking hard I was sure that it would be bleeding.

With Mia's head buried in my shoulder, I wrapped my arms around her. I wished we could stay like this forever with her beautiful face flushed from pleasure and me inside her.

I was in no rush to move. I hadn't felt this content in years even though the futon wasn't the most comfortable thing to be naked on. There would definitely be dog hair and wood shavings in my ass crack, but that's what showers were for.

Mia lifted her head a minute later with a small smile on her face. "When can we do that again?"

I laughed, feeling a lightness reach my chest. "I'm clearing my schedule for the rest of the day."

"Looks like I'll have to call Jared and tell him I'm working from home today. Sprained ankle and everything."

"Doctors orders," I said in a serious tone, letting a grin spread across my face.

She ran her fingers through my hair and shifted off me looking down at the wetness from both of us. "Shower first, at least for me."

She looked so fucking hot with my juices coming out of her. I wanted to tell her as much. I didn't give a shit if she showered. I loved how wet she was for me. The smell and taste of her like this drove me crazy.

"Mia, I couldn't care less if you showered. I want to get that fine ass of yours up to the house so I can show you what seeing you this way does to me. I want to taste you. Take my time fucking you nice and slow until you're trembling under me."

Mia's mouth formed an O, redness rising to her face. "That's so dirty but hot."

I stood up and found the T-shirt I was wearing along with my shorts, sliding them both on. At the same time, she threw on her shirt. It was like we were both under a spell, rushing to get back inside so we could explore each other again.

I noticed her wobbling a bit on the path into the house and scooped her into my arms. She went limp against me, unlike the last few times when she argued. This time she settled her head on my chest.

"I might be getting used to this," she chuckled.

I squeezed her ass, realizing she hadn't put her panties back on. "I could get used to having this ass under my palm. As a matter of fact, I think I should carry you everywhere from now on."

"I can get behind that," She cracked another giggle. "Get it... *behind* that."

"Wow, a dorky girl with an ass like yours. How did I get so lucky?"

I loved how easy it was with Mia. We could play and joke like we had been close for years. This woman had me wrapped around her finger and didn't even know it.

Chapter 22

Mia

IT WAS EARLY EVENING, and we'd only left Shawn's bed to let Remy out and rinse off in the shower. I was utterly exhausted but in the best way. We had made love for hours, slowly taking our time to stroke and graze every inch of each other. I had never, ever in my life felt so sexy or wanted. Shawn treated me like I was a buried treasure that he had to uncover.

I turned, locking eyes with the incredibly hot man beside me who was still panting from fucking me senseless a few minutes ago. "You going to be okay over there?" I joked pushing his sweaty hair out of his face.

He laughed, and his eyes lit up. I loved seeing the change in his demeanor when he was truly happy. After our shower this morning, we had both been frantic again. Crashing onto the bed, our dripping wet bodies molding against each other and soaking the sheets. I didn't know I could orgasm as much as I had today. Each one different, coming on in waves of pleasure or shooting through me like an electric shock. I wanted this every single day. Maybe not exactly this. We both had jobs we had to get to, but this feeling of mutual adoration. I never wanted it to end.

"I honestly don't know," he panted. "I thought I was in good shape, but that was before every drop of fluid had left my body."

As exhausted as I was, I licked my lips thinking about his fluid leaving his body. It had me clenching my thighs. I played with his patch of chest hair, rubbing it against my fingers and watching his eyes close peacefully. I'm sure he was more tired than me after his nightmare last night and not being able to get back to sleep.

It was then that my stomach gave a loud growl, and he popped his eyes open.

"Have we not eaten today?" I thought about it, and no, we had only had coffee that morning.

"I had all the fuel I needed," I joked. "But I am pretty hungry. I'm sure Remy is sick of seeing us lying around, too." I looked over at the dog, and he seemed happy sleeping in his bed in the corner of the room.

"Stay here. I'll go make us something." I admired the view as he got out of bed and threw on a pair of boxers.

"I can help." It felt weird to have someone serve me. "Remember, my ankle is doing much better." He made a sort of caveman grunt that implied to stay put as he went downstairs with Remy on his tail.

I stretched, getting up to clean myself up a bit. My body was sore, and I felt sticky all over. With a damp washcloth I cleaned my face and then wiped down the rest of my body. I tamed my hair back into a bun on top of my head and dug through my overnight bag for a change of clothes. I felt worlds better.

By the time Shawn came back upstairs carrying two plates of sandwiches and fruit, I almost felt like a new human again.

Perched back on the bed, we devoured our sandwiches side by side. "That was by far the best grilled cheese I've ever had." I wiped my greasy hands on the napkin Shawn had brought up.

He chewed and popped a grape in his mouth. "Grilled cheese is my favorite comfort food, especially with some bacon in there."

"I'll skip the bacon, but you can feed me grilled cheese any day." We laid back, stomachs full.

I should have been working on last-minute confirmations for the event tomorrow. I most likely had fifty messages from Lungberg in my inbox, but I didn't care. This was one of the first days in a long time that I didn't worry about work, my family, or even Kendahl. I took this day for me and Shawn. I stayed focused on the present and willing away my constant to-do list.

"So, you're going to join me in my misery at Sandy Hill tomorrow?" Knowing that Shawn might be there made me less anxious.

He shifted closer, turning to face me. "Ah, golf. The world's most boring sport," he laughed. "Normally there would be no way I'd go to something like that. Big groups and I don't mesh." He twirled one of my curls around his finger, giving me chills. "But, for you, I'll show up."

I beamed. "You don't have to play golf. Just come and have some food and hang out with the world's best accountant."

"Oh, I figured Lungberg would be busy schmoozing it up with everyone?"

"Ass." I punched him lightly.

"Will you wear the glasses?" He wiggled his brows.

"You'll have to wait and see."

He squeezed my side, pulling me closer. I could feel him already hard again through his boxers. "You're like the energizer bunny."

"What can I say? You and those glasses? They just get me fired up."

We spent the next hour wrapped up in each other's arms, laughing and sharing stories about our worst moments at work. I found out that while Shawn was apprenticing with his grandfather; he did a stint as a server. There were so many women that would slip him their numbers on the bills, even ones that came with their dates or husbands. I couldn't blame them. If Shawn was hot in his thirties, I couldn't imagine a twenty-something Shawn. He ended up being so uncomfortable with it that he asked to work in the kitchen instead, prepping and washing dishes.

The sun had set completely, and I needed to get back home. I didn't bring my outfit for the event and I needed to work a bit. The thoughts I willed away from the day were popping in my head to burst my happy bubble.

Reluctantly, Shawn walked me to my car after helping me pack up my things and adding one of his T-shirts to my bag. He said he wanted to picture me wearing it to bed tonight. Of course, I would. I already missed his smell and his warmth. But overall, I felt elated that we had this time together.

In the quiet of my apartment, I cleaned myself up and settled in for a few hours of work. The sheer number of messages I had from a day away from my phone was unreal. I sat there picturing myself waltzing into Lungberg's office and sternly telling him that I had a life and he needed to stop emailing and messaging me on my days off. Then I'd throw something at him, maybe my phone, but, no, I'd need that. I'd bring something else from my desk, something heavy enough to make an impact but light enough to not actually hurt him. I'd see his shocked face turn blood red, and I'd toss my head back with a maniacal laugh before turning on my heel and stalking out.

I scanned his messages. They all said variations of the same thing:

"Did you confirm with the club?"

"Don't forget so-and-so has an allergy to shellfish."

"What about the weather? Did you check to see if there were storms on the forecast?"

As if I could control the weather. I skipped over them all. If he trusted me enough to take ownership of this event, then he'd have to deal with not micromanaging me. A rush of adrenaline ran through me, sending butterflies to my stomach. Not the good butterflies. These were rabid butterflies that rammed against the walls of my abdomen. I'd never ignored my boss before. Not even when he was the most condescending prick in the world. But I heard Shawn's voice in my ear, calling me his fiery girl, and swallowed down the lump in my throat. I'd make this the best damn event Lungberg's ever attended, and he'd have no reason to remember me ignoring his messages.

After trading texts with Jared, where I casually evaded any of his questions about my personal life, I felt even more prepared for the next day. I'd catch him up on everything going on with Shawn, just not yet. We were both too busy, and this was too new. He'd read it on my face tomorrow at the office and Saturday at the event, especially once Shawn showed up. I'd have to keep my professional mask on around Shawn. Lungberg was already pissed, and he definitely suspected something between Shawn and me after the meeting in his office.

The only person I did call was Kendahl. She had texted me a couple of times and I didn't want to worry her. She answered on the first ring. "I was ten minutes away from storming your apartment to check that you were still living."

"I'm here," I laughed, "and very much alive."

"Very much alive?" Her voice softened, "Wait... That does not sound like the response of my best friend when she's been buried under a mountain of work."

"Well..." I hedged.

"Mia Rose Murphy, were you with Shawn?" Her voice had reached an octave that would make dogs and other small creatures howl.

"I was." I had to move the phone away from my ear as the squealing ensued. My phone trilled, and I saw that she was switching the call to FaceTime. I answered.

"Spill the details! How good is that hot man in bed?"

"Oh my God," I laughed, blushing. "That's the first thing you ask me?"

She took a bite out of something that looked like a cracker. "Of course. You haven't gotten laid in who knows how long. I at least need to know if it was good."

"What are you eating?"

"Cheese and crackers. I found this amazing cheese at that little gourmet supermarket I told you about the other day—" She cut herself off abruptly. "Wait a minute, you evil queen. Do not try to change the subject by getting me to talk about my love of cheese."

I puffed a laugh through my teeth. She was right. I knew Kendahl could go on about cheese. We shared that in common.

I told her everything. How, for the past two days, I'd been happier than I'd been in a long time. It wasn't just the sex for me. It was how he made me feel, strong and empowered, but still cared for.

"Girl, I'm over the moon happy for you. I told you that once you got out of your own way, good things would happen."

"I know. I'm glad I listened to you and told my anxiety to fuck off." I chuckled, "He's not perfect, but no one is. I know he has PTSD, and he keeps alluding to this big conversation we haven't had. He had a pretty bad nightmare last night, but I figure he can talk to me when he's ready. I know from Olivia that forcing those difficult conversations is never a good idea."

"Hmm." She bit into a hunk of cheese. "As long as you're sure he won't hurt you…"

"Deep down, I know Ken. Plus, that whole thing with PTSD sufferers being violent is a huge myth. You know I've always been so terrified of getting hurt, both emotionally and physically, but he takes such good care of me when I'm with him."

"I'm jaded too. But maybe you should try to find out more. There are ways to do it, without pushing him for info, you know."

I thought for a minute. He didn't have any family to contact, but there was Camila. She seemed to know him well, and there were for sure some feelings there, at least on her end. There was also Mark, Dina, and Coby, who seemed to know him at least a bit.

"I could talk to his assistant. I just feel like I'd be breaching his trust."

"Listen, if he gets angry with you for covering your own ass, then he's not as caring as you thought. I'll talk to Coby and try to find out what he knows."

"Okay," I said resigned. "Speaking of, how are things going there?"

Her face lit up. "We're still just talking. He's asked me out, but I'm not ready. I kind of told him the gist of what happened with Ben. He's divorced, and he gets it."

"Oh wow, a divorced guy? You haven't dated one of those before. I'm glad he's being sweet and understanding."

"I haven't dated a real man before either, let's be honest. I like the fact that Coby's older than me. He makes me laugh too, which is really what I've needed lately."

"I'm glad you're taking things slow. He seems like a good guy, but there's no need to rush things."

"By the way, did you ever ask Shawn about him?"

I cursed myself. "No, I forgot. I'm sorry! I'll be sure to ask him tomorrow."

"Operation ask people about our potential boyfriends commencing tomorrow."

I laughed. "I think we need to shorten that somehow. How about Operation Boyfriend? God no, that makes us sound like desperate twelve-year-olds on the hunt for our first boyfriends."

"I mean," she cracked up. "We're not that far off."

My laughter ceased after another minute. With the topic of Shawn taken care of I needed to tell her about the dark cloud on my parade.

"I forgot to tell you that my mom and Olivia have been messaging me. They're coming to stay in Florida for the summer." Not even chewing my bottom lip or biting my nails would help comfort me while talking about my family. Kendahl was the only person who knew about my complicated relationship with my parents, and all of Olivia's mental health issues.

She put her cracker down and drew her brows together. "Did they say why?"

"No, but they'll be staying at a house on the coast and want me to come to lunch on Sunday." I lowered my tone, "I miss Olivia and Alex. I've been a shitty sister and aunt lately, but I just can't deal with my parents. Not here and not now."

"Want me to come with you for emotional support?" Kendahl sipped from a glass of wine, licking her lips. "Remember that year when I came for Thanksgiving? You said it was the best one you'd had in years."

"Of course, I remember. That's because my parents don't always act like complete assholes when other people are around. At least not when they don't give a shit about impressing the guests. But no, you're dealing with your own stuff, and I don't want to drag you down. Anyway, it's been so long since I've seen them that I feel like I should probably go alone."

"I'm here if you change your mind. I have no plans on Sunday, other than going for a mani-pedi and binge-watching something on Netflix."

"That sounds amazing. Maybe I'll join you instead."

We ended the call, promising to text the next day after our detective work. After finalizing everything I possibly could, I shut my computer and stretched out on the couch thinking over my conversation with Kendahl and the past few days with Shawn.

I wished he was here, next to me, warm and solid. I missed Remy too, my furry little buddy. Did I really need to investigate Shawn's life? If this was a guy Kendahl or Jared was dating who gave off even a hint of weird vibes, I'd have already found out everything except his blood type and social security number. It wouldn't matter if their red flags were miniscule, like they weren't fond of dogs, or thought pineapple on pizza was gross. I'd be there, best friend googling like my life depended on it. Why was I so hesitant to dig deeper for myself? Maybe I was just afraid I'd find out that this thing really was too good to be true.

In a split-second, I unlocked my phone's browser and googled "Shawn Brooks, Palm Cove." I felt wrong doing this, but I was too curious. Kendahl had planted the seed of doubt in my mind. My screen loaded with links. There were a few social media pages with guys named Shawn Brooks, who were definitely not my Shawn Brooks.

I clicked a link that led to an article from a local paper about Shawn's business. They were raving about how he refinished an heirloom piece with quotes from his client. I beamed while reading it. He clearly loved what he did, and it showed by how his clients responded. It was a shame he had no website and didn't advertise. He could pick up work from all over the country.

Further down, another result caught my eye. It was from Tanger Funeral Home, a few towns over, and dated about five years ago. I clicked on the link and read:

Mr. and Mrs. Benson, along with Shawn Brooks, invite you to join them in a memorial service to celebrate the life of Michelle Brooks. The gathering will take place on April seventeenth at 11:00 a.m. at the Aviary Palm Clubhouse, Room C. Light refreshments will be served. Please bring your fondest memories of Michelle to share with family and friends. In lieu of flowers, the family asks you to please donate to The National Center for Victims of Crime.

Holy shit. I tossed my phone down. Could Michelle be Shawn's mother? I searched my brain for details from our last conversation. No, Shawn said his mother died when he was a teenager. This posting was from five years ago. It couldn't have been his grandparents, either. The timing and information didn't fit. Whoever Michelle was, I was sure that this was huge. I needed to talk to someone and find out more. My heart was hurting for this man who had been through so much. I texted him a quick goodnight before climbing into bed. My mind whirled with this new information, but my body was so exhausted that I was soon fast asleep.

If only I realized how chaotic my Friday would have been, then I could have done the smart thing and called in sick again. Too bad my ankle was only mildly puffy, or maybe I could have gotten away with leaving early. Shawn was to blame for my blissful state of unawareness and I let him know as much when I finally had a minute to breathe.

Me: *Have you ever considered kidnapping?*

I chewed my lip, smirking down at my lit-up screen.

Shawn: *I'm afraid to ask? Is this some new kink you want to try?*

I snort laughed and Jared gave me an 'are you okay?' raised brow.

Shawn: *Can't say it's a fantasy of mine, but I'd go buy a ski-mask just for you.*

This man. My chest relaxed for the first time that day and filled with a bubbly warmth.

Me: *How fast can you get that mask? I promise if you kidnap me from the office, I won't press charges.*

Reaching into my desk drawer I fished through my emergency stash of mini chocolate bars and scattered a few in front of me. Stress eating chocolate would have to do if being fake kidnapped wasn't an option.

Shawn: *I wish I could. Now you've got me thinking of you in a blindfold all tied up.*

Did I accidentally unlock a new kink? I squeezed my thighs together from the small pulses those thoughts brought on.

Shawn: *You're doing great, fiery girl. This event is almost over and then you can breathe easy knowing you kicked ass.*

I hoped he was right.

Chapter 23

Mia

DRESSED IN A LONG lemon-yellow sundress and strappy sandals, I surveyed the main banquet room at Sandy Hill Country Club. I had taken extra time on my appearance this morning, straightening my hair into long waves and applying makeup. With my career and reputation on the line and all our clients present, I wanted to put my best self, front and center. I was the first employee to arrive, which I figured would happen. Jared showed up a half hour later. Buzzing around, setting favors on a long table, and placing name badges for networking, I hardly had time to think about much else.

Jared stopped me near the silent raffle table. "I didn't get to tell you before, but you look amazing." He kissed both of my cheeks. "Everything is looking great. Lungberg's going to have to grovel to you after this."

I looked him over in his crisp, perfectly pressed linen button-down and khaki chinos. "You look amazing, as usual," I winked.

The heat outside was sweltering. I was grateful to be inside with the air conditioning and far from the golf course. Jared and I fluttered around, mingling with the club staff who were setting out food and pitchers of water while guests trickled in.

Our clients ranged in age and field so vastly that I wondered how they'd mesh, but so far it seemed to go well. By the time I spotted Mr. Bosch and his wife talking animatedly with Lungberg, all dressed in their golf finery, the banquet room was packed.

Lungberg didn't even acknowledge me as he passed me by, instead walking over to rub shoulders with a few clients at the bar. Fine by me. My day would be much better if I didn't have to converse with him.

When it looked like most of the name badges had been claimed and guests were settled at tables or golfing, I figured it would be safe for me to sit down and have a bite to eat. The buffet smelled amazing, and I kept seeing people walking by with plates of pasta.

I went over and loaded up a plate with creamy penne and salad then made my way to an empty table in the corner. I had been hoping Shawn would have shown up by now, but maybe he got held up with a client. My mind drifted back to the article from last night. I didn't know how long I'd be able to hold my questions in. Rushing him to open up was out of the question, but I was seriously curious.

Having avoided more than a few encounters of small talk, I made my way to the restroom. I needed a reprieve from the smile plastered on my face. Not that I hated this part of my job, but it was a lot. I didn't become an accountant for the social aspect.

The heavily perfumed restroom was decorated with a cushy pink sofa and wicker tables with magazines. I did my business and then plopped down on the couch slumping against the cushions. I only had a few more hours to go, and then I wouldn't have to deal with another event like this for a year. I grabbed my phone out of my purse to check my messages.

Shawn: *Running late, sorry. Be there soon.*

I breathed a sigh of relief. He sent it thirty minutes ago. I replied with a quick okay and a smiley face. I'd have to stay completely professional. I knew Lungberg already suspected something going on after our meeting, and he'd love to pounce on me for breaking some unknown HR rule.

That was when the bathroom door swung open and a beautiful, dark-haired woman walked in. I recognized her at once.

"Camila?"

She looked me over, and recognition sparked on her face. "Hi, Mia. I'm glad to see a familiar face. Are you hiding out?" She grinned.

"Eh, kind of." I smiled. "There are only so many conversations about Tiger Woods and the weather I can have before my brain explodes."

"That bad, huh?"

I nodded vigorously. "Did you come on your own?"

She leaned against the wall and slung her purse over her shoulder. "I brought my sister for company. She's currently doing rounds by the bar searching for a man without a wedding band on."

I shook my head. "Oh boy, I'm sorry for you."

"I'm used to it. She's been hunting for a rich guy since she turned eighteen." Her voice held an edge that told me there was more to this story.

"I knew a few girls like that in college."

I sighed, the conversation lulling. "I better get back out there. I wouldn't want to miss out on the cheesecake. I heard it's amazing."

"I know this may seem forward," Camila's face sobered before speaking further, "but between us, be good to him."

My eyes widened. I wasn't expecting her to bring up Shawn and me. "I will."

"He's a special guy, and he's been through so much." She frowned. "I've kind of had a thing for him for a while now, but clearly he doesn't reciprocate."

I stammered, starting to apologize.

"I'm not trying to be catty." A small smile graced her lips. "You seem nice, and I just want to see Shawn happy."

I didn't know what to say, so I nodded.

"I'll see you out there."

She turned and headed toward the stalls, her heels clicking on the tile floor, leaving me sitting there staring after her. I knew she had a thing for Shawn. It was obvious the day I met her. I'm glad she just wants his happiness even if that meant letting him go.

I barely noticed the man in front of me as I walked out of the bathroom and down the dimly lit hallway because I was still so focused on my conversation with Camila, which was surprising, considering he took up a lot of the space. He was tall, much taller than Shawn, but not nearly as large. He looked to be in his forties and was dressed formally, in suit pants and a button-down shirt. His dark hair, slicked back with gel, gave off a sheen in the sparse light.

I noticed the badge pinned to the side of his chest: Mr. James Sanders.

"Excuse me," I cleared my throat. "I'll just slip by you."

He eyed me, perusing my body slowly, and I stepped back. "You work here, gorgeous?" His slurring voice had a rough edge. I had never met this man. But apparently, he was one of our clients.

I forced myself to stand up straighter as I answered, "No, not here. My firm is hosting the event in the hall." He stepped closer, and I scanned the hallway for someone, anyone, to come and interrupt whatever this was.

"If I woulda known Bosch had a beauty like you in the office, I would have made it my job to come in personally for meetings.

I'm James. I own a few gyms in the area. You may have heard of them, Mr. Muscle Fitness." I hadn't, but I nodded anyway.

"Nice to meet you, James. I need to get back out there. My coworker needs my help with the silent auction."

He took a step even closer, cornering me against the wall now. "What's the rush? We were just getting acquainted."

I caught the sharp smell of whiskey on his hot breath. He was so close that I could see red veins in his bloodshot eyes. Instinctively, I turned my head, his breath hitting my cheek. My heart hammered in my chest. This was happening. This stranger was cornering me.

"I really need to go." I put my hands out to give him a shove, but he was one step ahead of me. He grabbed my wrists tightly, wrapping his bear claw hands around them. I puffed out a breath of pain. "What are you doing? Take your hands off me now."

"Feisty, I like that." I squirmed against his grip. This was my nightmare come true. With his hold so tight on my wrist, it would surely bruise. He yanked my hand down and shoved it against his erection. I opened my mouth to scream, but he slammed a hand over my lips before I had the chance. "This is what's going to happen. You're going to be a good girl and come with me into that men's room. I want to see what you have under that dress."

I frantically shook my head and kept trying to pry him off me somehow. *Fuck.* This was not happening. The men's room was only a few steps away and once I was in there, I knew there'd be no one to help me.

He stepped back from the wall an inch, one hand still on my mouth, the other gripping both my wrists tightly. I searched my brain for something from class, anything, to get me out of this. I felt him stumble and momentarily let go of my mouth to grab the wall for balance.

That was my opportunity.

I screamed as loud as I could. It startled him, and he staggered. *Fucking drunk asshole,* I thought as I slammed my heel down onto the top of his foot as hard as I could, and then I brought my knee up, crushing his balls with every ounce of strength I had.

He crumpled down the wall moaning and clutching his dick. "You fucking bitch!"

Camila was out of the bathroom now and rushing down the hallway. She took in the scene. "Mia? I heard yelling. Are you okay?"

Before I could answer, others crowded into the hallway. I looked up at them, breathing heavily. I needed to get the hell out of there. "Someone call the cops, please." The words came out in a whisper. Shit, the tears were coming.

I pushed past the confused crowd. One man was dialing a number on his phone, which I hoped was for the police. When I got out of the hallway and back into the brightly lit open room, I sank into a chair and looked out at all the people going about their afternoons, oblivious that I had just been attacked coming out of the bathroom.

That's when I saw Shawn, phone in hand, walking from the entrance toward me. He took a few steps forward but slowed, noticing the look on my face. I glanced down to where I was massaging my sore wrists.

As he moved closer, Camila pushed her way out of the hallway, searching for me.

"Some guy called the cops, and he's staying there to monitor things." She put a reassuring hand on my shoulder and the tears that threatened to release came rolling out. "Did he hurt you, Mia?"

Words were stuck in the back of my throat. Camila, in her heels and perfectly pressed dress, crouched down, so she was at eye level with me. I had only met this woman recently, but I was so grateful for her. She didn't press me to talk. Most people would want to be the first one to hear any gossip so they could spread it around, wearing it like a badge of honor, that they saw the whole thing happen.

I felt his presence, and Camila stood up, but not before she gave my shoulder one more squeeze. She said something low under her breath then left. Where Camila crouched seconds ago, Shawn stood bent over. He tipped my chin up so my tear-streaked eyes met his.

"Baby, what happened?" He sounded like he could commit murder. "Camila said someone attacked you?" His eyes bounced back and forth between mine, searching for answers.

"Fuck, I'm so sorry I was running late. I was trying to call you to see where to meet you."

He stood up to his full height, and he pulled me into his arms. They were warm, and he smelled clean and fresh like he had just showered. I buried my head in his shoulder and took a deep, sobering breath.

When I felt calmer, I pulled away to look up at him. My legs still trembled, and I felt tiny shivers starting throughout the rest of my body. The adrenaline rush I had had moments ago was fading.

"I was coming out of the bathroom... before, a few minutes ago." Breathing deeply and sniffing to clear some of the mucus from my stuffed-up nose, I continued, "This guy was blocking the hallway." I finished telling Shawn exactly what happened. Letting it out helped to settle my nerves.

"Where is he?" Shawn asked through clenched teeth as he took a step back to search the crowded area. I hadn't thought about the fact that Shawn would want to find and kill the guy who did this. I had to think fast.

"Shawn," I stammered. "The cops are on their way and the guy is being watched over in the hallway so he can't bolt. Please, just stay with me."

I saw the conflicting emotions on his face in the second he took to decide whether he wanted to stay and comfort me or if he wanted revenge. I didn't blame him. If someone tried to hurt him, or anyone else I cared for, I'd feel the same way. He looked away from me and his words came out slowly as if he was attempting to keep them from flying out in anger, "I'll be right back."

Shit, shit, shit.

The last thing I needed was an enraged Shawn beating the hell out of someone at my work function. He rammed a hand through his hair and stomped in the direction of the restrooms toward the exact spot I idiotically told him the guy was.

I stood up, smoothing my wild hair, and scrambled after him.

A couple holding wine glasses walked by, eyeing me with curiosity, but I paid them no mind. *Where were you a few minutes ago?* I wondered. This area was empty when I needed random people walking around.

When I made it to the restroom hallway, I noticed Camila was still there. She was talking to a nice-looking, extremely fit man in the ugliest golf shirt I'd ever seen. It was covered in flags from different countries in the world. This man had his thick hand wrapped around the arm of James Sanders, who was now slumped against the wall with his eyes half open. How drunk was this asshole? I know I didn't hurt him that badly, for him to be barely standing.

Shawn approached and exchanged a few words with flag-shirt guy and Camila before stepping in front of James. Shawn towered over the slumped figure, making the man who had seemed so sinister look like a toddler. I rushed to the area.

"Shawn, come on. The cops should be here any minute." But he wasn't hearing me. Camila and flag-shirt guy eyed me with sympathetic looks.

"You doing okay?" flag-shirt guy asked me. I glanced at his badge showing the name Tom. I'd have to find out more information later, so I can thank him properly.

I nodded, then continued pleading with Shawn to follow me back to the tables. When the cops arrived I'd need to give them my statement and get home. Hopefully without Lungberg or Bosch seeing me in this state. Camila, seeing that I wasn't getting through to Shawn, asked him to take me back out as well.

Shawn wrenched his fists together, his feet planted firmly in front of James Sanders. "Did you touch my girl you piece of shit?" I shivered at the tone of his voice and the veins of his neck that stood out. He pushed a finger into James' face, "I asked you a question."

James widened his eyes from the slits that they were and took in Shawn and his menacing stance. He slurred out, "Fuck you talkin' bout?"

"The fuck I'm talking about is you," he jabbed his fingers into James' chest, causing the drunk to stammer a step sideways, "laying your filthy hands on my girl." Flag-shirt guy, Tom, took this as his cue to step away, pulling Camila with him.

"Shawn," I pleaded. "He's clearly wasted. Let's just let the cops handle him, okay? I already kneed him in the balls so hard he won't be able to father children." Humor always helped diffuse a situation. This time, it didn't.

James squinted over at me with narrowed eyes, taking me in, and straightened. "Yellow dress? Yeah, I touched her. She grabbed my dick too," he spewed, spittle seeping into the corner of his lips. "That bitch wanted—"

Crack.

He didn't finish his thought. Shawn had reared back his fist and punched him straight in the face. James' head snapped back against the wall and blood poured from his nose. I had no doubt that Shawn had broken his nose.

James swayed on uneven feet, grabbing the wall for balance. Shawn was red with rage, pacing back and forth in front of him. He turned with clenched fists and reared back again.

"No!" I yelled, watching James cower like a scared animal.

While it made me ecstatic to see this piece of shit, who didn't even deserve to be called a man, get his ass handed to him, I didn't want Shawn to be the one to do it. He didn't need this stress and hurting someone would mess him up inside.

"Hey man, come on, you should back off." Tom's voice was calm and steady, as he tried leveling with Shawn. It didn't help. My breaths were coming in shallow gasps, watching the man I cared for so deeply lose it. There was nothing I could do to stop whatever hell he wanted to unleash. I was choking, air wasn't reaching my chest.

I watched Shawn rear back, ready to punch a near-unconscious man, when I slowly sunk to the floor.

Chapter 24

Shawn

Voices yelled all around me, but all I could make out was the pounding of my heart. Thick, red blood leaked from the piece of shit's nose and my flared nostrils picked up the metallic scent thick in the air. I needed to release this rage inside of me. Mia had gotten hurt. I wasn't here in time to protect her. I stared at his bloody face and vaguely heard groans of pain escaping his lips. He slumped over. *Not such a tough guy now, are you?*

He held his nose, moaning, and spit gobs of bloody saliva onto the floor. "You ssson of a bish," He sounded as if he had marbles in his mouth.

So he wanted more then. All I saw was red. Red on his face and red in my field of vision, like a tunnel focusing only on him.

Fuck it.

I reared my clenched fist back and connected it with his face for a second time. A release whooshed through me like a breath of fresh air. This would make it right. Guys like him didn't deserve to share the same air as people like Mia. I'd help her where I couldn't help Michelle.

My chest heaved, and beads of sweat trickled down into my eyes. Wiping it away, I noticed blood on my open hand. Was it mine or the scumbags? A pair of hands grasped my shoulders, pulling me a few steps back. I stiffened, twisting to shrug them off. A guttural growl escaped my lips. Whoever it was, was fucking with the wrong guy. I wouldn't take my eyes off the monster in front of me.

"Shawn, please stop," a desperate-sounding voice broke through the fog in my head. "The cops are coming. Please, Shawn."

I knew the voice. The anguish in it, the pleading. But no, it couldn't be.

"Michelle?"

I turned toward her. I knew what I'd see. I've replayed this scene in my head again and again. Her bloody lip, her torn dress, her eyes wide in horror while the faceless man held a gun to her head in the dark street. Only this time, her face wasn't bloody. I focused on the small details like Dr. Glover told me to do.

A yellow dress.

A brightly lit room behind her.

There were people this time, congregated around us like we were a circus act.

I blinked, and when I opened my eyes, my vision cleared.

"Mia?" Her name escaped my lips in a rasp that sounded nothing like me.

She took a tentative step toward me like I was a wild animal who would either fight or flee. She was afraid—of me. I held my arms out for her and she fell into them, burying her head in my chest. She was trembling all over, whimpers muffled from where her lips sunk into my chest. I led her away, not bothering to give the bleeding man on the floor another glance. If I looked at him again there was a strong chance that I'd lose myself a second time.

Two cops were led to the hallway by a bystander, who pointed at Mia and me, telling them something I couldn't hear. They pushed through the small crowd, not giving me a chance to lead Mia to the tables. She started to pull away from me to go speak to them, but I was reluctant to let her go. Her face was puffy and red, and a look of panic spread across her features.

"Shit," she muttered. I followed her gaze to an incredibly pink-faced Evan Lungberg, his teeth bared in a grimace. Mia looked from Lungberg to the cops to the man bleeding on the floral carpeting.

"Miss," one of the cops said as he approached her. He was an older man in his fifties who looked extremely annoyed to be there. "Come with me, please. I need to ask some questions about what happened here." He looked at me noting my bloody hands clenched at my sides. "You, too. I was told by a few witnesses that you were involved." I nodded, resigned to following him to a set of tables.

He took out a form and took notes on the story Mia told him.

While she spoke, I watched medics come through carrying a stretcher and various pieces of equipment. Another pair of cops followed them in, talking, in code, into their walkies. It took every ounce of strength in me to stay present. I rubbed the scratchy fabric of my shorts, feeling it chafe against my calloused fingers. I smelled the scent of delicious foods coming from the buffet, pasta sauce, loins of beef, and garlicky potatoes. My mouth watered despite the anxiety building in the pit of my stomach.

As Mia spoke, the cop kept glancing over at me, eyes narrowed. I put my head down to focus on my senses and to stay in the here and now until they needed to take my statement.

The officer rose. "I'm going to need the two of you to come down to the station."

Shit. I figured that would happen but hoped I could just take Mia home.

"Ms. Murphy, you can drive yourself if you wish." He glanced over at me with my head in my hands. "But, Mr. Brooks, I'm afraid I'm going to have to take you in."

I shot my head up. "Am I under arrest?"

No, I didn't do anything wrong. That monster hurt Mia, he was the one who needed to be arrested. Not me. I was defending her. I told myself this, even though the small voice in my head repeated that I, too, was a monster.

Another officer joined him. She was tall and about my age. He murmured something to her, as the scratchy sounds of their radios filled the surrounding silence. She nodded, taking out her cuffs. Before I knew what the hell was happening, the man began to pat me down.

"Mr. Brooks, you have the right to remain silent. Anything you say can and will be used against you in a court of law. You have the right to an attorney. If you cannot afford an attorney, one will be appointed for you. Do you understand the rights I have just read you?"

"Yes." This wasn't my first arrest, but the shock of how quickly this was happening was enough to drain all the blood from my face.

Handcuffs were slapped on my wrists, and I was led to the back of a squad car.

I watched Mia, her eyes wide in panic and fear, "It's okay, Shawn. I'll get help." Her boss met her side and started talking heatedly as they pulled me away. I didn't deserve her help, or anyone else's, for that matter. She was afraid, and I caused that. Monsters should be locked up.

It was a short ride in the sticky back seat that smelled strongly of old vomit and piss. We pulled up to the station. The female officer led me out of the vehicle with an arm on my back, pushing me forward. I didn't need to be led like I was some criminal who would flee, but I should probably keep my stupid mouth shut. The inside of the building smelled of cleaning chemicals and stale coffee. She led me into an open room lined with a few desks and chairs. Officers sat at most of them filling out paperwork or clacking away on keyboards. Looked like loads of fun.

She sat me down in a hard plastic chair with the cuffs in front of me cutting into my already sore wrists. My heart pounded, adrenaline making me vibrate my legs up and down in the chair.

Sitting at the station waiting around brought me back to my teenage years. I was always picked up for stupid shit like vandalizing a neighbor's mailbox or swiping a six-pack of beer from the deli. I never served any time. The worst I got was some community service and fines that my grandparents begrudgingly paid. I was such a little asshole back then with what I put them through. Seems like not much has changed, no matter how hard I've tried to be on the straight and narrow. They'd be ashamed of me.

The cops peppered me with questions. Many of them I couldn't answer. I had no idea how I ended up in front of that man punching the shit out of him. One moment I was walking into the banquet hall, searching for Mia, and the next thing I remember was her pleading and pulling me away. I told them as much, repeating that I have episodes of PTSD and that I'm under the care of a physician. They left me in the chair for what felt like hours while the officers consulted each other, paced around, and made calls.

I searched for Mia, but if she was there, they had her in another room. I hoped she was okay. I leaned my head back, eyes closed, when the tall female, Officer Diaz, sat down at her desk next to me. "I've spoken with Ms. Murphy and Ms. Torres.

They've both given me similar stories." She sighed and rubbed her temple. "Considering the nature of Mr. Sanders' injuries, he's decided to press charges. I do understand that Ms. Murphy was attacked, and she's pressing charges against him as well."

I nodded. I knew he would press charges. There was no way I'd get so lucky.

"There is a catch, and my partner is now discussing this with Ms. Murphy in another room. My colleagues at the hospital have relayed that Mr. Sanders is willing to drop all charges if Ms. Murphy does the same. Now, from an officer's standpoint, that's complete bullshit. He's clearly a predator who should be prosecuted, but the chances are if he presses charges, you could do time for aggravated assault where he may walk free."

My head was swimming with the words: *time, assault, predator.* No fucking way would I let Mia drop those charges. That piece of garbage would get off scot-free so he can prey on another innocent woman? God knows, he probably already had and just hadn't been caught yet.

Officer Diaz could see the turmoil on my face. "Listen, we're still running prints and information on Mr. Sanders. That could change things. In the meantime, sit here and I'll bring you a strong cup of coffee." She gave me a warm smile that didn't quite reach her eyes and put a reassuring hand on my shoulder before walking away. I wished I could talk to Mia. I didn't have to, to know that she'd drop the charges immediately if it meant I'd get out of there. I just needed to see if she was okay.

Diaz returned with a black coffee in a small Styrofoam cup. I eyed it and lifted my cuffed hands, reminding her of my predicament. "Oh yeah, I forgot for a moment there. Here," she unlocked my cuffs and I massaged the area where the cold metal cut into my skin, "don't go running on me. I don't want to deal with any more paperwork than I already have."

"Thanks." I lifted the coffee cup and took a tentative sip. It smelled like dirt and tasted like old motor oil, but it helped to soothe my scratchy throat.

The waiting was miserable. I tapped my feet, downed the coffee, and ran clenched fingers through my disheveled hair. Officers in different uniforms came and went, eyeing me suspiciously. Nobody gave a shit that I had been sitting here clueless for what felt like hours.

Day turned into night, and I still sat with Officer Diaz walking in and out to keep an eye on me. I was about to get up to ask someone else if I could go take a piss when she came back into the room flanked by the other officer from earlier. His lips stiffened into a straight line, and his thick, unruly brows furrowed. He cleared his throat.

"Mr. Brooks, I'm Officer Don Bowman." He slumped into the seat behind the desk, leaving Diaz to stand next to him. Exhaustion marred his face and all I could stare at were his bloodshot eyes. "It looks like all charges have been dropped. Once Officer Diaz and I finish these reports, you'll be free to go."

"What? You're telling me she dropped the charges?"

He hesitated, "She did. Mr. Sanders had nothing on his record and turns out you have quite a few things, albeit from years ago, but the situation wasn't looking good for you."

I stood up abruptly, clenching my fists at my sides. All words escaped me.

"We also looked into your past and saw the incident with your wife. My condolences." His hardened face softened at those words.

"That has nothing to do with this! That piece of shit wanted to rape my girlfriend. If she didn't protect herself, he would have done who knows what to her. This isn't justice."

I hung my head and slumped back into the chair. Resignation was winning over my anger after such a long day. I needed to talk to Mia, and, most of all, get the hell out of this station.

Diaz spoke up, "Sometimes these situations don't always work out the way we want them to. But I think Ms. Murphy made the right decision. Plus, Mr. Sanders is now on record and if he pulls anything again, he'll have a prior."

Huffing, I nodded. I guess that was a plus. Even so, none of this was fair.

"Just so you know," Bowman said, shifting in his seat, "Sanders' injuries were serious. He suffered a broken nose and a grade-two concussion."

"So maybe justice was served," Diaz said with a small quirk of her lips. "But don't quote me on that."

It was after nine in the evening by the time Mia and I left the station. Humidity still hung thick in the air causing my shorts to stick to me uncomfortably. She shuffled next to me, keeping a foot away like I carried a communicable disease.

"I'm sorry." I didn't know what else to say to her. I had royally fucked up. "I made everything worse. You didn't have to drop those charges for me."

We reached her car, and I slid into the passenger seat. She didn't respond at first, instead, she bit her nails while starting the car. Warm bursts of air shot out of her vents sending her floral scent wafting into the stuffy car.

She took a deep, steadying breath. "It was lucky we even had that choice. Of course, I had to." I went to interrupt, but she put her hand out on my chest to stop me. "Let me speak."

The air turned cooler as we sat idling, and I focused on a piece of her hair that hung down in front of her eyes, blowing in the puffs of air.

"There have only been a few moments in my life where I've felt as terrified as I was today. There's shit in my past too, Shawn. Shit, we haven't even scratched the surface of. But seeing you losing it the way you did and then getting taken away in handcuffs while I stood there completely helpless... it scared me.

We may be still learning things about each other but know this; when I care for someone, there's nothing I won't do for that person. But you also need to realize that it's not okay for you to let your anger take over that way. I had things handled. I want to see you taking better care of yourself. And jail? I'd lose you for good if you went there." She inhaled deeply through her nose before releasing the breath in a steady stream.

I bowed my head and covered my face with my hands, taking a few minutes to respond. "I'm pissed that he'll walk free."

She squeezed my thigh, driving toward my house. "Listen, I don't think having a broken nose, a concussion, and his balls slammed up into his body counts as scot-free."

Turning my head to watch houses pass by out the window, I held in a snort.

"I didn't get the chance to tell you how proud I am of you. They told me he was crumpled up like a squashed tin can before I even got there."

She shook her head but couldn't hide the grin that spread across her face. "Thank you but he was pretty drunk. I'm still trying to figure out how he had such a strong grip on me being that wasted."

"Sometimes booze make people all the worst kinds of fucked up. It's never an excuse to do what he did."

"Let's hope he never tries it again." Her hand squeezed the place on my thigh where it rested and I folded my palm over hers.

"Don't think I didn't notice you brushing off my praise." God, I wished I could have seen her in action. Not that I would have let that asshole get within an inch of her but some conflicted part of me felt happy that I wasn't there. Mia being capable of protecting herself had my chest swollen with pride. I reached out to adjust the strap of her sundress feeling her shiver beneath my fingertips. "You're incredible and I'm so fucking proud of you."

"Thank you." She released a breath, grinning.

As soon as we pulled into my driveway and her eyes weren't trained on the road I leaned across the center console and pulled her face toward mine, giving her a searing kiss. "I'll call you tomorrow, beautiful."

I turned away from her to get out of the car and inside so I could focus on my self-loathing. While I did everything to keep it together during the ride here and bring the focus onto her, I still wasn't finished punishing myself.

Then her car door closed and I turned around to see her following me up my front porch carrying her purse over her shoulder. She narrowed her eyes and frowned but silently followed. "What? Did you think I wasn't going to come in?"

Fuck.

I didn't want her to watch me spiral but I was too exhausted to fight her. Shrugging, I unlocked the front door pushing it wide open for her to come inside.

Chapter 25

Mia

When I pulled into Shawn's driveway and got out, his expression reminded me of the first time we'd met. That far-away look, followed by a grimace so deep I almost recoiled. He expected me to drop him off and get far away from him. That had to be it. I'd be lying if I said the thought hadn't crossed my mind, but I didn't want to be alone after everything that happened, and he shouldn't be alone either. That, and we needed to talk.

Remy rushed to the door to greet us, tail wagging. We were quiet as we took him outside to do his business. The tension was palpable. I embraced the quiet of the simple routine, both of us letting our minds settle down from the events of the day.

I knew I should call Jared to fill him in. He had been out on the course for most of the day, and likely had no idea what had happened. Kendahl would also be wondering how the event went. I'm sure there were no less than five messages from her in my texts. They were my best friends, but the thought of picking up my phone made me want to sink underneath a thick blanket and close my eyes for days.

Shawn looked as dejected as I'd ever seen him with his shoulders slumped and his arms hanging limply at his sides. Whatever strength he showed in the car when he praised me left him entirely.

"I'll get the shower ready for you." His voice was quiet and monotone.

I waited a few breaths, unsure if I should ask him to sit and talk. I wasn't used to our conversations being this awkward. I reached out for his hand, tangling my fingers in his. "What happened wasn't your fault."

He scoffed, "That prick would be behind bars if it weren't for me losing my shit."

Wrapping my arms around him and looking up into his stormy blue eyes I gave him a small smile. "You forget that he's a client of the firm. I have all kinds of info on him and his businesses." Realization shone in his eyes. "And my best friend also happens to work in public relations. I can imagine his business practices being as shady as he is. Karma will bite him in the ass."

Shawn rubbed his hands over my hair and rested his chin on top of my head, leaning in close. "You're too fucking good for me. Too smart, too beautiful, too strong. I don't know what to do to deserve you."

I sighed, knowing this conversation would go nowhere if I answered with my normal reply. So, I said, "Quiet that sexy mouth and get over here."

His eyes widened at that. He loved when I got feisty.

"Let's get you cleaned up and out of those clothes," I said in my most matter of fact voice.

"Mia, you should shower and rest. I can take care of myself. I'm fine." His eyes didn't meet mine. He was pushing me away, yet again, and I wouldn't let him. I needed him tonight just as much as he needed me. I stepped back from him, only a foot or so, but the way his face fell told me he thought I was leaving. He couldn't be more wrong.

I looked down at my wrinkled sundress like it was covered in grime. After the disgusting things Sanders said to me, the dress felt filthy. I slid it off my body and tossed it to the side. I'd likely never wear yellow again. Baring myself to Shawn was still so difficult. I knew my body was far from perfect. My breasts spilled out of my strapless bra, my ample hips, and my soft belly. If I was going to change my self-image, it needed to start with coming out of my comfort zone.

I glanced up at Shawn while trailing my hand toward the back of my bra to undo the clasps. His lips were parted, and his eyes were wide watching me hungrily. My bra dropped to the floor releasing my breasts. I could've sworn he could see my heart hammering against my ribs. The cool air had my nipples hardening almost instantly. I trailed my fingers down my breasts, slow and tantalizing, pinching my nipples gently. God, I was already soaked. I didn't even need to touch myself to know that.

Shawn moved back to perch on the edge of the bed, his eyes on me. He licked his lips and rasped my name. I pictured myself climbing into his lap and grinding into his hardness. Shivers coursed through me and we hadn't even touched yet.

I pulled my lemon-yellow panties off, leaving myself completely exposed to him. His mouth fell open and a gasp escaped his lips. I had shaved this morning leaving only a small strip of hair.

"Mia, get that sweet pussy over here." He reached for me.

"Language, Mr. Brooks." I tsked him wiggling my finger in front of his face.

I had one more surprise up my sleeve.

I dug through my purse on top of his dresser, grabbed my glasses, and put them on before turning back around to face him.

"Do you still want to take care of yourself?" I bit my lower lip, almost afraid of his answer, afraid that I wasn't enough, even though I could see what I did to him clearly written in his expression.

"Come here," he practically growled. Then he stood up and yanked his filthy shirt off, throwing it aside.

I almost doubled over in relief. I needed his hands on me, anywhere and everywhere. The second I reached him, our mouths crashed together, his tongue exploring every inch he could reach. I moaned into him. I needed to feel all his skin against mine, his hands fisted in my hair, palming my ass, my breasts.

I reached down to yank his shorts off, but he beat me to it, pulling them down, along with his boxers. His rock-hard cock pressed against my stomach. My mouth watered at the sight of him, and my insecurities washed away. Need pulsed through my body.

"Fuck me, Shawn," I whispered into his ear as I rubbed my palm up and down his shaft.

He quivered and his breath hitched. "You're so fucking hot when you tell me what you want."

I sat on the edge of the bed, pulling him to me, then running my palms over his hard abs and down lower. I wanted to feel his strong body on top of mine, having him take what he wanted from me. We needed this connection after the events of the day.

He placed slow, torturous kisses from my neck to my belly and continued lower until his face hovered right above my center. "You can't expect me not to devour your sweet, bare pussy."

Holy shit. I shuddered, needing to find release soon.

Shawn buried his face in my pussy and slid a finger through my wet folds. I jerked my hips up at the contact. I was so turned on I could scream. I grabbed the pillows above my head and opened wide for him. He swirled his tongue along my clit while plunging his finger deep inside me. The combination was incredible. Sounds I never knew I could make slipped through my lips making Shawn speed up at a punishing pace.

I was so close, every muscle in my body tightened. I yanked his hair and squeezed his face with my thighs as waves of pleasure rolled through me shattering me into a million pieces.

Shawn pushed himself back up my body, lips glistening with me. It was ridiculously hot. I ran my tongue along his bottom lip, sucking and tasting myself on him.

"See how good you taste, baby?" He uttered into my mouth. "That pussy is all mine."

Before I could say a word, he slammed his cock into me.

"Fuck yes," I groaned as my head pushed up into the pillows. He was so thick that a bite of painful pleasure had me hissing out in the best way.

"Your pussy is still quivering," he hummed. "It feels so fucking good." He thrust into me again and again.

We were delirious. Worked into a frenzy desperate to feel every inch of each other. I wrapped my legs around his back, but he grabbed them, still holding himself up, and positioned them so that they were flush against his chest, my feet resting on his shoulders.

At that angle, he reached deep inside me. I cried out as he rammed himself in and out. "Yes, harder." He was slamming into me so deep that his balls slapped against my ass. The sound of our bodies connecting and the fullness, I couldn't get enough. I pushed my hips up each time to meet him thrust for thrust. His eyes became glazed over and a look of concentration covered his face as he plunged into me, hitting spots I never knew existed.

"You... in those glasses." Our hips rocked rhythmically, my breasts falling to the sides. "Never take them off."

Unintelligible sounds escaped my lips as I climbed that peak again. My center tightened more and more as his cock destroyed me.

"I won't ever let you get hurt again." His eyes bore into mine, blazing. "I'm so sorry, baby. I keep what's mine safe." He sounded almost crazed with lust and fierce protectiveness.

"Yes...," words spilled out of me in between pants, "safe." With my hands around his back, I pulled him closer, deeper, scratching and palming his muscular back.

"Let me hear you say it." He slowed, sliding his cock out of me, not fully, but enough that it was sheer torture.

"Please. Shawn... say what?" Desperate with need, I tried to pull him back into me, bucking my hips up, begging for release. He stilled me with one palm against my hip.

"Say, you're mine."

"I'm yours." I didn't hesitate. I felt this beyond my heart and soul.

As soon as the words left my lips, Shawn flipped me over onto my stomach. My face pressed into the mattress, crushing my glasses against my nose. His strong hands pulled my hips up so my ass was flush against him.

He reached around to circle my clit with his fingers as he slammed into me from behind.

"Oh my God," I said, my voice muffled by the mattress. "So deep..."

I climbed higher and higher, again. My eyes scrunched, and the tension mounted in every muscle of my body. He was an expert with those fingers and that cock, fucking me and rubbing me in rhythm.

Suddenly, all the tension in my muscles uncoiled and my entire body trembled. My vision went black as my orgasm slammed into me.

"Good girl, come around my dick," he growled.

I was boneless, utterly spent, as I rode the waves of my orgasm. Shawn pounded into me harder and harder. He was close too. His movements became jerky and shorter but deeper. With my name on his lips, he drove into me, shuddering as he came. We didn't move. Shawn palmed my ass as his trembling calmed. Only then he pulled himself out of me, and his wet cock slid against my opening.

We collapsed against each other, my back to his chest, breaths still heaved out of us. I nuzzled into him, the top of my head reaching perfectly into the crook of his chin. He rubbed the scruff of his chin into my hair and planted a sweet kiss against the skin near my ear. Our limbs tangled together as he pulled the comforter over us. I could stay like this forever. Content and pleasantly exhausted, not thinking about anything else.

"My little siren," he murmured into my hair, "seducing me when I was trying to throw myself into a downward spiral. Is this your new tactic?" There was humor in his voice, and I knew my plan had worked. Gone was the self-deprecating man of earlier this evening.

I rolled over to face him, tracing along the sharp curve of his jaw and the outline of his lips. A small smile spread across my face. "It worked."

"I suppose it did." He took my finger into his mouth sucking it gently before placing a light kiss at the tip. "I think you might be the best thing that's happened to me in a long, long time."

"Look at you getting all mushy on me." I twirled a finger into his hair. "I think I have you beat, not only am I getting incredible orgasms but with a personal trainer to boot."

His face grew serious and his jaw ticked. "You know that this is more than just sex to me, right? There's no way I'm giving you up."

I pulled him closer and kissed the tip of his nose. The corner of his lips met that beautiful gaze. "It's hard for me to accept compliments and praise. I meant what I said earlier." He arched a brow, listening intently. "When I said I was yours. I want this. Us, together. I joke around, but that's how I handle things when I don't know what to say."

"I meant it too. You may regret letting me in, but I want this, and you, more than I've wanted anything for a long time."

We kissed tenderly, wrapped in each other's arms. I could glow with contentedness. Screw Lungberg and his threats to fire me. Fuck that rapey prick, Sanders. My parents and the looming luncheon could go suck an egg. Nothing would ruin this buzz.

"I'm sorry, again, about how I acted today." He didn't hold the same tone of insecurity he had earlier. "When the cops asked me what happened… I couldn't even tell them. It all felt like some weird dream. I saw red. It was everywhere, and I only felt this urge to protect. God, I was so angry when I realized I had failed you."

Without interrupting him, since I wanted to be sure he finished his whole thought, I responded, "Listen, I understand more about PTSD than you realize."

He moved a strand of hair out of my face, silently telling me to go on. I thought about the news article I saw, about Michelle. If I wanted Shawn to fully open up to me, maybe it was time I did the same.

"It's hard to talk about this." I swallowed the lump in my throat and flipped onto my back cradling one of the pillows to my chest. "I've told you a little bit about my family, and how my parents were never the greatest caregivers. My older sister, Olivia, was basically my surrogate mom. She's only two years older than me, but always seemed older than that." I hitched a breath, glancing over to meet his gaze.

"My parents were always trying to pit us against each other. Olivia was naturally athletic. She was so damn talented at everything she did. Got good grades, too. To me, she just seemed perfect. I always struggled in my classes, except math, and I was basically the last person to get picked for a team in gym class. I honestly think the only reason the cool kids didn't stuff me into my locker daily was because Olivia was my big sister and my family had money."

Shawn reached out to stroke my arm, listening intently.

I took another deep breath. "Anyway, something happened when Olivia was a senior." Suddenly my throat dried up and my tongue felt too heavy to move. Shawn noticed and got up to bring me a glass of water from the bathroom. I murmured a thanks and gulped it down in one swallow before I continued.

"In New York, we were having one of those rare early springs where the snow had melted and temperatures were hovering around fifty degrees after a long winter, so all the seniors were getting spring fever. Graduation was soon, and even the tame kids, like Olivia, were throwing caution to the wind and going out to parties. There was this spot that everyone called The Hill, ironically because it wasn't a hill at all, just a wooded area with lots of stumps where kids built a makeshift fire pit over the years.

"On the weekends, you'd find kids from a few nearby schools there, getting wasted and making out behind trees. Sometimes they'd bring tents and camp out under the stars. I always wondered if the cops knew about The Hill and just let the teenagers slide under the radar. I figured they'd be stupid not to know about it. No one was especially secretive about its location.

"Olivia told me she was going to her first real party. She was excited about it because a guy she really liked was going to be there. I remember her making sure I had eaten dinner. She took her time to get dressed super cute in a denim miniskirt and hot pink tank top. Temps over fifty in our town meant it was basically summer when it came to fashion. Her friend, Sasha, picked her up, and I went to bed a few hours later after watching a few episodes of *Friends*."

I was rambling and going off topic a bit, but Shawn was laid back, rapt with attention, stroking my hair causing my skin to pebble. It was soothing, and I needed his touch more than he knew.

My voice wavered like my body was protesting speaking the rest of the story. If only it ended differently like Olivia getting home a few hours later with a slight buzz from piss-warm beer and giddiness at kissing her crush. I clutched the pillow closer to me, bending my knees and letting them vibrate.

"When I woke up in the morning and peeked into her room to ask how the party was, I saw she wasn't home. Her bed was still made, her Care Bears still lined up against her pillows. I checked my phone for messages, but there were none. It was unlike Olivia. So, I tried calling her and texting her.

"She didn't get home until later that afternoon. The moment I saw her, I knew something was wrong. She was dirty, leaves and mud were smeared in her hair and all over her legs. But her expression... that I'll never forget. It was like her eyes were empty. Her bubbly personality was gone. She didn't remember what happened, only getting to the party with Sasha. She said there were so many people. Most of them she had never seen before. She remembered Sasha going off with her boyfriend and how she chatted with other girls from the volleyball team or introduced herself around. She had one beer. Someone gave it to her in a red plastic cup. She thinks it was a guy with dark hair, but that was the last thing she remembered about the night."

"Someone drugged her?" Shawn's face reddened and his fists balled up at his side.

I nodded. "Yeah, that's what we think must have happened. She woke up, freezing and alone in the woods about fifteen minutes from the main party area around five in the morning. Her phone was gone, so she had no way of calling anyone. She was so disorientated that she vomited when she tried to stand. That's when she noticed the blood dripping down her legs."

Tears leaked from my eyes. I hated to think about my Livvy waking up, scared and alone. I couldn't even imagine how she must have felt. Shawn pulled me to him, and I shook, letting the tears soak his chest. When I settled Shawn asked, his voice quiet and gentle. "Did she go to the hospital? Did they catch the fucker?"

A cynical laugh escaped my lips. "That's what most people would do, right? Go get checked out and file a police report. Well, my family isn't like most. Olivia was so shaken up that she locked herself in her room for two days, only coming out to use the bathroom. She didn't eat and wouldn't unlock her door even when I banged on it. I was young, I didn't know what to do, so I finally went to my parents. They hadn't even realized their own kid hadn't left her room for days—real parents of the year." I rolled over again and sat up, laying back against the headboard. I gnawed my lip and tried to stop myself from crying again.

"So, what did they do?"

"Well, they yelled at me for interrupting their conversation to start. Then, when I wouldn't quit, they finally agreed to go talk to Olivia. I waited outside her door pacing the hallway and chewing my nails down to stubs. When my parents left her room looking stiff and unbothered, I knew they either didn't believe her story or were going to sweep it under the rug."

"No fucking way."

"I wish I was kidding. I pushed myself in front of them, blocked the staircase and asked them what she said and what they were going to do. They looked at each other before looking down at me, like I was only an annoying child, and said that Olivia was fine. She was under the weather and needed to rest.

I remember crumpling onto the floor of the hallway and sobbing into my hands. These were our parents, the people who were supposed to care for us above all else.

Since Olivia's door was unlocked, I pushed my way into her room. Seeing her on her bed looking like a ghost of who she was, I'll never forget that moment for as long as I live." The scene replayed in my mind like a film.

"Livvy?" I approached her like you would approach a sleeping baby, watching every step I took in case a floorboard creaked and spooked her. I reached her bedside and sit down tentatively. She is lying on her side, staring off into space. The room is silent. Her usual playlist of pop music or background noise of cheesy MTV shows is nowhere to be found. The silence makes the air in the room heavier, which I didn't think was possible. I reach out to push

her dark hair away from her eyes. She jerks away at my touch. I wouldn't want to be touched, either.

"What did you tell mom and dad? Please tell me you told them what happened."

She is silent, but a single tear slides from her eye, dropping onto her pillow. I stare at the wet splotch as if it held all the answers I needed to make everything better. The answers to getting my big sister back and making this all go away. But, of course, nothing could fix what had happened.

She finally turns her gaze to me, eyes full of tears. "Just go, Mimi. Please, leave."

"She pushed me away more and more every day. I tried to care for her in the days and weeks that followed, but she wouldn't let me in. I'd go to her at night when I was woken up by her screams. She'd thrash around in her bed, covered in sweat, but nothing I did could wake her. When she finally went back to school, she stopped talking to everyone, even Sasha. She quit the volleyball team and walked around like a shell of herself. And then, about two months later, we found out that she was pregnant. There were only a few weeks of school left, but she quit anyway."

Shawn loosed a breath, letting everything sink in. "I know it's a lot," I sighed. "In the months and years that followed, things only became more and more complicated. Like I said, I am well versed in PTSD. Not that everyone has the same experience. Ugh, I'm rambling." I flopped back against the pillows. "I mean, I know what you go through isn't the same at all as Olivia's experiences, but I want you to know what I can and have handled." I turned toward him. "I'll do anything for the people I care for."

Not saying a word, he pulled me into his warm arms and held me. I felt safe and calm like nothing bad could ever happen to me again. I didn't want to know what time it was by the time we finished talking about Olivia.

Chapter 26

Mia

"Will you come with me to my parent's house tomorrow for lunch? They want to see me, and I...," I stammered barely able to complete the full sentence. I'm not sure what made me ask him. Maybe, it was my vulnerability after opening up? Maybe, I was tired of facing everything alone and shouldering the weight of it all. "I don't want to face them alone this time."

Once the question left my lips, I closed my eyes and snuggled up against him. The contact of his bare skin, warm against mine, comforted me. He drew his face close, placing a kiss on my temple, and whispered. "Of course, I'll go with you. I'd go anywhere and do anything you asked of me."

Exhaustion threatened to take me, pulling my heavy eyelids down. I smiled and let sleep fall over me like a warm blanket.

When I woke hours later, I stretched my limbs until I felt that pleasant ache then rolled over to find Shawn's place in bed empty and cold.

"I guess this is going to be a reoccurring thing," I muttered to myself. My thoughts whirled back to the previous day, and it all just felt unreal. No way did I rock throwing that party only to have it crash and burn with me almost getting assaulted and having my boyfriend end up arrested for beating the perpetrator senseless.

Then last night.

My cheeks heated thinking about the way Shawn commanded my body. Bringing my attention to my core, I could tell I was sore in the best way. I needed a shower though—desperately. Since Shawn wasn't around, I'd take care of that before heading downstairs to find him.

It was funny to me how comfortable I felt in this bedroom and this house, in such a short amount of time. I could envision framed photographs of Shawn and me on the walls, beaming hand in hand. Even the smells, the earthy, woodsy scent of Shawn mixed with the slight tinge of dog from Remy were like a balm to my senses.

Freshly showered and feeling like a human again, I found Shawn downstairs in the kitchen with Remy underfoot. He was wearing low-slung sweatpants, his chest bare while scuffling around the kitchen holding a spatula. Remy noticed me first and padded over my way.

"Whatever you're making smells amazing." I woke up ravenous and remembered that I barely ate yesterday amid all the chaos.

"It's a giant omelet: spinach, cheese, peppers, and onions, all the healthy stuff. Gotta keep your energy level up, if you get my drift." An amused grin spread across his face. "But first, coffee." He grabbed a giant mug from a hanging rack and filled it with the steaming nectar of the gods, thrusting it my way.

"Did I ever tell you," I said, adding milk and sugar to my coffee, "that you're my new favorite person? Especially when you feed me." I leaned in and brushed a kiss across his stubbled cheek. "Extra cheese on mine, please."

He chuckled. "I'm starting to see that I may have to compete with cheese for your love." My breath caught in my throat making me almost choke on the sip of coffee I had taken. Did he just say, *love?*

I pulled it together. "Keep cooking for me and making me coffee and you might keep first place in my heart."

"Noted," he said through a grin.

He plated up our breakfast and I couldn't help but stare at the way he moved with ease through the kitchen, even with Remy underfoot. Those sweatpants, loose enough to show the sculpted V-line along his hips hung dangerously low. One tug and they'd be sliding down his ass. I'd pull him to me and let myself run my hands over his carved abs... all the way down to...

"How's your coffee?" Shawn turned to face me holding my plate of food.

"Great," I squeaked, clearing my throat. He stared me down for a moment with a raised brow before sitting across from me to dig into his omelet.

I brought my attention back to my cup of coffee. Mia, you can't stay in bed all day, even though your body is telling you otherwise. *Simmer down.*

After stuffing our faces, we went back to my place so I could change. As much as I wanted to hibernate for the day, I couldn't back out of this lunch. Shawn wore a soft blue T-shirt that made his eyes pop and a pair of jeans. His booty looked edible. I was getting used to seeing him out of gym clothes, and there were zero complaints from me.

I drove, hoping it would help me focus on something other than my gnawing anxiety. I could tell Shawn felt the same way, as he kept clenching and unclenching his fists and bobbing his knees up and down.

I held his thigh reassuringly. "It's going to be fine. We'll go, make small talk, eat, and leave. Trust me, I don't want to converse with my parents more than I have to."

Running a hand through his hair, he placed his palm over mine. "The only thing I'm worried about is that I'll get pissed at them and say something I'll regret later."

A small smile played on my lips at his protectiveness. "I don't really care what you say to them. They're assholes."

"You say that, but I can see how much impressing them means to you."

I blanched, "No, not at all. I just… I don't know. I want them to see that despite their lack of guidance, I'm doing well. Great. Thriving."

"You are." He lifted my hand and placed a kiss on the top of my palm. "You landed me, didn't you?"

"You're such an ass." I smacked him and he laughed a deep husky chuckle.

It was a humid day, but there were only a few small puffy clouds scattered in the sky. I turned up the music, a mix of classic rock and alternative, and took in the sights of the coastal road. We quieted down again. The knee bobbing and fist clenching were kept to a minimum. Palm trees and live oaks lined the roadway making me feel like I wasn't merely twenty minutes from Palm Cove, but in an entirely different state. If I rolled my windows down, I'd undoubtedly smell the saltiness of the ocean breeze in the air.

My mind kept replaying the quick conversation I had had with Kendahl that morning while I was getting ready at my apartment. I couldn't tell her much, but we set things in motion for the downfall of James Sanders' career. This was the first time that having a best friend who worked in public relations came in handy.

Jared had messaged me a million times, freaking out once he heard about what happened. I called him back assuring him I was okay, and that Shawn was too. It was a quick catch up with promises to check in later and fill him in. He did promise to take Sanders file and accidentally lose all the information though. I struggled with that; I didn't want Jared to get in trouble, or even fired, for helping me. Knowing him, if I got axed, he'd go with me.

Refocusing my attention back on the man next to me, and the beautiful surroundings, I pushed the thoughts of Sanders and work away. I'd deal with all that tomorrow.

My GPS pinged letting me know we'd reached our destination. The house, if you could call it that, was more of an estate. The stark white limestone exterior and brown European-style roof looked like something straight out of a magazine.

"Holy shit, this house must have cost millions." Shawn looked out his window as we drove up the flagstone driveway and parked in front of a bubbling stone fountain.

"You're probably right. My father has friends in high places." I had never told Shawn that my father had started off his career as a high-profile defense lawyer, turned judge, and then turned politician. My parents were involved in so many foundations and elitist clubs by the time I was an adult I stopped trying to figure out where our money came from. My father commuted to Albany for most of my childhood but often stayed in New York City for weeks at a time, leaving us stuck in our snowy small town. This estate was probably owned by a politician or judge friend.

He seemed to be at a loss for his words. "I never realized you," he stammered, "came from this kind of money."

"Once I left the house, I was on my own. Don't let this show of opulence fool you," I scoffed. "My father pushed me to make my own way. Apart from paying for my college education, which I'm extremely grateful for, I've taken care of myself. I'd rather eat ramen every day than ask them for a dime."

"Your sister? Do they help her?"

I figured he'd ask that. After our talk yesterday, he surely had so many more questions about Olivia.

"They do. As far as I know, she still lives with them—her and Alex."

He nodded, and we walked up the perfectly manicured walkway to the door. I rang the bell and sucked in a deep breath. "You good?" he asked, squeezing my hand.

"Yup." My breath expelled like I was releasing air from a blown-up balloon.

My mother, Pamela, answered the door looking almost exactly the same as she did the last time I saw her over two years ago with frosty blonde hair cut into a wispy bob, styled with enough product that a gale-force wind couldn't have knocked a strand out of place. Her creamy skin was dotted with touches of makeup. The only signs of her age were a few faint lines at the corners of her eyes. Her signature amber perfume that she'd worn my entire life wafted toward me making my eyes water. I'd always hated it. She wore a navy-blue boat-neck blouse and pressed white linen pants, looking like she jumped off the pages of a Neiman Marcus advertisement. She eyed me with a slight frown and shifted her gaze to Shawn, shock widening her eyes before she greeted us.

"Good afternoon, dear, I'm so glad you could make it. You brought a friend, too, how lovely. I'll tell Carla to prepare another place setting."

Her saccharine voice made me want to grab Shawn and pull him back into the car. "Come in. Isn't this house exquisite? There are a few touches that aren't my taste, but it'll do for the summer."

We entered a foyer that was bigger than my entire apartment. The marble floors gleamed with light that was let in by the floor-to-ceiling windows. An ornate, twisting staircase ahead led to the second floor, and shining dark columns separated the foyer from the remainder of the lower level. But the real masterpiece was the ocean view that was front and center out of the enormous floor-to-ceiling windows in the back of the house.

"This place is great, Mom." I really was in awe as much as I loathed complimenting her.

"Yes, well, a home this size is something. It does tend to take one's breath away at first."

I heard Shawn snicker beside me. She turned to give Shawn an appraising look while leading us through the formal living space to the covered outdoor area.

"Mom, this is Shawn." I cleared my throat. "We met at a self-defense class I've been taking."

"Nice to meet you, Mrs. Murphy," Shawn jumped in. "Thank you for having me."

She barely acknowledged Shawn's statement, instead turning her head forward and leading us outside. "Yes, well, it would have been nice if my daughter would have told me we were having another guest. Nevertheless, it is nice to meet you as well."

The house took my breath away, but it was nothing compared to the outside. The entire area was like an extension of the interior. The real beauty, besides the ocean view, was the amazing infinity edge pool and spa beckoning me to jump in. What I had thought were all windows were doors that opened completely connecting the two spaces. An entire gourmet kitchen with a wood fire oven and bar was off to the side. There was a beautiful dining area and outdoor living room set up, complete with plushy pillows and a gas fire pit.

Seated on one of the sofas, phone in hand, was my father, Neil. My mother looked frozen in time; my father looked the opposite. Maybe she sucked his life force from him like some kind of youth-draining vampire. His hair was fully silver, and his face was lined far more than when I last saw him. He wore wire-framed glasses on his closely shaven face. I used to think all men shaved twice a day but then realized that it was only my father being obsessive about his appearance. I don't think I've ever seen my father with a five o'clock shadow. He stood up, smoothing out his khaki chinos, and came to greet us. We shook hands, a fake smile plastered on, as I said hello and introduced him to Shawn.

"Mia, so lovely to see you. Hi there, Shawn. Welcome to our home." I knew his handshake and robotic grin routine well. It was the same way he greeted his voters. "Let me just finish up some business," he lifted his phone, "then I'm all yours."

Doubtful.

My mother clicked her tongue with barely contained annoyance etched all over her face. I changed the subject. "Where's Olivia and Alex?"

She regained her composure and focused her gaze my way. "They're staying in the guesthouse. They should be over soon. If not, I can have Carla fetch them."

Man, I did not envy poor Carla.

"Oh, okay." Awkward silence commenced, and I fidgeted with the hem of my dress. I thought about what I was doing, then promptly stopped. My mother hated when I fidgeted.

"Well, since we're waiting for your father and Olivia, let's sit down and have a drink. I'd love to hear more about how you're doing."

I cleared my throat, glancing back at my father. As much of a prick as he was, I never enjoyed having my mother's full attention focused on me. With him there to distract her she never kept her line of questioning on me for long. We sat down at the outdoor dining table. Like everything else, it was solid and expensive looking, with intricate metal legs and a glass top.

A tiny woman, who looked to be in her sixties, shuffled outside from one of the open doorways carrying a tray in one hand and a pitcher in the other. She had a large tuft of salt and pepper hair that floated above her head. Smile lines etched her face and her eyes brightened upon seeing Shawn and me.

"You must be Mia," she greeted me with a heavy Italian accent. She placed her load on the table and sidled over to embrace me like I'd known her for years. Her gaze locked on Shawn. "And who is this handsome hunk? He reminds me of that Mitch from the watchers of the bay show." I suppressed a giggle as she reached out to squeeze Shawn's bicep through his shirt, while oohing and aahing. My mother cleared her throat and Carla jumped back a step. Shawn stifled a laugh and held his hand out, introducing himself.

"Carla, will you fetch Olivia and Alex, please?" She looked at her diamond-encrusted wristwatch. "They're ten minutes late."

"Yes, Ms. Pamela. I think they were at the beach this morning so they might be getting cleaned up."

She left as quickly as she came, so I called out, "It was nice to meet you, Carla," after her. I heard a muffled response in some sort of Italian. "Mom, she is absolutely delightful. When did you hire her?"

"She works for the Richardsons normally." After examining her manicure, my mother looked back up at me as if she were being forced to answer a difficult question. "They're the ones who own this estate, but they are spending their summer in the South of France, so they graciously offered it to us for a change of scenery."

I nodded, "Well, she's a delight." Shawn agreed next to me, nodding.

"Hmm, yes. She can be a nuisance, always seeming to be in my way, but she has the energy of a teenager. I don't know how she does it."

I silently willed Carla to come back and save me from this conversation as I asked my mother the question that'd been burning in my mind. "So, Mom, what brought you all down to Florida? Besides a change of scenery." I stuffed my hands under my thighs to keep myself from fidgeting.

Her eyes got shifty suddenly, looking back at my father, before meeting my gaze again. "It's not much of a story. John Richardson offered and we accepted." She tapped her fingers on the glass. "Lemonade? Carla makes it fresh from the citrus on the grounds. It's to die for with a splash of vodka."

More like half a bottle, I thought.

Shawn and I both said sure at the same time. The way my mother kept glancing back at my father and acting nervous was incredibly weird. Something was going on. They wouldn't just up and leave New York for the entire summer without a reason.

"So, Mia," she struggled to find a question like my life was so below hers that she couldn't possibly be interested in what I had to say, "how's work? Are you still with Mr. Lungberg? He's a wonderful man to be giving you a chance right out of school the way he did."

Wonderful? Maybe if you were comparing him to a wet mop. "Work is good. I just organized a client appreciation event that went well, and I am starting to take on my own clients."

"That's nice, dear," She nodded, still glancing over at my father every few seconds, who was speaking quietly yet fervently on his phone. "And you, Shawn? What do you do for a living?"

He took a sip of lemonade and coughed a little. "That has a kick to it, huh?" No response from her. He met my gaze, and I gave him a reassuring look. "I am a business owner, carpentry and refinishing. I also assistant teach at our gym."

"He does wonderful work, Mom. You'd love his custom pieces," I added brightly.

"I have some photos here on my phone." He pulled his phone out and scrolled, searching for a particular photo. When he found what he was looking for, a small smile crept on the corner of his lips and he handed the phone to my mother. She took it as if he was handing her something contagious and held it an arm's length away, squinting her eyes. "I don't have my glasses on me, but it looks lovely." Shawn started to explain the history of the photo when my father joined us.

His false smile was nowhere to be seen now. He sat across from my mother. "Where'd Carla run off to?" He reached for a glass and poured himself some water. "I'd love for her to make me an old-fashioned."

"Isn't it a bit early for that?" my mother snapped. I watched as the two of them shot each other daggers.

He leaned back and then turned his head to stare out at the ocean. "I'm on vacation, any time is the right time for a drink. Am I right, Shawn?"

Shawn shifted closer to me. "Eh, yeah, sure, sir."

"You'll join me, won't you? I got my hands on the best whiskey I've ever tasted. Must have been aged at least fifty years. Let's let the women talk about their hair and makeup and all that nonsense while we talk about real, important things."

Anger rose in my throat. He was still the same old, sexist asshole that he always was. His election-time speech about women having the same rights as men was an act. I squeezed Shawn's thigh under the table silently telling him it was fine, he could go. Thank God, Carla came strolling outside with my sister and nephew behind her.

Shawn and I stood up while my parents stayed seated having a whispered conversation across the table. Whatever they were discussing wasn't a happy topic since I could see my father's face turning shades of red that were only natural on pieces of fruit.

"I found these two, Ms. Pamela. I will go and get lunch ready now." My father stopped her, no doubt for that drink he wanted.

I took in my big sister before going to her and wrapping her in a hug. She looked healthy and different from when I last saw her. Her cheeks were rosy, and her hair was the usual deep brown but cut into a trendy wavy bob. She was still thin, much thinner than me, and lacking the muscle that she used to have when she was a teenage athlete.

"Livvy, it's so good to see you." It really was.

Inhaling her familiar scent of lavender and vanilla, I almost teared up from the comforting feeling of her hugs. I quickly remembered that she wasn't the same Livvy from my childhood, and depending on the day, she could be volatile or completely detached. This seemed like a good day. I could tell in the way she was carrying herself and hugging me back. We broke apart and she took me in and then Shawn, who stood next to me. "Looks like you're doing well, sissy?" Her brows raised. "Alex, come say hi to Aunt Mia."

My ten-year-old nephew, Alex, was now almost my height. He dragged his feet over from the sofa to greet us. He wore a polo shirt and navy-blue jean shorts with white boat shoes. His coffee-colored hair resembled mine, a mountain of springy curls atop his head. His face was dotted with freckles, covering almost every inch of his skin. He reached us and my sister gave him a stern look. Alex straightened up to his full height. They must teach new mothers how to perfect this face at the hospitals after delivery because I've seen so many mothers make the same expression. I had to cover my mouth to keep from laughing.

"Hi, Aunt Mia." Looking up at Shawn, he asked, "Who's this guy?"

We laughed, "Hi buddy, this is my friend Shawn."

Alex eyed him up and down, scrutinizing. "You ever kill anyone? You look like my favorite skin in *Fortnite*. I got *Battle Royale* yesterday. Killed like thirty people." Olivia shushed him and pulled him over to the table.

I had no idea what *Fortnite* was, but Shawn looked like he understood whatever Alex was talking about. "You get any legendary weapons?" Shawn asked, looking genuinely curious.

Alex beamed. "Oh yeah, loads. I love sniping. It's my favorite. Some of those weapons are so broken, though."

Shawn nodded. "Sniping's cool, but you gotta try using the pump shotgun."

While the two of them got into a lively discussion of *Fortnite* weapons, Livvy turned to me, smiling. "You know you just lost your date for the day, right?"

"Hey, whatever makes them happy," I laughed. "They may as well be speaking Latin to me."

She drank some lemonade and made the same face Shawn did. "Sour today." She watched Alex deep in discussion with Shawn. "It's nice to have someone else for him to talk about video games with. If I hear the word *Fortnite* anymore, my brain may explode."

As if he sensed we were talking about him, Shawn looked our way, grinning, and gave a thumbs-up while Alex kept talking.

"Let's sneak away later to chat." Olivia raised a brow at me again. "I want all the details."

It felt nice to have my sister back by my side again. Maybe it was my own fault for moving and letting our relationship slip. I carried a lot of guilt about that, but she wasn't an easy person to hold a relationship with, either.

Carla came back into the room holding my father's drink and a bowl of salad. I was starving. Breakfast felt like days ago.

My father nodded to Carla and thanked her gruffly before he downed a long sip. I was pretty sure you weren't supposed to drink whiskey like that, but what did I know?

"Well," my mother started, her voice raising a few octaves. "Let's enjoy this wonderful salad, shall we?"

Chapter 27

Mia

Lunch was tense. Tense wasn't a strong enough word for it. Lunch was unnerving. Stressful. Uncomfortable. I could look in a thesaurus and find many more synonyms for how I felt the entire time, but the only thing anchoring me was Shawn's hand on my thigh rubbing calming circles and the occasional looks of shared grief Olivia kept throwing my way.

Something was clearly going on between my parents. They were normally aloof and condescending toward me, but it was rare that they acted the same way with each other. My father downed three whiskey drinks within the hour-long lunch while my mother gave him dirty looks and kept anxiously tapping her fingers on the glass table, and she took barely two bites of her meal.

Alex eventually saved us from our misery when he announced that he was bored and asked if he could be excused to go play video games. My mother scolded him for being rude, but my father actually laughed a full-bodied hardy chuckle. My father agreed with Alex and then said he needed to take care of another business call.

Olivia and I helped Carla clear the table while Alex pulled Shawn into a nearby sitting room. It hadn't taken much convincing for Shawn to agree to play a few rounds of *Fortnite* with him. Watching them joke around and talk animatedly about how they were going to demolish people made my heart do a few flips in my chest.

"Hey, Mom," Olivia called to her from the kitchen. Mom was still outside, tidying up invisible messes and looking distraught. "Mia and I are going to take a walk on the beach."

She poked her head inside. "You don't have to yell. It's very unbecoming."

Olivia rolled her eyes. It felt like we were kids again, making fun of my mother's prim and proper ways.

"Can you keep an eye on Alex, please? He's in the sitting room with Shawn. They should be busy for a while."

"Yes, yes, go ahead you two. Go catch up." She flitted her hands at us dismissively and Olivia took my hand in hers leading me back outside toward the steps.

The mid-afternoon sun scorched the top of my head once we left the shade of my parents' covered patio causing beads of sweat to form behind my neck. Once we reached the shore it was like the air magically cooled a few degrees granting me relief with a gentle breeze.

I pulled off my strappy sandals as fast as I could so I could dig my feet into the wet sand. There was something grounding about sinking your feet into warm sand while smelling a salty ocean breeze. It could make me forget even my most pressing of troubles.

"This is paradise. At least once you get enough steps away from that hot mess up there," I laughed.

"They are pretty bad, aren't they?" My sister stared at the crashing waves with one hand twirling a strand of her hair. "I'm so used to them I don't even see it anymore."

"Is something up? They're the worst, but they're not usually focusing their nastiness at each other so much, right?"

"I'm not supposed to say anything," Olivia took a moment, chewing her lip, "but technically, anyone could find out if they looked online."

The wheels of my mind were turning. What was she talking about?

"Let's sit for a second," she sat and patted the sand next to her. I tried not to care that my dress would be covered in sand and that I'd most likely find it in crevices I'd rather not later. My sister was here and wanted to talk to me. "Did Mom tell you why we're here?"

"Not really. She basically just said they wanted a change of scenery. Why?"

Olivia played with sand as she spoke digging a little hole with her fingers. "Typical," she scoffed. "Well, our *perfect* mother cheated on our *dickhead* father."

My jaw dropped. "No way!"

"I kid you not," Olivia let out a dry laugh. "I suspect they've both been cheating pretty much the entire length of their marriage. It wouldn't surprise me if Dad had a secret family in the city or something. But yeah, she did. And you'll never guess who she got caught cheating with."

"Wait, let me guess. Oh my god. Was it the gardener? Or better yet, her personal trainer?"

"Not even close." Olivia shook her head and tried to hide her laughter.

"Pool guy? Pilates instructor? Repairman?" I rapidly fired out guesses one after another watching Olivia practically burst with the need to tell me.

Finally, she blurted out. "It was with Senator Gillis. A staffer caught them red-handed in her office."

It took me a moment before I fully digested this information.

"Wait a second. Did you say *her* office? Senator Gillis? I'm trying to remember a Gillis. Nothing's coming up."

"Yup," she said. "Mom was sleeping with a woman—a married woman who's also in politics."

Olivia fished her phone out of the back pocket of her denim shorts and pulled up a photo that she had screenshotted. The photo looked like it was taken at some fancy charity event. In it were my parents posing with another couple. My mother had her usual plastic smile on her face, just like my father, but the other couple didn't look as thrilled to be there.

"I don't even know what to say." I sat up straighter examining the photo.

"There's more." Olivia took her phone back. "I got a sneak peek at the article that's about to break. Someone sent it to Dad, and I happened to be in the kitchen with him when he saw it come through. Look." She swiped her phone and thrust it back at me. It was a blurry shot of a picture of my father's computer screen.

The headline read:

New York State Senator, Republican Elsa Gillis Doesn't Practice What She Preaches—A Breaking News Story.

I read on, completely shocked.

Information has leaked through an anonymous staffer this morning that Senator Gillis, best known for her anti-LGBTQ+ stances and her preaching of Christian values was found having sexual relations with none other than Mrs. Pamela Murphy, wife of New York's Attorney General, Neil Murphy. Both parties have declined to comment on the situation, but insiders report that Attorney General Murphy has taken a leave of absence at this time.

Scrolling down, the article featured more photos of both my mother and Ms. Gillis. They somehow managed to find an unflattering photo of my mother, which was rare. She never let herself leave the house without looking one hundred percent put together.

"Holy shit." I had no other response.

"Right? Of course, they haven't said a word about it to me. You know them and sweeping everything under the rug. I bet they're hoping that by the time they get back to New York everyone will have forgotten about this and they can continue like it never happened."

"You're probably right," I sighed.

We sat in silence for a moment dragging our feet through the sand and watching cool water fill the holes. "It's sad, though."

Olivia looked up. "What do you mean?"

"Them. How they live their life. We only get one life. Why would you want to be miserable for that many years?"

"It beats me," she answered shaking her head. "But I know I need to get Alex away from their toxic shit as soon as I can. That's the main reason I came down here."

I raised a brow. "Are you thinking of staying?"

"I am. They don't know, but I've been putting my resume out there to a few places. If I find something before the end of summer, we're going to stay."

"I'd love that." My face broke out into a mile-wide grin. "I can help. Just let me know what you need. And you're both always welcome to stay with me too if you'd like."

"Thanks, sis. I want to do this on my own, though. I have some money saved to help us start out." She looked out at the horizon again, a contented look on her face. "I really want to be close to the shore. There's something so peaceful about it, you know?"

I nodded. "I thought you were happy with Mom and Dad. I know you always agreed that they weren't the best parental figures, but if I knew you wanted to get out of there, I would have helped you."

"It's okay, Mimi. I'm a big girl now. I can take care of myself. And yeah, they suck, but I'm used to them and they're never around much. Alex and I usually get the run of the house. But, I want to get out of New York and make a fresh start for us. I'll admit it was kind of nice to have mom around to help with Alex. I think he may have softened her a bit."

I couldn't picture my mom and her white pants playing with a little boy, but then again, I couldn't picture my mother doing anything motherly.

I cleared my throat, emotion welling in my eyes. "I'm proud of you, Livvy. I'm sorry that I left." I took a moment to swallow the lump that had formed in my throat. "Do you forgive them? Mom and Dad, I mean. For not believing you, not doing anything."

A flash of sadness spread across my sister's face, her dark eyes shifted down to the sand. "First of all, there's nothing for you to apologize for. I understood why you needed to leave, and I don't hold that against you."

I started to interject, "Yeah, but—" but she cut me off.

"I wasn't done." She reached out and took my hand in hers. That small act brought the tears that were welling in my eyes out to the surface. I remember a time when she wouldn't touch anyone. She couldn't bear the feeling of another person's skin against her own. "You asked if I forgive them. The answer is yes and no. There were circumstances between our parents and me that I didn't want to lay on your already heavy shoulders. I learned that sometimes horrible things happen to us, sissy. Unspeakable, tragic things. But I've worked to push through those dark clouds to see the rainbow underneath. Without everything that happened back then, I wouldn't have my amazing son who makes me a better person every day. He is something to be thankful for. Whether I forgive them for not handling the situation the best way or forgive the man who did what he did to me it doesn't matter anymore. I've learned to let that go and to embrace the good that's come from our circumstances."

I let her words sink in. If she could forgive, then why did I still harbor so much anger and anxiety? I was still letting the past dictate my future, even though I'd made steps to change.

I wiped my eyes forgetting my hands were sandy. "Shit, I think I got sand in my eye." I blinked aggressively to no avail.

"Come on, let's go back inside and rinse your eye out," Olivia chuckled. "Alex has gotten sand in his eye twice already and we've only been here a few days."

"Great, so now I'm as bright as a ten-year-old."

"Hey, that ten-year-old is way smarter than me already, so consider yourself lucky to be roped in with him. He's inherited your math brain."

We walked back up toward the house, Olivia holding my hand so I didn't bump into a palm tree or fall in a ditch with my one good eye guiding me.

"By the way, back to our conversation."

"Yeah?" I turned to look at her, one eye squeezed shut like an old-timey pirate.

"I can tell Shawn is special. How long has that been going on?" I didn't know how much I was ready to share about Shawn, but I guess I promised her some details.

I drew in a thoughtful breath. "Not very long. We met at a self-defense class. He also randomly showed up at my job needing an accountant for his business. I really like him, but things are very new and have been complicated." Complicated was the best way to describe his back and forth behavior at first and the fact that he has something I know he hasn't shared with me yet.

"Hmm, complicated doesn't always mean bad."

We walked up the stairs brushing sand from our butts before stepping onto the patio, trying not to make more of a mess for Carla.

"He has... um..." I stammered, "PTSD. He's in therapy. Has been for a while, I think."

Olivia pulled me over to one of the guest bathrooms, opened a medicine cabinet, and handed me a bottle of saline rinse. While I leaned over to squirt a stream that rivaled Niagara Falls into my eyeball, she kept talking.

"Well, you know I've dealt with that. I know you were there for me through the worst of it. If he's a good guy, and he's actively working on himself then I don't see that as an issue."

I blinked, not feeling any more grit in there.

"All better?" Olivia asked, handing me a tissue. That stuff worked wonders.

"Yeah, I think I got it all out."

"Great. Let's go check on the boys. I hope Shawn isn't ready to pull his hair out."

We left a little while later with full bellies and hearts. I felt a renewed sense of hope after talking with my sister. If she could overcome so much and be doing so well then there's a chance for Shawn and me.

"Your nephew is hilarious. He's a piece of work, that's for sure." Shawn drove my car back toward his house.

"I'm sorry about him dragging you to play that game."

"No, I had a blast," he laughed. "At first, I was nervous because I've never been around kids other than helping out in the kid classes at the gym here and there. But it was fun. He made me give him my gamer tag so that we can play again. Apparently, I'm not a noob, whatever that means."

Shawn had a lightness about him I hadn't seen before. He drummed on the steering wheel to Lynyrd Skynyrd songs and sang along with me. When I told him about my parents, he almost had to pull over in disbelief. I was still pretty shocked myself, but like Olivia said, it wasn't like my parents acted like they were in love.

I wondered how my mother felt about this Gillis woman. Was she gay? Was she bisexual? Was it a one-time thing? I'd probably never find out. Hell would freeze over before I'd have that conversation with my mother.

Later that night we ended the weekend by ordering Thai takeout and cuddling on the couch while binge-watching Marvel movies. Or, at least, pretending to binge-watch Marvel movies, there wasn't much watching going on.

I also did a little digging on Coby for Kendahl. According to Shawn, he's a decent guy. He's divorced and a physical therapist. No red flags as far as Shawn knew except that he's kind of a lady's man. I'd have to relay that information back to my bestie.

Curled up in bed, with Shawn's warm body against my back and Remy's snores from his dog bed, I felt more content than I ever had. Even with the anxiety and stress of the weekend, I could breathe against him and know that everything was going to be okay. Maybe more than okay, as long as we had each other.

Chapter 28

Shawn

Another week went by and I had to pinch myself daily to see if I was dreaming. Mia and I had seen each other every day between classes and she'd been spending the night at my place. I had forgotten what it was like to be happy and have companionship. It was the small things like catching up about our day while we walked Remy side-by-side sweating in the early evening humidity or teasing her about eating cheese with every meal.

Of course, the sex was incredible too. My fiery girlfriend was getting more confident with me and coming out of her shell more and more every day. She got me so fucking hard with just a thought of that beautiful smile and those curves that I wanted to slide my hands over.

I messed around in my home gym while I waited for her to come by after work. Laying on my weight bench, the vinyl sticking to my bare back, I warmed up with crunches and leg lifts to get my core engaged. We were going to get ready for class and drive there together. Metallica beat out of my phone speaker as I grabbed the fifty-pound dumbbells and started a set of chest presses. I hadn't been keeping up with my normal workout routine since Mia entered my life. I've been too busy getting my cardio in other ways.

After three sets of chest presses, I switched to some chest flys, breathing hard with each exhalation. I was in such a trance that I didn't hear when Mia came inside until she hovered over me. She was dressed in a skirt that stopped above her knee and a button-down shirt tucked into it. A few of the top buttons were undone, giving me a peek of her delicious cleavage.

"Getting warmed up without me?" Her brows raised as she took in my bare chest slick with sweat. I sat up. I was going to grab my shirt to clean myself up a little, but with the way she was looking at me, I knew what she was thinking.

"I wouldn't dream of it," I said, pulling her toward me as I sat, my legs on either side of the weight bench. "It looks like you aren't dressed appropriately for a workout, though," I tutted. "I should help you with that."

"I think I do need your help with that." Her lips parted and a hot sigh escaped them.

Standing up, I pulled her shirt over her head, not paying any attention to the tiny row of buttons. I eyed her breasts greedily before unhooking her lace bra and taking them in my hands. My dick already throbbed from the simple touch.

I yanked off her skirt and panties, in one swoop, tossing them aside so my beautiful girl was bare before me. My mouth watered, needing to taste her. I gave her tight nipples a suck, one at a time, and she moaned my name. Her fingers tangled through my hair, pulling lightly, causing electric shocks to cover my skin with goosebumps. Our mouths collided, tongues tangling and sucking, while I crushed her against me. She was a fucking queen and deserved to be worshipped.

"Baby, get on this bench. I want to feel you coming on my tongue."

She shuddered, nodding and murmuring, and lowered herself to the bench. I tugged her down so that her ass was at the very edge, and I got on my knees for her. She was eager, her thighs parting, giving me a perfect view of her glistening pussy. I moved her legs up over my shoulders, loving the weight and feel of them against me.

"So wet for me already," I growled. I was hovering my face over her seam, and I wasted no time dipping my head between her legs. I consumed her like the greedy fuck that I was needing to feel her quiver and writhe against me. I slipped a finger inside her to rub the walls of her pussy in rhythm as I sucked and licked at her clit like an animal. She was so close, her tight pussy was clenching onto my finger.

"Fuck, Shawn... don't stop." Her hips bucked, and I met her pace, hard and fast, just like she liked it. One, two, three more thrusts with my finger and she came apart squeezing me like a vise. Her clit pulsed as I sucked it, gently, watching her ride every last second of pleasure on my face.

"Oh my fucking God." She sat up as much as she could, her beautiful face flushed pink and her hair going in every direction. I let her legs down and wiped at my soaked chin.

"Damn baby, you drenched the bench." Her wetness coated the vinyl. My cock was going to explode if I didn't get inside her. She stood up on wobbly feet, yanking my shorts down, and eyed me hungrily.

"Ride my cock with that soaking wet pussy." She visibly quivered, licked her lips, and then pushed me down on the bench. I loved how she responded to my dirty talk. She sucked my lip then my tongue as she straddled me and slowly sank onto my cock until I was fully inside her. "Fuck. You feel so amazing."

"So full," she moaned, rocking against me. The wet vinyl squeaked under my back with our movement. I'd never be able to lift in here without getting hard again.

My hands slid all over her body, massaging her breasts, grabbing her ass, and finally, guiding her hips as she ground against me. I thrust up, pushing deeper, needing to claim every inch of her.

"God, you're so deep, I can feel you in my stomach." Mia's mouth parted, and she tossed her head back. She brought one hand behind her to cup my tightening balls.

I quickened my thrusting. So close. She felt too good. I could be inside her forever.

"Mia—" I hissed out her name, wild and panting, as I spilled myself deep inside her. Her pussy pulsed milking every drop out of me as she collapsed onto my chest.

After a few minutes of nothing other than our ragged breaths for sound, she muffled a giggle into my chest.

"What's so funny?" I held her up to my eye level, raising a brow.

"We just had mind-blowing sex on your weight bench." She buried her head back into my chest, still laughing.

"Did I knock something loose in there?" I joked, joining her laughter.

"Maybe you did. I'm losing it." She lifted her head showing a beaming smile and I felt my chest crack open. Seeing her smile was almost as good as fucking her—*almost*. I lifted her, my cock slipping out of her, and scooted myself up so we were both sitting on the bench.

"This is going to need a good wipe down," Mia said as she looked down and swiped a finger over the surface.

"Eh, I kind of like the reminder of how wet I make you." I nuzzled her neck, giving her a nip and a kiss.

"So pervy," she laughed, reaching to pull her hair up. "Come on, let's go get cleaned up and ready for class."

"If you still have energy for class, I'm not doing my job right."

I gave her ass a little smack and followed her upstairs to get cleaned up and dressed, all the while thoroughly enjoying the view.

Every time Mia and I walked through the doors of the gym together, Mark gave me that stupid grin. Smug prick. That's why I loved him like a brother, though.

I led the class through our usual warm-up exercises and stretches before Mark came out to teach. I watched Mia and noticed the changes in her since that first day of class. I knew she still felt some anxiety every day in the hours before she came in, but once she got into her groove, it all melted away. Knowing what really brought her in here changed so much about the way I looked at her. I wouldn't dismiss anyone so easily anymore when they first came through here. You never knew someone else's story, their hardships, or their struggles. Who was I to have passed judgment on others for so long?

I walked around the room helping pairs to correct their form or show tricks to use more power. They were practicing a challenging combination of moves: elbow strikes and knee blows. This group was progressing fantastically.

Mia worked with her friend, Avery. Despite Avery being almost a foot taller than Mia and much more solid, she held her own. I rounded on them, smiling with pride as my girl knocked Avery back a step with her elbow strike.

I whispered into her ear, "I guess you still have energy after all. We'll have to fix that later."

She flushed and huffed a laugh, pushing me away so she could concentrate. Her husky, out of breath laugh had my cock's attention. I needed to go help someone else or I'd have to excuse myself to go make adjustments.

The steady beat of Mark's house music thumped through me as I breathed in the familiar scent of metal, sweat, and mingled deodorants. How was it possible that I could be allowed to feel this content?

I tried to memorize everything in that moment like a snapshot: Mia's breathy laugh, the sound of elbows striking pads, my Krav family grunting and breathing heavily, the smells, and even the way Mark stood in the corner of the room keeping one eye on his students while he held a conversation with Dina about something on her phone.

Dr. Glover had told me it was little moments I was missing out on by not being present. Maybe what he didn't realize was that I just needed a reason to stay in the here and now. I finally had her.

I paired up with Coby for the last drill of the night. Mark had us working on speed, lights out, and drilling combative moves as fast as we could. My pulse thumped like the beat of the music by the time we finished up.

"Gather around," Mark paced at the front of the room. "We have some bad news in our Krav family." Mia's eyes met mine, wide with concern. "About ten minutes ago, Dina got a text from Jill. They've had a house fire."

Murmurs started, as each of our gazes stayed fixed on Mark. "Both Jill and Kayla are fine. Thankfully, it happened while they were at work and school. Jill was on her way home after picking Kayla up from a friend's house. They were going to get changed and head to class but pulled up to firetrucks and rubble."

Mia leaned her head on my shoulder as I rubbed circles on her palm. Jill and Kayla were like family. Everyone here was. I knew Mia felt the same way.

Mark continued, "Dina and I are going to head over to offer support. If anyone wants to join us, you're welcome to."

I could see the emotion that swam over Mark's face and the slump in his shoulders. He was usually a stoic guy, but when something of this nature happened to people he cared about he was the first person to offer help.

"Do you mind if we stop by?" Mia asked, low in my ear. "I want to make sure they're okay."

Squeezing her in a side hug, I nodded. "Of course. We can follow Mark and Dina over."

A few of us made a caravan of sorts following Mark's Jeep the few miles to Jill's house. I looked over at Mia, in the passenger seat, biting her lip and twirling a loose piece of hair around her finger. "It'll be okay, baby. We're all here for them. Try not to worry too much."

Sighing, she squeezed my hand. "I know how hard Jill works to take care of Kayla all on her own. I can't imagine how they're feeling right now."

"I forgot that Jill's a single mom." Truthfully, I didn't know much about anybody at the gym, besides maybe Coby, Mark, and Dina, until Mia came into my life. With her influence, some of the other students have become like family.

"She is. She works two jobs to get by. Krav is the one thing that they splurge on. Although, I'm pretty sure Mark gives them a special rate, but I'm not one hundred percent certain."

That sounded like something Mark would do. He cared about teaching more than he cared about his finances. We were similar in that way, each of us barely knowing how to run the books for our own businesses.

We pulled into a mobile home community on the east side of town. It wasn't the best area, right off the interstate, but from what I could see in the dark, the landscaping was maintained and there was a small clubhouse with a pool for the residents straight ahead that was illuminated by a few blinking street-lights.

The thick, acrid smoke rose in the air. I smelled it before I saw it. We turned onto another street and it was like we had crossed an imaginary boundary into another world. A dense haze lingered in the air making it hard to see even a foot in front of me. My headlights barely cutting through the fog. It was there, straight ahead. Black smoke billowed from the decimated trailer, glowing embers were still being doused by a team of firefighters. My heart pounded the closer we got.

We pulled up, and Mia hopped out of the truck first covering her face with her hand to avoid breathing in the noxious fumes. I sat there taking my time breathing in and out, counting backwards from ten, and pressing my feet firmly into the floor of my truck with my eyes closed. But as soon as I opened them again, there they were—the flashing lights. Red and blue. The low wail rang out from a police car. I opened my door. I needed to be close to Mia to keep her safe.

I stepped out of my truck and the lights and sounds hit me like a ton of bricks. I felt myself slipping away back to the pavement on a sidewalk in Miami.

Where was Mia? I needed to get the hell out of here. I paced in front of the door of my truck. Finally, I leaned my head against the cool glass window. What the fuck did Glover say to do when this happened? I couldn't remember.

Images flooded my mind: Michelle on the ground, red thick blood, ambulances with sirens so loud, cop cars with lights that flared brighter than anything else in the darkness.

I looked up one more time and choked on the lump in my throat that was combined with the ashy taste on my tongue. The people were a blur. A solid mass of bodies illuminated by the red glow of the lights.

My hands shook as I opened the truck door and climbed back inside. *Fuck this shit.* I needed to get out of here. Coughing and sucking in breaths as I tried to calm my racing pulse, I turned the key and sped out of there before I could completely lose myself again.

Chapter 29

Mia

THE STING OF SMOKE in the air burned my nostrils as I followed Dina's small frame toward a group of people. Jill was there clutching a crying Kayla. Their trailer was a smoking mess of charred blackness.

"I'm so sorry, Jill." I said, mournfully, as I gave her shoulder a squeeze. She looked up at me, but I could tell her eyes barely registered the few of us there because of the shock of it all.

Kayla noticed a few of us arriving and wiped her eyes before turning to chat quietly with another teen from our class. Firefighters hauled hoses and circled the building while police officers shuffled around interviewing neighbors and taking notes. I turned to tell Shawn how upsetting this was but realized that he wasn't next to me.

"Shawn?" I hollered over the noise. It was dark and hazy, so it was hard to see. He was right behind me when I got out of the truck, or at least that's what I thought. Jill was repeating something over and over like she was in a trance. "What did you say?" I asked leaning in closer.

"How could this happen? Everything's gone."

My eyes filled with tears. I had no idea what to say. This was a tragedy, and I couldn't imagine how I'd be feeling. I rubbed her shoulder, glancing back every so often to see if I spotted Shawn.

"I'm so sorry, Jill. It'll be okay. We're all here for you."

I don't know how long we stood there watching the crew of workers secure the area. It wasn't until they packed up and left that I realized Shawn must be gone. It wasn't like him to not come find me to at least check in.

"Excuse me for a minute, Jill," I said. Dina took over, quietly talking to Jill with a hand on her shoulder.

I stepped away to call Shawn. Why would he leave without saying anything to me? The line rang and rang until his voicemail picked up. I hung up and dialed again. Still no answer. Something was wrong. I paced, pounding my feet through the pebbled street. My eyes stung, my chest ached, and now I was scared that something had happened to him.

I could have asked Mark and Dina for a ride home, but they were already taking Jill and Kayla home with them. I didn't really know the few other people still lingering around, not enough to get into a car with them.

I called Kendahl. I had no choice. She answered right away.

"Hey girl, sorry to bother you."

"What's wrong?" It was just like her to pick up on something in my voice.

"Nothing. I'm okay. I just need a ride home. I'm stuck without my car."

"Okay." I heard movement in the background. "I'm getting my shoes on. Where are you?"

I gave her the name of the trailer park and she was on her way. Before I rejoined the group, I tried Shawn. Again, no answer. I expected that, but I had hoped otherwise. I shot off a text asking if he was okay.

Mark saw me approaching and came to my side. "He bolted?" I looked up at him with a raised brow, so he added, "Shawn. He left?"

"Yeah, I don't know when, but he's not answering his phone. I'm worried. It's not like him to leave me like that."

Mark crossed his arms over his chest, his colorful rose tattoo gleaming by the light of the above streetlamp. "I could have guessed this would trigger him."

Shit. I was an idiot. I was so caught up and focused on comforting Jill that I hadn't even thought about Shawn having a hard time here.

"Oh God, you're right." The words came out in a croak.

"I don't know how much you know, and it's not my business," Mark ran a hand over his scalp, "but if I had known he was going to come here tonight, I would have stopped him."

"How bad is it?" I already knew how bad it could be after what happened at the country club. But this was something entirely different.

"I'm not really sure." Mark shook his head. "When I first met Shawn there were periods where he would disappear for a few weeks at a time. Dina and I would try to contact him, but he'd usually just send a text letting us know he was alive. He'd show up to the gym after days, or weeks, looking ragged but okay. We learned to just let him be. He always came back around."

I felt my face heat, anger creeping into my gut. Let him be? Seriously? What kind of friend would just let someone they cared about be alone while going through an episode? Images whipped through my mind of Shawn crying alone or pacing his living room. I wasn't that kind of person. He wouldn't be alone through this anymore.

Headlights came into view cutting through the haze. Kendahl's white Tesla pulled up a few feet away.

"That's my ride."

I hugged Jill and Kayla, telling them I'd see them soon. With one last pitied look from Mark, I turned to leave the group.

Kendahl had the air conditioner blasting, and it felt amazing to get out of the sticky heat and the smoky air.

"What the hell happened here?" she looked around, seeing the decimated trailer.

"I'll tell you everything, but first," I huffed a breath, "can we stop by Shawn's house? I need to check on him and grab my car."

She studied my face the clear worry in my eyes. "Yeah, of course. Lead the way."

I alternated between checking my phone every few seconds and staring out the window into the darkness.

Finally, Kendahl broke the silence. "I have some good news. I was waiting to tell you in person."

I hoped it wasn't about Coby and how happy they were. That was one thing I couldn't handle. "Yeah?" I said while keeping my face glued to the window.

"Claudia and I are taking care of Sanders."

Who was Claudia? With my frazzled brain, I couldn't think of anyone with that name. When I didn't respond, Kendahl continued.

"You remember my boss Claudia, right? I introduced you to her that time you stopped by my office. Tall, black hair cut in a short bob, sexy as hell for a lady in her sixties." Kendahl gestured with her right hand, almost whacking me in the shoulder.

Realization set in. "Yes, now I remember her."

"Anyway. After I told Claudia everything, she took it upon herself to dig up information on Mr. Muscle Fitness gyms and we struck a PR goldmine when we found Sanders' ex-wife."

That had me whipping my head toward her. "What did she say?"

Kendahl laughed, sounding almost like a cartoon villain. She scared me sometimes. "She gave up some juicy gossip about her dear ex-husband. A little something about insurance fraud and sweeping employee HR complaints under the rug. Once I got her chatting, she didn't stop. Apparently, Sanders did her dirty in the divorce and she's out for blood."

"What's that quote again? 'Hell hath no fury like a woman scorned'?" I asked, letting the news perk me up momentarily.

"Exactly." Kendahl reached across the console and held my hand. "Don't worry Mi, everything will work out in the end."

"Thank you for taking care of this." I couldn't agree with her but the distracting conversation helped me to not focus on Shawn for a few minutes.

Shawn's truck was in the driveway when we pulled up to his house. Thank God, at least he went right home. I gave Kendahl a quick kiss on the cheek and promised her I'd call her in the morning.

I had one thought in my mind as I sprinted up the front walkway to the door; Was Shawn okay? I had no idea what kind of mindset he'd be in. Clearly, it wasn't good, or I was sure he would have answered my calls and texts.

The motion-activated porch light kicked on. I had gotten used to being outside in the darkness all night; the light felt jarring. I rang the bell once, then twice. After a minute or two of waiting, I knocked—banged against the heavy wooden door. Remy barked loudly from inside the door.

Dammit Shawn, open up!

There was no doormat or fake rock with a hideaway key any-where to be seen. Shawn was way too concerned about security to leave his home vulnerable like that. I was not going to give up easily, so I banged again and again. Calling his phone in between bouts of banging on the door. My face was red, and every inch of my body was sticky with sweat, but I didn't care. He could push me out as much as he wanted to, but I wouldn't just lay down and let him.

With my phone on speaker, I finally slumped down onto the front step, giving my assault on the door a rest. His number rang and rang until I heard his brief voicemail pick up. I hung up and called again. I wished I knew what else to do. I could try to climb in the back, but again, I knew Shawn and his ritual of locking everything up like a prison. Maybe I should go home. Was that really what he needed right now?

I thought of Livvy kicking me out of her bedroom all those years ago, *"Just leave Mimi"*. It had killed me to leave her side back then. How could I leave Shawn now? This man who I was falling in love with.

My resolve sharpened. I pushed up from the hard step and went back to banging on the door. After what felt like another hour, I heard movement.

"Shawn?" I yelled, my face nearly flat against the door.

The scraping of a lock had me stepping back. He opened the door an inch and I took a sharp breath in. His eyes were completely bloodshot and swollen as if he'd been crying the entire night. His hair looked as though he'd dragged his hands through it over and over.

"Mia, please. You need to go." He spoke so quietly I could barely make out his words.

Tears slid down my cheeks. "Please, let me be with you. I can help, Shawn. You don't have to go through this alone anymore." I wiped my face with the back of my hand and tried to calm myself. I was here for him; I needed to keep it together.

He shook his head, shoulders slumped and head slung so low that his eyes didn't meet mine. I stepped closer to the door, reaching out and trying to hold him. He looked up into my eyes for just a second before rasping out, "Goodbye, Mia," and shut the door in my face.

I stood there, stunned. Did Shawn really close the door in my face when he clearly needed comfort? Maybe Mark was right. Maybe he knew Shawn best.

I shook my head. Resignation taking over. It went against every fiber of my being to leave him here like this. He looked and sounded like a wounded animal.

Breathing deeply, I gave in and fished my keys out of my purse. I climbed into my car to head back to my apartment. Was it possible that just a few hours ago, Shawn and I were completely fine? Better than fine, we were over the moon happy. Is this what a life with Shawn would be like? Would he constantly shut me out whenever a situation triggered him?

I navigated the dark roads, my mind whirling. Could I really have a future where I was on eggshells like this all the time? And what if I didn't even have a choice and Shawn shut me out for good? All these questions and more cycled through my head, pinging around like marbles against a wall. I made it back to my apartment on autopilot, going through familiar motions without registering anything at all.

After I finally showered away the grime that covered my body and was laying down in bed, I sent off one last text to Shawn.

Me: *Please, just let me know that you're okay. I care about you. I want to be there for you. You don't have to go through this alone.*

I turned over in bed, pulling my comforter up to my ears and forcing my eyes to close. Pictures of Shawn's tear-stained face filled my head as I fell into a fitful sleep.

Chapter 30

Shawn

I'D STAYED AWAKE ALL night alternating between pacing the floors and laying there staring up at the ceiling. Sun streamed into my bedroom window. The worst of it was over now. I inhaled a shaky breath that didn't quite reach my chest. I had known I wouldn't sleep last night. Every time this happened, closing my eyes only made it ten times worse. I'd see flashes of lights or hear sirens in my head. It would replay over and over like a never-ending circuit from hell.

Then there was Mia. She was relentless last night. I knew I did the right thing by

sending her away. I was a fucking lunatic, and she didn't need to see me like that. Hell, she was too good for me to begin with, and I'd been a selfish prick to not let her go earlier.

I had to do it, though. For her own good.

My phone was lying on the floor of my bedroom discarded. I powered it on with shaking hands, willing myself not to think too much about what I was about to write.

Me: *Mia, I'm breaking up with you. I can't be what you need me to be. This is what a life with me would be like... never knowing what will set me off. I'm fucked up and you don't deserve that.*

After powering my phone back off, I laid back on my cold sheets forcing my eyes closed. Finally, I saw nothing but blackness, sleep pulled me under like a good friend and I succumbed to it.

I woke to Remy nudging me with his head. "I know, I know, boy, you need to go out."

Darkness shrouded the house again. I must have slept all day. Sitting up, I took a moment to stretch. It felt like someone else had inhabited my body for the last twenty-four hours. My shoulders were stiff as a board, and my head throbbed.

Remy whined and gave me a look like he was about to do something he really didn't want to do. I jumped up and jogged down the stairs to open the back door for him to do his business. The poor guy. I had no idea when I last let him out. I vaguely remembered feeding him at some point this morning.

Just coming downstairs had me ready to go back to bed. I hadn't felt this drained in a long time. I let Remy back in and filled his food and water dishes. Glancing at the kitchen, I briefly thought about eating something too, but I had no appetite and cooking took more energy than I had, so I dragged my sorry ass back upstairs into my bedroom.

I should call Dr. Glover. He always said I could call him anytime. What would he really be able to do for me, though? I'm not in an active attack anymore, so I didn't need him to talk me off a ledge. He'd just give me another pep talk and try to get me to "stop punishing myself" and "live my life." Why should I get to live a normal life when Michelle was dead, and it was all my fault?

I didn't need to drag a beautiful woman like Mia down with me. She was so full of life, and ready for things I couldn't give her. Things like a normal relationship, maybe even marriage, and a family one day.

My phone seemed to stare at me, beckoning me to turn it on to see if she responded. Of course she would have, this was Mia, my fiery girl. I hadn't seen the meek and awkward Mia in a while. I hoped I was harsh enough to finally get her to see that I wasn't worth her time or her love.

I closed my eyes again, letting myself sink into bed. I tried not to think of Mia's beautiful body lying here with me not so long ago. Damn, it was going to hurt to lose her, but I'd do anything I needed to so she could have a happy life.

Chapter 31

Mia

It's been ten days. Two hundred and forty torturous hours since Shawn ended things. To say I've been going insane would be an understatement. I've tried calling. I've texted a hundred times. I've gone there and even sent Coby over, too.

Nothing.

He won't speak to anyone. While Mark says this is normal for him, I refuse to accept that and just sit by like all is well. But other than sending the fire department over to break down his door, there's really nothing else I could do.

I pushed my chair back from my desk, gazing out the window at the people passing by below. It was almost time to get out of here for the weekend. I desperately needed a day without Lungberg on my back or the cold shoulder I'd be given by everyone else.

Ever since the golf incident, Lungberg's been even more horrible toward me. He tells me daily that I ruined the biggest event of the year, and that I lost us an important client.

He's spread so many rumors about what happened that day that no one in the office but Jared will speak with me. Cathy hasn't even tried to show me any pictures of her grandchildren all week.

I turned back to my computer screen as I was needing to finish up a few forms before heading out to the gym. Jared was perched on the side of my desk, his kind eyes looking down at me. As much as I loved him, I didn't need his pity right now.

"Hey girl, you want to walk out together?"

"I need a few more minutes here." I stayed focused on my spreadsheet.

"Okay, I'll wait." He was using his placating voice, the same one he always used on Lungberg. It shouldn't piss me off, but it did. Yeah, I looked like an absolute mess. I had bags under my eyes, and I hadn't put on makeup or done anything with my hair in days. I almost wish I hadn't told him about things ending with Shawn.

"I may be a while. You can go." He leveled his eyes down at me, waiting for me to say more, before finally shrugging.

"If that's what you want. But you're not going to get off that easily. We will be talking about this," he gestured to me with his hand, "shit that's going on. I love you, girly, and I'm not about to let my office bestie drag herself into a downward spiral."

"I'm fine, Jared." I shook my head. "It's just been a long week."

"Well, you better call me later. You know I won't be dismissed this easily."

He turned on his heels, went back to his desk, and began to pack for the weekend. Normally, I'd find his sassiness charming, but today he had rubbed my last nerve.

Thank God it was almost time to zone out and punch pads.

Almost an hour later, as I was packing up, Lungberg surprised me by coming out of his office. I hadn't even realized he was still in there.

"Miss Murphy, I see you're still here. Good, good." He drawled, puffing his chest out.

I gestured down at the folded laptop in my hands. "I was actually on my way out." I hated being in such close quarters with him, especially this late, when Jared had already left.

"Yes, well before you go, I wanted to alert you to a change. I received a call from our client from the golf event, the one that you caused a scene with." My stomach dropped. "He's willing to keep us as his accounting firm, even after that whole mishap. He wants to come in on Monday and discuss his business with us in person. I scheduled him for eleven. I'd like you to apologize to him directly."

He couldn't be serious.

"Sir," I started slowly, knowing if I didn't think about each word out of my mouth, I would combust. "There is no way on earth that I ever want to look at that man again. He…" the words struggled to come out. "He tried to assault me."

Lungberg chuckled. He actually freaking laughed. "I'm sure it was all just a misunderstanding. You know how some men get when they have a few drinks in them. He assured me he meant you no harm. No charges were pressed against him. You can't treat the man like a criminal when he's done nothing wrong in the eyes of the law."

My mouth dropped open. Words tried to form, but they stumbled on my lips. This was exactly what was wrong with society. I didn't press charges because I couldn't, or Shawn would have gone to jail too. There was no point in explaining this to Lungberg. Clearly he didn't care about my safety or my well-being. I'd known that for years, but I'd still held out hope that maybe he'd retire soon, and I'd finally get to move up.

Enough was enough.

I took a step forward and stood up to my full height. "You know what, Lungberg, you're right. I can't treat him like a criminal." Lungberg's face relaxed into a lazy grin. "Because he's more than that. He's a predator. A vulture who preys on innocent women. He physically assaulted me, and if I hadn't had the means to protect myself, who knows what would have happened? If these are the clients you want to work with, then I'm done. I've put up with enough from you for years, and never complained once, but I draw the line at having to smile and apologize to my attacker."

His puffed-up chest deflated, and his eyes widened. The redness of his face crept up about three more shades toward a violet hue. "If you walk out of here, good luck finding another job in this county. Remember, Mia, I have friends in high places."

I began walking down the hallway. Halfway toward the elevator, I turned and forced my lips into a confident grin. "Fuck you. Fuck your friends. I quit."

I strutted out of there, head held high, ignoring whatever snide remarks he was hollering behind me. As I got into my car, I dug out my phone to call Shawn. He'd be so proud of me for finally sticking it to that asshole. But then I remembered and immediately slumped.

Telling Lungberg where to stick it had felt too good to let anything else bring me down. There was no room for more internal pity parties. I dialed Kendahl instead and gave her the play-by-play as I made my way over to the gym feeling like a total badass.

The gym was busy for a Friday evening class. I saw Jill and Kayla, talking with Evie, Anna, and Jake, and went to join them. It was the first night Jill and Kayla had been back since the fire.

"Hey everyone," I stood next to Jill to give her a side arm hug. "I'm happy to see you both back."

"Thanks," she smiled at me, but it didn't quite reach her eyes. "We were just talking about the shitshow that has been my week. I never realized how much paperwork and phone calls were involved after a house fire."

"I can't even imagine." On top of that, Jill was a single Mom who couldn't take off from her job for long or rely on a second income to help get them back on their feet. I wondered if there was something we could do to help them.

"You're welcome to stay with us as long as you need to," Anna chimed in. "I don't want you worrying about a place to stay."

"I appreciate you both." Jill gave her a grateful smile. "It helps that your place is close to Kayla's school. Once the insurance company gets to work and these loans I'm trying to get pan out, we'll be out of your hair."

The wheels in my head spun. I had looked into different grants and scholarships after Olivia had Alex and was thinking about going to college. There had to be some kind of aid for victims of house fires, especially for those who were single mothers. I didn't want to say anything yet, not without checking for myself.

With my newfound resolve to help Jill and Kayla filling my mind, I only checked the door once instead of the ten times I'd done all week searching for a familiar light brown head of hair.

I pushed out the doors coated in sweat and breathing heavily. Class was grueling, we worked in groups of four on ground fighting and other combative moves. I didn't get much time to speak to Jill, but I was able to pull Mark and Dina aside and let them know what I was thinking. We made plans to have lunch on Sunday and brainstorm some other ways to help them.

That left me sitting at home, all alone, on a Friday night. The upside was I could order in junk food and wear my most raggedy T-shirt while I researched aid for Jill and thought over fundraising ideas. On the downside, I'd much rather do this snuggled up next to Shawn's warm chest. I checked my phone for any sign from him. Just like the past ten days, the only notifications I had were the two thousand unread junk messages in my email box.

Should I text him again? I felt like a pathetic stalker, but it was too difficult not to reach out. His breakup text was absurd. The more I reread it, the angrier I got. I knew this would happen eventually, didn't I? I would open up and put myself out there, only to be found lacking. He said it's him, not me, that he's the fucked up one. Clearly, he didn't think I was the one, or he'd have let me in. We'd have worked through his past together.

I never thought getting ghosted would be the last nail in the coffin. In my mind, I expected something more dramatic, like finding out the guy I loved had started a whole other family in the Midwest somewhere—maybe Idaho. Or that he was leading an entire double life and was some sort of Mafia leader who killed and kidnapped people while only pretending to sell insurance. We'd have this huge fight where I'd slap him in the face and storm out, saying, "How could you? I gave you my heart!" in a voice that sounded like Scarlett O'Hara's at the end of *Gone with the Wind*. Maybe I've watched too many movies to feel like breakups should be a huge show of dramatics.

But being shut out completely? It's pretty much the most anticlimactic way to end a relationship, if you could even call what Shawn and I had that. Experience with relationships or not I knew that much to be true. We certainly had a spark. My face heated thinking about our last time together. I'd never look at a workout bench the same way again.

Without giving it another thought, I sent off one last text. If he answered me, great. If not, I was done reaching out. I needed to embrace this new version of myself that included telling Lungberg to fuck off with gusto and knowing my worth in a relationship.

Me: *Hey, me again. I don't know if you're even looking at these messages. This will be the last time I reach out. I'm sorry things had to end this way. You got your wish.*

Tears streamed down my face. *Come on Mia, be the strong independent woman that lives deep inside of you.* I hit send through a blurry mess of tears. There. I said my piece and now the ball was in his court entirely.

As I curled up in my bed, trying to make myself comfortable enough to get a few hours' sleep, I couldn't help but go over every detail of my time with Shawn in my mind. I really hoped I didn't just make a huge mistake in sending that text message.

Chapter 32

Mia

I woke up with a yearning to see my sister. Maybe our heart-to-heart awakened that part of me again. I'd shoved the need for her love and guidance down so deep after her attack that this feeling was foreign.

Kendahl had been giddy lately due to her budding relationship with Coby. I knew that she hurt for me when I told her Shawn ended things, but I didn't want to drag her down. She'd been through enough and deserved to be happy. No, it was Livvy that I needed.

I rolled over in bed to check the time on my phone. The light streaming through my window told me it was late enough to call her. That and the scent of Mrs. Vega's Saturday tamales seeping through our shared wall. She always made a few vegetarian ones just for me. I brightened, thinking of how sweet she was.

I clicked on Olivia's name deciding against FaceTime and opting for a regular call. "Mimi?" her voice cracked. "Is everything okay?"

I drew a breath in. Think of Mrs. Vega again. Bringing the tamales. Do not think about Shawn. It was no use. Hearing Livvy's voice opened the floodgates. I shuddered feeling salty tears leak out of my eyes.

"What happened? Do you need me to come over?" I could picture Livvy's brows furrowed with the crease in the middle of her forehead deepening. Our mother made the same look in the rare times she showed concern. Only she didn't have a crease anymore, thanks to Botox.

"No," I hesitated. "But can I come over?"

I heard her stirring on the line. "Of course. Are you sure you can drive?"

Nodding even though I knew she couldn't see me, I answered, "I'll be fine. I just," my voice wavered, "need to talk."

"I'll see if Mom can watch Alex for a bit. Come on over. I'll get coffee ready."

I moved around my apartment slipping on one of my T-shirt dresses, sliding my feet into flip-flops, and collecting my things. I said, "Make it strong. Be there in a bit."

Somehow, I made it to the estate bleary-eyed with my stomach in knots. It felt unnatural to go to Olivia when I was a mess like this. Between the years of my parents conditioning me not to bother her and my own instincts yelling that she needed me and not the other way around, I couldn't believe I made it here without changing my mind and turning around.

The salty ocean air filled my nose, calming my racing heart as I rang the bell to the main house. I realized too late that I should have gone directly to the guest house. Carla cracked open the door just enough to get a look at me. Her eyes widened as she took me in before stepping back to fully open the door.

"Miss Mia," she clutched her chest. "You gave me a fright. I thought to myself, who would come this early besides more of those people wanting trouble?"

People? What people? Had reporters found my parents all the way out here?

"But then I saw you and my heart went back to normal." She brought her arm around me and gave me a side hug. She smelled of lemons, sugar, and sunshine. "Everything okay? Your mama is upstairs. But your papa, he's out back."

I hesitated, wanting to tell her that I wasn't here for my parents. But the side hug she had me in was more like a death grip as she dragged me out back depositing me directly in front of my father. He looked up from his newspaper, his glasses perched on the edge of his nose. "Mia? What on earth are you doing here this early?"

He dropped the paper onto the table in front of him and appraised me. By the curl of his lip, he most definitely found me lacking. I shifted from one foot to the other glancing back toward Carla. I didn't know what to say to him. I never did. I'd usually follow Olivia's lead, or stay silent like a good, obedient girl, and hope that, maybe, I would get graced with an approving nod from him.

"You look a mess. What's going on? Did the paparazzi find you, too?" He stood up while lifting a shaking hand to push the glasses back up his nose. "I knew it was only a matter of time before they'd find me here."

Of course, he thought this was all about him. It was always about him. His career. His election year. His reputation. He never cared about us. Not me. Not Livvy. Not Mom. She was a pawn to him. A trophy wife, so we could look like the perfect little country club family. I could feel my face redden and my nostrils flared wide. I was tired of all the men in my life thinking everything was about them.

"No. I'm not here for you. Believe it or not, everything isn't always about you, Dad." I gritted my teeth. I could feel the anger bubbling to the surface like a Band-Aid being ripped off slowly. That bandage needed to come off. The festering wound underneath needed air to heal.

"You wouldn't know, Mia," my father assessed me with his eyes narrowed, "but I am in a crisis here. I don't need your childish tantrums. Your mother is upstairs. Go find her."

Assuming we were done, he reached out for his mug of coffee. I wasn't about to let him dismiss me that easily.

"No wonder Mom cheated on you. You're nothing but a selfish prick who uses his family. God forbid anything wreck Neil Murphy's image." My voice shook as I stared at him with cold rage. "You disgust me." I watched him choke mid-sip, coughing up droplets onto his white polo shirt.

"You have no idea what you're talking about and no idea what I've done for this family." He hacked into his hand again.

"I know enough." I clenched my fists. "You're camping out here in Florida. Biding your time. You're hoping to brush mom's affair under the rug, just like you did with Olivia's situation."

My chest heaved. I'd wanted to say those words to my father for ten years. They've brewed and churned in my chest for so long that it was like they were a part of me. They were a growth that gnawed on my soul, holding me down from the weight on them.

"You ruined everything. Why didn't you protect her? Why didn't you do the right thing by her?" My shoulders slumped, gravity pulling me down. I dropped myself onto the couch opposite him, not meeting his eyes. Anger was turning to sorrow and for the second time that day, I cried into my hands.

My father was silent. I couldn't see his face through my tears, but I knew he hadn't moved an inch. I let the sound of seabirds pull me back to the here and now breathing in the salty air through my clogged nostrils.

If it hadn't been so quiet, I might not have heard him speak.

"Is that what you really think of me?" Wiping my eyes, I could see him clearly. His head was down, a grimace lined his lips. "Mia, you may not understand the reasons behind every decision I've made but trust me on this." He swallowed hard enough for me to see his Adam's apple bob. "When it came to what happened to your sister, I had her best interest in mind."

"Right?" I huffed a laugh. "Because you and your election had nothing to do with it?"

He was full of shit. Nothing he did was for us. He wasn't man enough to let us decide what we wanted. Just like Shawn didn't let me decide if I wanted to be with him or not. He made that decision for me.

He raked a shaking hand through his hair. "I won't lie and say that my election had nothing to do with it. But what you don't understand, what you could never understand, was if what happened to your sister got out—she'd always be *that* girl. It would have made national news. Judge Murphy's daughter who was raped in the woods."

I choked on a breath hearing him use the word rape.

"She'd never be able to move on. And God forbid, Alex learned one day. Don't you see? I did what I did for Olivia. For our family. Your mother and I agreed it was what was best. You were a child, a girl... you were hurting for your sister. I knew you wouldn't understand." His ears turned crimson as he took a small sip of coffee.

I tried to see it from his point of view. Yes, it would have made the news since our family was in the spotlight. And yes, Olivia would have been outed. Instead of her assuming that her classmates had known she was different, stained... they would have known for sure.

Had I been wrong? This was not the conversation I imagined I'd be having after holding onto this pain for so long. Did my parents make the right choice? Olivia herself didn't harbor the pain and fear that I did anymore. From what she'd told me, she'd moved on with her life. Maybe I should too?

Numbness crept through my body settling into my gut. "I don't know Dad. I feel like nothing makes sense anymore."

I lifted myself up off the couch. There was nothing more to say to my father. Not today. Maybe he made the right choice in doing nothing for my sister? But I wasn't ready to accept that, let alone voice those words to him.

If I gave up everything I've ever believed about my family, then what would be left of me? It felt like I was resigning myself to it being okay for my father to make those decisions for Olivia, okay for Shawn to push me out, okay for Lungberg to have treated me the way he did for years.

I passed Carla making a fruit salad in the kitchen. My mouth watered at the scent of ripe strawberries and juicy pineapple. I barely registered her talking to me as I walked out the side door and down the path lined with hibiscus trees toward the guest house where I knew Livvy would be.

She greeted me with arms wide open enveloping me in a warm hug that I hadn't known I desperately needed until that moment. She smelled of lavender and mint, and the earthy scent of coffee floated through the open door. I let loose a sob into her chest and it went on and on until there were no tears left to be shed. All the while she rubbed my back, whispering comforting words onto my shoulder. We could have stood there for an hour for all I knew.

When I finally felt calmer, like I'd expelled every surge of emotion from my body, Livvy sat me down in the tiny sitting area of the one-bedroom guest house. A soft song I didn't recognize played quietly in the background. I sank into the plush armchair and savored a sip of coffee that Olivia fixed me just how I liked it.

"Wait..." I sipped again to confirm my suspicion, "did you add a sprinkle of cinnamon? I can't believe you remembered."

"Of course, I remembered." She twirled a finger through a lock of hair, smiling. "You started making your coffee like that in fifth grade." She sipped her steaming mug. "Way too early to be consuming coffee if you ask me. Maybe that's why you stayed such a teeny thing."

"Ha-ha, hilarious." I felt myself crack a real smile. The first one of the day.

We talked and drank, and I felt more alive with each precious sip. I told Olivia everything that had happened in the past week. How Shawn broke up with me by pushing me away. About Lungberg and my last straw at work. And quietly, I told her about the conversation, or outburst, with our father. She listened intently, gasping when I told her about Lungberg, and offering a sorrowful apology when it came to Shawn.

Once I rehashed the conversation with our father, she sat up, chewing her bottom lip.

"Mimi." Her expression paled. "I never told you this. But they asked me what I wanted to do that day, in my room. And again, after we found out I was pregnant."

"They did?" I set my mug down, heat flooding to my face.

"They did. And I told them I didn't want to do anything. I didn't want the world to know." She lifted her chin meeting my eyes. "I'm sorry I never told you. Back then, I needed you to be angry for me. I was so empty inside. I couldn't feel anything. All I knew was I wanted to disappear inside myself. I wouldn't have been able to do that if they dragged my name through the mud. I just—I'm sorry for what my choices have done to you."

This day was too much. I knew my sister didn't harbor the same anger I did. She had told me as much the last time I saw her. But I never would have guessed that she was the one who wanted to cover up what happened to her. God, I was an idiot. I sat there, mouth open, not knowing what to say. I closed my eyes to process what she had said. As if blocking out what was in front of me would help me sort through her words.

"Mimi, talk to me. I'm sorry. I just want to see you happy. Whether it's with Shawn or someone else, or by yourself. I need to see you happy again. Don't let what happened to me keep you from living your life to the fullest."

"Yeah," I acquiesced. "I need to process everything. That's all. You have nothing to be sorry for, Liv."

She steered the conversation back toward neutral ground as she was pulling out two yogurts and a bowl of strawberries from the fridge for us to munch on. I'd come here for nothing more than comfort and would leave here with revelations that have rocked my world.

Once my head cleared and food settled into my stomach, I realized I hadn't seen Alex around. "Hey, where's the little guy?"

Between spoonfuls of yogurt, Livvy answered, "He's a few houses over playing with a girl he met the other day. Actually, I have good news."

"I could use some of that right about now." I curled my feet under me and sat up straighter.

"I got a job." She squeaked the words out so high, I almost jumped. "It's a waitressing job, but between that and my savings we should be able to make do. I start next week. That's the house Alex is playing at, my new boss' house. He has a daughter who comes over on the weekends."

"I'm so happy for you!" I screeched. "Now I'll get to see my sissy and my Alex whenever I want. I can't wait to hear more about this job. Maybe you'll get to work in the kitchen too sometimes? You used to love to cook and bake. Do you still?"

I felt pathetic that I didn't know this much about my own sister, but we were changing that. Strained relationship be gone.

"I do. When I have time. When we eat with Mom and Dad everything is catered. But one of my best friends back at home was our in-house chef for a few years, so she taught me a thing or two." She blushed while adjusting herself in her chair.

I was so happy for her, and for myself. I had my sister back. Moving would be great for them. They'd have a fresh start, away from my parents. I'd have to get her to join Krav too. Baby steps, I was still working on Kendahl.

I left Olivia's place an hour later feeling like my emotions went through a laundry cycle. Everything was so jumbled up that I could hardly think. I was still upset and angry about Shawn. The thought of his breakup text message sent my pulse pounding. I didn't know what to feel about my revelations regarding my father and Livvy. Some bitterness, maybe relief that he wasn't the evil villain I had made him out to be for years.

I had a headache the size of Miami. At least with Olivia moving here, I had something happy to focus on. That and the fact that I no longer had to look at Lungberg's meaty red face anymore.

Back home, sweet Mrs. Vega knocked at my door, as expected, and hand-delivered some tamales with a kiss to each cheek. I settled on the couch with my plate and tucked my feet underneath me.

As exhausted as I was, helping a friend in need would make this awful, crazy week so much better. Research would help clear my head. I switched into accountant-Mia mode, and went to work typing and googling away on my laptop. Whether Shawn came to his senses was neither here nor there. I had other things on my plate. If he asked for my help and admitted his mistakes, then maybe I'd consider speaking to him again. But, for now, I would stuff myself full of tamales and focus on the bits of good in my life.

Chapter 33

Mia

"What if we planned a street fair?"

Dina and Mark both looked up at me, their eyes wide and questioning. We were sitting out on their beautiful back patio on Sunday afternoon, sipping margaritas and munching on chips and salsa. Dina with pad and pen in front of her, and Mark with his phone out while we tossed out different ideas to help raise money for Jill.

"What exactly are you picturing?" Mark asked, mid-chip crunch.

I took a sip of my frosty beverage. "I was thinking we can ask some local businesses to set up booths where they'd contribute a percentage of every sale to Jill's fund. I'm sure a few restaurants in town would get in on it, too. We can even find someone to play live music."

Dina stopped taking notes. "That sounds brilliant, Mia. You can count on us. We can set up a booth and do mini self-defense lessons. Maybe even raffle off a few memberships?" She looked at Mark for support, and he nodded, grinning.

"That would be amazing." I was getting giddy at the prospect of making this happen for Jill. If we could pull it off, it would be life changing for her.

"There's only one problem," Mark said between chips. "None of us have the time to go door to door around town soliciting businesses."

"Leave that to me." I had figured they'd bring that up. "You two just worry about your booth and I'll handle the rest. I already ran the numbers and made a few spreadsheets. I also contacted a couple of organizations and signed Jill up for some grants this morning. I should hear back within the next few days, but I know she'll qualify."

"You're an angel," Dina said, handing me the notebook. "You'll need this then."

"Thanks." I grinned at her. "To be honest, I quit my job the other day, and I'd love nothing more than to use my free time for some good. It'll help me as much as it'll help them."

"Was you quitting your job the right decision for you?" Mark asked.

"Best decision I've made in a long time." I beamed back at him.

"Cheers to that." Dina lifted her glass.

"Cheers." We clinked glasses. "And cheers to helping Jill and Kayla and setting up a cool town event that everyone will love."

Mark smacked his lips after he swallowed down half his drink. "I never cease to amaze myself," sipping the last drops, he puffed up his chest, "teacher, business owner, bartender—just call me Jack."

Dina raised a brow. "Jack-o'-lantern, you mean, because your head is the size of a pumpkin." She swatted him playfully and drained her glass, too. "You have a point about making good drinks, though."

Watching them tease each other should have made me smile, but it was almost too much for me to handle. They must have seen it on my face. "Have you heard anything from the other pumpkin head we all love?" she asked, grasping my hand in hers.

"No, not a word. I don't know. I'll have to move on." I didn't want to discuss this with them, but the words came tumbling out of my mouth like rocks rolling down a hill. "I really thought we had something special."

Dina turned to Mark and gave him a sad smile. "I wouldn't give up on him yet. I can't tell you what to do with your life, but we've known Shawn for a long time and there's not a better guy out there. He just needs someone with a lot of patience and understanding."

"I can read people like a book," Mark added. "It's one of my many talents." He waggled his brows. "Anyway, we can see that you're good for each other. You do have something special."

"Mark's right, which is something you'll rarely hear come out of my mouth," Dina said. I tried to turn my grimace into an actual smile. "Don't give up on him, yet. At least until you've heard the full story."

They're right that he hasn't really told me much about his past. It's always been a conversation that he's pushed aside for later.

I propped my elbows on the table and let my head rest in my hands. "Could you guys tell me even just a piece of the story?" I knew it was wrong to ask as soon as the question came out of my mouth, but I was curious and upset at how things were going.

Dina shook her head. "Listen, I would tell you everything if I didn't think what you and Shawn had was real. But it should come from him. Trust us, just give him time."

A sigh slipped out of my lips. "I hear you guys, and I want to give him all the time in the world to open up, but I don't like being ghosted and pushed away like this."

"I understand." Dina squeezed my hand lovingly. The gesture had me holding back tears.

"How about another drink?" Mark stood up, making his way over to the bar. "There's no way anyone can be sad while drinking one of my margarita masterpieces."

He was right. The rest of the afternoon went by with a series of funny stories about Mark and Dina's past, and more plans for the street festival. By the time I got home that evening, after sobering up on their couch, I had almost forgotten all about the empty hole that sat in my chest where my heart used to be.

By the next Friday, Jared and I had successfully signed up over thirty businesses for our charity festival. Jared had quit his job immediately after I did. When I apologized to him for how I'd been acting and we had a heart-to-heart talk about Shawn, he forgave me right away and offered his assistance. I don't know how I would have pulled this off without him. We made a damn good team.

We set the festival for the following weekend, which gave us only a week to set up a stage and finish obtaining the necessary permits with the town. Kendahl pulled her magical PR strings for me to expedite some of the red tape. She even managed to get one of the local bands she represents to agree to play the event for free. I felt so lucky I could burst. I couldn't wait until Jill and Kayla saw everything. Mark, Dina, and I had agreed to keep the plan a secret from her until the day of. I hoped she wasn't one of those people who hated surprises, because this would be a doozy.

While I was midway through planning one day, my phone rang. My mother was calling me. It was odd since we'd already had our obligatory catch-up conversation for the week.

"Mom?" I answered the phone and closed my laptop so I could focus.

"Hello Mia." I heard her swallow. "I've been thinking of our last conversation and about how you're helping that woman. Your friend." Her voice went up an octave.

"Yes, I'm running a charity street fair. What about it?" I was utterly confused. I hadn't realized my mother was actually listening to me when we spoke last.

"I spoke to your father, and we'd like to pledge $5,000 to your fund. We think what you're doing is," she sucked in an audible breath, "honorable."

Was I getting dizzy? Maybe my body was going into shock? Did she just say $5,000?

"Wow, Mom, that's... ah... amazing." I stuttered. "Thank you."

I chewed my lip for a moment contemplating my next words.

"How's everything going? I mean, with Dad and the umm... issue?" Scandal was more like it. What I wanted to say was, are you a lesbian now? Are you in love with that Senator woman? Should I prepare myself for a second mom? I would never come right out and ask my mother those things.

She hesitated, but then spoke in her normal, overly formal voice. "It is going as well as can be expected. Your father and I have agreed to separate, amicably. It's what's best. As far as the issue goes. Time will tell. We hope by the fall when we head back to New York, everything will have been forgotten."

I covered my mouth with the palm of my hand. My parents were going to get a divorce? I never thought they would have it in them. Maybe they'd stop being miserable shells of people after all.

"I hope everything works out for the best too, Mom. Thank you again for the donation. You and Dad are more than welcome to come to the festival. You can let loose and have some fun. It would be good for you."

I could picture her raised brow and her reaching to smooth out an invisible wrinkle on her blouse. She had never let loose before, but maybe this new affair-having version of her had some other skeletons hidden in her closet.

"I'll think about it. Look for a check in the mail. Have a good day, Mia."

When I ended the call I thought maybe, just maybe, there was hope for that woman. She could be happy for the first time in years, away from my father and his politics. If there was hope for her, there could be some for me too.

When I awoke on the day of the event, excitement bubbled in my chest. The sky was clear blue without a cloud to be seen. Scorching sunlight surged through my car windows making me wish I could control the weather. This is what I was missing all those years when Lungberg had been sucking the life out of me and treated me like garbage. I was running numbers and using my accounting skills, but this time, for a noble cause. If I could do this every day, I'd live a fulfilled life.

I parked my car and walked over to the blocked off Main Street. Showtime was in a few hours, and I had a ridiculous amount of work to still do. I tied my hair up on top of my head in a bobbing, messy bun and adjusted my teal sundress. It was time to make magic happen. I just hoped we had the turnout that we needed in this heat.

Chapter 34

Shawn

My phone had been going off for hours. Dina, Mark, Coby, and every other person who had my number practically begging me to go to some street festival that was going on today. I was changing my number as soon as I got the energy to leave the house. They were explicitly ignoring my rule to not call or text unless it was an emergency. I scrolled, passing Mia's unopened messages and opened the pdf that Dina had sent in her message. I figured I'd see what all the fuss was about.

If I spoke to Mia, or even opened that text box, I'd lose all my resolve and beg her to take me back. I missed her so much. When she banged at my door all those times, I'd had to go upstairs and shut the door to keep myself from giving in. I'd stare at the wall, each pounding knock reverberating through my nerve wracked body and will myself to ignore her. If I let myself get close enough to the door, I would've wrapped her in my arms and never let her leave again.

My screen lit up with a colorful graphic. The bold headline read ***Main Street Charity Festival*** and underneath in purple lettering *Shop, Eat, and Dance for a good cause.* There were pictures of a band, tacos, ice cream, one of those inflatable water slides, and jewelry scattered around under the headings. What the hell was the good cause? And why was every single person I knew going apeshit over it?

I propped myself up in bed, shoving a pillow behind my head, and texted Dina back.

Me: *Looks great. Can't make it, too busy with work.*

There. She couldn't argue with me when it came to work. Of course, that was utter bullshit since I had pushed off every one of my deadlines for another two weeks. I was skating on thin ice with a few of the clients, but most of them had used us since Gramps was alive and they knew we ran a small operation.

However, that didn't stop Camila from riding my ass. She wasn't thrilled when I texted her that I had to lay her off for the time being and that I'd contact her when I needed her again. She practically banged my door down after that. Just like Mia.

Fuck, I didn't need to think about Mia. I bet she would be at this festival thing. Maybe she'd even have a date. I buried my head into my pillow as I thought about her probably wearing one of her flowy sundresses. Like the one that showed off her tanned shoulders and delicate collarbone. Her hair would be up in a bun, beads of sweat on the back of her neck, and tiny curls escaping her hair tie as she walked. She'd be hand in hand with some other lucky bastard, and he'd buy her an ice cream cone and make her face light up when she laughed. An ache settled deep in my chest, like a hollow pit was widening and sucking my organs into it like a black hole.

"Fuckkkk," I groaned. Remy poked his head up at me from the bottom of the bed. I'd spoken out loud very little these days, so the sound of me groaning must have startled him.

"I'm doing the right thing, aren't I, Bud?" He tilted his head and plopped back down. "You're a real help."

Running the back of my fist over my eyes, I let the scene play again in my head. Only this time, it was me holding Mia's hand. Me, licking the tip of her ice cream cone causing her to scowl at me cutely the way she always did when I annoyed her. I'd push the tendril of hair behind her ear and kiss the remnants of vanilla off her bottom lip tasting her like I was starved, and she was the only sustenance I needed.

My phone dinged again breaking me from my thoughts. It was Dina.

Dina: *I call BULLSHIT. Enough is enough, Shawn. If your ass isn't there, then you'll have to answer to me.*

Damn, Dina meant business. Mark may be the scary looking one with a big bark, but it was Dina's bite that everyone watched out for. Leave it to her to call bullshit.

I ran a hand through my hair, thinking. I guess I could make an appearance. I'd go, let Dina see me, and head back home. If I had to make some lame excuse, I would.

I looked down at myself, wearing the same ripped T-shirt that I had been in for days. I sniffed my pits, and, holy hell, I was ripe. I'd have to do something about that before I let myself be seen by the outside world.

Taking a deep breath, I shuffled out of bed, knocking a few empty takeout containers to the floor, and went into the bathroom to get ready to leave the house. This wouldn't be easy, but maybe Dina was right. Enough is enough. I needed a push to leave my bed. I let myself think of Mia one more time, her perfect, full lips smiling before shutting the image away. She was better off without me, plain and simple.

An hour later, I was dressed in a comfortable, clean T-shirt and a pair of basketball shorts. Dina could drag me out, but she couldn't make me dress like I wanted to be out of bed. She was getting a clean Shawn, and that was something.

Getting into my truck felt foreign, like I was another person going through the motions: put key in ignition, turn engine on, put truck in gear. My mind quickly flashed back to the last time I drove, and my heart raced.

I slid the truck back into park and laid my head on the steering wheel. I took slow, deep breaths in through my nose and out through my mouth. Needing some fresh air, I rolled the window all the way down, despite the heat outside, and let the sounds of sparrows chirping in a nearby bush saturate my senses. A short distance away, someone was mowing their lawn, and children were screeching in their yard. The sounds filled me and anchored me to the here and now. Gripping the wheel tightly, I took one more belly breath and put the truck back in gear. I slid my sunglasses over my eyes to help them adjust to the brightness. Being inside for weeks had made the afternoon sun sear straight into my retinas like I was an ant under a magnifying glass.

I left the windows down the entire way toward Main Street and an entirely different set of sounds and smells invaded me as I parked a few blocks away. Holy hell, was this the same street I drove on almost every day to get to the gym?

Classic rock was being belted out from a stage that they'd set up in the parking lot of Krav Maga on Main. They lined tented booths up along the sidewalks selling everything from jewelry to toys. I saw signs for almost every small business in the area. In the next parking lot, a whole configuration of waterslides and bouncy houses took up every inch of space while giggling children screeched with happiness.

Scents of marinating meat and greasy goodness filled my nostrils and suddenly I needed to eat like my life depended on it. My stomach growled as I walked closer to the food booths and the crowd became denser. Everyone seemed to have the same idea I had.

I breathed in trying to focus in on one thing at a time. I hated crowds on a good day, and today wasn't one of those. Spotting my favorite taco shop's sign, I pivoted to head to their line.

After eating nothing but pizza and Chinese takeout for weeks, a fresh burrito and order of elote sounded mouthwatering. I had just secured my place at the back of the line when I spotted Coby's big head a few people ahead of me. He was arm in arm with a woman. Typical Coby. I made myself look busy by scanning my phone. I didn't feel like explaining to him why I'd been MIA for weeks. He'd bust my balls and try to get a rise out of me for sure. They turned to walk away, each holding a burrito and a drink when I realized who the woman was. Kendahl.

Shit.

If she was here, that meant Mia was definitely here, too.

I started scanning the faces around me. There were so many damn people. I didn't even realize this town had this many people living in it.

"What can I get you?" I jerked my head forward realizing it was my turn to order. My mind had gone blank. What was it that I was going to get?

"Taco and uh...," I mumbled, "a beer. Whatever you have cold."

The teenager taking my order asked me other questions. Whether it was about my order or just small talk I didn't know. My head whipped around searching the crowd for that familiar messy bun. I handed the cashier my credit card robotically, and she passed me my food. This wasn't even what I wanted, but it didn't matter. I'd have to find Dina and get the hell out of here.

My beer sloshed over the edge of the red cup as I hurried out of line and over to where it looked less crowded. The only thing going through my mind, as I trudged through the thick crowd, was shoveling my taco into my face and leaving. If anything, at least coming here got me out of another night of takeout. My growling gut would thank me even if this wasn't exactly the healthiest option. I was so deep in thought that I didn't see the person coming straight out of a porta potty next to me.

We collided with each other, and my entire beer spilled onto her chest.

"Fuck, I'm so sor—" I stopped in my tracks as I realized that Mia was standing in front of me, and I had just dumped a full beer all over her. Of course, this would happen.

She looked up at me, eyes wide. In that split second, I watched her face morph from embarrassment that she had crashed into someone to complete shock at seeing me to anger as she pressed her lips together in a straight line.

"Mia." Her name whooshed out of my lips like I had just been punched in the gut. She was more beautiful than my mind had conjured. Just like I had imagined, she was wearing one of her thin sundresses with her hair tied up. Her cheeks were rosy from the heat, and she had on just a smidge of makeup making her brown eyes stand out even more in the afternoon sun.

I snapped out of it remembering that I had soaked her with beer. "Shit, I'm sorry. Let me go get some napkins."

Frantically, I put my taco down on the edge of a booth a few steps away and headed back toward the taco stand. Before I could make it a step, Mia reached out, putting her hand on my shoulder, rendering me immobile.

"Don't worry about it. I'll go ask Dina for a shirt to throw over this. No big deal, it happens."

The tone of her voice sounded like it was, in fact, a big deal.

"Enjoy the party." She gestured out with her hand. With that she covered her wet chest with her other arm and stomped away from me.

Shit, shit, shit. Let her go. Stick to the plan.

As I watched her walk away from me a physical sensation so strong took hold of my limbs. Before I realized what I was doing, I followed her through the crowd.

Chapter 35

Mia

I'M GOING CRAZY.

That couldn't have been Shawn that smacked into me dumping an entire cold beer onto my chest. It must have been a figment of my imagination. Shawn had been a ghost for weeks. He wouldn't just nonchalantly show up at my street fair eating a taco like nothing was wrong in the world.

I glanced behind my shoulder, and Shawn was definitely there silently following me through the crowd like a frantic mother dog who just lost their pup.

No freaking way.

That man didn't get to remove himself from my life then show up with a taco and a beer like he didn't rip my heart out and drag it through the mud.

He looked terrible. I noticed the dark circles rimming his eyes, and his facial hair, thick and uneven. Even his clothes looked rumpled and oversized. I didn't allow myself a good look. That would have been too hard.

He was never Mr. Fashion, but he had always looked more put together than that. Serves him right. He should look crumpled and rumpled, and every kind of other word that rhymed with those. Frumpled? Is that a word? If it is, Shawn looked it.

My heart raced, and it had nothing to do with how fast I was cutting through the crowd toward the Krav Maga on Main booth. I had known, in the back of my mind, that Shawn would show up today. He was a part of the Krav family even if he'd been absent for a few weeks. I hadn't fully prepared myself for how I'd feel if I saw him again. I'd been too busy to even think about him much this week.

As I approached Mark and Dina's bustling tent every single person turned their heads to look at me then at Shawn behind me. Dina excused herself from a conversation with a couple who were looking at a brochure. She looked past me at Shawn.

"Glad you pulled your head out of your ass and made it." She wrapped her arms around him squeezing him tight. "I missed seeing this face around." Hand on her hip, she settled her gaze back to me. "What happened to you?"

"Beer happened to me." I leaned on their booth for support feeling like if I didn't my legs might just give out. I forced myself to keep my eyes away from Shawn. I couldn't look at his sad, pathetic face or my resolve might crack.

"I slammed into her." Dina raised a brow. "By accident. I didn't see her coming out of the bathrooms."

The band started an abnormally loud rendition of "Sweet Child O' Mine" by Guns N' Roses and Shawn had to raise his voice to be heard.

"Well, that's one way to make your presence known." Dina smiled slowly as Shawn tried to explain himself. She stopped him by squeezing his shoulder. "You still have your key, right?" she hollered over the singer crooning, "Oh, oh, oh, oh sweeeeeeet," holding the note way too long.

"Yeah, why?" Shawn yelled leaning toward Dina. She opened her eyes wide, as if to say, seriously, buddy? I looked between them reading between the lines. Digging my heels into the pavement, I put a hand on my hip.

"Dina, I don't need to change. I'm fine. I'm almost dry anyway, see. Practically shriveled up from the heat."

She grabbed my shoulder, and, damn, I forgot what a strong grip she had. "Get your cute ass inside and change. The hostess of the whole event can't be walking around looking like she just won first prize in a wet T-shirt contest."

Damn her. She had me there. I huffed, sneaking a look up into Shawn's eyes. He looked equal parts terrified and intrigued. He was probably picturing me in a wet T-shirt contest. I gestured to him with two fingers. *Eyes up here, buddy.*

He cleared his throat loudly. "Come on, I'll open the gym for you. I know where they keep their stash of extra clothes."

Not wanting to follow him but feeling like I was out of options we weaved our way through the crowd until we reached the locked door of the gym. Shawn shoved the key in and opened the doors to the dark space.

The air conditioning blasted me sending a shiver down my spine. I had gotten so used to being in the heat all day that the change in temperature felt extreme.

With the lights off and no one here, it felt like we had entered a completely foreign space. It was nothing like usual, with the bright fluorescent lights and the booming music. Especially when class was going and all you heard was the thwack of punches against pads and the huffs of people busting their asses. This was calm like a little sanctuary that only Shawn and I had discovered.

"I'll just leave the lights off." Shawn cleared his throat. "I don't want anyone to think we're open and try to come inside."

I nodded while shifting from one foot to the other.

"Let me go unlock the storage cabinet in the office. That's where they keep all the merch. There should be some branded shirt and short sets in there." He looked me up and down, slowly. "I'm sorry, again. I'm sure the last thing you want to be wearing is that stuff. I heard Dina say you organized this whole event. Congratulations."

Awkward silence followed as he fished through piles of black clothing pulling out a couple of things and handing them to me. His gaze lingered on me for another few seconds as I took what he offered.

"Thanks. I'm just going to..." I gestured to the bathrooms down the hall.

"Yeah, of course. I'll be right out here."

I went into the bathroom and locked the door. I plopped down on the toilet seat and put my head in my hands. Everything in me wanted to go to Shawn and sink my head into his chest. I missed him so much. His smell, the way he made me laugh, how thoughtful he was.

Shit.

Of course, the way he ghosted me was the opposite of thoughtful, but maybe Dina was right, and I needed to be patient and give him a chance to explain. That is, if he even wanted to talk to me at all. I pulled my soaked dress over my head thinking about how many times we've literally collided with each other. It seemed like a silly twist of fate for it to keep happening.

I had so much I wanted to say to him. When I quit my job, he was the first person I had wanted to tell. When I organized this whole event, I hoped secretly that he'd find out, so he'd give me that bright beaming grin and call me his fiery girl. He was the man I wanted to share my life with. There, I admitted it. I just had to see if Shawn felt the same way.

I opened the door, dressed in dry clothes, steeling myself for a difficult conversation. There he was, leaning against the wall of the hallway, looking about five inches shorter than he normally looked. I took one step out, then two, and reached out to run my hand against the rough stubble of his jaw. He let out an unsteady breath and I jumped back.

Damn, Mia, I said I'd talk to him, not come out here and paw him like a wild bear.

Before I could take another breath, he was crashing his lips against mine sucking in the very air that I breathed. His arms wrapped around me, and I reached up gripping onto his shoulders and running my hands through his messy hair. Our bodies were a tangle of limbs grasping each other like we hadn't felt human touch in years. I broke away, and immediately felt the loss of his lips like a stab to the chest.

"I'm so mad at you," I panted as I nuzzled my face into his chest. "Where have you been?"

He answered by capturing my lips again paying extra attention to my lower lip as he sucked it into his mouth. Thank God I was holding onto him or I would have lost my balance right there. My legs were jelly, and my core was on fire.

"I'm an idiot," he rasped through kisses. "I tried. I wanted you to forget about me. I'm too fucked up for you."

Grinding into me with each word, my body shook with need. I could feel how hard he was through his basketball shorts. Everything was intense, too intense. I couldn't think straight with him devouring me like this. But I didn't want him to stop.

I pushed my fist into his chest. "Shawn, please," I begged. "I need you."

It was as if hearing those words sent a spark of resolve into him. He stood up to his full height lifting me up, each palm resting on either side of my ass as he gave my cheeks a squeeze.

"I need you more than you know." He carried me into the dark gym, and, before I realized it, he deposited me down on the mats in the corner of the room away from any windows.

This was wrong. Anyone could walk in at any time. This was our gym. Our friend's business. But I was starved for this man, and I couldn't wait any longer.

"Touch me, Shawn." I pulled my shirt off over my head. That was quickly followed by my shorts as I tossed them to the side. Shawn's eyes widened and he licked his bottom lip. He looked like he'd never seen me undressed before and I was his favorite sight in the world.

Pushing me down gently onto the mat, he sucked and licked his way from my lips down my body paying extra attention to my hard nipples. A moan slipped from my parted lips. I hadn't realized how much I missed his touch. He took his time gently nibbling and running his rough palms up the length of my body.

I opened my eyes to see him propped up and staring at me intently. "You're the most beautiful thing I've ever seen."

"Shawn—" I started to object out of habit, but he cut me off.

"No. You are absolutely stunning, always, but especially when you're bare and moaning for me."

Holy shit. I was so turned on I knew I'd be dripping wet. It didn't take much with him. I pulled him on top of me tugging off his shirt and then helping him out of his loose shorts.

"I need you in me, Shawn. Now."

He was never one to deny me what I wanted.

I wrapped my legs around him, guiding his hard length to my center. He pushed himself into me with a hiss, filling me up to the brim. We became frantic again, tongues tangling, legs intertwined as he slammed into me again and again. I met him thrust for thrust, angling myself so my sensitive nub rubbed against him with each movement.

The mat became slick with our sweat, so much so that I had to push my feet down onto it to keep us from sliding across the floor. Shawn felt so good inside me, so right. God, I loved this man.

I loved him. This stubborn, infuriating, kind-hearted, beautiful man.

"Come back to me, baby." Shawn pierced my gaze with his blue eyes. "Come for me, show me how much you missed me. Show me how much you need me, like I need you." His words sent a pulse straight to my center.

I did need him. I did miss him. All of him, not just the incredible sex. I tilted my pelvis up; the friction driving me crazy. Shawn was throwing my leg over his shoulder when my whole body started to tremble and shake with my release. He pounded into me one more time hitting the walls of my pussy so deep that I spun out of control.

"Oh God, Shawn." I screamed his name and wrapped my legs around him tightly.

"That's right, Mia. Ride it out, love." The friction was too much, and I almost cried out from how sensitive I felt. Reaching up, I buried my face into the crook of Shawn's shoulder sucking and nibbling as I felt him buck deeper. "You're so perfect. Mia—"

He called my name as he spilled into me. We collapsed onto the soaked mat, legs draped over each other, faces buried in necks and chests. I was panting like I'd just run a marathon.

"Holy fucking shit." Normal language escaped me. I knew I needed to say many words, but my brain was utterly spent.

He racked a hand through his hair. "Yeah, holy shit is right."

We lay there, our breaths in sync. I forgot where we were or what we were supposed to be doing. There was only me and Shawn. Emotions swelled in my chest, and I didn't even realize it was happening, but tears started to stream down my cheeks.

Shawn sat up, and pulled me into his lap, rubbing my back for comfort. "Shh, baby. I'm so sorry. Oh God, I never wanted to hurt you. Please, Mia, let me explain."

I was sobbing now. Great heaving wails came from my throat as wetness coated my face. I tried to climb off his lap to get my clothing, but he held me firm in place. I didn't want him to see me like this. I didn't know what had come over me, but I couldn't hold the emotions in, not anymore.

Shawn cradled me in his lap whispering sweet words into my ear and rubbing my back. He was soothing me. This man, who was literally just coming out of a full-on breakdown was trying to make me feel better. I was still pissed at him, but I knew I shouldn't make this about me. I should get him to share his emotions, not the other way around. With my head in the crook of his neck the question I had been asking myself for weeks finally escaped my lips. "Why, Shawn? Just be straight with me. Why did you break things off with me?"

He slumped forward letting his hands drop from my back. This was it. He was finally leaving me for good. I pushed too hard, asked too much. Even though I knew I deserved to know, I shouldn't have asked right now. But then he did what I never thought he would do. With each palm on either side of my face he kissed me, gently and deeply, then broke away and said, "It's time I tell you about Michelle."

Chapter 36

Shawn

I NEEDED TO DO this. Mia's eyes looked wider than I'd ever seen them. If I had any hopes of her forgiving me she needed to know.

Nodding, Mia scrambled off my lap and started grabbing her clothes and throwing them on haphazardly. Her shirt was backward, which had the corner of my lips tipping up in a small grin. I pulled my shorts back on as well and leaned against the wall.

"Six years ago, I was married." She said nothing, but chewed her lip while waiting for me to go on. "Her name was Michelle. We met when we were kids and grew up together. She was a bookworm who always gave me shit for getting into trouble and for giving my grandparents a hard time. We dated for a year in high school, but then Michelle went off to college. It was a few years before we reconnected again, after she graduated."

I stood up, pacing the mat. It had been so long since I talked to anyone about Michelle. That part of my life felt so long ago it almost seemed like a work of fiction, like I was talking about someone else's past.

"We fell in love and got married shortly after. She made me a better man. Kind of like someone else I know." I tried to smile, but it didn't quite happen the way I wanted it to. Mia waited, still sitting with her hands in her lap, listening to my every word.

"It was our first anniversary, so I took her down to Miami. I was always so damn busy with the shop. I wanted to take a break, just us. Spoil her like she deserved to be spoiled. I got us tickets to a show and made reservations at a fancy restaurant. That was the first part of the plan that went down the tubes. The place lost our reservations, and they were fully booked up for days." I could see the wheels in Mia's mind turning. She always had a certain look on her face when she was deep in thought.

"We always loved to try out these little hole-in-the-wall ethnic restaurants whenever we could. Since, as you know, Palm Cove barely has a Chinese food place, Michelle was excited when she searched on her phone and found an Indian place with great reviews. It was nearby, and we already had a few drinks from before the show, so we kept our car in the parking garage and walked to the restaurant. Fuck—" I sat back down in front of Mia, taking her hands in mine.

"What happened, Shawn? It's okay. I'm here."

I drew in a shuddering breath.

"We ate and had a few more drinks. Practically closed the place down. The rest is fuzzy, still to this day, I don't know exactly what happened. But we started walking. It was dark, and the street was deserted. The last thing I remember was someone approaching us asking for money... it all happened so fast."

I hung my head low, trying to hide the tears that were sliding down my face.

"They hit me on the head. I think it was with a gun, but I never really found out. They knocked me out cold. When I woke up..." I gulped breaths, willing them to reach my heaving chest. "When I woke up, Michelle was on the ground a few feet away from me. They..."

Mia climbed into my lap, wrapped her arms around me, and held me tight. I breathed in her scent, letting her warmth surround me like a blanket, willing me to go on.

"They shot her. They...," a sob wracked my throat. I didn't think I could go on. I had to, though. Mia needed to hear the whole story. "They raped her and left her for dead. I couldn't protect my wife. I couldn't keep her safe." I rocked back and forth, gulping in air. "There was so much blood. I tried to save her. I screamed for help. It should have been me. Not her. She didn't deserve that. Not Michelle."

Mia's arms around my neck anchored me, holding me centered, so I didn't slip away again. I didn't want to tell her the worst part, if anything could be worse than what had already happened, but we were here, and I was bearing my heart for her. There would be no turning back now.

"I found out a few days later, after the autopsy, that she was six weeks pregnant." Mia sat back meeting my gaze, I couldn't look into her eyes. It hurt so badly. Tears streamed down my cheeks. "I was going to be a father."

I slumped down feeling the weight come off my chest. At the same time, all the air was sucked out of the room. Now, she knew. She could see what a waste of life I was. It should have been me that night. I'd give anything to trade places with Michelle. To give my child a chance to live.

We sat like that for what felt like hours. Mia in my lap, her arms wrapped around me while we both cried. We cried for Michelle, whose life ended so senselessly and too soon. We cried for my life, which changed irrevocably in that moment. Finally, we cried for our future.

Even with this out in the open, it would always be there, like a backdrop in our lives. This was the life of a victim. Every single victim lived two lives, the life before the crime and the life after. You would never be the same person again, not with the grief weighing you down. And not with the fear that the worst would happen again and next time you wouldn't be so lucky, or that someone else you loved would get ripped away from you.

We cried for all these things, but in the back of my mind, a glimmer of hope peeked through that maybe I could be enough for Mia. Maybe we could work through our grief and pain, and she would accept me for who I was and what I carried. I needed that hope just as much as I needed her.

Epilogue

Mia

Two Months Later

We took up the entire street in front of Jill and Kayla's new house. I beamed as I watched Jill shuffle around directing our Krav family and multiple hired workers carrying boxes and new furniture inside. The movers struggled to maneuver around the crowd.

The fundraiser had been a huge success. We raised over $10,000 directly for Jill, and that's not counting the grants she qualified for. She was able to rebuild a brand new mobile home on her plot with all the bells and whistles. One of the foundations that offered aid even started an account for Kayla to get her started at college in a few years.

I'd never felt more fulfilled than I was when we told Jill what we had done for her. The tears in her eyes and the hug I got made every minute of hard work worth it. The other plus side was that so many businesses loved what I did so much that they hired me on to do their accounting, saying they'd never met a bigger numbers wiz. Krav Maga on Main was one of those businesses.

I felt that unmistakable jolt to my stomach and looked behind me. Shawn was walking by holding a box, but he couldn't resist a butt grab on the way.

"Look at that box. My nephew could carry more than that." I teased him, wanting to see my favorite type of Shawn smile, the smirk.

"Oh yeah, if it's so light, let's see you carry it." He held it out for me, and I puffed up my chest, never wanting to give in to a challenge. I went to grab the box, but Shawn grabbed my side with one arm, lifting me up while still holding the box with the other.

"Put me down! You're just proving my point, you know. That box is extremely light," I laughed a full-body laugh that brought heat to my cheeks.

"I'll put you down, fiery girl, when you stop sassing me."

"So never?"

He placed me onto the ground and smacked my ass. I loved his playful moods. "I wouldn't want it any other way."

An alarm sounded from Shawn's phone and he grabbed it out of his pocket to silence it. I was so excited I almost couldn't contain myself.

Shawn drew a deep breath in through his nose and released it on a loud exhale. "I guess it's time. I've delayed this for long enough."

"Don't act so grumpy about it. A bet is a bet," I crooned, and I pulled on his hand toward Jill's house.

"I don't remember any terms of the bet saying I had to be cheerful." He crossed his arms over his chest and stomped up the porch steps.

I reached up on my tip toes to hang his gym bag over his neck once we reached the front door. "Go get changed and I'll meet you by the truck. I need to say goodbye to Jill."

He huffed and I saw a tiny peek of the Shawn I met at that first class months ago. Ill-tempered and brooding with a side of sweetheart underneath. "Fine. But you're going to pay later for this."

I waggled my brows at him as a warm breeze tickled my hair. "You mean it?"

After saying my goodbyes, I leaned against the side of Shawn's truck, waiting for him to come back outside. When he finally did, I had to bite my cheek to keep from doubling over in laughter.

Shawn stomped his way across the walkway wearing the same ruched booty yoga pants that he joked about wearing months ago. They were light grey, and tight enough to show every bump and bulge. On his upper body, he wore a white racerback T-shirt that read, *Namaslay All Day.* I found it online especially for him.

Lucky for him, the moving crew were the only people outside the house by the time he came out. Maybe he planned it that way, peeking behind the bathroom door to make sure our friends had come inside so he could sneak away. I knew he'd still be embarrassed but at least they were strangers and couldn't tease him every day.

"You look," I bit back a laugh, "so good. Can I see your booty? Do a spin for me please." I begged with my signature puppy eyes.

The teeniest of grins started at the corner of his lips and he obliged me. He even did a little twerk that had tears springing in the corners of my eyes from laughter.

"Now that you've had your fair share of ogling, let's go before we're late. I want to make sure we find a spot in the back."

We hopped in the truck and made our way across town and toward the coast. Shawn had me find a yoga studio outside of Palm Cove, to minimize the chances of seeing anyone he knew. That was a smart move on his part. Palm Cove was a small town where we ran into people we knew most days.

Sun Yoga Studio was in the center of a quiet shopping plaza with a dental office on one side, and a chiropractor's office on the other. Shawn got out and held his head high as we made our way inside.

Nag Champa incense burned in the open space, filling me with a sense of calm. I watched Shawn take in the differences between this studio and the Krav gym. The two couldn't be more different. Lights were dimmed instead of glowing brightly, relaxing meditation music played not bass thumping house music, and the instructor greeted us at the entrance with a warm pat on the shoulder and a smile versus Mark's gruff hellos.

Situated in the back on the room, we laid on our yoga mats in corpse pose for a few breaths before moving through a relaxing flow. As silly as it would have been to have Shawn be at the front of the room I was glad I was the only one who got to stare at his juicy peach in those leggings.

We moved through downward dog, child's pose, a few cat/cow poses, and warrior poses. All basic moves that were meant to help us relax and feel comfortable as beginners.

Every few minutes I'd peek over at Shawn and was pleasantly surprised at how well he was doing. For a guy who rarely stretched he was quite bendy.

When I wasn't peeking at him, he was breaking my concentration by whispering inappropriate things to me.

I'd be deep into child's pose and hear, "Don't you wish I was under you?"

Or he'd turn toward me saying, "Show me your downward dog later." At one point he coughed then rolled toward me saying, "I think the woman in front of me farted."

If he was aiming for me never asking him to a yoga class again, he'd gotten his wish. I couldn't keep it together. Every time I heard his deep seductive whisper, I'd blush and fumble whatever pose I was in burying my face into the mat to hide my laughter.

As soon as the instructor finished class with a '*Namaste*,' we bolted out of there. I lectured Shawn on the way home, but he obviously knew I wasn't serious by my barely contained grin.

After the long day, we settled on the couch at Shawn's house. Remy was curled up at our feet and Shawn's lasagna warmed in the oven. I'd managed to coerce him to keep on the yoga pants until bedtime and I grinned idiotically every time I saw his backside. I thought about how far we'd come in those couple of months since the festival and how different I was from the woman Shawn had first met.

I'm still anxious and scared before I go to class some days, but instead of hiding from that fear, I embrace it and let it make me better. I haven't kicked anyone in the shin for a while, so I consider that a win and I passed my level two exam last week.

Kendahl and Olivia even started coming to classes after I bugged them for the last month. They're in level one, but at least they get to partner with each other. Now my two favorite girls would learn how to stay safe and protect themselves. If they just learned the basics, I'd sleep better at night.

I reached over and placed my head on Shawn's shoulder angling for a kiss. "I love you, Shawn, more than you could ever know."

His eyes peered into mine and he stroked my cheek. "You saved me from myself. I love you so much. I don't want a day to go by where you don't know that deep in your heart and soul."

I kissed him savoring the taste of his lips. It was a fight to get here, but I'm a fighter, and sometimes we have to wrap our wrists, take our stance, one foot in front of the other, and battle for what we want. Love is worth the fight, after all.

Acknowledgments

Wow, I'm trying not to cry while writing this. I simply cannot believe, after years of dreaming and hard work, that I'm finally here writing my acknowledgements. Mia and Shawn would not be where they are today without the help and guidance of so many people who are near and dear to my heart. I apologize in advance if I cannot specifically name everyone.

First and foremost, Bobby. Your love and support have made my lifelong dreams possible. Yes, you ply me with endless inspirational quotes that make me want to hurl large objects in your direction, but deep down you always know what I need to keep at it. I love you.

Keesa, my true number one fan (you may not have the foam finger but I know it's true). From the very first paragraphs of Mia's story years ago, you've been there supporting me, giving amazing advice, and encouraging all the spicy peppers. I'm truly blessed to call you my best friend.

Tara and Breanne, my writing queens, the only people who have understood my midnight texts asking for another word that means core. I love you both so much. Keep on being amazing writers and thank you for your constant support and guidance. Don't worry Tar, I'll make sure someone has hard lips next time.

Of course, my Krav partner for life, Crystal, this book would simply not exist if it wasn't for you pushing me out of my shell and telling our anxiety to fuck off. I can remember the exact moment that Mia and Shawn's story popped into my head, which was probably why I ended up in a neck brace instead of rolling the way I was supposed to. You've been there from the very first page, offering support and feedback (no more Little One ever) and I'm forever grateful.

Steph, Andi, Denise, Liz, Connie, Kristi, Kim, Devon, and Tiffany- you've all been amazing cheerleaders and have helped me reach my goals more than you know. I'm so grateful to have you all in my life.

To my editor, Brittany, who helped my manuscript reach its true potential. Thank you so very much. Enni, my cover artist, I'm in love with your beautiful work. You were so worth the wait.

Skyler, Lucas, Riley, and Robbie. You're the reason I keep dreaming and doing what I love. Never stop following your passions. Always fight for what you love and know that you're stronger than you believe. Riley, this book wouldn't be here without your special note. I'll keep it always.

Lastly, you, my lovely readers- I'm so grateful that I get to share my words with you. Thank you from the bottom of my heart.

About Author

Lauren lives in Phoenix, Arizona with her full chaotic family. When she's not crafting her next happily ever after, you can find her playing taxi to her teenagers, being pulled by her two large dogs, and when she's lucky reading with a cup of coffee. *Fight For It* is her debut novel.

www.ingramcontent.com/pod-product-compliance
Lightning Source LLC
Chambersburg PA
CBHW021410310726
48971CB00005B/1282